THE
TOWERS

To Madelyn, who blooms like the summerflower, and who is proof to me that sometimes words of love fail, and the only thing for it is to get married, and use the rest of one's life to try to explain.

Table of Contents

CAIRN MERIDIA

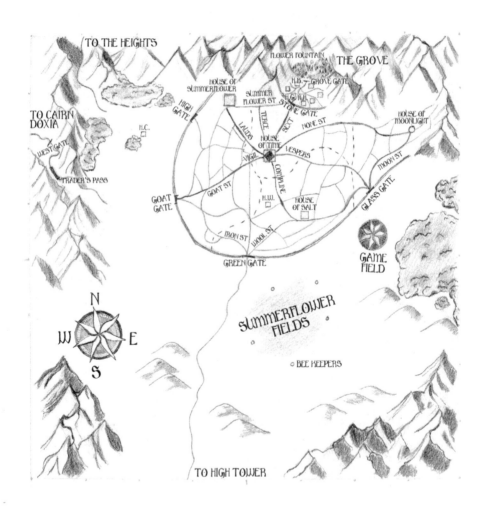

ONE HUNDRED TOWERS

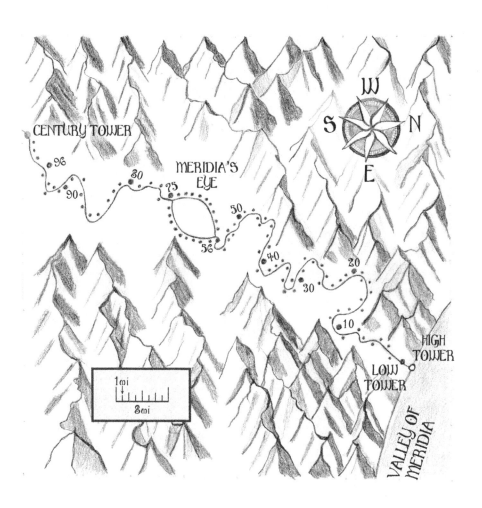

PROLOGUE
The Whispers in the Grass

This is how it came to pass.

The first men lived in a land of wealth and plenty, where they built palaces of glass and gold, and grew stone trees as tall as towers, and learned many deep mysteries of the magic of shame and grace. But calamity came upon them swiftly. Fire rose from the depths of the earth, burning their lands and blackening their skies.

So they built great ships of stonewood, ships as big as cities, and into these ships they put the work of their hands, the wealth of their families, and many seeds and animals. They set sail east, across the Endless Sea, and lost themselves on the falling waves. For many years they sailed, heading toward the sun, harvesting the fierce creatures of the sea and drinking rainwater from the skies, until whole generations of their children were born and grown and aged and died, all with no sight of land.

Then one day, a great storm took them. The wind blew cold and fierce, and the water came crashing against their ships in waves as high as mountains. When the storm finally left them, many ships were lost, and the fleet was scattered to all corners of the sea. Only three of the ships had stayed together, lashing themselves to one another in the storm. And the three captains of these ships were siblings, different in appearance and stature. Tarn Harrick was a mighty hunter and warrior, brave and bold, who knew the way of bow and spear. His sister Tani was a sage of wisdom and power, beautiful in appearance. She carried a book from the burning lands, and often she was studying it, learning the power of shame and grace, and the magic of the stone trees, which comes from Ior. For in those days all knowledge was in one book. Their younger brother was a builder, and he knew the ways of binding wood and stone. He was a man of short stature and handsome appearance, and his true name is lost, he who would be called Tjabo.

Soon after the storm, the captains came at last to the land of Nora, and there they found a second endless sea. But where the one they left was made of water, this sea was made of grass. For the land of Nora was flat and empty, and nothing but grass covered it, from the rising of the sun to its setting. There were no rivers or lakes, no mountains or valleys, no trees or shrubs or flowers or thorns, but all was grass, and the grass was all. It grew taller than the height of a man, though there were no men to see it, nor birds nor mice nor goats.

But there were other things in the grass. Dark things.

Some of the people refused to leave their boats. Having known nothing else their whole lives, they wanted to return to the sea. But Tarn Harrick led them forward, saying, "Our grandfathers left their land many years ago, fleeing the fire and ash that fell from the sky. They took to the sea, seeking some new place to make their home. And we have sailed our whole lives to fulfill that desire. And now, we have been driven here by a storm. Our masts are shattered and our sails are riven. Shall we take to the sea again, and perish in the depths because of our fear? Come, follow me and my sister and my brother, and we will show you how to make a new home on this sea of grass."

And Tarn took up the ancient swords of the land of his fathers, and he and his kin waged war on the grass with them, cutting a wide swath down to the bare earth. They took apart their boats and built a city with the wood, putting their homes on stilts that rose above the grass.

For the men found that the place was not wholly deserted. Dark things moved in the grass, things which had lived long years in the land of Nora and had grown strong in their own magic, the blood magic of the grass sea. And these things came to the city of men in the night, whispering a strange tongue, like wind through the grass. If a man wandered too far away from the city, the dark things took him, carrying him away to some foul place, from where none returned. And sometimes Tarn fired his bow at the dark things, who would shriek and vanish.

So the men of the wooden city knew some peace, and lived in peace with each other. They planted the ancient seeds of their stone trees in the cleared ground, and the seeds quickened and grew, rising up like a ring of towers around the city, their bark thick and their leaves wide. The men took fish from the shore and found which grasses were good to eat, corn and wheat and oat, and which were good for goats, clover and sedge and dropseed. They kept their water barrels full of rain, and at night they kept watch against the things which moved in the grasses and slunk around their city, whispering.

Now Tarn married and had three sons and three daughters. And he led the defense of the city and was content. From sunrise to sunset, his sister Tani studied her book. She learned much of the seven graces of men, and the seven shames, and the power of the stone trees, which is from Ior. She, too, took a husband, and she bore a daughter, who she named Meridia. And she taught her daughter the secrets of the book and all her magic. And she was content.

But the youngest brother was not content. He remembered the stories of the great palaces and castles, palaces of marble and gold and obsidian— grand, beautiful things that had once graced his grandfather's land, before the fires came from the sky. He looked on the growing stone trees with disdain, and began to wander through the grasses by day, circling further and further away from the city, walking on tall wooden stilts. Always he looked for a break in the grasses, a sign of mountains or forests, things he knew from paintings and stories. Tani cautioned him, saying, "Surely, the creatures of the grass will take you, and then you shall die."

But he scoffed at her, saying, "You are all cowards and fools. Will you sit by the sea forever, and fear nameless things? We are the sons and daughters of great men. Let us do great things." Most closed their ears to his urging, but some listened and became like him, ill-contented with their humble wooden city.

Then one day, the man went far, far out into the grasses. And when night came, he did not return. Tarn grew afraid for his brother's life, and so he told his three sons to light torches, and the four men went out into the grasses with their bows and spears, looking for the man and calling his name, the name which has been forgotten. But there was no answer save for the whisperings of the dark things, and the sigh of the grass.

Some years passed, and the city grew quickly in size. The stone trees rose higher and higher, drinking the rain and eating the sun, and many children were born who had never ridden on the sea. Then one day, the man who had vanished in the grass returned, and all of the men and women who had been taken by the dark things over the years were with him, much changed. They were gaunt and wild-eyed, and sometimes they forgot the tongue of men and whispered the grass language. Tarn's brother told the people of the city that he had indeed been taken by the dark things, who seized him as the sun was setting, when he had wandered too far afield. Deep underground they had taken him, to their endless tunnels and burrows beneath the grass. Of what happened to him there, he would not say, except that they had taught him their language and sent him back with the other men they had taken. He took the name Tjabo, which means 'King,' and often he would sleep in the grass with the others, letting the dark things caress him through the night.

One day his sister Tani came to him and said, "If you can indeed speak to the grass creatures, tell them to leave us in peace."

And Tjabo said, "You are wise and powerful, sister, and you know many things. Yet you are a fool in this. The children of the grass are not our enemies, but our friends. They only wish to show us how best to live here, to help us let go of the old things and embrace the land as it is. Tell Tarn to put up his bow, and let them come into the city. For they have promised to fulfill all of my dreams." But his brother and sister refused him, for they did not like the change in him, or the men and women who were with him, or the name he had chosen for himself.

Now Tjabo and his followers went throughout the city, and found other men and women who looked on the wooden city with disdain. And they gathered in secret places, where Tjabo spoke of the grass unending. "Rise early in the morning, and set your face toward the sun," he said to them. "And walk until the sun sets behind you. Then arise the next day, and do the same. And again the next. Let your feet walk through the grass for a generation of man, and you will not see the end of it, still it will go on before you in rippling waves, yellow and green. Turn north or south, and you will see the same. The grass is all, and all is the grass. But only follow me, and I will fulfill your dreams." With such words he whispered despair and hopelessness into their ears, and gained their allegiance.

Now a great sickness fell on the city, and many children were taken ill. And the people went to Tani and her daughter Meridia for help, for they knew the ways of the book and the magic of the stone trees, which is a healing magic. And the two of them spoke words of power over the children who were brought to them, imploring Ior for help, and made them teas from the leaves of the stone trees. Yet many fell ever deeper into sickness. It seemed as if a darkness had settled in their eyes, for they looked on the world like the shades of men, without care or passion or love. They moved like listless things, shuffling and sighing on their beds, and complained of cold while they burned with fever.

Tjabo went again to his sister Tani and said, "Did I not tell you that your knowledge is old? See, this sickness is a sickness of the new world, a sickness of the grasses. Let me take the children to my friends, for I know their magic will be able to cure them. For their magic is a magic of the blood, a magic that can change us for the better."

"The dark things of the grasses are no friends of ours," Tani said. "If this, indeed, is a sickness of the grasses, then no grasses will be able to cure it."

"So be it," Tjabo said.

But he and his followers waited outside her chamber night and day, and when a child was brought to her that she could not cure, they spoke to the child's parents. And many fathers and mothers gave their children to him freely, for they feared death more than the darkness in their children's eyes. Tjabo took the children out to the grasses, and there they spent a night listening to the whispers. And when they returned, they burned no longer with fever. But the darkness in their eyes was deepened, and their faces were grown wild as Tjabo's. They lost their fear of the grasses and wandered through them in the night, with Tjabo often at their sides, teaching them the grass-tongue and showing them the black things that moved through the fields.

So Tani went to her brother and said, "Tarn, look at what has happened to our brother, the one calling himself Tjabo. He has said, 'The grass things will heal us and fulfill our dreams.' But he has brought us a nightmare instead."

But Tarn grew angry with her and said, "What do you want of me? Will I raise a hand against my own brother?" Though in his heart, he knew that she spoke true.

Then one night, a messenger came for Tani, saying, "Please, come quickly, my sister is near the point of death." So she rose and took her book with her, leaving her daughter to sleep. But a second messenger met them on the way, weeping and saying, "Our sister has died. There is nothing more you can do for her." So Tani returned home.

Now as she approached her dwelling, she saw a dark man emerge from her doorway. She hid herself, to see what the man would do. The moon came out from behind the clouds, and she saw that it was her brother, whose name has been forgotten. On his back, he carried a person, still and silent, and Tani saw that it was her daughter, Meridia. So she followed close behind Tjabo, slinking in the shadows, for she thought, "If I see that Tjabo is the cause of this sickness, surely my brother will join me against him," though she was afraid for her daughter.

Tjabo went to the edge of the city, past the stone trees, which groaned and shook as he passed, though there was no wind. And when he had left the trees, he whispered the grass tongue, and the dark things came to him. They surrounded him in the grass, and he stood Meridia before them in the light of the moon, but Meridia did not move, or seem to know where she was. And Tani stood close by, watching.

Tjabo spoke the grass-tongue again, and the things in the grass whispered with him. And Tani saw a shadow come out of the ground. It grew and thickened in the moonlight, until it seemed to stand with a life of its own. And then it reached out and touched her daughter, who cried out in pain and despair.

With a shout, Tani rose from her hiding place and spoke the words of the book, words of power, and Tjabo was thrown down as if by some giant fist. The whispering of the dark things was broken, and they fled into the grass, letting Meridia fall. Tani rushed to her daughter, hoping that there was no darkness in her eyes.

But while she was looking to her daughter, Tjabo rose from the grass with a shepherd's crook in hand. He struck his sister on the head, over and over again, whispering, whispering, until she lay dead at his feet.

Then Tjabo spoke the language of shame, and the staff began to glow with a terrible blue flame. Ribbons of fire shot forth from the crook like arrows, and Tjabo began to burn and kill, destroying the wooden houses of the people and setting the stone trees aflame. And with every death the fires burned hotter and higher, consuming the city like a wild beast. Many joined him, the men and women who had listened to him speak of the unending grass, and the children with dark eyes, who had been taken into the grass. For Tjabo had been plotting with them for many days to destroy the city.

Now Tarn heard the commotion, and saw the glow of the fires in the night. And many people fled to him, saying, "Your brother has gone mad! He has killed your sister, and now he besets us with some strange and evil fire. He is burning the stone trees and killing, and other men and women and children have joined him."

When Tarn heard what was happening, he roused his three sons, and bade them take up their bows. As swift as the wind they ran, and came to a grove of stone trees ahead of Tjabo. Tarn hid behind the largest of the stone trees, and he set his sons behind others, for he thought, "Only a foolish man would try to stand against a bow of flames. We will strike from the shadows." And Tjabo came to the grove, but he did not see Tarn and his sons hiding. So Tarn whistled, high and piercing, and they drew back their bows, arrows flying forth as quick as lightning. One struck Tjabo's right eye, and one his left. And again, one struck his right arm, in the crook of the elbow, and one struck his left. And Tjabo dropped his staff and screamed in pain, and it was like the screaming of the earth. And Tarn drew back his bow a second time to pierce Tjabo's heart, but the ground beneath Tjabo opened up, and a dark thing of the grass snatched him away, pulling him into the earth. When Tjabo had fallen, his followers were afraid, and they fled, vanishing into the grass.

Tarn took up Tjabo's crook, and found that its fire still burned. The people brought his sister Tani and her daughter Meridia to him, and Tarn and his sons and all the people wept for them, for they thought Meridia was as dead as her mother.

But when their tears fell on her face, Meridia opened her eyes and sat up. And behold, one of her eyes was as dark as the earth, and the other was as bright as a star.

Tarn took up the fiery crook and said, "Meridia! Listen to me. The men and women and children who followed Tjabo had dark eyes, and I see your right eye is as dark as theirs. But your left is as bright as your mother's once was. Have you come back to us as his child or as hers?"

She said to him, "Put away your staff, uncle; I am still my mother's daughter. Tjabo came to me in the night and whispered some spell, which cast me into deep and troubled nightmares. He took me to the grass and spoke again, and a shadow rose up from the ground and touched me. But before it could consume me, my mother struck Tjabo down, and I fell as if dead. The part of the shadow that had entered me tried to kill me indeed, but I fought against it with the wisdom of my mother's book. I trapped it within my right eye and spoke to it. See, I have learned much from it. Now I understand the dark things and their ways. I know the names of their creatures and the language of their blood magic. I know the lies they told Tjabo, and the lies he passed on to you. They have promised to fulfill his dreams, and the dreams of all that follow them. They have promised freedom and greatness. But their greatness is lower than the grass, and their freedom is lived in chains. And the dream they would bring to pass is nothing but a nightmare."

Tarn and the people were greatly troubled at this, and they said, "What shall we do? Tell us, and we will follow you."

Meridia turned toward the east, where the sun was beginning to rise. "Look to the sun," she cried. "And listen to the lie that Tjabo told. He said, 'A man could walk for a generation without leaving the grasses.' But this is a lie. The grasses do not go on forever. Ten days walk in that direction lies a great river, which flows out to the sea. Follow the river to the north, and the land will rise around you in foothills and forests. You will hear birds sing in the trees and wolves howl in the night. A month's journey will bring you in sight of mountains, jagged and rocky on the horizon. It is to those mountains we must go. For Tjabo and the dark men will surely return, and when they do, they will overwhelm us in the grass."

"How shall we reach this place?" Tarn asked. "For we cannot leave the grasses in a single day. Surely when night falls, the dark things will come and kill us."

"Look to your brother's staff," Meridia said. "For it holds an ancient power, the power of shameful things. Through the murder of my mother, Tjabo has brought forth fire to burn us. This was the power that destroyed the land of our grandfathers. They fled to escape this fire, but the fire has followed us here. Now see, Tjabo's shame will be our salvation. We will burn a path through the grass, and when the dark things come, we will chase them away with a staff of flames."

And so the people ripped their city apart and made wagons with the wood, and into these they put food and weapons, the old and the infirm, and children too young to walk. They hitched their wagons to their goats and to their own shoulders, and followed Tarn and his sons, who went before them with the fiery crook, burning a path in the grass. By day and by night they walked on ashes. And when they had to sleep, they slept on ashes. Always the dark things surrounded them, and if the fire slacked for an hour, they came, stealing men and women away. But Meridia moved among the people tirelessly, encouraging them with kind and brave words.

At last, they reached the river and turned north, finding everything just as Meridia had told them. The dark things left them, trapped in the grass, and the people fell to the ground exhausted. But Meridia roused them saying, "Come, we cannot stay here. The dark things cannot come here, but men now serve them. The men will come for us soon if we linger."

So they set off again, through the foothills and forests, until they saw the mountains on the horizon. Black and harsh they were, and above them rose the Insurmountable Heights, the cliffs that vanish in the clouds. With faltering steps, the men went up into the mountains, stumbling and weary. They had no knowledge of rock and high wind and sudden storms, and many died in the passes. But Meridia led them on with strength, taking them through narrow ways.

At last, they came to a wide and fertile valley, high up in the mountains, lush with the red and white of the summerflower and alive with the hum of bees. Meridia called a halt and said, "Here at last we have found our home. This valley is lush and beautiful. Tarn my uncle, turn a circle in this spot, and tell me what you see."

So Tarn turned in a circle and said, "Mountains rise around us like a stone wall."

"And what of the breaks in the wall?" Meridia asked.

"There are two," Tarn said. "One in the south, through which we entered the valley. It is narrow and difficult to climb. The second is to the west, and we do not know where it goes, save that it is even steeper, and goes deeper into the mountains."

"Hear what I say," Meridia said. "Let us settle here. Let a tower be built at the southern pass, to hold the way against the nightmares that Tjabo and the dark things will surely send to destroy us. And let a few men, the best climbers and runners among us, be sent along the western pass, to see if it opens to the south. And if so, let a tower be built there also. For a few men can hold a narrow way against many, and so protect the others."

Tarn and the others agreed with her, and they built a tower of stone above the southern pass, secured with a gate of iron. And men were sent along the western pass, to follow it as long as they could.

Now Tarn was growing old, and he mourned his sister. So he went to his niece Meridia and said, "Let your mother's memory not be forgotten. When she was grown, she took a husband and bore a daughter. And she taught her daughter the secrets of the shames and graces of men, and the magic of Ior's stone trees, all of which you now know. And indeed, you have surpassed your mother, for now you know the blood magic of the whispering things as well. But behold, you have no daughter to whom to pass on your wisdom. So let the people be your daughter and pass your wisdom onto them."

And she said, "What would you have me do?"

Tarn said, "Write for us, therefore, prohibitions—that we might know what is good to do and what is evil, that our sons and grandsons might live in this land in peace and prosperity, and that the nightmare of the grasses may never take us again. Show us how to remove the power of shame, so that none can rise up to burn us with fire."

So Meridia wrote the Prohibitions, as Tarn had asked, one hundred in all. The people read them and lived by them, and their prosperity grew.

After a time, Tjabo returned to them, as Meridia said he would. With him were a host of dark men, armed with stone axes and clubs, and other, darker things that sickened the eye and chilled the heart. For they had become creatures of the blood magic, and the blood magic had twisted and changed them, so that they were no longer men. And where once Tjabo had been a man of fire, now he was a thing of ice, and the cold came with him, biting and bitter. Where his eyes had been were only two black stones, and strands of grass were wrapped around his elbows. Blood leaked from beneath these strands and froze into red icicles, which hung from his elbows and dropped to the stone ground.

When Tjabo saw the stone towers the people had built, he treated with them, saying, "What have you done? You have burned the homeland of the grasses and set the whisperers against you. Through me they would have made their peace with man, but there will be no peace with you now. They have sent us to kill and destroy you utterly. And they will never stop, for their memories are long and their hatred runs deep."

The dark host surged forward, with Tjabo at their head. And old Tarn Harrick his brother stood against them, with his three sons and the staff of fire. A host of good men stood with them, wielding the swords of their fathers, the swords which had cut the grass down to the earth. Long into the night the battle raged, with many men falling on both sides. And when the sun rose in the morning, the battle had turned against Tarn and his sons, for their enemies seemed to gain strength with every death. Such was the power of the blood magic, that lent speed to their hands and strength to their arms.

When hope was almost lost, Tarn sent for Meridia and said to her, "The enemy is at our gates! Soon they will freeze the iron and break it, and they will wash over us like a flood. Is there nothing you can do to help us?"

"What many men cannot do, one man may accomplish," she replied. "What would you give up for this people?"

"I am old and my hands are weak," Tarn said. "Whatever I have left is for this people."

"So be it," Meridia said. So she directed her uncle to stand at the gate of the tower. She kissed him on his forehead and on each of his hands.

And Tarn said, "Strike me in the eyes and in the crooks of the elbow.

For perhaps if my brother sees me thus, he will remember the love we once bore for one another, when we still rode on the sea."

So his sons drew back their bows and struck him with the last of their arrows, once in his right eye, and once in his left. And again, once in his left arm, near the crook of the elbow.

And it was Meridia herself who loosed the fourth arrow, which struck Tarn in the right arm. As she loosed, she spoke a spell of power, the most ancient she knew. Tarn's blood spilled out on the ground, and the tower stones began to glow with a white brilliance, as if a shaft of starlight had fallen to the earth. The dark men who saw the light were struck dead at the sight of it, undone by the power of Meridia's spell.

And Tjabo alone was left alive, for he was blind, and his stony eyes did not see. He raised his fist to Meridia and said, "Let your victory grow sweet in your mouth, for your years are short. Mark me. Seventy years this victory has won you, the length of one man's life. Then I will raise up another host, greater than the first, and we will destroy you. And if that host fails I will send another, and another, until all of your towers are cast down and your people lie dead." Then he departed, back to the dark things that whisper in the grass, and the deathly cold went with him.

The people mourned for Tarn, their captain, and they laid him to rest in a grove of stone trees. They built a fountain over his body, and Meridia spoke words of power so that the fountain would never run dry.

Now in those days, the men they had sent to the west returned to them and reported all that they had seen. "We have followed the paths for many miles and many years," they said, "And have walked them from beginning to end. See here, to the west lie six other valleys like this one, fair and fertile. They are open only to each other, and to the south by narrow ways, much like the way that leads into this valley."

Meridia heard their report. Then she gathered the people and said, "Look, there are still many of us, and there are seven valleys. Let us go, each to a different valley. For surely Tjabo will seek to destroy all of us, and it may be that if one of the cities is destroyed, the others might yet survive." And so the people split themselves into seven groups, three led by Tarn's sons, three led by his daughters, and the seventh group which stayed with Meridia. And those who were leaving set off to hold and secure the other valleys, and to build towers in them according to Meridia's instructions. They took the Prohibitions with them, and lived according to them, for the people saw that they had made their city prosper, and had grown them in beauty and strength.

After fifty years, Meridia had grown old, and knew that her time was nearing. So she sent for the leaders of the six other free cities, and they traveled the mountain paths to see her. She said to them, "How do your people fare?"

Tarn's eldest daughter Doxia stepped forward with her companions and said, "We have done everything according to your instructions. We keep to the Prohibitions, and if one shames herself, we take the power of the shame from her, that she might not use it against us. We have built towers and trained our sons in war, and Ior grows our stone trees ever taller." And the others stepped forward in turn, and each said the same.

So Meridia said, "It is well. My death approaches, and there is much I still have to teach you. I would not leave you defenseless against the nightmare that is coming back for you."

And they said, "Mother, tell us what we should do."

Meridia sent for pen and paper, and gathered all of the scribes of the city to her. She took out her mother's book, and read to them in secret what it contained. Some wrote the secrets of dreaming, some the secrets of grace and shame, some the secrets of justice, some the secrets of time, some the secrets of bow and spear, and some the secrets of plants and animals and made things. And to some she revealed mysteries. The scribes wrote down Meridia's words and made books. And when these books were completed, she called the people to her again.

"Appoint for yourselves six leaders from each city, and send them to me," Meridia said to them. "And send to me also one man from every house, whoever is master there." When the people had done so, Meridia gave the books to the leaders of the people.

And she said to them, "Here I give you these books, which contain the wisdom of our ancestors and the knowledge of shame and grace. To each of you I give one book, so that no one might boast of the knowledge of all things. Rather, all the leaders of a city will need the other leaders, and each city will need the other cities. And of the most powerful books, nothing they contain may be copied or written elsewhere. But to all cities and to all men, I give knowledge of the graces of Ior, of their magic and power, and of their goodness for all things."

And the people said in reply, "We will treasure these gifts always."

And Meridia said, "Stay in this valley, keep watch, and endure. For I have put a great power on it, to shield you from the Nightmare. I say to you, should the Nightmare enter this city, even the trees and animals will come to your defense."

So when Meridia had at last finished her work, she rose early in the morning. And, taking nothing but her goat with her, and a little water, she set up into the mountains, toward the Insurmountable Heights, where Ior dwells, the cliffs that are lost in the clouds. For she thought to die honorably, reaching as high as she could. And the people named their city Cairn Meridia in honor of her.

After seventy years had passed, the Nightmare came again to Cairn Meridia, larger and more terrifying than before, though Tjabo was not with them. The people remembered the mysteries that Meridia had revealed to them, and they threw the Nightmare back, breaking it against their towers.

Ten years later, the Nightmare came to the second free city, the city of Cairn Doxia, and there too, the people stood against the darkness and defeated it. So it went with all seven of the free cities. Every ten years the Nightmare attacked a different city, and the people fought against them, using the secrets of their great mother Meridia. So each city lived seventy years in peace before the Nightmare came again.

The dark men of the grasses spread, making their homes all over the land of Nora, and building palaces of gold and glass and marble, all that Tjabo had coveted. But Tjabo himself lived beneath the ground with the whispering things, and with their blood magic they extended his life beyond the count of years. The dark men sent their sons to him, and they all served the Nightmare. And just as Meridia had said, their greatness was lower than the grass, and their freedom was lived in chains.

And the men of the valleys kept watch, and endured.

Part One

Neither more nor less than one hundred towers shall shield you from the Nightmare. For each tower is a Prohibition, and each Prohibition is a tower. And the towers alone can save you from the death the Nightmare brings.
— The First Prohibition

And he will be like a living tower, a walking stone, a sword of light. He will wake from the Nightmare as one forever Unshamed, destroying all bonds. He will wake broken and alive, ever bleeding, ever dying, ever laughing, ever smiling. And he alone will save you from the death the Nightmare brings.
— From *The Mysteries of Meridia*

CHAPTER ONE

Blood on the Rocks

The blood trail stretched out ahead of them, following the shattered rocks of the mountainside toward the valley, near a mile below them at this point. The sun was high in the south, and Garrett was sweating under his heavy white wool. But fog still gripped the valley floor, in spite of the heat, sitting just below the treetops like a dark gray blanket.

"I don't like it," Cringe said, wrinkling his pug nose and frowning. "Doesn't smell right to me. Can't you smell it?"

"It's just blood," Garrett said, though privately he was thinking much the same. It looked odd somehow, the blood. Too wet. "No more than a few drops."

"You said it makes a trail?" Crack asked Garrett, bent over the blood. The big man was sweating even more than Garrett, his massive shoulders hunched.

Garrett nodded. "I didn't follow it far, but it leads down the mountain for a quarter mile or so at least."

"I'm telling you, it smells rotten," Cringe said again.

Cringe wasn't his real name, of course, no more than Crack's was his. Sergeant Floramel had given them those names when they'd entered the Tower Guard together. Akrin and Krayken, their real names were, brothers from House Haeland. They were house brothers, not related by blood.

And it showed. Where Cringe's face was shallow and pinched, Crack's was broad and bulbous, and his neck was as thick as a ram's. A red petal decorated Crack's breastplate, a sign of the grace of bravery, the blessing of Ior's strength. Cringe had the silver petal of faith on his chest, and Garrett's own was emblazoned with the orange of diligence. There were plenty of men in the guard who possessed none of Ior's graces, but the scouting teams always included one brave man, one diligent, and one faithful. Brave to fight, faithful to see, diligent to run.

"I smell our dinner," Crack said finally, straightening his big frame. "We haven't had a good bit of meat for days. That bow of yours has been useless."

"Can't shoot what isn't there," Cringe said, which was true enough. Cringe was the best shot in the company though, Garrett had to give him that. He'd seen the man bring down a streaking falcon at a hundred yards, just as easy as throwing a rock downhill. And he was a good tracker. Better than Garrett, anyway. The grace of faith did that, gave men a feeling for things, sharpened their senses in odd ways. But the mountains had been eerily quiet during their descent out of the high passes, deserted of all life save for the flowers and moss. They'd seen neither hide nor hair of game for nigh on a week.

"May be a pronghorn nearby, injured by a cougar," Crack said. "It can't have gone far."

"There's not a lot of blood," Cringe said. "Just drops. Probably not enough to really hurt it."

"Who cares," Crack said. "It's fresh blood, so the thing is close. And all the better if it's not ravaged. We'll take it clean, and sup on venison tonight."

"I don't like it," Cringe said stubbornly.

"You can shove your likes," Crack grunted. "Seeing as how I've got the command here. We're going after some meat."

There was nothing Cringe could say to that, so he fell in behind his house brother, still glancing about and sniffing the air like a ferret.

The blood trail rolled out ahead of them, sometimes clear and bright red on the rocks, sometimes fading away on darker ground, but never disappearing completely. It led them lower and lower downslope, and stuck mostly to the trail. Crack led the way, with his house brother close behind. Garrett took the rear, mopping his brow. Winter snow still held the high passes they had left, but here in the foothills spring had come in force. The air was ripe with the smell of wet earth and grass, and spring flowers dotted every crack and crevice of the mountainside, white chickweed and yellow glacier lily and bright red widow glass. Beautiful to look at, though it was dangerous to look too long. The foothill paths were cracked and treacherous, full of loose gravel and rotten stone. Garrett's mother always said that Tarn Harrick had broken the mountain to pieces when the first free men came, just to make it harder for the Nightmare to follow. But Garrett thought it likely had more to do with the constant freezing and thawing here. Ice was the only thing stronger than the stone. Ice and time. They had both ravaged these lower passes for generations, and a false step here could drop a man twenty feet, or pin him beneath a boulder as big as a house. Old Ahab, the castellan of Century Tower, had gotten his foot trapped that way, trying to raid a ptarmigan nest for eggs. He'd lost the leg for that, though he'd kept his life. Garrett supposed he'd have made the same trade, if it came down to it. But it was best to keep one's eyes on one's footing, and not on the flowers.

"It's leading us to Tarn's Bridge," Cringe said suddenly, and Garrett realized he was right. Goats and pronghorns and birds had many paths into the mountains, but men and Nightmare had only one: Tarn's Bridge. It wasn't a bridge in truth, but a narrow path that hugged the south-facing cliffs in a long, steep ribbon of stone, no wider than a man's shoulders. The bridge was two miles long at least, and spilled out onto the valley below, amid a tumbledown of boulders and rockfalls. Garrett had been on it once before, and had no desire to relive the experience.

"What's that?" Cringe said, pointing to a small hollow off the path. "Huddled under the overhang."

"Might be our pronghorn," Crack said, leading them over to investigate.

It was. The body was seemingly untouched, no wounds or injuries, no blood on the ground, save for the same few, scattered, wet-looking drops. From the size of the antlers, the animal looked like it had been full-grown in life, but in death it was little bigger than a newborn fawn, more a husk than a corpse, shrunken and dry.

And there was something else too, a horrible smell, something strange and rotten that made Garrett gag, bile rising in his throat.

"There," Cringe said. "You've got to smell that."

"You quit your complaining," Crack growled. "That nose of yours is going to get you in trouble."

"You must smell it," Cringe said. "Garrett?"

"I smell…something," Garrett admitted. "Could just be rot, but…"

Crack glared at him over Cringe's head, but his expression softened soon enough. "Well, might be I smell something, too," he muttered. "What of it, then? It's a dead body."

"The smell of an open grave," Cringe said. "And hot blood rotting on the ground."

Garrett looked about uneasily, loosening his dirk in its sheath. He knew what Cringe feared now. Every boy and girl in Cairn Meridia knew what a trail of blood and the smell of an open grave meant.

Horror.

"Don't be a fool," Crack said, and Garrett realized he had just spoken the word aloud. "Ain't no horrors this close to the mountains, as you seem to have forgotten. They stay in their tunnels down south and bloody their knives on slaves."

"Except when the Nightmare comes," Garrett said.

"Which ain't for another twenty years," Crack said. "Or have you forgotten how to count, too?"

"The neck," Cringe said. "Look at the neck."

He pointed at a single, dark line running vertically down the pronghorn's neck. *That's where the knife would have gone in*, Garrett thought. The knife that drinks blood.

"There, you see," Cringe said, the fear palpable in his voice. "What else kills that way, if not a horror?"

"Rock lions kill at the neck," Crack said.

"Wound is too neat," Cringe said. "And no rock lion would leave prey uneaten."

"Krayken, might be we ought to arm ourselves, whatever it is," Garrett said.

Crack sniffed the air again and prodded the pronghorn with his foot. The hide ripped like brittle paper, exposing a few yellow ribs. "Right," he muttered. "Arm up then." He pulled a pair of stout, thick handled axes from his pack while Cringe strung his bow and nocked an arrow. Garrett had nothing but his dirk, and that he left on his belt. He could pull it quick enough if need be, and he wanted his hands free in case of a fall.

"Keep a clear head," Crack said. "If it's a horror, it's our job to deal with it. With any luck, it's slipped and smashed its hooded head on the rocks already, but if not…"

If not they would have to fight it, and kill it if they could. The Tower Guard was sworn to protect Cairn Meridia with their lives, and destroy any creature of the Nightmare on sight. They were two weeks hard march from Cairn Meridia though, and far from any tower. Alone.

They started down again, moving slower now because of the weapons. More dead animals dotted the path along the way, a few at first, and then more and more, coming closer together, until they lined the path in a gruesome trail of corpses—hawks and hares and weasels, pronghorns and rabbits and white-pelted goats, black foxes and tree bats, even a brown bear. Every one of them was drained of blood, every one of them had a knife wound in its neck. The bear was so shrunken that it looked no bigger than a dog, its great, shaggy coat hanging loose on its bones. And the smell was near overpowering, and waxing stronger as they drew closer to the bridge.

"He's killed all the animals," Garrett said. "That's why we haven't seen any the last few weeks."

"It," Crack corrected. "Horrors ain't men. Not any more. And more likely most of the animals have fled. They know the smell of the Nightmare better than we do. Likely these are old kills."

He's admitted it's a horror we're tracking, though, Garrett thought. He didn't know if that made him feel better or worse.

The path took a sharp turn to the east, down a steep slope of treacherous gravel and scree. They slid down on their butts, feet first, Crack and Cringe still holding their weapons at the ready. A pile of animal corpses greeted them at the bottom. The men had no choice but to break their fall on them, boots crushing the poor dry things beneath their weight. Garrett scrambled over the top of a pair of wolves, holding his breath as corpse dust billowed up around him. At some point in their descent, the warmth of the sun seemed to have faded. Fog still gripped the valley below, though Garrett saw wind start to move the tops of the trees, and he could hear the sound of it whispering.

Whispering.

"Garrett!" Crack barked.

He looked up, and there it was, not a dozen paces from him. The horror.

It was a stooped figure, thin and hunched and clad in inky black wool. Its face was hidden behind a red mask, painted with the snarling face of a demon, and in its hand was a small, slim dagger, slowly dripping blood. It looked just like a horror from the books. Somewhere far off, Garrett was amazed by that. Exactly like it did in the books.

"Feather it!" Crack said.

Garrett heard the twang of Cringe's bow, and an arrow whistled over his head, taking the horror full in the chest. The thing didn't seem to notice. It shuffled forward, staring right at Garrett, whispering, whispering, mask grinning its horrible grin, knife dripping. The daggers always dripped blood, men said, even when the horrors hadn't killed for a long time. Some said it was sorcery, and some that the horrors cut themselves often, to keep it fresh. The stench of death was overwhelming; Garrett groped awkwardly for the dirk at his belt, trembling. *When did it get so cold?*

"Garrett, get behind us!" Crack said.

Another arrow buried itself beside the first, but the horror paid it no attention. Garrett couldn't seem to get his fingers to work properly. It was no more than five steps from him now. He could hear the whispering clearly, a strange rushing that he felt like he could almost understand. His breath was fogging in front of him, his sweat had turned to ice on his brow. The horror lifted his bloody dagger.

And then Crack was between them, broad and bull-necked, swinging an axe in each hand. The horror hissed and slid backwards, supple as a willow. Crack came hard after it, trying to crush the thing under his weight. It slipped away again, but a third arrow whistled over Crack's ear and sprouted in the horror's neck. *How many is it going to take?*

Garrett realized he finally had the dirk in his hand, though he couldn't remember drawing it. Anger flooded through him, washing away the fear. He had just lain there like a babe, shivering and cold. Even Cringe was fighting. His little dirk wasn't much use here, but maybe if he got behind the thing...

Crack gave him little chance though, continuing to press the attack, axes spinning in his hands. The horror fell back and back, staying out of reach, knife probing. Another arrow took it in the knee, and finally this one seemed to bother it, slowing its steps. With a roar, Crack leaped and brought both his axes down, burying them in the horror's shoulders. It fell to its knees, and a final arrow slipped past Crack's side and took it in the eye. The hooded figure collapsed, and the whispering went silent.

Then Crack slumped to the ground, and Garrett saw the knife in his gut.

"Krayken!" Cringe said.

They knelt at his side, Cringe holding his brother's hand. The knife was buried to the hilt, but no blood leaked out. *The knife that drinks blood.* Garrett grabbed hold of it and tried to draw it forth, but he might as well have been trying to pull it from stone. Crack looked like he was shrinking, his face sinking in on itself as the knife drained him dry. A horror's blade never failed to kill.

"Leave it," Cringe said, pushing his hand away from the knife. "He's climbing the heights now."

"I'm sorry, Cringe," Garrett said, forgetting to call him by his real name. "Your brother fought bravely. Braver than me. You both did."

"Garrett, look," Cringe said, pointing over the valley. "Ior help us, look."

He looked, and at first he thought the fog had merely darkened, turned from dark gray to full black. But the sun was shining brightly, and the fog was moving in a strange way, boiling like water in a pot. Then he saw the banners waving in the wind, the glint of sunlight on steel, and realized he was not looking at fog.

He was looking at an army.

It can't be. His mouth had gone bone dry. There were twenty years yet. Twenty years of peace.

But the Nightmare had come.

Garrett was on his feet, fear in his legs. "We…we've got to get back to the city," he said. "We've got to warn them."

"You go," Cringe said, pulling arrows from the horror's body. "I'm staying with my brother."

"Don't be an idiot," Garrett said. "He's dead."

"I bloody well know he's dead," Cringe snapped. For a moment Garrett thought Cringe might strike him, but the anger faded from his face and was replaced with a strange, calm expression. "You're much faster than me, Garrett. I'll only slow you down."

"So follow behind on your own," Garrett said. "You'll still beat them to the city. If that's where they're going," he added lamely. *Could it really be happening now? Decades too soon?*

"I love my brother," Cringe said, looking at Crack. What used to be Crack. He was shrunk up to almost nothing now, just like the animals had been. "It's what he would have done. I'll meet them at the bridge. They'll have to come up single file, and I'll have good cover. Might be I can slow them down a day, a few hours. Give the city more time to prepare."

"Your bow would be more use in a tower—"

"Every man is a tower that stands in a narrow pass," Cringe said.

"Don't quote the bloody Mysteries to me," he said.

"I love my brother," Cringe said again. He pulled the knife from Crack's dusty belly, and handed it to Garrett. It came out easily enough, now that its work was done, the skin collapsing around it to form a thin black line. "Take this to the General. He'll believe you."

"But Cringe, I mean, Akrin—"

"Love is one life laid down for another," Cringe said, resolved. "I love my brother. And he loved me. You understand?"

He didn't, but he saw the look on Cringe's face. They stared at one another for a moment.

No more than a moment.

Then Garrett took the knife, slipped it in his pack, and set off at a run. It was a two week journey to Century Tower. He aimed to be there in five days.

He did not look back.

CHAPTER TWO

The Meeting of the Masks

They came alone, and remained alone, hooded and masked in robes of deep black and dull gray. Many carried baskets full of food, honey bread and potatoes and jars of milk—meals for their husbands in the Tower Guard. Foolishness, that. Baskets were unique, identifiable. Saerin carried nothing but her quill, and that she usually kept hidden, tucked under the folds of her robe. She rarely had occasion to say anything, nor a desire to. Silence was its own mask.

A few candles burned in sconces on the wall, but no fire was lit, and the early spring chill clung to the stone walls and floor. Jars of honey stood in neat stacks along the walls, with wax combs on wooden drying racks taking up the bulk of one corner. A bee keeper's cellar, obviously, though Saerin did not know which one. She had little occasion to go to the summerflower fields, this far out of the city, and two of the women in green masks—the Whip's guard—had blindfolded her besides, once she had reached the outskirts of the fields, leading her the rest of the way in by the hand. They would lead her out the same way, once the meeting was over.

That was always the worst part, the blindfold. Always. Somewhere in the back of her mind, Saerin always expected to find the High Defender waiting for her when the blindfold was lifted, white bearded and cold eyed, his immense bulk hovering over her, ready to come crushing down. Tonight she had been almost certain of it, even taken the time to repeat the Prohibitions silently as she walked, preparing her heart for a try at repentance. Destined to fail, of course. She would die the first moment the Heartspell touched her.

But when the blindfold was lifted, she had found, like always, only Masked Ones like her, silent and shuffling. It was a large gathering tonight, almost fifty already, and more were still coming, crowding the others into the center of the room. A few sat on empty barrels or squatted on the floor, but most stood, or leaned against a wall if they could find the space. Too many. It would take forever to lead them all out again once the meeting was over. The Whip must be planning a big announcement. She had been hinting at it for months now, dropping a word here or there, a plan that involved some real action, more than just facilitating lust in the young, or despair in the old.

Saerin squeezed herself between two of the drying racks and watched the rest of the Masked Ones being led in. She had seen many of them before, recognizing them by the marks of shame they carried. A person was known by their shame, here, where masks hid their faces. Saerin always took time to memorize the marks when she had a chance, sorting and noting, putting a name to their muffled shapes. Names were useful things.

She recognized a good many of the people here, and there were a good many more besides that she did not know. There was Sapphire Ring, short and thin, dressed in a robe of pale silver, her mark of greed glittering blue on her gloved finger. An important person, Saerin guessed her to be, perhaps a House Master's wife, or a Dreamer. She carried herself with a certain authority. Next to her was Summerflower Wine, the phial at her side full of a liquid that was such a deep red that it was almost black. Every few minutes her hand would reach for it, caressing the clear glass as if of its own accord. The dagger twins, Black Dagger and Stained Dagger, with their squat bodies and broad hips, stood together in the corner, as always, weapons belted at their sides. The others gave them a wide berth.

And then there were the sisters of the overflowing house of lust, as Saerin thought of them, women with strips of soiled bedsheets tied around their waists and arms. Blue Trim and Gold Thread and Cross Stitched, Black Hem and Many Rips, Thick Wool and Thin Wool. And on and on. Saerin carried such a token herself. Not her real mark, of course; she'd cut the white linen from the hem of one of Zoe's dresses, stained it with a bit of sour milk. Her own mark was tucked away safely in a pocket sown inside of her dress, the stone hard against her skin. But it was always best to play another part, blend in as much as possible. Attention could get you killed.

Another figure was led in. She wore a man's robe, but a few strands of straight black hair had escaped from beneath her hood and trailed down her mask, well below her chin. Several of the others near her touched their masks lightly, searching for hairs of their own. The mask blocked all sensation to the face, of course, so one had to feel with the fingers. A sensible practice, though it marked one out as a woman immediately—if you were paying attention, anyway, which Saerin always was.

And they were nearly all women, that she was sure of. Even the ones wearing men's robes were too slight and feminine to make it really convincing. Men had a certain way of standing, a set to the shoulders and head that was difficult to imitate without practice. And none of the "men" ever looked at the other "men" with much more than a glance. Real men sought each other out in mixed company, shared their privileged place with one another, even in silence. They were easy to pick out, and Saerin had seen no more than two or three in all the meetings she had been to. And why would men take a mask, after all? Cairn Meridia did not hate them, and so they did not hate it.

Thick and Thin Wool walked in front of the drying rack, cutting off most of Saerin's view of the door, not seeming to notice that she was there. They were almost certainly sisters, Thick and Thin Wool, and nearly as big as most men. Saerin had just begun edging her way out of the racks to get a better angle when there was movement at the door. People scurried backwards, pressing against one another, giving the newcomer plenty of space.

The Whip had arrived.

She was dressed like the others, in a simple robe of gray, with boots of supple, black leather and bare, pale hands. Unlike most, she let her hair flow freely down the side of her face in shimmering brown waves, flaunting her femininity. Her mask was the color of blood, and open at the mouth. The small whip she always carried was coiled loosely at her side, its three tips barbed with small diamonds. She was the founder and leader of the Masked Ones, or so she claimed. Saerin suspected she might be a figurehead for someone else, someone that preferred to stay in the background and rule from a distance. That's what Saerin would have done, had she been in charge. Well, Saerin never would've started something like this in the first place, but if she had… There were advantages to staying in the shadows. At any rate, the Whip gave the orders. And they were best followed quickly. Those diamond tips weren't for show.

Then Saerin let her gaze slip past the Whip, to the pair of green-masked guards coming behind her, and the man they were dragging between them.

He was a small man, clad in the blue uniform of the tower guard, though he wore no breastplate and carried no weapon. Blood matted his hair to his skull and stained his face, clotted and dry. Bruises decorated his face and neck, and his fingers seemed to be frozen at strange angles. He might have been handsome once. The green masks dropped him face down in the center of the room, a sack of meat in human form, and the Whip stood over him, one supple boot resting comfortably on the back of his neck.

Another green mask came in, carrying a large piece of parchment and an easel. They set it up against one wall, and everyone moved around to be able to get a better look at it, crowding each other, but staying well away from the Whip and the still figure beneath her. No one ever spoke aloud at meetings. Too much risk in someone else recognizing your voice. Everything that needed to be said was written, scrawled on parchment and held up for all eyes to see. The record was burned at the end of every meeting, the ashes scooped into a bucket by one of the green masks and carried away, Saerin knew not where. Her attempts to follow them after the meetings had proved fruitless and frustrating.

The Whip removed her quill from a pocket of her robe and held it up for attention, an enormous thing, made of a black swift feather. Everyone was already looking at her. She dipped it in the ink pot the guard held out for her, and wrote swiftly on the parchment, in the large, flowing hand Saerin had come to know well.

The time has come, she wrote.

A sigh passed through the masks, like a cool breeze rocking a field of summerflowers. There was a trace of tension there, too, a breeze hovering on the edge of a storm. The silence was expectant, waiting. The Whip began to write again, and as she wrote, the tension in the room rose and rose, like a climbing flame. Saerin had put on the mask six years ago, at the age of fourteen. In all that time, the Whip had ordered many things, all of them against the Prohibitions, all of them shameful. Some had even been fatal.

This was madness.

"But surely we'll all be killed!"

There was a collective intake of breath. It was Sapphire Ring. The fool had spoken aloud.

The Whip smiled and set her quill in the ink pot. Her blood red mask made the smile entirely humorless—the grin of a demon.

"Some of us certainly will be," she replied aloud, to Saerin's surprise. Her voice was warm and smooth, like a draught of sweet, burning wine. "But the time for hiding and shirking, for small things done in the shadows, for burning our words in the fire—that time is ending. The time is coming when our voices will be heard." She kicked the still body under her foot. "Look on this, masked ones, and see what is coming to the leaders of this city. As we have done to this lamb, so shall we do to them."

There was a different kind of silence, a stunned silence of shuffling feet and darting eyes. *A lamb*, Saerin thought. *What kind of woman kills a lamb?* Sapphire Ring pushed her way through the crowd, stepping up to the inkwell.

Our numbers are growing, Sapphire Ring wrote, thinking better of her outburst. *Fear keeps the silence, fear and hatred of what should be feared and hated. But fear can break the silence as well as keep it. Command this, and someone will break. Someone will run to a guardsman or a keeper. The masks will come off.*

"Are you so careless?" the Whip asked, still speaking aloud. She stroked the weapon at her side. "Who here knows you?"

They will be ready for us, Sapphire Ring wrote, and Saerin nodded, thinking much the same thing. Did the Whip plan to kill the High Defender with a single blow? Even if everyone in the room with them was a fully trained soldier wielding a firebrand, the Guard would crush them like a nest of beetles.

Why should we do this thing? Sapphire Ring finished writing.

"Have you forgotten so quickly, *sister?*" the Whip asked. She snorted, fingering Sapphire Ring's boy cloak. "Indeed, we are nearly all sisters, here, are we not? The ones without a voice, without power. Too ashamed of our womanhood to wear our own clothes."

The Whip looked around the room, directing her words to the crowd. "You ask why we should do this thing. Tell me, *brothers*, when a man and a woman are caught stealing a few kisses in the moonlight, which one is sent away by the Unshamers with a few prayers, and which one is left screaming on the floor?"

There was no response from the others, and the Whip laughed, a throaty, liquid sound.

"We live in a city broken by shame," the Whip went on. "A city broken by fear, where those who would choose freedom are forced underground like moles, too scared to show their real faces, or speak with their true voices. Where tyrants reign, clinging to a set of foolish laws choked with the dust of a thousand years. I ask you, is this the mark of a good city? Is this how we are meant to live? Centuries we have survived in this valley, fearing the Nightmare, dreading the day when our sons and lovers are sent to die on the towers. And for what? Seventy years of peace, they say."

The Whip spit on the dead body of the lamb to show what she thought of peace. "But it is merely seventy more years of hate," she said. "Seventy more years for the Unshamers to spoil our sons and torture our daughters, to send them to the ground weeping, to fill them with hatred for themselves, all for the crime of a few extra hours taken in rest, or an extra sweet taken from the pantry, or a bit of pleasure taken in their beds. How many of you came to us after such a torture, or for fear of one? How many of you found your mask on the steps of the House of Summerflower?"

There was a general shifting and murmur of agreement at this question, and Saerin restrained herself from joining in. The pain of Unshaming was something they all knew, and feared.

"You chose power and action over silent suffering," the Whip said. "You chose your sisters and daughters over masters and Unshamers. You each swore an oath, to work toward the end of them all, to take your justice for what they have done, to you and your families. I offer you that justice now. It is yours for the taking, if you will only have the courage to stretch out your hand."

The Whip waited a moment, grim beneath her mask, still caressing the hilt of her namesake at her side.

Then she spoke again. "But if you will not do it for justice," she said. "Then do it for peace. For I bring you a new word now, from the mouth of Tjabo himself."

Another wind rippled through the crowd, this one uneasy. The name of Tjabo was not spoken lightly.

"Yes, Tjabo himself," the Whip repeated. "The so-called enemy of Meridia. Yet he has offered us what our supposed Defender never could. *Peace.* For when we have rid ourselves of the chains of the High Defender and his black-coated lackeys, when we pledge our fealty to the true king, then the Nightmare will have no need to trouble us any longer. We will have one and the same master then, Tjabo the true king, a kinder master than this city has ever known. You have heard, each of you, what I have told you of the south, how the people live as men and women ought, free from the chains of the Prohibitions and the tyrants who cling to them.

When the High Defender is dead we shall live as they do, in a city without Unshaming, without epitimia, without the sound of screaming filling the halls of the House of Summerflower. A world where no one will be forced to follow the Prohibitions at the point of a knife."

Silence greeted this, at first, and Saerin found her eye drawn to the corpse at the Whip's feet. And then Sapphire Ring wrote, in a trembling hand, *But to kill so many…*

"Perhaps you should carry a mark of cowardice as well as greed," the Whip sneered at her, smiling her humorless grin. "You would suffer a hundred injustices daily to avoid shedding a dozen drops of blood? For the sake of a thousand deaths you would throw away ten thousand years of peace? You cannot see past your own fear. Our power is far greater than any of you know. Nor will we need to face the full brunt of the Defender and his thugs. For there is a surprise waiting for them, marching soon over the mountain passes.

"The Nightmare is coming."

There was a moment of absolute stillness. And then Sapphire Ring laughed, a deep, hollow noise with just the hint of a ragged edge. A few others joined her, though their laughter, too, was uneasy.

The Nightmare is twenty years away, Sapphire Ring wrote. *Have you taken leave of your senses?*

The smile never left the Whip's face. Swift as a streaking merlin, she struck Sapphire Ring's neck. Blood blossomed out, a sickening red spray that disappeared in the red of the Whip's mask, a few specks dotting her lips. Sapphire Ring dropped, falling atop the body of the lamb, and there was a quiet rush away from the pool spreading around her, women lifting their robes above the redness, picking their husbands' baskets off the floor.

The Whip had already forgotten her. She held up a knife, slick and dark, and began to chant, words fell and strange. They sounded a little like the words of Unshaming, but where those dropped and cracked like falling stones, these ran all together like grass in a field, so that Saerin could not tell one word from another. For a moment, her mind was thrown back to another place, another time, when she had said such words herself. The stone in her robe grew cold against her chest, and she saw the face of a young man, and felt the brush of ghostly lips upon her forehead.

But Saerin pushed the memory away, and wriggled her way fully out from behind the racks, standing behind Thick Wool's shoulder, trying to get a better look. She was a tall woman, Thick Wool. Saerin attempted to push her a bit out of the way, but she took no notice of her. A strong woman, too.

The Whip's incantation rose and rose, and the knife began to glow, first deep red, then orange, then a yellow that lightened steadily until it was almost white. With a final cry, the Whip plunged the knife into the prone body of Sapphire Ring. She twitched once more, and went still.

The Whip pulled her knife free. A faint shimmer of red flames now licked the edges of the blade.

"The time for hiding is over," the Whip said. She pointed the knife at the parchment carrying Sapphire Ring's last words. Scarlet fire shot forth from the tip, burning the parchment to glowing ash and cinders, along with the wooden easel that held it. Saerin could feel the heat from where she was standing.

"I heard four voices laugh with this one," the Whip said, pointing to the corpse. "The first people to kill one of those four will get a weapon like this."

There was a moment of shocked silence. And Saerin felt, in that moment, the fate of every woman in the room hanging in the balance, saw every masked face pull back, as a choice was presented to them.

And then four figures broke for the door at once: Gold Trim and Summerflower Wine and two others Saerin did not know. They didn't make it far. There was a mad struggle, screaming and cursing. Gold Trim went down under a trio of women, the Dagger twins and one other, their blades working furiously. Summerflower Wine caught a pot of honey to the face, the red clay shattering as the sticky-sweet liquid sprayed out, and then she too vanished beneath the press of a handful of bodies, Many Rips and Black Hem and others. The green masked guards took the last two at the door, one with an axe in hand and one with a silver mace, hacking the runners down with a flurry of blows. It was not quiet. And Saerin realised why they were meeting so far outside of the city that night.

She moved to the left of Thick Wool, as if to get a better view. The door was across the room, some fifty feet away at most, and unguarded for now. But a press of bodies lay in between, any one of whom might give her away at the wrong moment. Sapphire Ring was right; the Defender would rip them all apart like wet paper. But Sapphire Ring was also dead, and Saerin had no intention of joining her. She was no warrior, to seek out glory in battle. Life was the only glory she cared about. She had to get out of there without being seen. Slow and patient as a ghost, that's how she needed to move, easing through the crowd like a drop of water through rocks.

The Whip began to chant again, moving from body to body. Red flames popped up one at a time, the power of fire taken from the shame of murder, their light casting strange, flickering shadows on the walls. The rest of the women shuffled back a bit, pockets of space opening up around the bodies. Saerin slipped through them. Patiently. A few feet at a time. How long before they understood what was happening here?

When the Whip had finished, some ten others held firebrands of one kind or another, knives and hatchets and strips of bloody cloth, even a broken shard of the honey pot. They stood behind the Whip like proud soldiers, clutching their new power in stained hands.

"The Nightmare is coming," the Whip said again. "And this time it comes with a fury as yet unknown. It will break the Guard, and the House of the Summerflower. The black bell will ring from the House of Time and the House of Moonlight will crumble. And when the High Defender turns to fight the darkness in front of him, we will slip our cloaked dagger in his ancient back. He will die, and we will burn the Prohibitions to ash and the Mysteries to cinder. And there will be a new order, free at last from the Nightmare without, and the nightmare within."

She thrust her dagger out, and the crowd split down the middle to get out of the way, opening up like a tearing seam. Fire flew out like a lance, burning a black line down the middle of the stone floor. Saerin grabbed a random woman by the shoulder and shuffled with her, just managing to reach the half closest to the door. For the first time, she noticed that Thick Wool was right next to her still, her blond hair falling across her face. She had followed Saerin across the room. She was smart as well as big, then. The woman that Saerin had grabbed shoved her away, and she let herself be pushed back and shouldered aside by a few of the others, trading a few bruises for a few more precious steps toward the door. She caught a glimpse of the green masks moving back toward the entrance as well, Axe and Hatchet, she called them, by the weapons they held in their hands. Saerin risked moving a little faster, slipping along the back wall now, stepping in the small spaces between honey pots.

"The time has come to choose," the Whip said. She burned another line across the first, making a cross on the floor.

"You will all make a heart oath tonight," the Whip continued. Closer now. Into the corner and up the near wall. The Green Masks were moving too slowly. *Just a little more time.*

"A heart oath to serve and obey me against the High Defender, unto to death," the Whip said. "Any woman who does not make the oath will be treated as this one." She spit on Sapphire Ring's swathed back. "You, there, trying to leave unnoticed," the Whip said. She turned and pointed directly at Saerin. "You will die first."

Saerin froze, her throat seizing. The green masks were nearly to the door, but only a few women stood between her and the night air. She could make it if she ran.

But the stone in her cloak burned cold against her chest, and terror held her in place like a chain.

"Bring her here," the Whip said, and three of the women between her and the door came toward her.

And past her. They seized Thick Wool by the shoulders and pushed her forward through the crowd. The Whip hadn't been pointing at Saerin. The Whip hadn't even noticed her, small and slim and quiet. But the big woman with the blond hair stood out like a pearl in mud.

"Wait," Thick Wool pleaded. "Wait, please. I wasn't leaving. I'd never betray anyone here."

Ignoring her, the others wrestled the big woman down to her knees in front of the Whip, at the place where the black lines crossed. Her hood fell back, and her hair spilled out around her, gold and red in the light of the Whip's dagger.

"Who wishes for the honor of killing this one?" the Whip asked the crowd. There was a shuffling and cursing near the front of the room as several women tried to push forward. Saerin heard a yelp of pain and the sound of a mask cracking, and then there was one woman standing in front of the others, a big woman, with a thin strip of wool tied around her arm. A woman who was, Saerin thought, almost certainly the sister of the woman kneeling on the floor. Saerin tried to find the strength to move again, to unstick her feet from the cold stone.

"Good to see you so eager," the Whip said to Thin Wool. She made a subtle movement with her hand, and a second knife appeared in it, slim and gleaming, but without fire. She held it out to Thin Wool, who took it by the hilt.

"Let go of me!" Thick Wool screamed, heaving and shaking. "I'm one of you, damn it. I'm not the one you want." The others kicked and beat her down, holding her in place as she struggled.

And Saerin realized that she was at the back of the room now, with nothing between her and freedom. Axe and Hatchet had paused to watch the execution, and the crowd had flowed past her, leaving her alone. She took a silent, trembling breath, and gathered herself. It would have to be quick and quiet. It would have to be the moment the woman died.

Thin Wool seized her sister by the hair, pulling her head back, exposing her dark throat to the open air. She stood behind her victim, so that Thick Wool couldn't see her, didn't know who was taking her life. Saerin wondered, in that moment, whether that was a mercy or a cruelty.

"I'm not the one you want!" Thick Wool screamed again.

The cold steel of the knife gleamed.

Thin Wool took a deep breath, and launched herself at the Whip, vaulting over her sister's head.

And flames the color of blood took her in the chest.

Holding her breath, Saerin eased the door shut behind her, slipping into the night. A brave woman at heart, Thin Wool. And a fool.

Saerin strode away from the beekeeper's at a light jog, orienting herself in the night's darkness. She would not sleep tonight. There was much to—

Saerin ducked and rolled to the side, hearing the whoosh of an axe pass over her head. The woman had been nearly silent; only the sound of a few pebbles had given her away. She shouted for the others and came at Saerin again, who darted to the side and broke for the open field. Axe swung wildly and missed her by a foot, but she reached out with her other hand and snapped it closed around Saerin's cloak. Saerin went down in a heap, dragged under by the bigger woman's weight. Scrambling madly, she wrenched and twisted, managing to pull her knife free from under her cloak. She stabbed at the woman's face, but Axe flinched back in time, and took a graze on the ear, a shallow cut from lobe to tip.

Her axe came around again, whistling toward Saerin's kneecaps, but she rolled away with all her strength. Saerin felt the robe tear along the shoulder and then she was free, and running, the woman shouting curses at her back as she struggled to untangle herself from the empty robe. Saerin moved like a deer, alive.

CHAPTER THREE
Awake in the Dark

As he did every morning, General Jair Thorndike woke in total darkness. The stones of the Low Tower were knit together closely, and no light could reach his chamber, buried as it was in the center of the old keep. Years ago, this room had been a holding cell for prisoners, men and women who had been caught committing grievous crimes and who had refused to be Unshamed. It was the closest thing Cairn Meridia had to a dungeon, though it was five stories up, at least. And for a dungeon it was spacious, nearly twelve feet square and ten high. Prisoners had been kept well fed and watered, of course, and free of chains. It was the darkness that was the real enemy, oppressive and choking, making the room feel little bigger than a coffin. A coffin of shame. Most lasted no more than a few days before they started begging to be sent to the House of Summerflower.

Jair had lived in it since his eighteenth birthday, when Praeses had pinned the marble tower of generalship to his uniform. The next day he had commanded the cell to be cleaned and swept out, the prisoners moved to a well-lit chamber near the top of the tower. He had filled it with a simple straw mattress, a chest of clothes, a wash basin, and a chamber pot. There were no candles or books, no fireplace, and no bath. He was not there to be comfortable. He was there to make the darkness his friend. Or at least earn its respect as an enemy.

Jair judged it to be some time between first and second vigil, still at least an hour before sunup. The walls of the Low Tower were too thick to allow the ringing of the city bells through to his chamber, but Jair had spent three years of his youth in the House of Time, embedding the steady marching rhythm of the clocks into his bones. It was said The Clock himself could tell the time of day or night down to the second, and Jair did not doubt it. There was more to that gray-cloaked man than it seemed. Jair himself had never done any better than five minutes, but that was good enough for him. Enough to wake him in the morning, anyway, when darkness and silence sealed him off from the rest of the world.

He rose from the bed and moved confidently around the room, dressing himself for the day, trimming back the night's growth of beard with his razor. The blade flicked back and forth quickly, expertly in the dark. He knew the layout of his room by memory and each of his uniforms by touch, small rips or imperfections in the seams, the feel of the stitching. They were little different from one another, anyway—a small array of blue shirts and tan trousers, leather boots and gloves. The white breastplate of the Tower Guard went over his chest, identical to the breastplates of his soldiers, save for the colored petals of the heart flower design and the marble tower on his shoulder. The petals were for the graces of Ior, seven in all: purple patience and red bravery, silver faith and golden chastity, orange diligence and blue humility—and the green petal of love, the source and summit of all other graces. Jair had mastered six of them by his fifteenth birthday. Though the last, humility, had taken him three years to earn, far longer than any of the others. But he had learned.

He hung a simple short sword from his waist and tucked his pipe and tobacco pouch in his belt. The pipe was part of the uniform—the most important part, really. *You are not a machine*, Praeses had told him once. *So do not let your men think you are. Men have no love for machines, and no respect, either.* The High Defender had his hounds, Patience and Diligence, to prove his humanity, and they had certainly won him respect, if not love. Jair had his pipe.

Ridi was waiting in the hallway as usual, a lantern in one hand and a stack of papers in the other. The lantern was nearly shuttered, and only a faint line of light leaked out from its base, but after the hours of darkness in his room the beam seemed bright as sunrise. The castellan stood like a spear, eyeglasses perched on the end of his pointed nose. He gave a tight salute with the hand holding the papers and then fell in beside Jair as the two men began the winding journey through the tower's innards to the mess hall.

The Low Tower was a veritable ant's nest of twisting passageways and spiraling stairs. Traders and visitors to Cairn Meridia often marveled at the height and grandeur of the High Tower, but if the real strength of the guard could be found in any one place, Jair thought it was in the Low Tower, short and squat and brown. The stone of its walls was rough and undressed, and built so cleverly that it looked like part of the mountain itself, a weathered outgrowth of old rock. Walking through the midst of it was like walking through a series of caves, barely shaped by the hand of man. Many of the guardsmen believed it to be the very tower that the first Nightmare broke against, when Tarn became the first lamb. Jair had no way of knowing whether that was true or not. Even Oded likely didn't know, though Praeses might have the answer in one of those books of his. It didn't matter. What men believed was more important than what could by proved from history, and Jair was content to let the men believe in the sacredness of the Low Tower. They would fight better with the memory of Tarn Harrick giving strength to their limbs.

"I trust you slept well, sir?" Ridi said, the same thing he said every morning.

"As well as always," Jair replied. "What do you have for me today?"

"There are a few orders that require your signature," he said, waving the papers. As long as Jair had known him, Ridi had never once met him in the morning without a stack of papers, though he never seemed to consult them, just waved them around for emphasis. Likely his weak eyes would be unable to read them in the low light of the lantern, anyway. "The Eighty-First is requesting the new pikes, so we'll need an official order to the armorer."

Jair smiled. "Captain Cyril has finally come around? He always did have more sense than most Blackwings." The Eighty-First was a full day's ride down the southern road, but Jair made a mental note to make a personal visit sometime soon. It was hard to get to all one hundred towers with any regularity; they were laid out along the southern road like a line of stone ants, each a mile or less from its fellows, though the road twisted and climbed through the mountains so much that no more than one or two other towers was usually visible from any of them. "How many does that leave with the old pikes?" Jair asked.

"Seven, sir," Ridi said. "Towers Twelve through Fourteen, the Sixty-Third, the Sixty-Eighth, West Gate, and the High Tower, of course."

"Excellent," Jair said. "We may convince them all yet." They started down a steep set of stairs, lit from below by a glowing brazier. The shifting coals made rippling shadows on the wall.

"I am sure I do not need to remind the General that he could simply *order* the remaining captains to implement the new pikes if he wished," Ridi said.

"A man who is forced onto the right path will abandon it at the first sign of tough climbing," Jair said, for what was likely the hundredth time. "They'll see the right of it eventually."

"As you say, sir," Ridi said, moving on to the next item. "The Golden Games will be contested today after second terce."

As if Jair didn't know. They only came once every fifty years, after all, a last celebration to mark the final year of rest, before the twenty-year preparation for the Nightmare began.

"There are a number of rumors going around that you intend to contest the quindo," Ridi continued.

"And do you put any stock in these rumors, Ridi?" Jair said, smiling.

"The General is always full of surprises," Ridi said, and Jair laughed. "Inspection for the Sixth Tower today," Ridi continued. "Captain Lorrin says they'll be drilling from lauds until terce. Several of the men are competing in the games, so he wanted to give them plenty of time to get to the grounds before preliminaries."

"What is he drilling today?" Jair asked.

"Sudden loss, I believe. And star fall." Those were the names of the drills, designed to fight against different creatures of the Nightmare.

"Tell him to have the men run through pincushion, too," Jair said. Tower Six was less than an hour's ride away, so he'd have time to do a full inspection. "And send a crate of clay pigeons. I want to watch his gunners shoot."

"As you say, sir," Ridi replied.

The business of the morning rolled on. Jair broke his fast in a small dining room off the mess hall, a plain meal of honey bread, goat milk, and porridge. As General he could have had meat with every meal, but he never felt right eating more than his men. He might begin to think himself better than them.

"I have the report you requested on grace acquisition," Ridi said, pulling a few papers out of his stack and setting them on the table where Jair could read them. They were covered in tables and charts, filled with Ridi's spidery hand. "Approximately one quarter of the current guard has acquired a grace of some kind," Ridi went on. "With perhaps half again that many claiming to be in the process of acquiring one."

"How far along are they?" Jair asked. It took a year and a day to earn a grace, a year and a day of keeping every related Prohibition. And there was no way of knowing if you had actually done it until you presented yourself to the Unshamers, and let the Heartspell test you.

"Most are at least six months outside of the testing," Ridi said. "As expected, the vast majority are attempting to acquire bravery, with diligence running a distant second. I'm afraid we have very few attempting love, or humility."

"We shall need to encourage them," Jair said, scanning the pages. The graces were of utmost importance to the defense, especially love. Bravery was more impressive, of course; Jair had seen brave men that could shatter rock with their bare fists. He had done it himself a time or two, when he had first been empowered. But love did a bit of everything that the others did, and, even more important, it was the best defense against the cold hand of despair.

When the morning business was finished, Ridi set a number of papers in front of him to sign and seal.

"Who is my squire today?" Jair asked, as he lit his morning pipe.

"A Private Harn, of House Floramel," Ridi replied. "A bit timid, but devoted. He just took his vows as a lamb."

Every General before Jair had a devoted squire, someone to clean and mend and run errands, someone to do all the little things that were beneath a General's attention. Jair had no need of cleaning and mending; he could do that himself, and preferred to. So he let Ridi choose him a different squire every day, as a way of getting to know the men. He learned far more about his troops from his squires than he ever did on inspections.

"Honor to the lambs," Jair said. Then he asked, trying to keep his voice as casual as possible, "Any traders come through yesterday?"

"Just one—a southerner from the Pratum hills," Ridi said. "The guard at the West Gate let her through late last night, but she hasn't attempted to come into the city. It's likely she spent the night up on Trader's Pass."

"What is she carrying?" Jair asked.

"The usual leather goods and cooking herbs," Ridi replied. "There are a number of interesting seeds as well, and the inspection reports more tobacco than I'm like to credit. I suspect she caught wind of your liking for the stuff."

Jair suppressed a sigh of relief. *Nothing like waiting until the last minute, eh Willow?* he thought. "Well, I won't disappoint her, then," he said aloud.

"Shall I send Pym to fetch her, sir?" Ridi asked.

"No, let her sleep," Jair said, grabbing a third slice of honey bread. "Send her to me once she is turned away at the gate."

"As you say, General," Ridi said, tucking his papers up under his arm. "I'll take my leave then, sir." He turned away for a moment and then paused. "Quite lucky for you, I think," he said over his shoulder. "To have a trader come through the high passes this early in the season."

"Ior's blessings never cease," Jair said, waving the castellan away.

"So it would seem," Ridi said, and vanished in a rustling of wool and paper.

CHAPTER FOUR

Trader's Pass

It was fifty years since the last Nightmare, still twenty before the next, and the morning dawned clear and crisp on the valley of Cairn Meridia. The spring grasses stood tall and thick in the pasture, slicked with the barest hint of frost, and the wind from Trader's Pass carried the smell of running water and growing things.

By luncheon the grass would be dry and the ground hard. A good day for a race.

A good day to win a race.

Bryndon knew he was going to win. Cael was quicker off the line, perhaps, Drem was stronger. But today was Bryndon's day. He could feel it in his bones, see it in the morning rind of ice on the surface of the washing barrel. As long as he could get there in time for the first heats, anyway. Father had sent a message home, telling Bryndon to start grazing the herd on the new clover around Trader's Pass, and that was a long way to drive and feed and water a dozen goats, especially goats as ornery as theirs. He'd have to get them back by terce if he wanted to have time to wash up and grab some food before walking to the racing fields. And he wanted his legs fresh when he arrived.

One sharp tap with the butt of his crook, and the ice broke. He splashed a bit of the water on his face and neck. Then he slipped his hands under the surface and held them there till they turned white, flexing his fingers as much as possible, whispering the Prohibitions through clenched teeth. Gran had taught him this. When the Nightmare came, it brought coldness with it: wind and hail and thundersnow, and even with wool-lined gloves, men sometimes found their hands too frozen to squeeze a trigger or grip a pike. Bryndon did not intend to be one of them. Besides, it made waking Robin up far easier.

When he reached the twelfth Prohibition, he could stand it no longer and pulled free. He took a furtive look around and then dried his hands on one of the saddle blankets. It wasn't Prohibited, so he didn't feel too bad, but he knew Master Florian wouldn't approve. Well, Master Florian disapproved of most things, Prohibited or not. Touching the saddle blankets. Eating between meals. Laughter. It was hard to believe he was Father's brother.

No matter. Master Florian wouldn't be on the towers when the next Nightmare came. He was a man of the Golden Generation, born five years after the end of the last Nightmare, and he'd be too old to fight when the next came. He didn't have to train his hands to melt frost like a hot poker. He just had to whip children when they annoyed him. Bryndon smoothed the blankets out, careful to leave no wrinkles.

He slipped back inside. Sleep still gripped House Claybrook, and would until true dawn, when the sun summited the eastern peaks and cast its full light upon the valley. All was silent, save for Kian's quiet snoring, which sounded like the thrum of a beehive. The still forms of the Claybrook children lay scattered across the sleeping room, wrapped in woolen blankets, little Digon wrapped up so tight that he was almost impossible to see. Teagan and Rhys were sharing a cot again; they must have changed places in the night. Master Florian would definitely not approve of that, house siblings or no. Neither of them had been Unshamed for lust, of course, and everyone knew they'd get married eventually. But still. Not a risk Bryndon would have taken, especially not for a girl like Teagan, who couldn't even bake a decent loaf of bread.

Robin's usual cot was empty. *Must've had another bad dream...* She'd always been prone to them, black visions of milidreads and shrieks and darkstones, minions of the Nightmare that she was far too young to have seen. Gran thought she might be a Dreamer. Bryndon hoped she was not. Dreamers had to live in the city, in the House of Moonlight. They had to wear purple robes and sleep during the daytime and forswear all family and children. It was no life for a woman, even one so odd as Robin. He found her sleeping in Mother and Father's bed, her bright red hair matted to her pale forehead with sweat, her small form curled up like a babe in Father's extra cloak. They were both long gone, of course, Mother to her work in the scullery, Father for his guard on the Ninety-Sixth Tower. He had been gone almost three weeks. There was something about the smell of the bed that was comforting to Robin though, even when empty.

Bryndon shook her gently by the shoulder. "Robin," he whispered. "Wake up, sis."

Robin's eyes fluttered open for moment, then closed again as she snuggled down deeper into the blankets.

"Come on, red bird," Bryndon said, shaking her a bit harder. "It's race day, and we've got to take the flock up the slopes. Hurry now."

"I'm sleeping," Robin mumbled, pushing his hand away. "Ten more minutes."

"Now you mind me," Bryndon said. "Father says you're to mind me. Come on, after the race I'll buy you a honeycomb with the winnings."

No response from Robin, who looked like she had fallen asleep again.

"Alright then," Bryndon said. "You leave me no choice."

He shoved two ice-cold hands under the blankets, clapping them to Robin's back and neck. With a hiss she jerked up, slapping him away furiously.

"No messing around on race day, sis," Bryndon said, scooping her up, cloak and all. He dumped her at the foot of her cot. "Get dressed. If you're not outside in ten minutes I'm coming in after you. And next time my hands won't be so dry."

Nine and half minutes later, they were opening the gates, and Robin was very pointedly not speaking to him. The goats were as eager to get to the fields as he was, pushing past one another, small bells jingling around their necks. All except Bumble, who bleated and paced around the stall, hollow-flanked. Bryndon felt her udders, which were heavy and full. She would kid soon, probably within the week. Father would be pleased. The house had no debts to pay at the moment, and he'd likely be able to keep one of the kids this time, maybe even two if Bumble had triplets. Bryndon filled her trough with fresh water and left her behind. Kian would feed her when he woke up.

"Keep them close," Bryndon called, hurrying to catch Robin and the rest of the herd. His legs felt strong and loose as he ran. "We're heading all the way to Trader's this morning, and the foxes might be high enough up the slopes now to cause problems."

Robin said nothing, just tapped Lunker back in line, a little harder than necessary, her small mouth tight. She had a lot of emotions for one so young. Bryndon ran to her and knelt down, enfolding her in a tight hug.

"Thank you for coming with me," he said. "I'll get you that honeycomb, okay? I promise."

"You really think you can win this year?" Robin asked.

"I know it. Today, I'm the fastest boy in Meridia."

Robin kissed him on the forehead. "So humble, mud head," she said, using her nickname for him. Red bird and mud head, they called each other. House Claybrook's best. "Lunker's wandering off again," she said.

Bryndon smiled and stood, trotting after Lunker, who was tearing up chunks of purple clover. Sometimes it was hard to tell which of them was older.

They pushed up the lower slopes, treading carefully on the grass, which had gotten slick with dew and melting frost. All was quiet, save for the tinkle of goat bells. Even the stoneflies slept.

Soon the ground turned rocky and steep, the grass shorter and wider spaced—small, lush islands amid a sea of moss and lichen. A path appeared, switchbacking up the mountainside. Here it was paved with pieces of flat, white marble, leftovers from some grander, more important buildings in the city proper. Father claimed they were hundreds and hundreds of years old, the stones, worn smooth with the tramping of generations of goats and men. Many were missing or cracked, sitting loose in their niche, and in need to repair. The goats managed easily, while Bryndon and Robin picked their way up with care.

"Did you dream last night?" Bryndon asked.

"Once," Robin said. "It was darker than usual."

"What was it?"

"I was looking for the General," Robin said. She spoke as if to herself, her red hair hanging curly and loose around her shoulders, blowing a bit in the morning breeze, staff tapping the stones at her side. "He was sick, and I carried a bottle full of medicine that would cure him. But I walked through a black fog, and could not see. Then a man grabbed me from behind and wrapped me up in a blanket made out of the fog, and he threw me into a dark cave to die."

"You died in your dream?" Bryndon asked.

"It's happened before," Robin said, sounding unconcerned. "I don't mind. Because when I die, I wake up."

Bryndon took her hand and kissed it. It was warm and callused. "Well, you look strong and healthy to me now," he said. "Here. I brought us some breakfast."

They shared a hunk of brown cheese between them, continuing to climb. Soon they passed over the summit of the path and began their descent into Trader's Pass. Here true dawn had already come, and the narrow valley lay before them bathed in golden sunlight. Father was right about the pasture. The sedge and blue wildrye were in full bloom, thick and high, patches of it up to his knees in some places. Bryndon let the herd graze freely.

"Keep them away from the caves," Bryndon called out to Robin, as she wandered away with the herd. He took a seat on a moss covered rock, resting his legs. "And don't you go in either. It's filthy muddy in there, and Master Florian will whack you good if you come back with your clothes all soiled again."

Robin gave no sign that she had heard, but Bryndon knew she would mind him. Well, he thought she would, anyway. At any rate, she was well away from the cave entrance, a small hollow opening on the south side of the canyon. He'd explored the caves with Kian all the time when he'd been younger, throwing mud balls and playing courage. Sometimes he missed those days.

Bryndon jumped off the rock and took off his boots, flexing his toes in the high grass. He'd spent the winter running barefoot on cold stone, toughening his feet to the consistency of fine leather.

He bent down, staggering his legs, one hand resting lightly in front of him, the other held tight at his side. He'd have a lane to himself, in the finals, room to fire out unimpeded. Lean forward, almost to the point of falling, make your legs catch up. Start like a rock tumbling downhill. That's what Gran had told him, and Gran knew everything, or claimed she did.

Robin spotted him from a distance. "Ready!" she called out.

Bryndon slowly extended his hand backwards, above his head. Fingers loose. Head steady.

"Loose!"

Like an arrow from a bow he flew, body bent, heels flying. Thought vanished, and there was nothing but the air rushing past his ears, the grass breaking in front of him, and the slow burn of blood in his legs. He knew again that he was going to win. He saw the others fading, lagging, even Drem, the line within his reach.

Then his foot struck something hard and warm in the long grass, and he was sprawling, sliding, his teeth clicking shut on his lower lip. He tasted blood and mud and wet grass and his only thought, relieved, was that his legs seemed unhurt.

"Bryndon!" Robin cried. He sat up and saw her rushing over, little legs pumping.

Then another figure rose out of the grass, and Bryndon saw what he had tripped on.

It was the ugliest woman he had ever seen.

Bryndon rose to his knees, spitting mud. He could taste blood welling in his mouth, hot and metallic. The woman he had tripped over was standing up, knife in hand. When she saw Bryndon rising from the grass, however, she slipped the knife back into the green sheath at her belt.

"Are you hurt, child?" the woman said, walking over to him. She was slim and strong looking, with broad shoulders and a powerful stride. Her clothing was close fitting and drab; whatever color it might have once possessed had worn away long ago, and now it consisted of little more than a motley of brown and gray. She wore trousers like a man, and her face was not quite as ugly as Bryndon had initially thought. It had none of the noble beauty of the city, but it had the look of health, and intelligence, and hard use. Her skin was an unnatural array of colors, splotched with patches of green and brown, like moss-covered bark.

"I am alright," Bryndon said, struggling to his feet, looking at her warily. "You're a southron, aren't you?"

"My face gives me away," she said, smiling. It wasn't an unpleasant expression; the green and brown seemed to meld together like the shadows of leaves on a forest floor. "Though I am no slave of Tjabo's. I'm a trader from the Pratum Hills, here at the mercy and forbearance of the High Defender of Cairn Meridia, Praeses High Tower. Or so the guards at the West Gate were quick to inform me."

"Did I kick you hard?" Bryndon asked.

"I've had worse from my goat," she said, rubbing her side. Her voice was odd, lilting. It reminded Bryndon a little bit of birdsong. "Such is my punishment for hiding in the grass like a beast. Peace, little one." She bowed to Robin, who had come alongside Bryndon.

"What were you doing lying there?" Robin asked, frowning her small frown.

"I traveled long into the night before I found this place," the southron said. "And I was so tired when I did reach it that I curled up and fell asleep at once in my blankets."

"Didn't you hear us calling to one another?" Robin asked.

"I did, little one, but I thought it was a dream. It has been many weeks since I have heard another human voice."

"Don't call me 'little one,'" Robin said, her back stiff.

"Robin," Bryndon chided. "This woman is our guest."

"Not yet, she isn't," Robin said, which was technically true. They had shared neither bread nor fire with her, and had no responsibility to be welcoming out here, on the mountainside, not according to the Prohibitions.

But the woman took no offense, seeming amused rather than annoyed. "Forgive me, my lady," she said, bowing again. "You have me at a loss. I am Willow Peeke, traveler and trader, and I am at your service."

"Peace be with you, Willow Peeke," Bryndon said, before Robin could say something else rude. "I am Bryndon Claybrook, and this is my true sister, Robin. We welcome you in the name of the Free Cities and House Claybrook, by the mystery of the stone trees of Ior, under the guidance of—"

"Are you the Nightbringer?" Robin interrupted, pointing her staff at Willow's chest.

"Robin!" Bryndon said, aghast. "What a rude thing to ask a person!"

"I'm afraid I don't know enough to be offended," Willow said. "Who is this Nightbringer?"

"She comes before the Nightmare," Robin said. "Gran says she'll be a strange woman, who comes from the mountains and who can speak to animals. She says the Nightbringer will have a worm in her left hand and a mask on her face, and seven braids of dark hair, one for every Shame." She looked pointedly at Willow's hair, which was, indeed, done up in seven dark braids, bound with green ties.

"So Gran says," Bryndon said.

"So everyone says," Robin replied.

"You listen to too many myths," Bryndon said. "The Nightbringer is part of neither the Prohibitions nor the Mysteries, just some rumor from the Dreamers. And even if she was real, she wouldn't be here for another twenty years. And it's insulting besides. Suppose someone called you the Nightbringer."

"It sounds like someone to be wary of," Willow said. "But I don't come from the mountains, my lady Robin. I come from the lowlands, far to the south of here, across rock and snow and ice, in the foothills of Pratum, where Tjabo's princes hold sway. There the trees grow thick and high, higher even than the tallest of your towers in some places, and from the tops of the highest of them one can look for miles and miles to the south, over a sea of unending forest, broken only by the River Osku, which flows toward the Chained Cities like a shining blue road."

Willow sighed. "But it is many years since I have seen the green lands of my home. I am a trader now, and long miles I have walked in the mountains, bringing goods from the lowlands to the seven Free Cities, and from city to city. The seven braids in my hair are to honor them, and the seven virtues. Three of the cities I have laid eyes on in my life, and Cairn Meridia will be the fourth, and fairest of them. Or so I am told, and believe it to be true, for the men of the Free Cities seldom lie. I cannot speak to animals more than any other human, and as for the worm and the mask." She spread her hands, to show they were empty.

"Do you have any seeds?" Robin asked, still suspicious.

"I wouldn't be much of a trader if I didn't, would I?" Willow said. She reached into her bag and pulled out a single seed, holding it out in the palm of her hand. Robin stepped forward to examine it, and Bryndon followed, trying not to appear too eager. New seeds were always the most interesting things the traders brought. Some people preferred books and scrolls; Master Florian always made a show of considering them, anyway, whenever any new ones came in. But there were always a dozen bidders for the seeds, and most times Shepherd Pilio had to be called in to distribute them justly.

The seed in Willow's hand was oblong and large, perhaps half the size of an egg. Small flecks of white dotted the pale blue of its husk, so that they looked almost like clouds in a summer sky. Willow whispered a few words, breezy phrases Bryndon couldn't quite catch, and poked the seed with her finger. For a moment the blue of its husk seemed to glow. And then, with a tiny cracking sound, the seed split, and a green tendril poked its way into the sunlight. Up it grew, thickening and twisting, sprouting as it climbed, small filaments and leaves and bunches of tiny red flowers, which looked like bells. Robin reached out and stroked one of the flowers with her finger. Pollen dropped from it like rain, dusting her skin with gold, and the scent of sliced apples wafted through the air.

Then Willow whispered another command, and the little plant slipped downward, reversing its growth. The flowers folded up and vanished, and soon there was nothing on her hand but a large seed, glowing a soft blue.

"What manner of plant is that?" Bryndon asked, unable to keep the wonder out of his voice.

"*Heliantumim* men call it in the south, though it has no true name among the mountain people. I have heard it called 'scarlet bell' in Cairn Imerin, and 'blood drop' in Cairn Doxia, and I like neither of these, for the flower is more noble than these names, and the name of a thing should match its nature. When planted, it will stay six years in the ground, spreading its roots deep and wide, and in its seventh year it will grow nearly fast enough to see. It will not reach the heights of your stone trees, nor the beauty of the summerflower, but it is a hardy thing, and useful. The pollen soothes burns and cuts, and grants deep sleep and pleasant dreams, especially for those whose minds are torn."

"It is wonderful," Robin said, looking at the pollen on her finger.

"Consider yourself lucky," Willow said. "It is quite rare for *heliantumim* to flower so strongly under the growing magic alone. I have never seen it before."

"Perhaps you should call it 'robin's bell,' then," Bryndon said. "For the plant seems to have honored her."

"No," Robin said, her voice confident. "Its name is dream bell."

"Dream bell," Willow repeated, smiling. "So be it." She slipped the seed back in her bag, and glanced up at the sun. "Come, the morning wanes. I have traveled far to come to the city, and I wish to see it soon. I have a pack wether as well, who I left to wander free last night in my haste to sleep, and I must find him."

Bryndon blinked and looked around. He had forgotten about the herd. And the race! They had lost precious time. He scampered through the clover, rounding up the goats one at a time, driving them to the spring to drink. He had a small moment of panic when he couldn't find Lunker, but he spotted him halfway up the eastern slope, trying to pull the tender blue flowers off a thorn bush. Bryndon had to nearly drag him by the neck to get him away from it, whacking his flanks with the staff.

But soon the whole herd was fed and watered, and they started back down the mountainside, Bryndon on the right, Robin walking with Willow on the left. Robin's earlier animosity seemed forgotten, and the two chatted like old friends. Robin was confusing sometimes.

Bryndon pushed them as hard as he dared, but the way down was more dangerous than the way up. Willow's pack goat was nearly twice the size of the largest of their herd, and laden down with two enormous saddlebags that bulged out on either side, so they were forced to move slower than usual. He judged the sun past terce by the time they reached the gentler, lower slopes of the valley. No time to wash up. Still time to walk to the racing fields, though, if they kept a good pace the rest of the way. The ground had dried out wonderfully, firm and springy underfoot.

The slope eased, and Bryndon lengthened his stride, whistling and tapping at the goats lagging behind, pushing the herd ahead.

"Robin," he said. "Run ahead and check on Bumble for me. Make sure Kian fed her this morning."

"Willow and I are talking," she said. "She's telling me about her home."

"You mind me now," Bryndon said. "Remember what I said."

"Perhaps you'd better go," Willow said. "Come find me in the market later and I will tell you more of the south."

Robin shook her head and muttered something under her breath, but she set off at a jog, the crook swinging back and forth with her stride. Bryndon and Willow were left alone. He stole a few glances at her as they walked. She looked to be about twice his age, perhaps a little younger than Mother.

"Do you carry many seeds from the south?" he asked, breaking the silence. "Or many maps or pearls?"

"Much of each," she said. "And other things beside: leather fire gloves from Cairn Doxia and cooking herbs from Cairn Elendon and much tobacco. Though not as much of anything as I would like, of course. I have traveled three years in the mountains, now, and much of my packs are filled with the gold and gems of your people, destined for trade in the south."

"Haven't they enough gold of their own in the south?" Bryndon asked.

"More than enough," Willow replied. "But they are always hungry for more, especially the gold of the mountains, which is far purer and more beautiful than southern gold. And the beauty of gold is one of the few beauties that southrons appreciate. Seeds are rather lost on them."

"They are to be pitied," Bryndon said. "Living in chains, without the Prohibitions to guide them."

"Ah yes," Willow said lightly. "We southrons are certainly an unenlightened race."

Bryndon flushed. "I didn't mean. I'm sure you aren't like that," he said. "I just meant—"

"I know quite well what you meant Bryndon Claybrook," Willow said, voice flat. "I have heard much the same thing in all the Free Cities."

"It's not that I blame them, I mean, you," Bryndon said, feeling like he was botching the whole conversation. "You don't have the Prohibitions like we do, so it's just that, well...you don't have the Prohibitions," he finished lamely.

"True, we do not," Willow said. "Though it may surprise you to learn that my people do not need a woman dead a thousand years to teach us not to be greedy."

"I—Do you have many of the dream bells?" he said desperately.

Willow snorted at the abrupt change in subject, but let it go. "Half a dozen, at most," she said.

"I should like one for our House," he said.

Willow glanced at him, and he tried to keep his face expressionless. "I shall put them for sale in the market soon," she said. "Your House will have as good a chance as any other, I expect."

"Yes, I suppose," Bryndon said. He brushed a bit of dirt off his pants that wasn't there. Willow stayed silent, as if knowing he had more to say.

"You'll need someone to act as a Shield for you," Bryndon said. "If you want to start trading right away."

"Shield," Willow repeated slowly. The word sounded strange in her mouth, like she was saying it for the first time. "I have heard this word before, but I do not know it. It is a person?"

"A Shield is a…a Shield," Bryndon said, shrugging. "Someone to take responsibility for any shame you might incur. All must follow the Prohibitions in Cairn Meridia, or be shamed. Foreigners are no different. But it is cruel to ask a foreigner to obey what they do not know. So when one comes to the city, a citizen must serve as Shield. You share their roof and their food, and they share your shame."

"But am I not a guest of all citizens?" Willow asked. "Such was my status in the other Free Cities."

"I do not know what other cities do," Bryndon said. "But in Cairn Meridia, you are only a guest if you are in need. I assume you have plenty of food? A tent of some kind?" He waited for Willow's nod. "If you have food and shelter, you are not in need. You'll have to camp in the mountains and wait till you run out of food. And throw away the tent, I expect. Otherwise they won't let you through the gates without a Shield."

Willow scratched behind her goat's ears, thinking. "Shaming and Unshaming," she said. "This is very painful, yes?"

Bryndon nodded, rubbing a spot on his ribs. He did not hear screaming.

"And the Prohibitions are many and complex, such that a foreigner is likely to break one?"

"Usually," Bryndon admitted.

"So the Shield offers body and spirit and food and shelter, and the foreigner repays him with pain and suffering." This time it was not a question. "This seems a very unfair trade for the Shield."

"It is a gift," Bryndon said stiffly. "Gifts are not trades." Then after a moment, he added, "Though, sometimes, the trader may also give a gift to the Shield, something to show her thanks."

"An exchange of gifts," Willow said. She sounded amused again. "This seems like a trade to me."

"It is a gift," Bryndon insisted. "If the trader decides not to give, that is not Prohibited."

They were nearly home now; Bryndon could see the tall form of Master Florian talking to Robin about something, her arms crossed in defiance. He mentally counted the coins tucked away in his pillowcase, wondering if he had enough for two honeycombs.

Bryndon cleared his throat. "I could do it for you," he said. "I'm fifteen, and that is old enough to serve as Shield."

Willow stopped and grabbed his shoulder, turning him to face her. With an effort, he met her dark eyes, trying to keep his face calm. This time, he did hear the sound of screaming, and though he knew it wasn't real, knew it was just in his head, his side started to hurt again, a dull ache that made him want to lay down on the grass and hold his breath until it passed. The pain of Unshaming never really left.

"And what gift would you ask of me, Bryndon Claybrook?" she asked.

Bryndon felt tiny beads of sweat leaking out of his forehead. "I would ask for no gift for myself," he said. "But my sister is troubled by dreams. She…she is almost certainly a Dreamer, and in eight years she will be sent to the House of Moonlight, forever apart from her kin. I know that means nothing to you, but I would spare her that." When Willow said nothing, he added, truthfully, "And I thought, perhaps, you might help me learn a little more about the south."

Willow smiled again, though this time she seemed pleased rather than amused. "For your sister, then," she said, extending a hand.

"For her," Bryndon said. They shook, and Bryndon felt the hard shell of a seed pressed against his palm. He put it in his pocket without a word.

CHAPTER FIVE

Something Missing

Saerin woke to the sound of crying.

"Don't start that with me," she heard Master Usper's cold voice in the hallway. "Tears won't help you now, girl."

Saerin's eyes felt like they were filled with sand, red and gritty from a few hours of restless sleep. The first glimpse of sunlight immediately gave her a headache.

"But-but please, Master Usper," the crying voice said. "I swear I didn't lose it this time."

"So I suppose it got up and walked away on its own did it?" Master Usper said. The voices were getting closer, and Saerin could hear the sound of footsteps in the hall. "How stupid do you think I am, girl?"

"Not very stupid at all," the voice hastened to say, and Saerin recognized it as Zoe.

"Not very stupid at all," Usper repeated, his voice dropping dangerously low. "How nice of you to say. I suppose you think me just stupid enough to believe that you hung your cloak nicely in the closet like you're supposed to instead of losing it again and *lying* about it to save your miserable skin."

Saerin slipped out of bed quickly and pulled a simple dress of gray wool out of the wardrobe. The black swift wing of House Blackwing was embroidered across the breast.

"But I *did*, Master Usper, I did," Zoe said, right outside the door. "Hang it up, I mean, not lose it or lie about losing it, neither."

A pounding began on the bedroom door as Saerin belted the dress around her waist. She checked herself briefly in the mirror, smoothing her yellow hair and trying to look as awake as possible. Master Usper didn't care much for his charges sleeping in past lauds. It was best to play the diligent daughter. She pinched her pale cheeks to give them some color, and padded barefoot to the door, throwing open the latch.

"Master Usper," Saerin said, feigning surprise and dropping a curtsy. "Forgive me, I was at my mid-morning prayers. Why Zoe!" she said, pretending to see her for the first time. "Whatever is the matter with you?"

"Oh, there's a question for the wisdom of the aged Wizard Oded himself," Usper said, shouldering his way into the room. He was small for a man, barely over five feet tall, and every inch of that was stretched tight across his bones. Zoe followed behind him, her green eyes glistening with held-back tears, wearing an identical dress to Saerin's, though cut four inches longer and three wider around the hip.

"Eight years old when we took you in, girl," Usper rattled on. "And already I could see you would bring this house nothing but shame. Told old Master Vestus the same, I did, told him to leave you for the Silverfeathers, or the Claybrooks. 'This here is a *lesser* girl,' I told him. 'So let a lesser house take her.' But he was old and soft-hearted and told me not to make such a fuss. 'Her father says she's a good-hearted girl, just a might forgetful,' he says, so I shut my mouth proper like an under-castellan is supposed to and roomed you with a right, gracious Blackwing girl like Saerin. I thought a girl near your age—maybe some of her good breeding might rub off on you. But no, you've proved of lesser stock, just as I thought, and brought nothing but shame and misery on House Blackwing from that day to this. 'Forgetful,' ha!"

He threw open the wardrobe door, revealing a number of dresses and shifts, shoes and belts and head scarves, all of Saerin and Zoe's clothing hung up neatly and properly on opposite sides of the wardrobe, like mirror images.

Except where Zoe's robe should have been hanging was nothing but an empty hook.

"And there, the proof. Lost! Your only cloak lost, and you have the nerve to suggest that someone *stole* it," Master Usper said.

"No, no," Zoe said. "Please, Master Usper, I was only asking if maybe someone borrowed it, or took it for washing, or—"

"*I* am in charge of sending out the washing," Usper said, turning abruptly. "And everyone else in this house has a robe of their own, as you know, and no need or occasion to sneak into your room at night and steal yours."

"I only meant—"

"*Shame*, I name it," Usper said, pointing a finger up at Zoe's trembling nose.

There was a moment of silence as Usper let the word sink in. Zoe's pale skin flushed scarlet. "No, please, Master Usper, I swear I—"

"*Sloth*. And *pride* besides," Master Usper cut her off. "A diligent girl keeps her belongings and tasks in order. A humble one thinks of others instead of always thinking of herself, or whatever it is that fills that puffy head of yours. Buttons and needles, baskets and bowls, my own personal bottle of summerflower wine. Forgotten. Lost. Misplaced. And now this." He pursed his lips together in what Saerin would have sworn was a suppressed grin. "I think it's high time we sent you to the House of Summerflower, girl. A nice, long visit with the Unshamers ought to straighten you out."

"Please," Zoe whispered. "I hung it up right here last night. Saerin and I went to the services at the Grove, and *she* forgot her head scarf, so I got home first and—and I hung it up *right here*," she pulled the hook down and shook it. "And then I went to bed, and Saerin came in and…well, you must have seen it, right Saerin?"

Two sets of eyes turned to look at her, and Saerin thought of the last time she had seen Zoe's cloak, clutched in the hands of a green-masked terror of a woman, a woman trying to chop off her legs with an axe.

"Saerin?" Zoe asked again.

"Well?" Master Usper said, tapping his foot.

Zoe looked at her, her lips silently moving.

Please, Saerin.

Saerin looked at the floor. "Oh Zoe, dear," she said. "I'm sorry, sweetheart. We'll find it today I'm sure."

Zoe burst into tears. And this time Master Usper didn't stop his grin from showing.

CHAPTER SIX
A Shield

The Goat Gate guarded the west entrance to Cairn Meridia, and was manned by three old Timekeepers in the gray robes of their order, two of whom were nearly always sleeping. The gate itself was small and white and topped with a set of dull bronze spikes, etched with the text of the Prohibitions in tiny runes. The text was impossible to see from the ground, but Father had told Bryndon about it many years ago, one of the first times he had been allowed to come to market day. He remembered riding on Father's shoulders up to the gate, hands entwined in Father's wavy black hair.

Keeper Loric was awake and on duty when Bryndon and Willow arrived, just as he had been when Bryndon had first come riding through the gate. Robin trailed along behind them, intent on getting the promised honeycomb as soon as possible. Loric laughed when Bryndon told him his intention, knitting his bushy eyebrows together, then he puttered around the gatehouse for a few minutes, gathering the necessary materials and muttering to himself about the follies of the young. He seemed not to realize that Bryndon could hear him, or didn't care.

"Hold out your hand," Loric said, when he returned to the gate.

"What?" Bryndon said.

"Can't hear me?" Loric muttered. "And they say I have bad ears. YOUR

HAND," he said again, and seized it.

There was a quick flash of steel, and Bryndon sucked in his breath as blood blossomed out of a shallow cut on his palm.

"Now yours, my lady," Loric said, turning to Willow. "And be thankful you found someone so foolish," he added, not quietly.

Willow accepted the cut without a word, and Loric directed them to hold hands, letting the blood mingle. Though her face was a patchwork of brown and green, Bryndon found Willow's blood was as red and warm as his own. Willow, for some reason, seemed to find the whole thing highly amusing. Robin looked on with rather morbid interest.

Loric turned to Willow and said, "You must swear to the following oaths, or you will not be allowed to enter."

"Very well," Willow said.

"Do you promise to trade no books?" he asked.

"I do," Willow said.

"Nor make any weapons of shame?"

"I do."

"Do you swear to obey the Prohibitions? To serve as Stranger when the Nightmare comes? To pluck no summerflowers from the valley floor?"

"I do."

Loric grunted, apparently satisfied, and wrapped a length of cord around their wrists and hands, binding them together.

"You know the words?" Loric asked Bryndon.

"Huh?" Bryndon said.

"THE WORDS," Loric said again. "DO YOU KNOW THE WORDS THAT BIND YOU AS SHIELD TO THIS FOREIGN WOMAN?"

"No," Bryndon said. There seemed to be a lot of things he didn't know about being a Shield. The cord bit into his flesh uncomfortably.

"THEN REPEAT AFTER ME," Loric said.

"We can hear you just fine," Willow said coolly.

"Why are you making me shout then?" Loric grumbled. "*I*—wait, what's your name again, son? Rindie?"

"Bryndon," he said. "Bryndon Claybrook. This is Willow Peeke."

"Ah, yes, the sergeant's natural son. I remember you now." He didn't seem to acknowledge Willow's name. "Repeat after me, then—*I, Bryndon Claybrook, do solemnly bind myself to this woman.*"

"I, Bryndon Claybrook, do solemnly bind myself to this woman."

"*As shield against despair and wrath and all other shame.*"

"As shield against despair and wrath and all other shame."

"To take the penalty for her, should she break the solemn peace of the Prohibitions."

"And to present her back at this gate, unblemished and blameless, when her time here is done."

"Her blood is now my blood, and her flesh is my flesh."

Loric grunted and unwound the cord from around their wrists. "It's done then. This stays here as proof of your vow," he said. "When she leaves, you'll have come back through here to see it burned."

And he waved them through the gate, the trader and her shield.

CHAPTER SEVEN

Shem Haeland

Shem slipped under the pine limbs, green needles pricking his neck. Under the dark eaves, the ground was soft and dry and brown, layered with years of dead cones and needles. *They are like me*, Shem thought, and took a moment to appreciate the idea, kneeling to the ground and letting the dead needles run through his fingers. He was not dead, though, just old and brown and dry, his skin wrinkled like new leather left too long in the sun. He noticed a blue vein tracing the bones in his hand and poked it with a finger. It popped back at once.

At least the blood in my veins still flows true. He gave thanks for his blood and stood, brushing the dirt from his hands. It was important to give thanks. *Neither more nor less than one hundred times shall you give thanks for your blessings each day. For each tower is a thanksgiving, and each thanksgiving a tower. And the towers alone can save you from the death the Nightmare brings.* That was the twenty-third Prohibition. Some men, even some Unshamers, claimed that Prohibition meant little more than "Give thanks often," but Shem made it a point to reach one hundred every day. Else it was too easy to let the thanksgiving lax and the blessings slip away unnoticed.

He had risen before the dawn, put the finishing polish on his sabre. It was carved in the traditional fashion, as always, from a single piece of stonewood taken on the winter solstice, polished with beeswax, summerflower honey, and lamp oil. He'd used a double handful of crushed summerflower seeds and six eggs to make the paint—two thin bands of red around the hilt and two more toward the tip. The colors of House Haeland. One of his best ever, the sword, light and strong and balanced, and he was appropriately proud of it, giving thanks to Ior for the blessing of hands to shape, eyes to see, and wood to work. He had only the grip to finish now, and for that he had sought out a good, strong pine tree, on the rolling hills east of the city.

He stripped the bark from the south side of the trunk with his knife, exposing a strip of wet, brown sap. Carefully, he pressed the bare hilt of the sabre against the sap and rolled it back and forth, covering it with a fine, even layer of the sticky substance. When it was fully coated, he sat on the ground with his back against the trunk, and pulled a strip of soft, white goat leather from his pouch. Starting in the center, he began to wind the strip around the handle, crisscrossing back and forth in an intricate web. He hummed a hymn of praise as he wound, and the leather stuck fast to the sap. Shem gave thanks. His grip would be firm. Many of the younger men bound their hilts with hide glue these days, claiming a tighter seal between leather and wood. They were missing the point. Some things should be done a certain way.

He ducked back under the branches and started the long walk back to the city, a few miles away. The sun was just barely topping the eastern slopes of the mountain ring wall, and the air was cool and damp. He had a few hours still, to make the morning rounds, and good weather to do it in. He slashed at the air and grass as he walked, moving through the sword forms, thrust and parry, cut and block, testing the new grip. Practicing his gratitude.

As the sun rose over the mountains, Cairn Meridia stirred and stretched and yawned forth her people, filling the cobblestone streets with the click of boots and the swish of wool, goatherds from the outer houses, delivering the morning milk and eggs, baker's boys walking behind movable carts, overflowing with flat honey bread cakes and oat bread big as a man's head, old widows and young maids, lines of boys headed for the daily Recitation of the Prohibitions in the Grove and tousle-headed young girls with empty buckets heading for the wells. Meridia was known among all the Free Cities for the beauty and grace of her buildings, the great stone houses with white and red marble facades, the bright and shining glass, the delicate stonewood carvings that decorated every shutter and door. Even the more humble buildings of red brick had a certain elegance about them, Shem thought, the care of long years spent crafting and shaping, until every ounce of beauty was wrought from the stone.

Shem gave thanks for it all as he walked. He went to the well first, the biggest one on the Grove Road, outside House Haeland, dipping and hauling the heavy buckets for the littler girls, watching for fighting or bickering in the line. While the girls waited, he made them say three things they were thankful for, and asked after their parents. Taisia's father had been promoted to Captain of the Fifty-Third Tower, and the poor girl was distraught over the whole thing, since it meant four more weeks away from home. Little Lena, whose head was barely taller than the well, told him her mother was sick, and begged him to go visit her if he could. Pretty Alessia confessed to him in a low whisper that Cael Greenvallem had promised to wear her favor in the races that day, and she wanted Shem's opinion on whether he would win. He gave Taisia a bit of crystallized summerflower honey, Lena a promise to visit when he could, and told Alessia that Cael was a fine runner, but he wagered Bryndon Claybrook was the one to beat this year. She sniffed and shared *her* thought that a *boy* like that from an *outer* house wouldn't dare. Shem made her say six things she was thankful for before surrendering the full bucket.

As he was finishing up, he saw Zoe of Blackwing rush by, her shoulders hunched, her back bare of a cloak.

"Zoe, dear," he called out.

She turned back to him, and he saw her face was red and, in spite of obvious efforts to wash and cover it up, tear-stained as well.

"Where are you off to this morning, my dear," he said, walking beside her. "I'm going to visit a few friends near the House of Summerflower, and I could use some company."

"Oh, of course," Zoe said. At first she walked stiffly by his side, but after a little while, she put her arm on his. They were nearly identical in height. "How are you today, Lamb Shem?"

"Just Shem," he said. "I haven't been a lamb in some time, dear. Slow down a bit, if you don't mind, I'm not as young as you."

"Sorry," Zoe said, slowing her steps. "Master Usper says it's proper to grant a man his title, even after he's left the Guard."

"Master Usper was always one for adding unnecessary rules where friendship might otherwise break them down," Shem said. "Where is your cloak this morning? It's too early in the season to be walking around without one."

Zoe's face broke a bit, and tears gathered in the corners of her eyes. "I lost it again, Lamb…I mean, Shem. Forgot it at the Grove last night, Master Usper says, but I swear I hung it up in my closet like I was supposed to. Really, I did, no matter what Master Usper says. Only this morning it wasn't there, and Saerin says she didn't see it when she came to bed." She drew a deep breath, and Shem felt a shudder run through her. "I'm to go to the Unshamers," she whispered. "For pride and sloth, Master Usper says."

"Ah…" Shem said, reaching over to pat her hand. "That seems an injustice."

"I—Master Usper only wants the best for me, I'm sure," Zoe said.

"You are very kind, Zoe dear," Shem said. They passed through the Stone Gate, a high arch of dark gray granite, knit together so well that it was nearly impossible to see where the individual stones joined. A few guardsmen stood on the narrow battlements above them, keeping an eye on the current of people passing in and out. "I was merely saying it seemed like an injustice to *me*," Shem continued. "You will have to do what he says, I'm afraid, but do not fear the Unshamers. Perhaps Ior will grant you courage today, if you ask for it."

"But only men of the Guard are given the grace of bravery."

"Where did you hear that nonsense?" Shem said, snorting. "No, don't tell me, I know who it was. The very *first* act of bravery was by a woman, Zoe, when Tani fought her brother for her daughter Meridia. Think of her, and be strong. Ah, here we are."

He stopped in front of a low brick smithy, gave Zoe a kiss on the cheek, and bid her farewell. She hugged him in return and set off again, standing a bit straighter than she had before.

Shem directed a silent blessing at her retreating back and then turned to the smithy. Though the sun was well up, no clink or clack of hammer on steel came from the anvil, and no coals were burning in the forge. A black piece of fabric was hung over one window. Shem knocked firmly on the door, and after a few moments, the door opened, revealing a great bull of a man, only five and a half feet tall, but seeming nearly as wide across the hip.

"Well met, Shem," Old Bael said, taking his hand and practically dragging him through the door into a massive hug. "It is good to see you."

"And you, Bael," Shem said to the bigger man's chest. "Let me breathe for a moment, son."

Old Bael dropped him sheepishly. He wasn't old in the normal sense.

"Old" Bael was thirty-five years younger than his father, whom everyone had called "Young" Bael since the days when the word actually meant something. At that time, Young Bael's *father* had been Old Bael, and the current Old Bael had been nothing but a babe in arms. Shem supposed the next boy in the family would be Young Bael again, at least until someone grew tired of the whole game.

"I don't have a long time to stay today," Shem said, patting the wooden sabre at his side. "But I told Drem to come by this morning with a bit of iced sweet milk."

"He's come already," Old Bael said, nodding. "Father was right pleased by that, thank you. Happiest he's been in nigh on a week."

"Good," Shem said. "I'll stay and talk for a bit, then, if he's awake."

Shem found Young Bael in bed, sitting up and reading the *Mysteries of Meridia*, her teachings on the graces of Ior. Young Bael had the build and bones of his son, but the sickness in his chest had weakened and shrunk him almost to the size of a normal man, and his skin hung loose from his cheeks. Still, his eyes were bright and alert, and he did seem in good spirits.

"Never actually read this before," Young Bael said, holding up the *Mysteries*. "Only had to memorize the Prohibitions when I was a boy, you know, and never really thought there was much more to living than that and my forge."

"The meditations on love are my favorite," Shem said. "Lambs often recite them before the crucible, to strengthen the will." Then he added, "At least, that's what my Captain always told me. Never had a chance to experience that myself, of course."

"Aye, we're Golden men both," Young Bael said. "Though the years have worn heavier on me than you. A forge will do that to a man. Going to win the sabre again this year?"

"We shall see," Shem said, standing to take his leave. "I haven't faced younger men since I left the guard. I'll return tomorrow, and give you the blow-by-blow."

"Bah, forget that," Young Bael said. "I'll be there. Old Bael's going to contest the shot put title, you know, and I've got a cart all lined up to take me out to the game fields, like a little baby in arms."

"Good," Shem said, clapping him on the shoulder. "Then I'll see you soon."

The rest of the morning passed in a steady blur of people and streets as Shem made his rounds, leaving a kind word here, a few sugared peanuts there. Near twenty thousand people lived in the valley of Cairn Meridia, and Shem did his best to know as many of them as he could, and to know them as well as he could. One of the common houses had lost half their chicken coop in a fire, and Shem stopped for half-an-hour while Master Grinder and his boys ripped the old one out and replaced the damaged fence, whacking at the chickens with his sabre to keep them out of the street. Then there was nothing for it but to give the young men a lesson on swordsmanship, setting them all to strike and parry with sticks of burned wood from the fence, before Master Grinder shooed them all on their way to the Grove for the morning lessons. Shem stopped briefly at the Silverfeather's to ask after Wynn, and told Rahel he would visit her daughter Ruby soon, who was still confined to the Low Tower, refusing Unshaming. And on it went.

By the time second terse rang out from the House of Time, Shem had worked his way to the Glass Gate, where he joined a crowd of people heading for the game fields. Here in the Moonlight District the city was newer, less than a thousand years old in some places, and the red and white marble buildings of the Grove District were replaced with smaller structures of polished bluestone and granite. Colored glass was everywhere in this part of the city, showing all manner of things—scenes from the histories of Meridia, icons of the seven graces—even depictions of bread and wine, goats and cheese and trees, celebrations of the beauty of small and everyday things. He saw the bent back of Elsie Claybrook, whom everyone called Gran, and fell in alongside, offering his arm.

"There's a kindness," Gran said, taking his arm. Shem noticed, however, that she put very little weight on him, and carried a full basket in her other hand. "It is a long walk across the city for an old woman like me. Why, I had to leave the house near sun up to get here by this time."

"Ior has blessed you with much."

"Aye, a sore back and a trick knee, and don't think I'm not thankful for both," Gran croaked. "They remind me that I'm still living."

"And how is your family?" Shem asked.

"Loud and snotty, grumpy and joyful, by turns," Gran said. "The Sergeant spends too much time away."

Shem nodded. "A boy needs his father," he said.

"Bryndon?" Gran said. "That boy is foolish as a billy goat and always will be, 'til he's got a good wife to settle him down, anyway. It's Robin that needs her father. The girl's half-mad for him, and likely a Dreamer besides. But she's got no one to look up to, no one to teach her how to use her strength properly. Except me of course, and I'm old as dirt," she added, and Shem smiled. "Anna does her best, but she's stretched thin," Gran went on. "Trying to care for a family that lives near thirty miles apart, with all the extras."

The "extras" were the foster children from the common houses, boys and girls without places of their own. House Claybrook took in many of them, for such a small house.

"You've told him all this yourself, no doubt?" Shem asked.

"Do I look a fool to you? No, don't answer that," she said. The crowd was getting bigger and coming closer together as they neared the gate, and Shem slowed his steps. Gran snapped at a fat stonemason for stepping on her toes, giving him a solid whack with her basket. Shem heard the sound of metal clicking together inside it.

"And what of you Shem Haeland," Gran said, turning back to him as if nothing had happened. "How is the life of a castellan these days?"

"I am grateful for the work," Shem said. "Keeping the books and minding the storehouses and keeping all in order. House Haeland was kind to honor me with it."

"Found yourself a wife yet?" Gran asked.

Shem laughed. "I'm sure I would look a fool in a marriage cloak now. A little old man with summerflowers in my hair."

"So find someone young and tall to balance you out," Gran said.

"Are you making me an offer?" Shem said, then ducked as the basket came whistling at his head. But Shem heard her chuckling under her breath, and when they resumed walking she leaned a little closer, and patted his arm a bit more often than strictly necessary.

They passed through the gate, waved through by a harried looking Timekeeper, who seemed more intent on keeping himself from being trampled than watching the gate. Once past it, the crowd spread out across the valley, streaming in a slow moving river to the game field.

"You're a good man, Shem," Gran said, finally. "We need more good men to become husbands, show the boys how it's done. It's near a shame to waste yourself on bachelorhood."

Shem sighed. "I will not say I have not considered it," he said. "But lambs do not marry."

"You're in luck then," Gran said. "Because you are not a lamb."

"So I tell myself," Shem said. "But it always sounds like a lie."

The Game Field was laid out on one of the few flat stretches of ground in Meridia Valley. White and blue flags blew lazily in the wind, marking the giant ring that made up the competition area. It was near a half-mile across, and a mile and a half round, split into seven oblong ovals that circled the center like petals on a flower. The games would be split among them—fencing in one oval, races in the next, shot put, archery, dance, quarterstaff, and quindo—each had their place. Wooden benches stood in lines along the edges of the petals, and Shem helped Gran find a seat among them, facing the racing oval. The benches were already nearly full of spectators, mostly old women and nursing mothers. There were too few seats for everyone else. The games came but once a year, and the Golden Games only once every fifty. Nearly everyone would be there at some point during the day, everyone who wasn't on the towers or visiting the Unshamers. Some of the women near Gran claimed the General himself would be contesting the quindo, though how they knew that was a mystery. Shem thought it unlikely—as well claim the Wizard meant to pull a bow. The Six Rulers of Cairn Meridia had no time for games.

As the morning wore on, the steady river of competitors and fans continued, wandering over the field, or settling in at the best vantage points on the slopes of the surrounding hills. Shem recognized more than a few: Gilda the washerwoman, Cael Greenvallem, short Master Usper of House Blackwing. As he was walking toward the sabre field, he spotted Aaron Stonepillar, who waved to him and wandered over, a sack of iron shots slung over his shoulder.

"Well met, Shem," Aaron said, clapping a hand to Shem's shoulder. Shem would have sworn that his boots sank half an inch into the soft ground. Aaron Stonepillar was thirty years younger than Shem, and near five stone heavier, a bull of a man from head to toe. An axe handle could rest between his shoulders with room to spare.

"Well met," Shem replied, slipping out from under his meaty paw. "Will you be taking home the honors again this year, you think?" Aaron had won the shot put ten years straight, since Tavys Whitelimb had turned trader, and left for Cairn Doxia and the other Free Cities. He hadn't returned since, though that wasn't unusual for traders. The West Road was hard and difficult; snow blocked the paths for much of the year, and the mountains were full of dangers. The cities were full of women, too, and Tavys Whitelimb was young and strong. Most likely he had taken some girl to wife, and settled somewhere to start his own house.

"There's a few of the young men who might surprise," Aaron said, rolling one of the shots in his hand. "Old Bael is finally coming into his own. And you? Sabre again this year?"

"Until I cannot lift a sword, or carve my own blade," Shem said. "It will be good to duel younger men again. I have fought in the aged division too long."

"There's talk the General will contest the quindo," Aaron said.

"Talk from the old women, you mean," Shem said.

Aaron smiled. "They've been known to talk a bit. Still, I think they may be right about this one. Care to make a wager on it? My shot against your blade."

"What am I supposed to do with a hunk of iron like that when I win?" Shem asked.

"Trade it; bury it; give it to the Tower Guard and let them drop it on the next darkstone that walks by, for all I care."

"And what'll you do with my sabre if you win?"

"I'm in need of a good toothpick," Aaron said, showing his teeth. "Now I'm off for a look at the ring. Last year it was three inches too small, and I nearly fell on my face on the first throw. Shame not."

"Shame not," Shem said, watching the big man stride away. *Give it to the Tower Guard, and let them drop it on the next darkstone that walks by.* Perhaps he should. It would be the only contribution he would be able to make to the defense of the city. He shook his head, gave thanks for his life of peace, and set his feet toward the sabre field.

CHAPTER EIGHT

The House of the Summerflower

The House of Summerflower was a rambling, one story structure of a few score rooms that sprawled across the top of Summerflower Hill like an open hand. The house was set a ways apart from the rest of the city, and where elsewhere the cobblestones and marble pavement ruled underfoot, here the grass was allowed to grow green and lush and bright. It circled the great house like a living kirtle, spotted with the red and white summerflowers that were its namesake. White marble formed the front facade, its surface painted with scenes from the founding of Cairn Meridia, the building of the first towers, the piercing of Tarn Harrick, and wise Meridia bent over her scrolls, imparting the nature of grace and shame. The full text of the Prohibitions was interwoven through the scenes, engraved in the marble long ago and periodically renewed during the tenth year of each peace.

The rest of the house was red brick and white mortar, though only faint hints of red ever peaked out from behind the covering of deep green ivy. Zoe walked the path up to the house with heavy feet. She had been praying continuously since she had left Shem, thinking of wise Meridia and asking Ior to grace her with courage to face the Unshamers. She did not *feel* very brave, though. Saerin had been to the Unshamers once, and had come back from the experience subdued and quiet. Zoe's few timid attempts to engage her in conversation about it had been rebuffed sternly, and she had let it go.

Massive oaken doors guarded the entrance to the house, one of which was thrown open. A young, dark-skinned Unshamer stood guard, a small black slate in his hands. He was a handsome man, dressed in the robes of his brotherhood, half milk white and half blood red, the colors split straight down the center. Zoe curtsied as she approached.

"Name and house?" the man said, sounding bored.

"Zoe of House Blackwing," she said. "I'm here to beg Unshaming of the brotherhood." Just like she had learned in her childhood lessons.

"What shames have you committed?" he asked, writing her name on the slate.

"I misplaced a number of things of my house—" she began.

"Lust, wrath, pride, cowardice, despair, greed, or sloth," he said, cutting off her prepared speech.

"What?" Zoe asked.

"Haven't you ever been here before?" he asked, looking at her like she was a small, annoying bug.

She shook her head. "Not for Unshaming, sir. Of course I was taken here as a child—"

"Shames must be recorded under one of the seven prohibited categories," he said, cutting her off again. "Which one of them did you commit?"

"Um…sloth, sir," Zoe said. "And pride."

He looked at her contemptuously.

"Pride?" Zoe said.

He grunted and waved her through. "Take as much time as you need in the waiting room, then go through the first door on the right," he said, making a few tallies on the slate. "There's a bit of a line this morning, so you may have to wait."

"Thank you, sir," Zoe said, dropping another curtsy, but the man had already forgotten her, turning his attention to a fat scribe in a silver coat that had come up behind her.

She walked through the entrance hall, where a number of people waited, some sitting on benches that lined the walls, others pacing nervously, preparing themselves to enter. Most were women, and most had their hoods up, hiding their faces. A mosaic covered the floor, showing the House of Summerflower itself, silhouetted on its hill by a setting sun. She remembered it from her one trip to the house as a child, when old Master

Vestus had taken House Blackwing's children to tour the house library and see a bit of how the Unshamers lived. She still missed Master Vestus. The old man had been one of the few people who had ever shown her any kindness, taking her in when the common house her mother had belonged to finally disbanded. Saerin was nice enough, most of the time, but she was a distant room sister at best. There always seemed to be part of her that she didn't want to share with Zoe, something she kept to herself. A secret only true Blackwings were allowed to know. And Master Usper…

Zoe shivered and prayed again for courage, setting her shoulders and wishing she had her cloak, so that she could hide her face in her hood like everyone else. She still felt vaguely betrayed by her cloak's absence, as if it had, indeed, gotten itself off its hanger and wandered away. She *had* remembered to hang it up properly last night. She had. She didn't care what Master Usper said.

No, that was no good. She must *make* herself care what Master Usper thought. Otherwise she would be unable to repent properly, and the Unshaming would be difficult and painful.

Well, it's no good waiting here, she thought. Better to have it over and done with. She passed by the rest of the shamed and took the first door on the right, as the brother at the entrance had instructed. Then she stopped, right on the threshold, and found herself in the biggest room she had ever seen.

The Room of Unshaming.

It was airy and well-lit. Sunlight filtered through a number of open skylights in the ceiling and Zoe noticed a few birds had built nests in the skylight recesses. The sound of their singing echoed occasionally off the marble walls, sounding cheerful and happy at the prospect of spring.

But mostly, Zoe heard screaming.

The screaming was coming from a woman in the center of the room, an older woman dressed in a robe of rough-spun black wool. She was on her knees in front of a half-circle of seated Unshamers, gripping her head with clawed hands, twisting and writhing. Zoe noticed her hands and face were glowing pale blue from the magic that infused her. Heartspell, the Unshamers called it; it laid bare the truth of a person's shame. The Unshamers did not move, simply watching the woman as she screamed. They seemed detached somehow, as if they weren't really looking at her at all, but past her.

Zoe heard the door open behind her and scuttled out of the way as the fat scribe bustled in.

"You in line?" he asked, when he saw Zoe.

"What?" she said.

The man made an annoyed grunt and brushed past her, placing himself in line behind a young man, waiting near the woman. Zoe took a place in line behind the scribe. She felt faint. The woman on the floor went silent for a few moments, body wracked with convulsions. Then she started up again, harsh and howling by turn. The young man in line ahead of her was no more than fifteen or sixteen, and looked as pale and sick as Zoe felt. The scribe seemed to take it all as a matter of course, shifting impatiently and rubbing a small gold ring on the pinkie finger of his left hand.

The Unshamer in the center of the circle stood, and Zoe watched him for a moment before realizing with a start who he was. He was small and lithe and old, and wore the red and white robe of his order, worked with silver and gold threads. The pale skin on his head shone like a polished egg in the sunlight, except where a few strands of white hair still clung to the surface. But it was his eyes that were the most striking, a blue so pale they were almost white. There was only one man in Meridia with eyes like that: the Wizard Oded, master of the House of Summerflower and leader of the Unshamers, one of the six rulers of Meridia. And perhaps the most hated.

Oded held up a small figurine, a woman made of porcelain, carrying a babe in arms.

The shame object.

Zoe had never seen one before. Like all Meridians, she knew the basics of the process. When a man or woman went to the brothers, their shame was taken from their bodies and placed in an object, usually something associated with their crime: a staff that had been used to strike a friend might be used as an object of wrath, a bucket someone had failed to fill might be an object of sloth. Usually the objects were destroyed in the process of Unshaming. For the worst shames, though, a different spell was used, one that would preserve the object and imbue it with power: fire for wrath, wind for pride, lightning for lust. The objects were then sent to the towers, where they were stockpiled as weapons for the next Nightmare. Saerin had told her that sloth objects could cause sickness and greed objects fear, but they were no good against the Nightmare, and so were never made. And cowards, of course, were never allowed in the guard.

The figurine in Oded's hand glowed with the same blue light as the woman, and, as the Wizard raised it higher, the light waxed and shone, and the woman's cries grew louder and louder, crescendoing with pain, until

Zoe clapped her hands over her ears to shut out the horrible sound.

Then there was a silent, concussive pop, and the figurine shattered into dust, scattering across the floor. The woman's screaming ceased, as if her breath had been taken from her body, and she collapsed.

"You have been freed from the chains of your shame," Oded said. His voice was as dry and dusty as his appearance, and sounded barely louder than a whisper after the woman's screams. "Go now, my daughter Gwyneth, and shame no more."

The woman named Gwyneth didn't move. By all appearances she was unconscious, or dead. No, not dead. The Unshamers almost never killed people, unless they had murdered or raped, and were unrepentant. Oded coughed a bit and gestured to a few of the other Unshamers, who picked the woman up by her shoulders and feet, and carried her from the chamber. A young boy in the blue robe of the acolytes scurried forward with a broom and pail, sweeping up the porcelain fragments.

"Let the next son or daughter step forward," Oded said, settling back into his chair.

The young man hesitated for a moment, looking at the door where the Unshamers had disappeared with the woman. The scribe cleared his throat loudly, hands on his hips. When the boy still failed to move, he pushed his way past and went to one knee in front of the Wizard. He somehow managed to make kneeling look arrogant. The boy hurried from the room, leaving Zoe the lone remaining supplicant.

"Wizard Oded, by the Prohibitions, I, Gryn Silverfeather, repent of what I have done and beg Unshaming," the scribe said, sounding impatient. "Test my heart, and let justice be done."

The words were ritual. Every child in the city was taught them at an early age, though Unshaming wasn't allowed until after a child's thirteenth year.

"Your humility becomes you, my son," Oded said. The reply was ritual as well, and there was no trace of irony in his voice. "You are guilty of crimes against the Prohibitions of Meridia. You have thrown yourself at the mercy of the House of Summerflower, and beg to be tested in the presence of witnesses. Step forward."

He did so, and another Unshamer met him, placing a hand on the scribe's heart. The scribe would confess his shame, next. Then the Unshamer would use the Heartspell to see the truth of the person's crime, and declare an epitimia. That was the real trial of Unshaming, the epitimia. Saerin had told Zoe once that it was a special word, *epitimia*, something from Meridia's books, and that it didn't really have a translation in the language of the valley. The epitimia could be anything, though usually it was something difficult and painful, some sort of sacrifice the person would have to make in order to be freed from their shame. Some were actions, like alms giving, prayer, service, or fasting. Some were trials: pain, anguish, torment. Some made a woman scream in agony before collapsing unconscious on the floor.

"Confess your crime," Oded said.

"Lust," Gryn said. That was all.

Oded coughed. It sounded like the snapping of a dry twig. "Perhaps you wish to say a bit more, my son. Complete freedom can only come when—"

"No thank you," the scribe said. "You may proceed."

Oded remained silent for a moment, and Zoe could have sworn his white eyes tightened with anger. But the emotion flicked across his face so fast, she thought perhaps she had only imagined it.

"Very well," Oded said, his pale face blank and dry once again. "Unshamer Halat, you may proceed."

The brother with his hand on the scribe's heart—Halat, Zoe assumed—began to speak. Zoe did not understand the words, but she knew it was the magical language of the far land across the sea, the land of the blackened sky. Men called it the music of Meridia, and Zoe could understand why. It was both musical and rigid, like a song made of rocks, and as Halat spoke the scribe began to glow a pale blue. Zoe waited for him to collapse or show some sign of distress, but the scribe simply stood there, as impatient as ever.

"Brother Halat, by the power of wise Meridia's Heartspell, you see this man's heart, and know his shame," Oded said. "Will you set him free?"

"I will," Halat said.

"What epitimia do you prescribe?" Oded said.

"Let this man pray," Halat said.

Zoe stifled a noise of surprise. *That's it?* she thought. *That's his whole punishment?* She knew the Unshamers were much harsher with women than men, of course, though it hadn't always been that way. Saerin claimed there were records that showed the situation had been reversed throughout most of Meridian history, with men receiving the harshest epitimia. In the last twenty years or so, however, it was the women who suffered the most, far, far more than the men. Some said the High Defender was behind it, others said it was Oded. A few mentioned The Clock, as well, though what the master of the House of Time had to do with Unshaming was not something Zoe had ever understood.

"And what is the object of his shame?" Oded said.

"His marriage bed," Halat replied.

The scribe gave a start at this, and now it was his turn to look shocked, which turned very quickly to anger.

"Very well," Oded said, nodding his approval. "Gryn Silverfeather, you must return to your home and recite the Prohibitions on lust twenty times, holding your marriage bed in your hands, and when the object of your shame unravels you will be set free."

"Witnessed," said the Unshamer to Oded's right. "It is just and merciful."

"*It is just and merciful*," the rest replied in unison.

"My marriage bed?" the scribe said. "My entire bed?"

"It is not necessary to lift the object," Oded said. "If you simply touch it with your hand—"

"I'm not worried about lifting it you—Wizard Oded," he said, fists clenched. "You are telling me I have to destroy my entire marriage bed? Do you know how much that will cost to replace?"

"Brother Halat has deemed it a proper sacrifice for you," Oded said. "Perhaps if you were more truly repentant…but the decision is made."

"Wouldn't a set of sheets be more appropriate—" the scribe began.

"The decision is made," Oded said, and Zoe heard power in his dusty voice for the first time. "The Heartspell will remain on you until such time as your bed is destroyed by its magic. I urge you to do it quickly. The magic will begin to pain you the longer it is upon you, and if you wait too long you may find that your bed is insufficient to relieve the agony. If you wait longer than a month, it will very likely kill you." Oded offered this last bit of information as if discussing the weather. The scribe opened his mouth to speak again, but Oded cut him off. "You are dismissed," he said. "Go in peace, and shame not."

The scribe's teeth clicked shut. He bowed stiffly and stalked off at once, skin still glowing faintly. The door slammed shut behind him.

And the Wizard Oded turned to Zoe.

"Let the next son or daughter step forward," Oded said.

Zoe walked forward, head down, feeling the eyes of the brothers on her. When she reached the center of the circle, she sank to her knees. She saw the stone beneath her had been worn smooth by thousands of other knees like hers; there was even a slight depression, a kind of double socket in the floor.

"Wizard Oded, by the Prohibitions, I, Zoe of House Blackwing, repent of what I have done and beg Unshaming," she said, staring at the ground. Her voice echoed strangely in her ears. "Test my heart, and let justice be done."

"Your humility becomes you, my daughter," Oded said, and Zoe thought she detected a hint of kindness in his voice. "You are guilty of crimes against the Prohibitions of Meridia. You have thrown yourself at the mercy of the House of Summerflower, and beg to be tested in the presence of witnesses. Step forward."

Zoe rose and stepped forward, just as the scribe had done before her. To her embarrassment, she found herself looking down at the seated Wizard in front of her, and noticed a few patches of dry, dead skin on his bald scalp. Would the Unshamer know that she was looking at Oded's head when he used the Heartspell on her? Best to think of Master Usper, and try to be as repentant as possible.

Halat stood again and laid a hand on Zoe's chest, singing the music of Meridia.

At first, Zoe felt nothing. Then it was as if something else became present with her—something or someone. It was in the room with them, it was standing next to her, it was touching her skin. Then it slipped inside her, quite easily, with no resistance on her part. Not that she could have resisted. It was overwhelming, the presence, awful and wonderful at the same time, and she-he-it filled her like water, and it knew everything about her, all at once, and Zoe felt herself begin to sweat. And yet it was wonderful, too, a relief almost, to be with something that she did not need to hide anything from.

And then Zoe could feel Halat, standing next to her, could feel his mind and will, connected to her by the presence, seeing a little of what it saw, knowing a little of what it knew. But only a little. If the presence could see her whole self, she felt that Halat could only see a pinhole. She had no idea how she knew this, but the lack of explanation didn't seem important. She knew it like she knew her own face in a mirror.

"Confess your crime," Oded said.

"I lost my cloak again," Zoe said. She had been dreading this part, not knowing if she was going to make a fool of herself or be able to explain the situation correctly or clearly enough. But the Heartspell made speaking easy. She said the words because they were the right ones. "I hung it up in the closet, and in the morning it was gone. Master Usper thinks I forgot it again, but I didn't. I don't know where it went, but he says I'm prideful and slothful and so I need to be Unshamed."

Some of the Unshamers exchanged glances. Oded plowed on with the ritual. "Brother Halat, by the power of wise Meridia's Heartspell you see this woman's heart, and know her shame," Oded said. "Will you set her free?"

There was a long, silent pause. Then Halat said, "I will not."

Oded registered only the barest hint of surprise on his lined face. "What reason do you give for denying this woman justice and mercy?" he asked.

"The loss of this cloak does not hold her in shame," Halat said. "Her conduct was not Prohibited. There is no justice to be done, no mercy required."

Does that mean I can go? Zoe thought. But then Oded spoke again.

"Child, is there any other shame that you should confess?" Oded said.

Before that moment, Zoe would have sworn that there was nothing else. But once the question was asked, she found herself thinking of dozens of other things, times she had violated the Prohibitions from her girlhood up to that very morning. And from her lips the words came forth, and she said, "I have failed to thank Ior one hundred times yesterday. And many days before that."

Why did you admit to that? a part of her asked. *You could have left here free and clear.*

But Oded nodded and smiled, and this time there was real kindness and approval on his face. "Well done, daughter," was all he said.

"She speaks truly," Halat said. "I will set her free of this shame."

"What epitimia do you prescribe?" Oded said.

"She has neglected her labor in thankfulness," Halat said. "Let her labor, then, in recompense. Let this one feel the pain of childbirth for one hour."

What did he say?

"And what is her object of shame?"

"A lock of hair from her head shall serve," Halat said.

"Very well," Oded said, nodding his approval. "Zoe of House Blackwing, you must undergo an epitimia of pain. While I hold your lock of hair in my hand, you will feel the pangs of childbirth for one hour. Then you will be free."

"Witnessed," said the same Unshamer to Oded's right. "It is just and merciful."

"*It is just and merciful,*" the rest replied in unison.

Halat pulled a knife from the sheath at his side, and cut a small lock of hair from Zoe's head.

"Have you any children, daughter?" Oded asked, as Halat held the hair out to him.

"No, Wizard Oded," Zoe said.

"You had best sit," Oded said, taking the hair in his wrinkled fingers. "You will be on the ground soon anyway."

Then the lock of hair began to glow blue, and Zoe sank heavily to the floor as the pain blossomed in her gut. It was not long before she, too, began to scream.

CHAPTER NINE
The Golden Games

Saerin shifted her basket to her other arm and tried her best to look bored.

"He picked me a bouquet," Alessia was saying. "Blue flag and glacier lily and summerflowers, of course. And he tied it up with green silk ribbon, and oh Saerin you should have seen it, it was so beautiful. And he was so handsome, wearing his feast day clothes and polished black boots. They're made of kid leather, you know, he told me. And Madge put the flowers in a little blue vase with some water and salt, and I just could not stop looking at them, you know, they were just so beautiful."

"Hmm…" Saerin said, turning a little further away from her younger house sister. They were sitting on the soft grass near the front rows of the sabre field, watching the afternoon bouts. Rani Redcrag was dueling an older, brown-skinned man Saerin didn't recognize, someone from House Haeland by the colors on this sabre. Both men were stripped to the waist and sweating in the sunlight. Rani had the reach and seemed stronger, but the wrinkled old man was picking him apart with ease, his movements far tighter and more subtle than Rani's sweeping blows. A number of red welts stood out on Rani's pale skin, and a few of his wounds trickled blood.

"Of course he'd already gone to Master Usper and told him his intentions," Alessia droned on. The girl was insufferable, and far too conscious of her blonde good looks. "He's very proper like that. And strong and handsome. Did I tell you he's wearing my favor in the races today?"

"Only three times," Saerin said, but the girl took no notice.

"He said he would win for sure, if I gave him my favor. Oh, he *must* win," Alessia said. "That would just be so perfect. I'm sure Master Usper would approve the match if he won. Then I'd be a Greenvallem and I could make apple tarts for supper every night and all of our children would have a house of their own forever."

Saerin turned further away, so the girl was practically talking to her back. Rani swung too wide again, and the old man slipped his blade down Rani's sword arm, snapping the point against the wrist. There was a sharp crack, and Rani's sabre fell from his nerveless fingers. The crowd shouted its approval, clearly favoring the old man.

"Not that he wouldn't approve it anyway. House Greenvallem is so honorable," Alessia said. "Did you know the Low Tower castellan is from House Greenvallem?" Saerin said nothing, and Alessia went on, "They say he's the General's right hand, that he knows the exact strength of the guard down to the last uniform, that he never forgets a number."

"They're fairly easy to remember," Saerin said. "One, two, three, and so forth."

Alessia blinked, then frowned. "Oh you know what I mean," she said. "You ought not to be so sarcastic. It's not lady-like. There's a reason you don't have a husband yet, and only the one suitor from Silverfeather."

Saerin let that slide, and watched as the fencing official handed the old man the victory coin. Worth a week's wage, those coins, and the victor of every tournament bout received one. Champions could earn half-a-year's keep during the Golden Games, depending on how many entries there were. The crowd applauded politely, and there were a few shouts of "Shem! Shem and Haeland!"

Saerin felt a tap on her shoulder, and looked up to see the stiff figure of Master Usper had joined them. She did not have to look up very far.

"Has Tomos competed yet?" he asked, not bothering with any greeting.

"There's one more bout before his," Saerin answered. "But he hasn't arrived yet, that I've seen." She gestured towards a large wooden sandwich board, covered with sheets of thin paper, filled with cramped writing. "The schedule is over there, if you care to look," Saerin said.

"Master Usper," Alessia said, her voice sickly-sweet and wheedling. "Do you think I might be able to go watch Cael race soon? He's wearing my favor, you know, and—"

"What have you seen so far?" he asked Saerin, ignoring Alessia completely. "Anyone to worry about this year?"

"That one is skilled," Saerin said, nodding to the old man. He was taking a long drink from the water jugs, still bare chested. A tall woman with silky black hair stopped to speak with him briefly, and he bowed politely to her.

"Shem Haeland," Master Usper nodded. "He used to draw water for Zoe when she was a lass, taught her all manner of slothful behavior. His time is twenty years past."

"He ripped Rani Redcrag apart," Saerin said. "Why have I never seen him before?" Shem was shaking his head and gesturing to the black haired woman. Then, to her surprise, he turned in their direction and pointed right at her, saying something she couldn't hear.

"He's won the aged division every year since he retired from the guard," Master Usper said. "But the Golden Games are open to all men of age."

"He is the best to fight so far," Saerin said. The woman was walking toward them. There was something about her that tugged at Saerin's memory, something about her walk perhaps.

"If he faces Tomos, he'll wish he stayed home," Master Usper said. "No old man is a match for the High Defender's swordsman."

"Master Usper," Alessia said. "Did you know that Cael Greenvallem is wearing my favor today? I was hoping—"

"You are to stay here with Saerin," Master Usper said. "I need her here to watch for challengers, and I can't spare anyone else to look after you."

"I don't need looking after," Alessia said. "I'm almost thirteen and a half."

"You'll speak no more about it," Master Usper said. "Or about Cael Greenvallem." Alessia looked furious, but she said nothing else, retiring into a sullen silence. There was no arguing with Master Usper when he used that tone. "And who is this?" he said, under his breath, though not quietly enough to keep Saerin from hearing it.

The black-haired woman had reached them, and she dropped into a low curtsy. "Excuse me, but are you Master Usper?" she asked. She was dressed in a light dress of blue linen, the crossed arms of House Whitelimb sown small and delicate on her chest.

"I am," Master Usper said. "And you are?"

"Delighted to have found you," the woman said, laughing. The laughter was bright and charming, but her mirth didn't seem to reach higher than her smiling lips and bare teeth. "I believe I have found something that one of your young house daughters lost." She reached into a purse at her side, and there was a rippling of fabric unfolding in the wind.

Zoe's cloak.

Saerin locked an expression of mild interest on her face, and glanced lazily at the woman's left ear. Her hair covered most of it, but when the breeze lifted it for a moment...

She saw the thin red line, from the top of her ear to the bottom, where Saerin's knife had scratched her. Saerin knew this woman. She had tried to kill her with an axe.

"What's this?" Master Usper said, eyeing the cloak.

"I was walking back from my devotions at the Grove last night, and stumbled upon this fine cloak, just sitting lonesome in the middle of the street. I'm afraid I tripped right over it, quite literally," Axe said, giggling again. "So it's a bit worse for the wear. There is a rather sizable rip." She held up the cloak and stuck her fingers through a hole, wriggling them like pink worms.

"What makes you think it belongs to my house?" Master Usper demanded.

"Didn't Zoe lose a cloak last night, Master Usper?" Alessia asked. "Why, it's a wonder it was found."

"You hold your tongue, and let your elders speak," Master Usper said.

"But I was only—" Alessia said.

"Silence, girl," Master Usper snapped. Saerin restrained herself from giving Master Usper a look. *Why did he suddenly seem so eager to defend Zoe?*

"Zoe, is it?" the black-haired woman said, smiling. "A beautiful name. I should like to return it to her in person, if possible." She glanced at Saerin, and raised her eyebrows a bit. "I don't suppose—"

"Zoe is not here," Master Usper said, answering the unspoken question. "And it is true she lost a cloak, but I doubt this is it."

"It seems to bear a striking resemblance to...forgive me, I do not know your name," she said to Saerin.

"I tell you it is not hers," Master Usper said, saving Saerin from having to answer.

Axe bared her teeth again in a rigid grin. "Of course, if you say it is not hers..." she said. "Forgive me for being indelicate, but I do not expect a reward or gift of any kind. It is a pleasure to be able to simply serve you in returning it. Perhaps you should look at it again."

A bit of the stiffness went out of Master Usper's shoulders. *Of course, he was just worried about a reward*, Saerin thought. He didn't care about Zoe at all.

"Well now that I look at it closer," Master Usper said, snatching the cloak from the woman's hands. She let it go without a word, but Saerin noticed her fingers flex briefly. "Perhaps it is hers after all."

"I should love to return it to her in person," the woman said.

"I sent her to the House of Summerflower," Master Usper said. He had already stuffed the cloak into his satchel. "To beg forgiveness for her pride and sloth. You may consider the matter settled." Then he added, as if the words were being drawn out of him with a pair of pincers, "Thank you for your kindness."

"Of course," Axe said, dropping another curtsy. "I shall leave you to your swordplay. Farewell," she said, giving one last look at Saerin before she turned and strode away.

"What a nice woman," Alessia said brightly. "She forgot to tell us her name, though."

She didn't forget, Saerin thought. Even in the daylight, Masked Ones did not show their true faces. Saerin kept her gaze fixed on the woman's back, memorizing as many details of her as possible. House Whitelimb. She wondered how long it would take the woman to find Zoe. And what she would do when she did.

Saerin hopped to her feet. "I want to walk around a bit," she said.

"You're supposed to stay here and watch the matches," Master Usper said.

"There's no one that will be able to stand against Tomos," Saerin said, truthfully. "You're wasting your time with these *swordsmen*." She gestured to the current opponents, a few potbellied goatherds from the outer houses, wielding what looked like ancient, hand-me-down stonewood sabres. They used their swords like thin clubs, hacking at each other viscously. Master Usper snorted in disgust. Whatever else he might be, the little man had a good eye for swordplay.

"I suppose you're right," Master Usper said. "Still, be sure that you are here this evening for Tomos's victory. House Blackwing will need to show its strength."

"Does that mean I can go watch the races?" Alessia asked. "You know that Cael Greenvallem is wearing my favor today?"

"Who?" Saerin asked.

"Cael Greenvallem," Alessia said, looking confused.

"Never heard of him," Saerin said, stalking off into the crowd, following the path the black haired woman had taken.

She slipped through the gaps in the shifting crowds easily, standing up on her toes every once and while to try and catch a glimpse of the light blue dress. She assumed Axe would head for the city immediately, probably wait outside the House of Summerflower for Zoe to come out. At least, that's what Saerin would have done.

She finally spotted her next to the quindo field, standing on a small ridge on the east side, watching the teams compete. Saerin slipped behind a portly looking scribe in a silver jacket and pretended to watch as well, keeping Axe in the corner of her eye.

The quindo field was torn up already. Massive divots pockmarked the grass, many of them filled with fine brown sand. The Whitelimb team was playing guard, and it looked to be going badly for them. Only three of the seven circles were still in their control, and the men of House Bluestone were threatening to overrun another, pushing out all but one guardian, a squat, muscular man with more hair on his arms than his head. He had chosen the shield, and was blocking a fury of blows from the Bluestone's axe man.

It was a fascinating game, quindo. Saerin had played it often as a girl, before Master Vestus had died, and Master Usper had prohibited her from continuing on the grounds that it was "unsuitable for a woman of her bloodline to muck about with the neighborhood boys." She had been too small for any position but knife, but she had been exceptionally good at that, using her size and quickness to slip through blockers.

"Who do you think will take it?" said a voice behind her.

Saerin jumped and turned to face a slender, long-legged man, dressed in the black and violet of the High Defender's personal guard. Before she could open her mouth to reply, he had enveloped her in a tight hug, clasping his arms around her shoulders. His embrace was a bit bony, but warm.

"Wynn!" Saerin said, pushing herself away. "What are you doing here?"

Wynn Silverfeather brushed his shaggy brown hair out of his eyes. "Aren't you happy to see me?" he asked, taking her hand in both of his. Then he shook his head. "No, I'm sorry, that was unkind."

"Of course I'm happy to see you," Saerin lied. "You took me by surprise is all. I thought you would be with the High Defender."

"That's where a guard belongs," Wynn said, nodding. "But he gave Tomos leave for the day—to compete in the sabre, as I'm sure you know.

And since our houses are so closely tied together, he thought it appropriate to let me come as well, to root him on."

"How kind of him," Saerin said, glancing away to make sure the green mask hadn't left yet. She was still watching the match, hands folded behind her.

"Yes, he is much gentler than most people realize," Wynn said.

There was a long pause, and Saerin pretended to cough a little, for lack of something better to do. She could feel the old weight again, hanging between them, the weight of shame and longing and rejection, the specter of a slim book of black leather and a shining green stone. She fought off memories of a blood-slicked sword, and wished desperately that she could make an excuse and leave. The old questions still lingered behind his brown eyes. But the green mask was not moving, and Saerin had nowhere else to go.

Then Wynn turned abruptly and faced the match again. "So, who do you think will take it?" he asked again. "The Whitelimbs seem to be stiffening up finally."

"The hairy man is good," Saerin said, happy to escape into a safe topic. "But he puts too much weight on his front foot. The axe should be turning him instead of trying to batter him into the ground."

Wynn nodded. "Think you could slip past him?" he asked.

"I slipped past you all the time, didn't I?" Saerin said.

"You did," Wynn agreed. "You always were a better soldier than me."

"I was certainly a better general," she said. The axe was showing signs of tiring, whacking at the wooden shield more wildly. Other members of the two teams shouted encouragement, unable to join the fray until one of the men broke point. "You could never think beyond the target in front of you."

"Not much has changed," he said. The hairy man was starting to drive the axe back, moving straight ahead, pushing against him with the shield. Saerin glanced at Axe again. She seemed to be speaking to another woman, a woman with flowing brown hair, though the angle was too sharp for Saerin to make out her face.

"Actually, I was sort of hoping to run into you here," Wynn said.

"Is that so?" Saerin said, not really paying attention. She could almost see the other woman's face. If she turned just a little bit...

"It is," Wynn said. "I'm not sure if you remember this, but my fifth year is coming up. It's in a few days, actually."

"Your fifth year?" Saerin said. The woman turned briefly, but another man crossed in front of her before Saerin could get a good look. She clicked her tongue in frustration.

"Five years since I joined the Defender's guard," Wynn said. "I'll be taking my vows soon. Vows for life."

"How wonderful," Saerin murmured. "No one deserves it more than you."

"No, Saerin, that's what I'm trying to tell you," he said. "I'm not going to take the vows."

"Oh don't be stupid," Saerin said. The other woman had gone, leaving Axe alone. She took one last look at the quindo match, where the hairy man had driven the axe out of the third circle, bringing his team's quarterstaff back into play. The quarterstaff was in the hands of an athletic looking youth with short, curly black hair. He could have been the shield's son. The green mask turned and walked away.

"I'm not being stupid," Wynn said. "You always think I'm being stupid. I've never been more sure of a thing in my life."

"Then you're definitely being stupid," Saerin said. The green mask was walking quickly, moving toward the city. "I'm sorry, Wynn, but I've got to go. There's something—"

"Saerin, I still love you," Wynn said.

She stopped dead for a moment, then laughed. "Now I know you're being stupid," she said. "I'm sorry, I really do have to go—"

"Saerin, look at me," he said, grabbing her by the shoulders and turning her.

"Don't touch me," Saerin said. She could hear the chill in her voice, the dead cold. Memories flooded through her, the ghosts of pain and fear.

"I—I'm sorry, I didn't mean…I love you, Saerin. That's why I came here today, really, to tell you that. To tell you that I still want to be your husband."

"You still want to be my husband," Saerin repeated. "How wonderful for you. Perhaps you have forgotten that I never wanted to be your wife."

She watched Wynn shrivel up like a leaf. "That's not what you said before," Wynn said. "And I thought, perhaps, now that you're a bit older…"

"No," Saerin said.

The roars from the crowd could not penetrate the silence between them. Tears brimmed at the corners of Wynn's eyes.

"Don't you dare cry," Saerin said.

"Still?" Wynn whispered, ignoring her. "You still believe it? After everything I have done?"

"Watch what you say," Saerin said. "We wouldn't want anything shameful getting back to the High Defender."

"I have been to the House of Summerflower," Wynn said, wetness streaking slowly down his face. "Can you say the same?"

"You know the answer to that," Saerin said.

"You know I would never say anything," Wynn said, drawing closer to her. "No one knows that we took the book—"

Saerin hissed and jabbed a knuckle into the soft part of his abdomen. "How dare you speak of that," she whispered. "You swore to me, never again."

"That was a mistake," Wynn said. "By Ior, these six years were a mistake. We were meant to be together, Saerin, me and you, until death. I don't care what you thought you saw in that stone. You can't live in fear."

"It was fear that drove me to your arms, Wynn Silverfeather," Saerin said. "And then I saw what a weak, pathetic thing you really are, a jumped up boy who can't think for himself, who can't see the truth of a thing until it's staring him in the face. Run back to your High Defender. He's the only wife you'll ever have."

And then she turned and stalked away without another word, before he could see her own tears begin to flow. She was halfway to the city before she remembered Axe. And Zoe.

Willow did her best to ignore the stares. She should have been used to it by now: the open mouths, the frank looks, the hushed whispers behind cupped hands. Four years it had been since she had left her home, four years trading in the Free Cities, where most of these smooth skinned northerners had never seen anyone who was born south of their own city gate. Half of the Meridians treated her like a child, and the other half seemed to think she might bite them. She was a rarity here, a curiosity, and there was no way to hide her patched skin. Not that she cared to try. She would not sweat under a raised hood just to hide what she was. Let them stare.

On the racing field in front of her, Bryndon was lining up for another heat. It was his fourth or fifth race of the day, Willow wasn't sure. She found the whole spectacle a bit confusing. There were races in Pratum, of course, but much longer, miles and miles through the forested hills instead of this few hundred feet on soft grass. And everyone started at once. There was no gradual whittling down of competitors. Willow thought the whole exercise rather pointless. Bryndon was clearly going to win. No one else had finished within five yards of him.

She didn't know what to think of Bryndon. For the hundredth time, she wondered whether she had made the right decision in accepting his "gift" to act as Shield. He was as full of his own righteousness as any Meridian, but there was something else there, too, something she couldn't quite place. There were times when he seemed genuinely ashamed of that self-righteousness, when he let a little bit of doubt slip in and humble him. And he was certainly curious about the south, asking her all kinds of questions in the lull between races. It was nice to talk about home for awhile. She thought of home often, these days, for this was certainly her last journey before she set her sights for the passage south. She would be a rich woman when she returned, rich enough to get herself a husband, certainly, though she suspected her childbearing days were behind her, by choice, though not by nature. That was all to the good. She did not relish taking another child to the house of grass.

"Have you given thanks any more?" Master Florian said, tugging at her elbow. The man had stuck to her side like glue as soon as Bryndon had introduced them. He seemed to consider it his personal job to insure that she followed every one of the Prohibitions, whether she wanted to or not. "Remember that you must do it one hundred times a day," he continued.

"Oh yes, ten more times," Willow lied. "It is an edifying practice." She had learned early on that the word "edifying" had a magic sort of effect on Master Florian. It made him nod and hum with pleasure, and it made him say—

"Edifying, yes, I'm so glad to hear that," he said. "That's exactly the word I would have used myself. Your count is now up to seventy-five, so you are quite close."

His last update had pegged her at fifty, so it seemed Master Florian had given her credit for an extra fifteen expressions of gratitude somewhere along the line. Probably for using "edifying." The real magic of the word was that he largely left her alone after she said it, and let her talk freely with Robin. The girl was a treasure, full of all the fascinating insights of the young. And there was something else about her too, something strong and strange. An "old soul" she would have been called in the south. Willow had asked her about the dreams Bryndon had mentioned, but the girl had gotten quiet, withdrawn, and Master Florian had interrupted them at once, looking around to see if anyone had overheard them and frowning like a toad. She got the feeling he didn't like Robin's dreams either, though for entirely different reasons than Bryndon. At the moment, Robin sat contentedly at Willow's side, ripping up strands of grass and whistling through her thumbs.

The red-bearded man who seemed to preside over the races cried out for general quiet. Willow could hear the sounds of clacking wood from the sabre ring, the hum and rumble of people watching other events all over the game field. A slim rope stretched in front of the racing men, about waist-high on most of them, tied to a set of posts on either end of the starting line. The rope and posts were twisted together in an ingenious way, so that when the starter pulled a second cord, the whole apparatus snapped flat to the ground, letting the runners pass over the top. The first time she had seen it, Willow was sure the men would trip themselves at once, but no one had yet. They all seemed to measure their first strides perfectly to get across it.

"Ready!" the bearded man called out, holding the starting rope taut.

The runners bent low on the line, one hand on the ground, the other high in the air. Bryndon was in the center, looking simultaneously coiled and relaxed.

Without a word, the bearded man pulled. The posts snapped to the ground with a whoosh and a thunk, and the men were flying over the line, bent low, arms pumping. A burst of noise from the crowd followed them, a frantic energy launching the runners down the straightaway. Bryndon was half a foot ahead by his third stride, and the lead just grew from there, his bare feet flashing as he pulled away. Robin jumped and cheered, clapping her hands and whooping, even doing a small dance with Master Florian, who spun her round twice before he noticed Willow smiling at them and abruptly stopped to encourage her to give thanks for Bryndon's victory, for the continued health of the other competitors, and for the generally edifying experience of breathing the air of Cairn Meridia.

"He's going to win for sure," Robin said, as Master Florian put her down. "Don't you think, Willow?"

"He is winning every heat easily," Willow agreed. Bryndon had stopped to shake the hands of the rest of the competitors, thanking them for a clean race. It seemed to be a ritual of some kind; the winners of all the heats had done the same, though Willow had noticed that most of the races were *not* clean. A few of the men in the earlier heats had very deliberately tried to trip Bryndon, and he had thanked them just the same, as if nothing had happened. "No doubt they've been promised gifts by other houses," Bryndon said, when she asked him about it. "The great houses fight for honor at the games, and hope to insure that their champions win the top prizes. So if a lesser house has no true contender, they may receive a prize goat, or two dozen yards of fine fabric, as a gift from a more competitive house. No one is told to trip anyone, but…that is the way things normally work out."

"This is not Prohibited behavior?" Willow asked.

"I suppose it is," Bryndon said, shrugging. "One of the Prohibitions on falsehood probably applies. But no one really cares all that much. Only a Master can send someone to the Unshamers, and they usually let it go. Kian—that's my house brother—was always quite good at tripping people, when he was running. It was really the only thing he was ever good at. That's how we got Bumble, actually, from house Redcrag."

Willow would never understand Meridian customs. They could be absolutely rigid on some things, and loose as a fat woman's skirt on others. She supposed it must be exhausting, trying to remember and enforce all hundred Prohibitions, continually confronting friends and family with their shames. No wonder they let a few things slip. She pulled a piece of honey bread from her pocket and munched on it.

"What's that light?" Robin said, intruding on Willow's thoughts. She was pointing toward the city gates, at a press of spectators watching the quindo field.

Willow shaded her eyes against the sun, but saw nothing. "I don't see any light," Willow said. "Is it coming from the city?"

Robin shook her head. She had a slightly unfocused look, and her eyes twitched back and forth in tiny arcs. "It's right in the middle of the crowd," she said. "How can they not see it? Like a little star."

"I'm not sure," Willow said. "Perhaps—well, look now. They seem to be doing something." The crowd was moving and bending, circling around some central point like a flock of birds. Cheers began to go up—chants of someone's name. Willow couldn't make it out. Then the crowd parted, and she knew.

The General.

General Jair Thorndike was much as she remembered him, tall and solidly muscled, with thick yellow hair cut short to his scalp, his stride somehow both loose and purposeful. He looked older, a bit more filled out, but otherwise he was the same, with all the noble beauty of the Free Cities. She had not known who he was, that first time they'd met. She'd been in the market of Cairn Doxia, trading for seeds and gold, and Jair had been wearing a plain brown robe and weather-stained traveling gear, not the blue and white and gold of the Meridian guard that he wore now, sparkling in the sun. Even so, he had made an arresting figure then, as now. The truth of Jair Thorndike couldn't be hidden under a few clothes and some dirt.

"Well, Robin," Willow muttered under her breath. "There's your light." Jair was heading directly for Willow and Robin, approaching at a steady walk. His movement was like wind through a field of grass; the people around him bowing low as he passed by. Robin reached up and took Willow's hand. It was warm and small.

"Peace, General Thorndike," Willow said when he reached them, bowing like the others. "It is an honor to meet you. Thank you for allowing me into your fair city."

"Peace be with you, Willow Peeke," Jair said. To her surprise, he bowed to her as well. "You are most welcome here. I am told you have a great deal of tobacco to trade."

"The General is well informed," Willow said. "The guards who searched my saddlebags at the gate must have been paying attention."

"I shall pass along the compliment," Jair said, straight faced. "I wonder if I might negotiate a large purchase for the Tower Guard."

"Of course," Willow said. She looked around significantly at the crowds, who were all clearly listening intently, staring at the General with looks of rapture and fear. Master Florian was pale as milk. "Perhaps we might find a more private place to discuss business? I wouldn't want everyone to see you stoop to haggling."

"Haggling is a noble art," Jair said, smiling. "Wise Meridia practically instituted it among us, when she split the books among the people, and forced each man to need his fellows. But perhaps you are right. Come." He gestured toward the hills behind her, and Willow left Robin with a few murmured words, telling her to congratulate Bryndon, and tell him where she had gone. Then she fell in stride behind Jair and followed him.

They walked in silence for a time, and Willow realized that she had not really experienced weight of people staring, before, not like this. Every eye was drawn to them like iron to a lodestone, and no one bothered trying to hide their gawking. Everyone else was doing it too, after all, so they had the safety of numbers. She couldn't blame them. She was sure they made an odd-looking pair.

"You almost didn't make it," Jair said, breaking the silence once they were out of earshot of the crowds. "I trust my messenger got through alright?"

"She reached Cairn Doxia just before the winter snows last year,"

Willow said. "Bit of a snob, that one, though she delivered your message. I would have left right away, but the passes were choked with drifts. Then I ran into a storm on my way here. One of the coldest I've ever been in. The wind was falling off the Heights like an avalanche." She shivered just thinking about it. "There was a time when I was preparing myself for the end."

"It sorrows me to put you in harm's way," Jair said.

"Well, it's over and done with now," Willow said. "Still, it was a risk, coming this early in the spring, one I wouldn't have taken unless you had sent for me, with your cryptic notes, even with the price you promised me. So, the question remains. Why *did* you send for me?"

"My tobacco stores were running low," Jair said.

"So stop smoking so much," Willow said. "And send for me in the summer, when I won't have to chase a pair of cougars out of their cave in order to keep warm. Besides, you would not have promised a full set of books of the graces, just for tobacco."

"As I said," Jair said. "It was absolutely necessary." Willow was about to repeat her question when Jair spoke again.

"You took a Shield," he said. "A young boy, I'm told." There was no anger in his voice, but Willow felt a chill nonetheless. It was the same tone Bryndon's mother had used, when he had introduced them at House Claybrook. She hadn't been excited at the prospect of her son exposing himself to more possible shame.

"It was his choice more than mine," Willow said. "He informed me that he was old enough to serve. Fifteen he is, no boy."

"Only a boy of fourteen would think a fifteen year old is not a boy," Jair replied.

"It seems to me that I have chosen well," Willow said. "There may be no faster man in Meridia, boy or no."

"Do you know you have put him at great risk?" Jair said. "It would have been better for you to choose someone a little more experienced."

"How could I know he is at risk, when you won't tell me what I'm doing here?" Willow asked, annoyed. Jair was very pointedly not looking at her. Then, realization striking her, Willow laughed. He wasn't worried about Bryndon at all. "*You* wanted to be my Shield, didn't you," Willow said. When Jair said nothing, Willow laughed again. "I'm flattered General, but I don't think the rest of your people would have liked watching you take a southron wife."

"I have no intention of marrying you," Jair said stiffly. "The Shield ceremony is not a wedding, as much as it might resemble one in the south. But it would have been best for me to act as Shield. I can protect you far better than a young boy—very well, a young *man* from a small house on the edge of the valley can. No matter how fast he is."

"And what, General Thorndike, do I need protection from? Especially here in the free city of Cairn Meridia?"

Jair stopped walking, and turned abruptly back to the game fields. They had come higher up than Willow realized, and the field was laid out below them, the summerflower design standing out in contrast against the masses of people. He scanned the field, as if looking for something.

Jair was silent a moment before answering. "You asked me why I sent for you. It is a fair question, and I would gladly answer it, save that I mistrust my own motives for doing so."

"How so?"

"Because they are extremely selfish motives," Jair said. "I sent for you as a last resort, Willow. There is a possibility, a remote possibility, that you will be extremely useful to me in the near future. It is my sincere hope that I am wrong about that. That you will be able to conduct your normal trade and return home in the full of summer, bringing the books of the graces to your people. But if I am right…"

Again he broke off. When the silence had stretched to its breaking point, he said, "If am I right, I fear you may be the only hope we have of living to see the summer." He held up his hand to forestall her question. "That is all I wish to say on the matter at this time. You have made your choice, and I shall have to keep watch on you from afar. A Shield is binding until you depart us forever. Or until one of you dies," he added, not quite as an afterthought.

She watched a man fall heavily to the ground below them, legs swept out from under him by the butt of his opponent's quarterstaff. There was a distant sound of applause, and the victor helped his opponent to his feet for the second bout.

"Go about your business as normal," Jair said. "Trade with the people, endure the strange looks, and try not to get young Claybrook in trouble. Ridi tells me his father is a good sergeant. And a good man. In a few days, you will know whether I have need of you or not. And either way, you will get the payment I promised."

"Very well, Jair Thorndike," Willow said. "If that's all you have to say about it." She turned to face him, squaring her shoulders. "I believe we still have that large purchase of tobacco to negotiate."

"Indeed we do," Jair said, tapping the pipe in his belt. "How good of you to remember."

"The offer will have to be a generous one," Willow said. "Selling in bulk always leads to a loss."

"I think we can reach an agreement," Jair said. "I have a number of fine amber stones, golden and beautiful. And light. Very light for the journey home."

"My hearing is getting worse with age," Willow said, cupping her ear. "Did you say 'amber' or 'diamond?'"

CHAPTER TEN

The Source and Summit

When the sun had begun its descent into the western mountains, and the House of Time was ringing second none, Wizard Oded called a halt to the Unshaming for the day and rose from his chair, joints creaking and popping. It was warm in the Room of Unshaming, and many of the supplicants and other Unshamers were sweltering, but Oded liked the heat. The blood of a man thinned as he got older, and Oded was perhaps the oldest man in Meridia. No sweat stood on his bald head.

He left through the Unshamers' door, walking with slow, small steps, his hands folded together in the sleeves of his robe. The halls of the House of Summerflower were stuffy and dark. There were no windows in this part of the house, and the only light came from a few sputtering candles, set in sconces along the wall, the ceiling above them stained black with soot. They were cleaned once a year, the ceilings, but centuries of use had made that task almost meaningless. The stains were buried deep.

A few beetles scattered as Oded approached, the sound of his feet startling them out of their insect afternoons. They flew ahead of him like a little processional. They lived in the ivy, the beetles, as did myriad swarms of ants and ticks, aphids and flies and the spiders who preyed on them all, even a kind of large blue moth that most of the Unshamers called "crooks" after the blue flame of Tarn's legendary flaming shepherd's crook.

The insects were certainly a nuisance, getting into the food and linen and especially the books. The books were the biggest concern, and Oded made sure the librarians took special care to inspect every volume weekly for signs of attack. But they were a nuisance to all equally, and if he could endure them in his seventy-fifth year of life, so could the younger men. Besides, such things were integral parts of their unique brotherhood, annoyances that served to knit them together with a common bond of mild distaste. The ivy was as much a part of the House of Summerflower as the bricks it covered. Indeed, Oded privately suspected its roots were buried so deeply into the walls that it was likely impossible to remove without bringing the whole building down with it.

Ahead of him, the hall split in three directions, and Oded took the leftmost fork, knowing Unshamer Raul would be with the acolytes at this hour. A crook detached itself from the wall and fluttered to his shoulder, wings beating slowly. Oded shrugged and coughed, but the little moth took no notice, cleaning its antennae with its forelegs.

"Excuse me," Oded said, coughing politely again.

The moth looked back at him, silent.

"Fine," Oded sighed. "Be that way."

Oded paused briefly at another intersection, nodding to Garis and Grymm as they passed, a handful of scrolls under each of their arms. Studies of the Prohibitions, perhaps. Though, knowing Brother Grymm, they were just as likely to be adventure tales of Tarn and Meridia, or accounts of the games.

"That man should have joined the Tower Guard, and become a scout," Oded told the moth. "I think he is ill-contented here."

The moth flexed its wings in silent agreement.

"But then, he is not alone in that," Oded continued. "Some of us are called to pleasurable work, and some to dutiful work. The first must find discipline in his joy—the second, joy in his discipline. Yet the second is the more difficult and elusive task I think. Still: *Neither more nor less than six days a week shall man and woman labor under the sun, for the laborer builds the tower and the laborer mans the wall. And only the towers shall save you from the death the Nightmare brings.* We are prohibited from undue rest, and so we must not desire it."

The moth shared no opinion on the labor of men, having its own labors to worry about.

"The slothful complain of their labor, but the Prohibitions are just. There is some rest for us here in the valley, and more on the Heights, whether we go there in body or spirit," Oded said. "My own predecessor was killed in the Nightmare, of course, along with the rest of my brethren. I still remember…"

But whatever Oded still remembered, he did not share it with the moth. It seemed to have no hard feelings on the matter, however, continuing to ride comfortably on his shoulder.

"Nigh on fifty years have I labored as Wizard here at the House of Summerflower," Oded told the moth. "And, truth be told, it has been more duty than joy. Unshaming is thankless work, hated work. And the burden of leadership is heavy, especially for an old man like me. The real question is, what is best for the House of Summerflower? For that is my real labor. Unshamer Raul is a good man, trustworthy, well liked by the acolytes and brothers both. Generous with the people, just and proper in assigning his epitimia. Praeses may disagree with him, I suppose, but I think it best that someone did. I have given him his way for far too long…"

Oded trailed off, limping his way forward. He was approaching the Acolytes Room, and he could hear the muffled voice of Unshamer Raul, giving the day's lesson. The Acolytes Room was on the north wing, furthest away from the noise and hustle of the streets, a place of contemplation and quiet. Oded shuffled to the doorway, watching the class silently for a few minutes with the crook on his shoulder.

It was one of the largest meeting spaces in the house, the Acolytes Room, next in line behind the Room of Unshaming and the banquet hall, decorated with paneled walls of carved stonewood and a high, vaulted ceiling of polished bluestone. The near wall was taken up by a giant, thin slab of black slate, near twenty spans high and three paces wide, and it was here that Raul gave lessons to the acolytes, scratching on the slate with his thin chalk. Oded saw Raul had written the tenth Prohibition on the slate in his bold, looping hand: *Neither false weight nor false measure shall you use to steal from your brother. For a man who tricks his brother thus is bound by the shame of greed, and its power shall rule over him.*

"Here we see another example," Raul was saying to the boys, chalk dust in his coal black hair and beard. There were twenty acolytes in all, ranging in age from seven to thirteen, nearly all of them children of the great houses, sent by their parents for the honor of brotherhood. "Where wise Meridia has not only given us the Prohibition by which we are to conduct ourselves, but also, along with it, a deeper mystery and principle. Who can tell me what the power of greed is?"

A boy of perhaps nine years popped to his feet at once.

"Panic," the boy said. "It makes people scared."

"That is true in one sense, Dillus," Raul said. "But all things may be seen two ways. Indeed, the fear that comes from an object of greed is a powerful form of magic. But magic simply unlocks the true nature of a thing or a person, manifesting it in a different way, that one might see it and know it clearly. And if there is no magic to bring the power of greed out of a man, it remains in him all the same. The magic of greed can terrify an enemy without, but the power of greed will always terrify a man from within. A bolt of lightning can cleave stone, but lust has already torn asunder the man who wields it. So it is with all the shames. Pride is a blowing wind, wrath a burning fire, sloth a corrupting sickness. Cowardice gives a man an eye for evil, a kind of cunning that can only see how best to fear his neighbor. And worst of all is despair, which turns a man's heart to ice and stone. As love is the source and summit of all other graces, so despair is the source and abyss of shame, for by it a man cuts himself off from all hope of goodness, and thereby plunges willingly into all manner of other vices. That is why the creation of despair objects is strictly Prohibited, for such objects often take on a life of their own, driving their wielders to suicide."

Raul broke off his lesson as he finally noticed Oded standing silently in the doorway.

"Wizard Oded," he said, bowing. There was a shuffling of feet and scuffing of chairs on the stone floor as the rest of the boys rose to their feet as well, then went down on one knee.

"Find your seats," Oded said, limping into the classroom. "You'll ruin your knees if you stay on the floor too long." A few boys eyed the blue moth curiously as he passed, but none did anything more than look. Oded knew he was a sort of mythical creature to these boys, same as Wizard Oxyna had been to him when he was an acolyte. They would likely not be surprised if he kept a moth as a pet, or pulled one out of his ear, for that matter.

"It is an honor to have you here, Wizard," Raul said.

"You were speaking of despair," Oded said, finding a chair of his own at the head of the room. "The source and abyss of all shame, you said, I think rightly."

"I am pleased you agree," Raul said.

"And of special importance for the Unshamer," Oded went on. He turned to the acolytes, meeting their eyes in turn, boys and young men in the blush of youth, with dreams of wearing red and white robes, trimmed in silver. "You are all here because you wish to become brothers of the House of Summerflower, Unshamers, with the power to keep a man's shame from harming the city. But consider well the path you would travel, else you may find it too much for you to bear. For this is no easy task. The smith and the washerwoman look at you with envy, and think your burden light. But you will soon know the truth. Day after day after day you will sit in the Room of Unshaming, and the people will come to you. And day after day after day you will listen to their shames. Sons who struck their fathers, brothers who raped their sisters, mothers who hate their children, tradesmen who cheat their customers. You will hear of cruelty beyond tears and lusts beyond what your stomach can stand. Men will confess themselves to you and beg for Unshaming, and when you give them the key to their freedom, you will see nothing but fear and hatred in their eyes. And then you will see them again the next year, or next month, or next week, with more stories of evil that they will pour into you like acid into a jar."

No one stirred. Every gaze was glued to Oded, save perhaps the moth, which still seemed unconcerned.

"That is your labor here, if you go on to become brothers of this house. To set your mind on evil continuously. To consume it like bread and wine. To take it as your wife. It is a marriage that leads swiftly to the chill of despair. What good is it, you will ask yourself, to free a man from his shame in the morning, when he will simply become a slave to it again in the evening? Is man not destined to be ashamed? Is my work not in vain? And as despair slowly tightens its grip on you, mercy and love for the poor souls who come to you will flee, and you will find yourself seeking, not to free them, but to crush them. To levy epitimia so heavy and painful that they will never dare shame themselves again. You will hate them for their weakness and become blind to your own. You will do petty wrongs to your brothers, and console yourself with the lie that you are not as bad as they. Then a man will offend you in the street, and you will strike him down in anger, or a young woman will ensnare your boyish heart with a glance, and you will whisper sweet words to her in the darkness of your sheets. And you will go weeping to your brothers for freedom from wrath and lust, when in truth you are a slave of despair, your heart has turned to ice. And the fire of wrath and the lightning of lust are the weapons with which you try to break despair's grip. Try and fail."

Oded coughed dryly as he drew a piece of chalk from his breast pocket. He had a dozen different coughs, each with its own character and purpose.

He turned to the slate wall, and carefully drew a figure on it.

"More than fifty years I have spent in labor here, longer than nearly any other Wizard in written memory. And in that time I have seen many brothers crushed by the weight of despair. I have tried many different things to save them, many epitimia and much counsel. But I have come to understand, finally, that there is only one thing that succeeds, succeeds where all else fails."

He finished his sketch, stepping away so that the others could see clearly.

"This is the summerflower," he said. "The emblem of Cairn Meridia. For the summerflower always blooms with seven petals, one for each of the graces that Ior gave to man. And always one petal springs forth first, and the others grow from it. The men of the guard color it green on their breastplates, green to symbolize life. And you all know what it is, of course."

"Love," said an older boy.

"Love," Oded repeated, nodding. He didn't know the boy's name. "Love is the first and best. It strengthens, heals, endures, humbles, sees clearly and acts wisely. Every man, woman, and child in Meridia knows this, and is bored with it. But an Unshamer must never become bored with it. You must always be excited about love, passionate about love, diligent in your practice of love, nurturing it like the summerflower, that the other graces might grow in you, and despair might never find a way in, to freeze and crack your soul. For when the Nightmare comes with its snow and wind and ice, there is one plant in the valley that the cold never harms. But always it grows green and beautiful as if in the height of summer, for it is strengthened by love."

Oded tucked the chalk away and sat down again, heavily. The moth stirred from its perch for a moment, hovering above him, and then settled back down. He had not spoken that much in years, and he felt thoroughly used up.

"We shall end our lesson there for today," Raul said quietly. He was looking at Oded as if he had never seen him before. "Each of you spend an hour of silence in your room, and think on what Wizard Oded has said. Dismissed."

The acolytes rose and departed, each bowing deeply to Oded on their way out. He nodded to each of them in turn, trying to see how well the lesson had sunk in. They looked much as they had before.

Soon the room was empty of all save Raul. Oded gestured for him to take a seat, and prayed to Ior for the strength to say what he must.

"You have put my teaching in its proper place today, Wizard Oded," Raul said. "I have never seen the boys so impacted by a lesson."

"You have hopes for them?" Oded asked.

"I have hope for every boy that comes to us," Raul said. He had a heavy, round face behind his beard, and Oded could see the care Raul had for his charges etched in every line of it. "I think, perhaps, five of them might make it to full brotherhood. Though it might be more, if you were to speak in my classes more often."

"Perhaps I would scare them all away instead," Oded said.

There was a brief silence. Then Raul said, "I think, maybe, you had some other reason for coming here today."

Oded sighed. "You think rightly. I have thought long and deep about this, and I do not say it lightly. Sometimes, in my weaker moments, I think perhaps I am being tested and tried, yet all the same, I cannot shake the feeling that this is the right thing to do."

"What is that?" Raul said.

"When Meridia was old and used up, she did not wait for Ior to take her spirit to the Heights. She set out for them herself, body and soul, and left her city to the care of younger men."

Understanding dawned on Raul's face. "Wizard Oded, you cannot mean—"

"You think me eloquent when I speak of the perils of despair, and so I prove to be," Oded said. "For I know despair first hand. It has been with me since the day Praeses rescued me from that tower of death, and I found every one of my brothers lying crushed on the ground. Long years I have fought it, and lived with it, and now I am old, and cannot fight it any more. So I must go."

Raul shook his head. "We all must struggle with the shames of our hearts. You have much more to give us, Wizard Oded, much more to teach us."

"I was never meant to be Wizard," Oded said. "Do not gainsay me. It is true. I was made for a life of following better men. But there was no one left besides me, and so I did my work dutifully, and trained up the next generation of Unshamers to take my place. Tried to follow the guidance of the High Defender. My time is passed, Raul, but yours is just beginning. Soon, I will depart for the Heights, following in the footsteps of wise and blessed Meridia. And when I am gone, you will be the one to step into my place, to lead us through the next Nightmare. Twenty years still remain to you to prepare. I have let us become a weak and sleepy house; I have let fear guide our epitimia when love should have done so. You must wake us up, and train brothers who will be strong in love and faith. That was something I never could do."

"But you cannot leave us," Raul said, and Oded was surprised to see tears in his eyes. He had not known he was that well loved by the young schoolmaster. "You are the only Wizard the men of this house have ever known."

"Do not weep for me," Oded said, patting the younger man's hand. "I am finally going where I belong."

The moth fluttered off of his shoulder, rising toward the light of the windows set high on the walls. Oded watched it go, feeling like something was missing.

Then he said, "I go to join my brothers in the warm embrace of death."

CHAPTER ELEVEN
Beacons and Bells

Garrett stumbled and fell.

He barely noticed.

It had happened so many times that it seemed simply part of the journey. Put one foot in front of the other. Fall. Get up and do it again. His hands were raw and ripped from catching himself on the rocks, and little drops of blood and bits of skin decorated the trail behind him.

No sleep the first two days. He had plodded through the mountains steadily, grinding out mile after mile, taking a few rushed drinks from flowing streams or a few mouthfuls of snow, chewing on jerky 'til it disintegrated in his mouth. Always the vision of that sea of darkness below him gripped his brain, the Nightmare coming too early. At times he wondered if he had imagined it, if he was going crazy, seeing visions and dreams made real. But then he remembered Krayken shrinking down to nothing before his eyes, and Akrin with his bow on his shoulder, heading for Tarn's Bridge. And the thought pushed him on, up and down, switchbacking his way to Cairn Meridia, the mountains piercing the blue sky above and below him.

Then he had slowed. At first he hadn't believed it, had just sort of watched his body failing him with a detached amazement, wondering why his feet were dragging, why he had only made a mile and a quarter when he should have made two. Then for the first time since Ior had strengthened him with the grace of diligence, he had felt tired, he had wanted to stop. The pain came soon after, a twisting in his gut, a sharp pounding in his feet. By the third day, his legs were black and blue from hip to ankle, bruised and swollen. Eventually, he realized his choice was between rest and death.

So he'd slept an hour on the third day. Another hour on the fourth. The falling had started sometime then, between the third and fourth day, as he had picked his way down the Stone Shoulders in the night. Then a shameful five hours on the fifth day, underneath the spreading limbs of a small mountain cedar. He had woken from that sleep panicked and terrified, shivering in the night cold, thinking another horror was waiting for him outside the shelter of the tree limbs, with its dripping knife. He'd lost another hour to that fear, clinging to the trunk and mumbling prayers around his tears, until he came back to his senses. The Nightmare was still weeks behind him. He could move swiftly and (relatively) tirelessly, a man alone who knew the mountains better than the city he was born in. The Nightmare had massive hordes of troops, darkstones in their heavy armor, creatures unused to the elevation and the narrow, treacherous ways of the mountain paths.

So he'd let go of the trunk and set off again, eating the last of his food on the run, as the bruising moved into his back and the pain covered him like a garment.

Six days.

Seven.

He lost track of where he was, no longer sure that he was still moving in the right direction, or how far away he was.

All thoughts of the Nightmare fled from his mind. Then the rest of his thoughts followed.

And there was only the mountain, and the pain, and a small voice in his head that told him to put one foot in front of the other, to catch himself when he fell, to get up and do it again.

The sun was descending the western sky. He would have to sleep again, but the little voice told him not yet. Not quite yet. Just move your feet once more. Once more. Once—

A fresh wash of pain exploded in his head, and Garrett found himself on his back, looking up at the sky. He'd run into the mountainside. Delirious and blind, he'd run straight into the mountainside.

Get up, the voice said.

He rolled onto his side, dry heaving on the ground.

Get up.

The strength went out of his arms, and Garrett found his cheek pressed against the smooth rock of the path. A bit of clover grew in the cracks.

Get up, Garrett.

"I don't think so," Garrett said. Or at least he thought he did. He couldn't seem to tell what was inside his head and what was outside.

Garrett.

"I'm not getting up," he said, stubbornly. "I've come far enough."

But he *was* getting up. Hands were under his armpits, hauling him to his weary feet. Then he saw the helmeted head of a Sergeant he didn't recognize, looking at Garrett with something like horror in his eyes.

"Garrett, is that really you?" the Sergeant said. He had the voice of Sergeant Floramel, but that couldn't be right. "What in Ior's name happened to you? Where's Crack and Cringe? What's going on?"

Garrett blinked and looked at the mountain wall he had run into, made of dressed stones and white, weathered mortar. Then he looked up, and saw the firing ports in its side, from which a few faces looked down on him curiously.

Century Tower.

He had made it.

Somewhere, he found the strength to weep.

There was a flurry of activity, men moving and calling, orders given and received. Garrett passed through it like a babe in arms, carried about by his brothers, comprehending almost nothing.

Then someone laid him down on a bed and shoved a cup into his mouth. Garrett drank, and the liquid tasted bitter and acidic. The pain inside him seemed to intensify, yet his head cleared, and he saw that he was in his old bunk. There were the three black stones his kid sister Lena had given him, and there was the figurine of Tarn Harrick he had gotten from his father when he had entered the guard.

And there was Sergeant Floramel, holding the cup, asking him a question, over and over again, the same question.

Sometime later, Garrett slipped into a black, bottomless sleep.

And high up on the top of Century Tower, Sergeant Floramel lit a massive signal beacon. He took a handful of powder from the bag that was slung around the beacon and threw it into the fire. The flames changed from red to green, and burned hotter and higher and brighter, until it was almost more than Sergeant Floramel could stand. He looked north, where tower Ninety-Nine stood, near a mile off, and waited.

Then another green flame rose from the top of Ninety-Nine, and Floramel breathed a sigh of relief. He went below, calling for a mount and a skin of summerflower wine. Then he set a rolled blanket in front of him and spurred his goat toward Cairn Meridia, chasing the signal fires.

They passed ahead of him with great swiftness, faster than the speed of a striking merlin, lighting the path with a line of twinkling green flames. Tower to tower. Height to height. And each man who lit a beacon recounted the years since the last Nightmare, and wondered. Few, if any, thought the Nightmare had come again. But they were a people who kept watch, a people who followed orders, even when they didn't understand them.

So they lit the beacons, and watched for the next tower in line to respond. And then they rushed below, and asked their sergeants what was going on. And the sergeants called their captains, and the captains cleared their throats and told everyone to wait and see. If the Nightmare was coming, a rider from Century Tower would be along shortly.

And everyone watched the road. And strained their ears for the sound of goat hoof on stone.

Bryndon sat in the grass near the starting line, alone in the midst of the crowds. A pleasant sort of weariness was in him, the ache of muscles stretched and warm. He was happy, and trying not to let it show. Not a few would-be champions had been sent to the House of Summerflower by envious competitors for showing too much pride before the finals, for failing to display the humility required of all Meridia's citizens. Cael, especially, had been watching him closely since the quarters, as had that shrew of a house master, Usper Blackwing, who Bryndon was fairly sure resented every man over five feet tall and every woman that dared to breathe. He had already tried to provoke Willow a number of times, "accidentally" stumbling into her on three different occasions, and repeating a few choice things about southron complexion in her hearing. It was the first time in his life that Bryndon had been thankful for Master Florian, who had stuck to Willow's side like a flea on a goat, fending away gawkers and worse. He was a harsh man, Master Florian, but he was loyal.

And he knew, like everyone else there, that Bryndon was going to win.

Bryndon stood and touched his toes, bouncing a bit, feeling the spring of his muscles. It was nearly time to start. Dirk, the head marshal, was speaking with a few of the other race officials, discussing the details of the finals. There were ten of them in total, besides the starter, one to watch each competitor, and ensure that the race was clean and fair. Each was chosen from the competitors' houses, and with Master Florian occupied, Kian had been chosen for House Claybrook. Robin had found that quite funny, and told him several times not to fall asleep at the finish line, else his snoring might cause a false start. Bryndon was glad for him; it was a great honor, and Kian was not often surrounding himself with honor, a trait he had in common with the rest of House Claybrook.

Bryndon felt a hand tug at his elbow, and looked back to see Robin's flaming red hair. He took one look at her face and knelt down to her level, hands on her shoulders.

"Robin?" he said. "Robin, what's wrong?"

She didn't answer him.

Once, a mountain lion had wandered down to the valley, taking goats and chickens from the fields. A group of twenty men from the outer houses had tried to track it down and kill it, but had failed completely. So Father had come up with a plan to entrap the thing, staking their goat Boots out on the mountain at night, and surrounding him with crossbowmen. "He's older than you are Robin," Father had said, when Robin had come crying to ask whether Boots would be killed. "He's watched twelve of his kids born and suckled, and now he's watched three of them get dragged away in the night by a screaming mountain lion. If there's anything close to love inside a goat, then Boots would probably *want* to be the one out there on a stake. Love is one life laid down for another."

So they had waited with Father that night, sticking close to his side, as they usually did when he was home from the towers. And Robin watched the shadow of the big cat slink towards Boots with a look of terror and wonder on her face, a fascinated dread.

Now she looked the same. Her eyes were focused, but not on Bryndon.

"Robin?" he said again, shaking her a bit. "Talk to me, red bird. What's going on?"

"I don't know," she said finally, sounding confused. "I feel like I'm dreaming. Look there," she said, pointing south. "Do you see the fire? It's burning across the field, blackening the sky with smoke. No one else seems to see it."

Bryndon looked, but saw only the rows of spectators, the officials breaking up their meeting as Dirk approached the starting line. Kian gave him an encouraging wave, and Bryndon returned it.

"There's no fire," Bryndon said, turning back. "Where's Willow? I thought you were going to stay with her."

"She's talking to the General," Robin said, waving distractedly to the crowd, still looking to the south. "You're sure you don't see it? Sometimes—sometimes it isn't there. Maybe that's why…"

"The General?" Bryndon said. "What's she talking to the General for? You're not making any sense, bird."

Dirk began to call for the competitors of the final race to step forward, reading out their names and houses, assigning lanes. He looked over at Bryndon inquisitively, and Bryndon gave him a wave of acknowledgment to show he had heard.

"Look, sis, I have to go," he said. "Find Gran or Mother and cheer for me, okay?"

"Bells," she said, gripping his arm as he tried to pull away. "Can you hear the bells?"

"There are no bells," he said, starting to get impatient. The other competitors were lining up, practicing their starts. People were looking at them askance. "No bells and no fire. Let go now, and sit with Gran."

"Listen to me!" Robin screamed. A small, shocked silence formed around them at her outburst. Bryndon opened his mouth to shush her once again.

Then he heard the bells.

Ringing out from the House of Time.

The silence in the crowd spread. Voices fell and the sounds of laughter cut off suddenly, until only the bells could be heard, ringing, ringing, booming and braying. On and on they went, the bells, and Bryndon found Robin's face buried in his chest, her hands on her ears. The competitors and judges looked at each other, at the crowds, back to each other.

And then, unmistakably, they heard the sound of the black bell.

Few in the crowd had ever heard the black bell before. And even those who had heard it had lived fifty years since then, fifty years in which to forget the sound.

But even so, every soul there knew what it was.

It sounded, perhaps, like any other bell. And yet its ringing was fell and terrible, as a mother's cry might sound like any human voice, and yet when she laments over her fallen child, her wail of grief sends a shiver through all who hear it. So was the black bell of Cairn Meridia, that warned of the coming of the Nightmare. It cried over the city with metallic rage and sadness, and none who heard it could doubt its meaning.

Fourteen times it rang over the city, shaking its houses and shops, its paved streets and crystal windows, and each toll was worst than the last, until Bryndon saw that Robin was not the only one holding her ears in pain.

Then at last the ringing stopped, and there was silence. A silence more profound than any Bryndon had ever heard, as if the mountain itself was holding its breath.

And then the crowd found its voice, and a wordless cry moved through it like a rushing wind. Bryndon gripped his sister tightly, feeling suddenly that this mass of people was a dangerous thing, a beast that might spook and trample them.

"To me!" a voice said, rising above the others with authority and power.

Every eye turned to the racing field, where a tall man was striding out from the crowd into the center of the runway. He walked with a purposeful stride, lithe and muscular, and he was garbed with the uniform of the Tower Guard, his white breastplate emblazoned with the seven-petaled flower of the Heart Fountain. All seven petals of the flower were colored, and a small pin on his shoulder flashed and caught the light of the setting sun. General Jair Thorndike.

"Heed me, people of Cairn Meridia!" Jair called out. "You have heard the black bell of the House of Time, the herald of the Nightmare. Do not let it steal your faith, or lead you down the path of despair. It is fifty years since the last Nightmare, and we expect, still, to have twenty more years of peace before the next comes again. Yet if that is not so, if the Nightmare has indeed come, we will meet it head on, and with the graces of Ior we will prevail. Therefore, do not be afraid, for we are strong, and we are ready."

Silence greeted this. And then, from the crowd came a cry of, "Thorndike! Thorndike and the Guard!"

Others took up the cry, and soon the fields were ringing with it, the roar of five thousand throats.

Jair held up his hand for silence once more, and when at last the cries died out he said, "Return to your homes now, and do not fear. The Six will meet this very night, and discover the truth of this. And each man, woman, and child will know his duty by morning. Go now, and shame not."

The crowds broke remarkably quickly, streaming back to the city in a shifting mass. Bryndon spotted Willow walking toward them, confusion on her face. And Bryndon realized, with a sinking feeling in his gut, that there would be no final race today, no moment of glory for himself and House Claybrook. The black bell had snatched it away.

"Bryndon," Robin said, tugging on his sleeve. "Does this mean I can't get a honeycomb?"

CHAPTER TWELVE

The Six Become Seven

Night had fallen, and darkness ruled in the Grove of Cairn Meridia. The moon hung thin and sharp overhead, its pale silver light washing out Bryndon's plain and youthful face. Willow sat cross-legged on the soft grass, resting her hands on her knees. Bryndon paced next to her, absorbed in a seemingly unending process of attempting to straighten his hair. He looked exhausted.

"You're never going to get it to look right," Willow said. "Too much running. It looks like a busted bird's nest."

Bryndon frowned at her. "That's not very helpful information," he said, squashing it down again. "I just don't see why we're even here."

"The General says come, we come. The General says wait, we wait. I would think a good Meridian would know that."

"Robin said you two were talking, earlier," Bryndon said. "What were you talking about?"

"Tobacco, weather, diamonds," Willow said.

"That's all?" Bryndon said, sounding suspicious.

"That's all that need concern you," Willow said.

"I'm your Shield," Bryndon said. "You ought to show me a bit of courtesy."

Willow snorted.

"At least you could stand and talk to me like a normal person," Bryndon said. "Instead of sitting on the ground like a tired old woman."

Willow rose slowly to her feet, and made her lowest, most dramatic bow, the kind she might have reserved for a prince. "Shield Bryndon," she said solemnly.

"Oh, shut it," Bryndon said, and sat down.

They sat on the crest of a low hill, in the center of the rough half-moon shape of the Grove. Below them lay the Flower Fountain, sitting at the center of a shallow, perfectly round depression, like a white pearl at the bottom of a grass bowl. It was much simpler than she would have expected, a marble pool separated into seven smaller basins, like the petals of a flower. The same pattern as the game field. Small carvings decorated its sides, figures of men and women acting out the seven shames and the seven graces, interspersed among images of stone trees. Bryndon said it was the oldest thing in Meridia, except for the stone trees themselves.

The Grove was deserted, save for them. After the ringing of the black bell, Jair had swept them away, leading them through the heart of the city with practiced ease. Then he had taken them through the Grove Gate, left them on the hill, and told them to wait. Two hours had passed since then, and Willow's pockets were growing noticeably absent of food. These Meridians seemed to live on little more than honey bread and potatoes.

"Do you think the Nightmare has really come?" Bryndon asked.

"I do not know," Willow said, shrugging. "I know little about the Free Army."

"The Free Army?" Bryndon asked.

"That is what the Nightmare is called in the south," Willow said. "At least, that's what the lords call it, when they decide to steal more of our sons and daughters for its ranks. The Free Army, sent to free the people of the north from the slavery of the Prohibitions."

"They think *us* slaves?" Bryndon asked, dumbfounded. "But *they* are the ones, I mean…" he sputtered out, realizing who he was talking to. He always seemed to forget that Willow was not a northerner. She supposed she should be flattered.

"Only the very foolish believe that," Willow said. "Though there are plenty of those to be had in the south. Just like here."

"Well, at least we're waiting somewhere pleasant," Bryndon said, changing the subject. He had the grace to look embarrassed, at least. "I used to come to the Grove often as a boy, you know, for lessons. Not that I was any good at them. Robin's the smart one. Usually, I would just stare at the stone trees."

"They are a marvel," Willow agreed. The stone trees rose around them like sentinels, dark green and brown shadows lit by the soft moonlight. "They'd be worth coming to Meridia to see by themselves, such massive living things so high up. How do they grow so tall?"

Bryndon frowned a little, thinking, and then shrugged. He clearly had never considered it before. "It's always been thus in Cairn Meridia," he said. "A few miles from here the ground is rocky and hard, but in the valley the soil has always been deep and soft. The wheat grows full and the stone trees grow strong." He paused for a moment, and then added, "Though some people say it's because of Tarn Harrick's spirit."

"Tarn who?" Willow asked.

"Tarn Harrick was Meridia's uncle," Bryndon said. "He died in the first Nightmare, and was buried here, under the Flower Fountain. People say Meridia put a spell on the Grove, when he was buried, so that his spirit would always be ready to defend the city in need. They say it's his spirit that makes the trees grow tall, that he waits inside every leaf and twig."

Willow looked at the stone trees again. A spirit in a tree. The idea was not unfamiliar. There were people in Pratum that still worshiped tree spirits, though they were supposed to be wild things, the spirits, given to petty tricks and violent tantrums. She did not think she would enjoy being stuck in a tree for a few thousand years. A cool wind rustled the dark leaves, and Willow turned back toward the fountain, suppressing a shiver.

"What did Jair mean, when he said the Six would meet tonight?" she asked. "Who are the Six?"

"The heads of the Great Houses of Meridia," Bryndon said. "They sit in council over the city, enforce the Prohibitions and resolve disputes."

"Like lords?" Willow asked

"*Lords?*" Bryndon replied, looking confused. "What is that?"

"Barons and nobles and princes and all that," Willow said. "Kings and queens."

"Like Tjabo?" Bryndon said. "No, nothing like that. The Six are chosen by the people, and empowered by Meridia's books."

He saw her blank look and went on. "When Meridia left, she gave each of the Six a different book, containing the wisdom and power to rule. The Wizard's book teaches one how to Unshame, the General's teaches one how to fight, and so on. Each is given a bit of wisdom, but not all of it. That way they all need each other. Though nobody knows what's in the High Defender's book."

"What does the High Defender do?" Willow asked.

Bryndon opened his mouth, but before he could reply there was movement at the far end of the Grove, and Jair came striding out of the trees, dressed in a new, more formal looking uniform. Bryndon sprang to his feet, and Willow followed more slowly.

"My apologies for the long wait," Jair called out, waving. A thin, stiff-looking man with spectacles perched on the end of his sharp nose walked a bit behind him, a sheaf of papers in his hand. "I'm sure you are both hungry. Bryndon, you've had a taxing day."

"Thank you, General," Bryndon said, bowing three or four times. So far that was all he had said when Jair was around. Thank you, General. Jair could probably bleat like a mountain goat, and Bryndon would just say "Thank you, General" and try to smash down his hair more.

A number of soldiers emerged from the trees behind Jair, carrying baskets and jugs, torches and planks of wood. Lots of interesting smells came wafting out from the baskets, and the jugs sloshed promisingly. The soldiers snapped together the planks of wood with practiced ease, creating a massive, low table and a number of stools. Willow wasted no time taking a seat, and a few buttered rolls. Bryndon sat next to her, selecting a red sausage.

"The others should be here shortly," Jair said, taking a seat of his own. The stiff man remained standing.

"Others?" Willow said, around a swallow of cold milk.

"The beacons have been lit, and the black bell has rung out from the House of Time," Jair said. "The Six must gather and discuss what is to be done."

Willow saw Bryndon freeze with a bite of sausage half way to his mouth. He looked from Willow to Jair and back again.

"What's wrong?" Willow said.

Bryndon swallowed and put his sausage down. "I had forgotten…I'm not hungry," he said. The blood had completely drained from his cheeks.

"You really should eat," Jair said, a look of pity on his face. "It is good food."

"No thank you, General," Bryndon said, and pushed away from the table.

Jair sighed and scooted closer to Willow, taking a chicken leg from the basket. "I have much to make up for, to that one," he said.

"He likes seeds," Willow suggested. "And his sister."

There was more movement at the tree line, and a few figures slowly emerged. Jair put his chicken leg down and moved to greet the newcomers, exchanging kisses on the cheek. Two of them were close to Willow's age, but the third was an old man, wizened and thin. All were dressed in strange robes that were half red, half white.

"The Wizard Oded," said a dry voice behind her. The spectacled man had spoken. "Master of the House of Summerflower. He is near eighty, fair and wise in his own way. And the High Defender's man to the core."

"Is he?" Willow said, eying the man up and down. "And who might you be?"

"Ridi Greenvallem," the man said, bowing slightly. "The General is going to be occupied with pleasantries, and he asked me to keep you informed."

"Well met," Willow said, inclining her head around a mouthful of the General's chicken leg. "Who are the men with him?"

"Brothers of the House of Summerflower," Ridi said. "Unshamers Raul and Halat. Most think one of them will succeed Oded when he finally dies."

As the brothers were taking a seat at the far end of the table, more men arrived, the leaders of Cairn Meridia and their retinue. Ridi named them all as they entered, speaking quietly, below the general chatter of the greetings.

"Shepherd Pilio, Master of the House of Salt," he said, naming a portly, balding man with spectacles the size of smalls moons. The hair that was absent from his head seemed to have migrated to his chin, enriching a full, curly beard of brown, streaked with a few traces of white. "He manages the herds, flocks, and crops of Meridia," Ridi went on. "Sets the rules for the guilds and merchants, and resolves trade disputes among the houses. A good man for a trader such as yourself to know. He supplies the guard as well, and tends to go his own way, which is always whatever way is cheapest. The three with him are his eldest sons."

A tall, graying man with a sharp widow's peak was next, dressed in flowing purple robes. "Weaver Tarius, head of the House of Moonlight," Ridi said. "A bit flighty at times, but a staunch supporter of the General."

"He's alone," Willow said, sucking on an apple.

"All of the Dreamers are women," Ridi said. "This is no place for them."

"Perhaps I should leave," Willow said, to which Ridi said nothing.

A hazel-haired man in a rich gray robe was next, hems trimmed with silver thread. He was altogether unremarkable in appearance, which Willow thought the most remarkable thing about him, his face neither handsome nor ugly, his body neither thin nor fat, his height average, his eyes the same color as his hair—though he did have a certain rigid set to his mouth and nose. "The Clock," Ridi supplied. "Master of the House of Time. He keeps the count of hours and the years between Nightmares, and his Timekeepers guard the city gates and investigate accusations of crime and shame."

"His name is 'The Clock?'" Willow asked. "What kind of name is that?'"

"All the Masters of the House of Time are named 'The Clock' when they assume their post. Their old names are wiped from the records, forgotten and obscured. Though some people can't help remembering," he added. "He supports the High Defender in most everything, though often his ideas tend to becomes the Defender's in short time."

"Why are you telling me all this?" Willow asked, but Ridi did not answer her.

Finally, a large group entered the clearing, and Willow did not need Ridi's whispers to know that this was the High Defender.

He was older than she expected, but tall and broad. His hair and beard were snow white, and cut close to his dark skin. He was dressed much like the General, in a soldier's jacket and trousers, but where Jair's clothes were plain, the High Defender's were richly embroidered with thread of gold and scarlet. A pair of white and brown dogs ran around his heels, and seven fearsome looking guards in black flanked him on either side, each carrying a longsword slung over his back.

"Praeses High Tower," Ridi whispered. "First among the Six Rulers of Cairn Meridia. His seven guardsmen and his dogs, Patience and Diligence. He and the General are often at odds. You should stand."

Indeed, the rest of the men in the clearing were on their feet as Praeses exchanged greetings with the Six Rulers. He met Willow's gaze briefly, and she was struck suddenly by the depth of his eyes, like inky black pools in the torchlight. Then he turned away to greet Weaver Tarius, and she realized that she had briefly forgotten to breathe. She took a few swallows of summerflower wine.

When the pleasantries were over, the Six took seats around the table. Willow sat as well, flanked on either side by fat, bearded Shepherd Pilio and Jair. Though the other attendants stood behind their leaders' chairs, no one seemed to think it amiss that Willow sat next to the General. Praeses spoke first.

"The Six have gathered," he said, his voice deep and powerful. "Who mans the watch upon the Towers?"

"Captain Nils of Century Tower has the command, High Defender," Jair replied. "Until our meeting is finished."

"And how long before the Nightmare comes again," Praeses said, this time speaking to The Clock.

"Twenty years, two hours, forty-three minutes, and seven seconds," The Clock replied. Even his voice was plain, neither deep nor high.

"Yet the black bells rang out from the House of Time," Praeses said. "How is this so?"

"The beacons were alight," The Clock said. Though he sounded a bit defensive, he never seemed to lose his same, rigid expression. "Had I been present when they were first spotted, I would have called a meeting before panicking the people with their fell tones. As it is, my men acted without my consent, and rang the bells. I'm afraid we may have ruined the Golden Games for nothing."

"Your Timekeepers did their duty," Praeses said. "For that they are to be commended."

"Yes, give them all an extra copper for the poor," Shepherd Pilio said. "In the meantime, I'd like to know whether the Nightmare is *actually* on its way to crush us like a bug or not."

"Impossible," The Clock said.

"Absolutely," Jair said simultaneously.

"There are still twenty years, two hours—" The Clock began.

"One of my scouts saw it with his own eyes," Jair said. "Twenty years or no, the Nightmare has come."

"Is this scout present?" the Wizard Oded said, his voice old and careworn. With a start, Willow realized that bald man's eyes were nearly white, bleached of color. "I should like to question him."

"I'm afraid he was too weak from his journey to risk moving him here," Jair said. "Sergeant Floramel took his report. Sergeant?"

A tall man in a travel stained uniform stepped forward, his face dominated by a massive, bushy brown mustache.

"If it pleases the Six," Sergeant Floramel said, bowing. "Scout Garrett Common arrived at Century Tower this evening, directly before vespers. He was alone, and greatly distressed by his journey, but I questioned him for some time, and he was very sure. The Nightmare is coming. Not eight days ago they were in the foothills of the southern mountains, approaching Tarn's Bridge. Garrett saw them with his own eyes, he did."

"Does not each scout have two companions?" Oded wheezed. "Why did they not return as well?"

"The three of them fought a horror on the mountain side," Sergeant Floramel answered. "Crack got a blood-knife in his gut, and Cringe…beg pardon, that's what we call 'em at Century. Privates Krayken and Akrin are their real names. Private Krayken died, and Private Akrin went to hold Tarn's Bridge, apparently."

"That seems foolish," Oded said. "Why not return with this Private Garrett?"

It was Jair who replied. "One man can hold Tarn's Bridge for a long time," he said. "The way is narrow and dangerous and steep, and there are many places that can be blocked with rubble and attacked from above. It was my intention to station men on the Bridge before the next Nightmare, and bleed the enemy before he came within sight of our towers, but that opportunity is lost to us now."

"Still, surely one man could not delay them any significant length of time," Oded said.

"Akrin loved his brother," Sergeant Floramel said. "He loved him very much."

Silence descended on the Grove. They had great respect for love, the Meridians, that was one thing Willow liked about them. Though their idea of what 'love' meant sometimes seemed to differ greatly from hers.

"His sacrifice is noble," The Clock said. "If it is true. Yet we should consider other possibilities as well."

"Such as?" Praeses asked.

"Sergeant Floramel, you say that Scout Garrett was unable to come to us himself," The Clock said. "Why?"

"He wasn't in any state to be moved," Floramel said. "Poor lad's been running near nonstop for a week. Even with the grace of Ior, I don't know how he did it. He could barely speak at first."

"I see," The Clock said. "And given this state, you did not think to question whether the man might be delirious? Crazed from his journey?"

"Begging pardon, sir," Sergeant Floramel said. "That's what I thought at first as well. But he had this." He pulled a knife from the sheath at his side, and stabbed it down into the wooden table, where it stuck, quivering. It was a small, wide bladed knife, and the light of the torches gleamed wetly on the drops of blood running slowly down its length. Willow had seen a knife like it once in her life, in the house of grass. She shivered and tried not to think of that. The whispers in the dark.

"A horrible sight," The Clock said. "But by itself, it proves nothing. The man could have fought a horror and gone mad with fear, he could have met with a small force and then gotten confused and misspoke in his illness. There are any number of things—"

"He tells us he saw it with his own eyes," Jair broke in. He had lit a pipe, and a haze of smoke drifted around his head. "I have given orders for five additional scouting teams to travel south and report back on the truth of his statement. In the meantime, however, we must prepare for the worst."

"High Defender, surely we do not want to cause a panic," The Clock said.

"Indeed, the Prohibitions are often disregarded with the approach of the Nightmare," Oded agreed. "Perhaps some restraint in judgment might be in order."

Praeses thought in silence a moment before answering. "I agree with General Thorndike," he said, and Willow felt Jair relax at her side. "If this scout speaks truly, we have precious little time, and we must make use of all of it."

"Thank you, High Defender," Jair said.

"But how is that *possible*," Shepherd Pilio broke in. "Near two millennia we have been throwing the Nightmare back, and they have *never* come early. Seventy years to the day, every time. It makes no sense."

"It makes perfect sense," Weaver Tarius said. It was the first time the tall man had spoken, and his voice had a strange, misty quality to it, like he was just waking up from a long nap. "But you are forgetting your history, Shepherd."

"I have the present to worry about," Pilio said. "And at present, I'm wondering why your Dreamers haven't warned us about this, if indeed it is true. Seems like a pretty big thing to miss."

"We accept only what Ior gives us," Tarius said. Willow decided he would have been handsome twenty years ago. "The dreams of my house have been troubled of late, full of masks and flame and nameless men. There has been much sickness. Perhaps this is the reason."

"You said something about history?" Willow said.

Every eye turned to look at her, and Willow took another bite of chicken. "Willow Peeke," she said, waving the bone in greeting. "I'm the woman. Forgive me if I intrude."

"Peace be with you, Willow Peeke," Tarius said, bowing slightly in his chair. "I speak of the Mysteries of Meridia, the book wise Meridia set down for us at the founding of our city, that we might know how all came to pass, how to live in the present, and what is to come."

"We all know the story," Pilio said. "What's your point?"

"Yet you have forgotten it," Tarius said. His voice never lost its calm detachment. "Seventy years it was before the Nightmare attacked Cairn Meridia a second time, but after that, the attacks came every ten years, one against each of the Free Cities, before returning again to Meridia."

"If my math is correct, seven cities at ten years a piece still comes out to seventy," Pilio said, snorting.

"If there are still seven cities," Jair said.

Pilio looked at Jair with open shock on his face. "You can't mean... What are you saying?"

"Ridi," Jair said, calling the man forward. "How long has it been since we had a trader come bearing goods from Cairn Jarth?"

Ridi shuffled a few papers around and read off one of them. "Ronan Hearth, in the ninth year of the twenty-eighth peace," he said. "Some sixty-eight years ago now."

"And what of Cairn Creta?" he asked, though Willow was sure he already knew the answer.

"Two came through in the twelfth year of the twenty-eighth," Ridi said, this time not bothering to consult his papers. "Brothers seeking to exchange wise Meridia's book on the shame of cowardice. House Blackwing agreed to the trade, in exchange for a house book on the building of towers."

"None since," Jair said. "No traders or travelers, no refugees or messengers. Nothing but silence from the west."

"There have been long silences before," Praeses said, petting one of his dogs idly. They made an odd pairing, the massive man and his dogs. "The mountain paths are treacherous and the way is long."

"Not like this," Jair said. "Never longer than a few decades, at most." He leaned forward, meeting each of the other's eyes in turn. "The Nightmare is a cycle. Ten years of peace, and then it comes to the next city. If there are seven cities, then each has seventy years. But if two of the cities have been destroyed...It is fifty years since the last Nightmare. They would be coming for us."

Silence stretched thin as they glanced from one to another. A few of the men with The Clock exchanged whispers.

"This city is ill prepared," Jair said. "We have little more than five thousand men at arms in the guard, a mere six hundred of which are gunners. Before the last Nightmare we fought with twice that number, and still it took the actions of two heroes sitting at this table with us to stem the tide at the Fifth Tower." Willow looked at Jair in surprise. Two heroes, did he say? There were only two men at the table old enough to be alive and fighting fifty years ago. She could picture Praeses as a fighter, but surely not dried up little Oded.

"We must act, and we must do it quickly," Jair went on. "If we are wrong, and this scout is delirious or lying, then we will have lost nothing. But if the Nightmare *is* coming, then every second counts."

Pilio slapped his meaty palm against the table. "By Ior, the General speaks sense. I'm for making the declaration."

"I agree," Tarius said. "The signs are clear."

Oded looked to Praeses for a moment, coughing dryly.

"This threat must be taken seriously," Praeses said. "We should make the declaration."

Oded's shoulders slumped, like someone had just loaded a boulder onto his back. Then he simply nodded.

"Very well," The Clock said. "As I see the rest of you are in agreement… The Timekeepers will read the decree tomorrow morning, once an hour, every hour, beginning at lauds." He crossed his right arm over his chest. "The Nightmare has come," he said.

"*The Nightmare has come,*" the rest of them repeated.

"Then let us begin," The Clock said. "There is much to do."

"There is first the matter of this council," Oded broke in. "The Prohibitions require six in times of peace, people of the city. But in times of war a seventh must be added."

"Ah yes," The Clock said quietly. "We see now why the General has brought his guest."

"Are you talking about me?" Willow asked.

"*And she shall not be male,*" Oded intoned in his dusty voice. "*And she shall not be of the city. And she shall be called nothing but Stranger.*"

"Master Ridi," Praeses said. "Are there any other traders in the city at the moment?"

"No, sir," Ridi replied. "It is still exceptionally early in the season, and Willow Peeke is the first and only one to arrive."

"Excuse me," Willow said, looking from face to face. None of them seemed to want to meet her eyes. "Excuse me."

"Very well," Oded said continuing to ignore her. "Then as it is written in the Prohibitions, I move that the Six become Seven, and Willow Peeke be raised to Stranger."

"Seconded," Tarius said.

"What are you all talking about?" Willow said, slamming her mug in frustration. "Who's a stranger?"

"All in favor rise," Jair said. He and Tarius were the first, but one by one they all stood, Oded and Pilio and Praeses, and finally The Clock grudgingly rose to his feet, shrugging as if to say that this madness was out of his hands.

"It is done," Jair said, a note of triumph plain in his voice. "She is now one of us, with an equal voice."

"How interesting," Willow said. "Because no one seems to be listening to my voice at the moment. *What is happening?*"

"You have been given a great honor," The Clock said, finally answering her. "You have been made the seventh ruler of Meridia, as the Prohibitions require." He turned to Jair. "We are surely blessed, General, to have a female trader come to us so early in the year," The Clock said, smiling ruefully. "One wonders if some plan of Ior was not behind it. Or if perhaps someone had information he was not sharing with the rest of us."

"As you say, The Clock," Jair replied, face impassive. "No need to cause a panic without further information. But I thought it best to be prepared."

"Well it's a good thing you did," Pilio said. "Else Oded would probably insist we send for one before any work could get done."

"But—but..." Willow sputtered. The food in her stomach had turned to a ball of ice. "I'm not...I mean—I'm a *trader*. I sell seeds and tobacco and fine leather gloves. I don't belong here."

"You do now," Jair said. "I'm afraid you agreed to it when you took a Shield and entered our city."

Willow thought back to the strange ceremony at the gate. It had reminded her so much of a wedding, with the cords and vows. And the old Timekeeper had asked her questions. *Do you promise to trade no books? Nor build any weapons of shame? Do you swear to obey the Prohibitions? To serve as Stranger when the Nightmare comes...*

"You can't be serious," Willow said, her gut dropping. "That's ridiculous. I had no idea what I was saying."

"The words are the important thing," Oded said. "They carry the power of the vow."

"If you wish, you can refuse," The Clock said. "But I'm afraid there are penalties for that."

"Like what?" she said. "I'll leave happily, if that's what you mean. I don't fancy being here with the Free Army knocking on the door anyway."

"The penalty for oath breaking is death," Oded said, coughing.

"You would kill me for agreeing to something I didn't even know I was doing?" Willow asked. "What kind of justice is that?"

"The death would not be yours," The Clock said. "The guilt of a guest in our city is born by their Shield."

Everyone turned to face Bryndon, who looked like he was going to be sick.

"Perhaps you'd be willing to stick around for the young man's sake," Tarius put in.

Willow did not know what to say. *This can't be happening*, she thought. *I'm in a dream or a hallucination.* And then, closely on the heels of that thought: *Damn you, Jair Thorndike.*

"I say we take a short break and send for some more food," Jair said. "We shall need to be here late into the night, and I think Willow might want a moment to prepare herself."

"I'm in favor of that," Pilio said.

The others murmured their agreement, and there was a shuffling of chairs and an outbreak of talk as they rose and turned to speak with their servants and attendants. Willow rounded on Jair.

"You knew," Willow said. "You knew this was going to happen."

"My last resort," Jair said. "I had hoped I was wrong."

"Damn you," she said. "Damn you to Tjabo's deepest pit. You know I'm not going to kill an innocent boy."

"I had intended to give you the option of killing me," Jair said. "An option I am now glad you do not have. But it is done."

She turned with a growl to Bryndon, who was looking at her like she was a poisonous snake deciding whether or not to bite him.

"Stop looking at me like that," she said.

"Stranger Willow," Bryndon replied, bowing.

"Oh, shut it," she said.

CHAPTER THIRTEEN

Someone Missing

Saerin ran the brush through her hair, humming softly to herself. She was not thinking of Wynn. She was very pointedly not thinking of Wynn. She was thinking of the Nightmare and the black bell, the tangles in her hair and the stock of herbs in the house pantry. The Whip had been telling the truth. The Nightmare had come, and twenty years early. Everyone with half a brain would eventually figure out what that meant: that Jarth and Creta had been destroyed, that the seventy year window of peace that Meridia had enjoyed was over forever.

That Meridia was doomed.

The city had barely survived the last Nightmare. The guard was undermanned, the Unshamers were weak, some of the towers themselves were still in need of repair. And somewhere out in the city, the Whip and her captains were plotting their strike from within. Saerin didn't need her stone to see that the city would fall. And when it did, anyone without a mask on her face would be butchered where she stood, or worse—dragged south to the grasslands and given to the whispering things. If even half of the stories about those dread tunnels were true, Saerin would rather spit in the Whip's face than go down into them. At least the Whip would eventually kill her.

How to rejoin the ranks of the Masked Ones, though, now that she no longer knew the location of the next meeting? She'd have to think of a way soon. She could act the part of a rebel as well as she could a loyal daughter of Meridia, but there was no telling how quickly the attack would be planned, and she would need to know as many details as possible if she was going to be able to blend in with the others. Blend in and then fade away after it was all over. Perhaps she'd even be able to stay in the valley. The Whip seemed to think she would be put in charge of whatever new leadership Tjabo's army installed, which meant there could be a life for her here, of sorts. If she could make it through the battle unscathed.

When her hair was done, she tied it up for the night and blew out her candle. The house was silent as a graveyard. Zoe's bed was still empty, the quilt neatly folded over it. She had not returned from the House of Summerflower. Saerin knew she never would. She did not think about that either.

Part Two

When the time of her passing drew near, Meridia prayed to Ior, that he might show her the true enemy of man. For seven days and seven nights she prayed, neither eating food nor drinking anything but water, until at last Ior looked with favor on her faith and spoke to her in a dream.

He took her up to a place upon the Insurmountable Heights, and there he told her to look out over the land below her, to the sea of grass, where the dark things live. And though she was far away, she looked, and behold, she saw the dark things clearly, crawling on their bellies like snakes. Yet they looked to her like men, twisted and bent low.

"Is this the enemy of man, Exalted?" she asked.

And Ior said, "Look closer, dear one."

So she looked again, and this time she saw a cave by the edge of the sea, where the sea of grass and the sea of water meet each other and the river Osku empties itself into the water. And though the cave twisted and turned and no light reached beyond its first turning, still with the grace of Ior her eyes could see to the heart of it. And there she saw Tjabo enthroned in the earth in darkness, his blind eyes watching the dark men who followed him. And the men whispered their worship of him in the language of the grass.

Again Meridia turned to the Exalted Ior and said, "I see blind Tjabo. Is he then, the enemy of man?"

But Ior said, "You have seen without understanding. Look once more, child."

So a third time Meridia looked, and once again she saw Tjabo sitting enthroned in the cave that no light can reach. But now she saw through his body to his very heart. And, behold, within his heart was a cold that seemed deep enough to swallow the world. And it was like a living thing, fell and terrible, for the cold looked upon her as she looked upon it, and Meridia felt as if she would die, as if her blood would freeze in her veins and her heart turn to stone.

"Of what are you afraid, child?" Ior asked, for he knew what she saw and felt.

"You have shown me the enemy of man," Meridia whispered, for it seemed her breath would not come. "What is this cold that so consumes my mother's brother?"

"It is a small and pitiable thing," Ior said. "Look one last time, and you shall see."

And Ior placed his hand upon her shoulder. So one final time Meridia cast her gaze to the cave and the heart of cold, and this time she saw that Ior had spoken truly. For with Ior's exalted hand upon her, the cold that seemed so vast and powerful to her before was like nothing, in truth. And Tjabo upon his throne and the dark men below him were like shades of gray, each like the others, so that it was almost impossible to tell them apart.

And Meridia asked in wonder, "What is this thing, that seems so powerful and yet is powerless in truth? What is it that brings such cold to a man's heart and turns him as gray as stone?"

"It is despair," Ior said. "Of all the shames of men, you have seen the most deadly, for despair is the opposite and enemy of love, and so it is the enemy of man. Yet is it not a powerless, pitiable thing? For if love is everything, so despair is nothing, and nothingness cannot harm the faithful. Yet still, be wary of it, for it chills the hearts of those who embrace it, who lose faith and know no love. That is why the Nightmare always brings the cold. Because every soldier in it has chosen complete and utter despair, and they are as cold as death. But the one who keeps faith and love will be warm."

"Love is one life laid down for another," Meridia said.

"You have spoken truly," Ior replied. "And know this also, that faith is the assurance that such love will always prevail."

And then Exalted Ior ended the dream and sent Meridia back to her chamber, where she arose and gave thanks, and broke her fast on honey bread, praising the wisdom of her master.

— From *The Mysteries of Meridia*

CHAPTER FOURTEEN
The Darkstones

The young mountain goat walked across a sliver of stone, searching for moss and lichen. The wind blew high and strong out of the north, but she moved across the cliff face easily, trusting her hooves. Snow still clung to patches of the mountain here, hidden underneath small outcroppings of rock. But there was also food, and the goat filled her belly, for the memory of winter was still fresh.

She climbed higher, heading toward the rest of her tribe, which dotted the cliff face above her, small shapes of white against the dark mountainside. The wind blew her a whiff of a strange smell—a bitter, rotten odor. The goat shook her head, unsettled. Not a cougar smell, or a man. But predatory.

She climbed over a ridge line, and looked to the south, where the man-trail wound beneath her, a quarter mile away. The bad smell grew much stronger, and the goat saw a line of creatures on the trail, thousands and thousands, like an army of giant black ants. They were shaped like men, and walked on their hind legs. But they were much bigger than any men the goat had ever seen before, nearly twice as big, most of them, and their skin looked like it was made of black, shiny stone. The goat watched them pass below her, confused at such a sight.

One of the darkstone-men looked at her, and pointed. He pulled a strange thing from his back, like a little tree, straight and pointed. He took a few steps, and then the tree was flying at her like a bird, streaking through the air. It clipped the stone a few feet below her, and skittered away, tumbling down the mountainside. The goat snorted and climbed higher. The darkstone-men seemed dangerous. She heard another tree hit the stone to her right, and she quickened her pace, scrambling up the mountainside. Soon the trees were falling around her like rain, one passing so close to her that it scraped a few tufts of hair off her hide. There was a bellowing from the darkstone-men, and the goat bleated alarm to the rest of her tribe. These were worse than men.

Finally, she climbed too high for the trees to reach. A few more clattered off the cliff face below her, but that was all. The goat watched the line of darkstone-men march onward, heading north. Then she went back to her feeding.

For some hours they passed below, through the afternoon, into the night, and for much of the next day—an endless, unbroken stream of black. The goat and her tribe stayed well away. And after the army had passed, they were largely forgotten.

CHAPTER FIFTEEN
A Voice

It didn't take long for Willow to begin to hate Ridi Greenvallem. It wasn't the castellan's fault. After that first night, when Willow had found herself accepting one seventh of the leadership of a city she had first laid eyes on that very day, Jair assigned Ridi to be Willow's guide and assistant, a job that apparently required Ridi to follow her around like a second shadow, talking constantly about the history, economy, and defense of Cairn Meridia, emphasizing his points with deliberate thrusts of his sheaf of papers. Jair had given her a pair of guards, too, serious young men in the white and gold of the Tower Guard. They told Willow their names, Clud and Glew, and answered any direct questions she asked them with as few words as possible. Other than that, they seldom spoke, and seemed to have no personality, other than their fondness for constantly sharpening their swords with a dark whetstone that they shared between them.

Their silence was far preferable to Ridi's continuous dry hum of facts and dates, however. Willow had never met a man who could talk so much, especially one that wasn't talking about himself. He had shown up the first day before dawn, mere hours after the first meeting in the Grove had ended, knocking quietly but insistently on the door of House Claybrook until a furious Master Florian had opened the door in his dressing gown, demanding to know who was calling at such a shameful hour. When Ridi told him he was there on behalf of General Jair Thorndike, to assist Willow Peeke, the declared Stranger of Cairn Meridia, Willow thought his eyes might pop out of his skull.

"Stranger?" he said, looking from Willow to Bryndon and back again. "When in the world did this happen?"

"Last night," Willow said. "I'm as surprised as you. Apparently I was their only option."

"But, that means…the Nightmare really is here," Master Florian said, clutching his dressing gown.

"The General has sent out scouts to confirm," Ridi answered. "But we are confident. The declaration will be read today."

"How horrible," Master Florian said, his voice sounding choked. Then remembering himself, he turned to Willow and bowed. "Stranger Willow," he said. "It is an honor to have you in our house."

"There'll be none of that," Willow said. "I'm no lord. Just a fool who was tricked into this by a conniving—"

"Perhaps we should be on our way," Ridi interrupted smoothly. "The High Defender has called for another meeting of the Seven in an hour."

"What for?" Willow asked.

Ridi looked confused. "To prepare the city for the Nightmare, of course," he said.

"Didn't we take care of all that last night?" Willow said. "We were there for ages."

"I'm afraid there is quite a bit more to come," Ridi said. "But do not worry. I promise to assist you in every way."

Willow had expected Ridi to lead her and Bryndon to the Grove, but instead they had gone to the House of Salt, a massive, square structure of granite fronted by a broad stone staircase that spilled out onto the street. The House of Salt was the trade center of Cairn Meridia, and it seemed full of frantic men wearing identical pairs of spectacles. That first day was miserable, sitting in an uncomfortable wooden chair from morning to evening, listening to an endless stream of merchants and weavers, smiths and goatherds, beekeepers, well wardens, scribes, house masters, and captains of the guard. They spoke of weapons and uniforms, provisions and deployments, tower repairs and night curfews. Most of it either made little sense to Willow or else was mind numbingly boring. Often their petitions would start off making no sense, and then slowly transform into boring as Ridi explained to her what was going on.

Decisions were made by vote. Those who supported a decision would stand, those opposed to it would stay seated, so that Willow soon felt like a windup jack-in-the-box, forever popping up and down. Her chief pleasure was in disagreeing with anything that Jair proposed.

As time went on, however, and that first long day bled into the next, and the next, she found it harder and harder to continue to disagree with the General. Of the other six members of the council Jair was by far the one she found herself agreeing with the most. Each was given a chance to speak on every issue, and Willow learned much from what they said. Praeses was a hard man, with little mercy or humor. Tarius seemed to have a good heart, but he spoke with little force or conviction, often relying on Jair to speak for him. Shepherd Pilio spoke often, usually about cost, and he seemed to wield a great deal of power in such matters, denying many petitioners due to "the state of the city treasury," often while brushing crumbs out of his beard.

Oded usually just agreed with whatever the High Defender said. Unless someone happened to suggest something that departed at all from the traditional way of doing things, at which point the old man would often employ all manner of coughs in suggesting that the council might, perhaps, be better suited in considering a course of action that was less... ahem... unconventional. The first time he had said this Willow had laughed aloud. The rest of them had looked at her like she was a braying goat.

"Oh come now," she said, when it was her turn to speak. "This woman is asking to visit her son. Surely there is no harm in that?"

"The soldiers have duties," Oded replied stiffly. "They do not need distractions from women-folk. Besides which, each soldier is already granted one night to spend at their house of origin before the Nightmare. That is the traditional night of rest, and it has proven effective for centuries. Let us not throw such things aside lightly."

"I agree with the Wizard," The Clock said, which was not a surprise. "We should have great confidence in that which has stood the test of time."

If there was anyone in the council that Willow found herself *disagreeing* with the most, it was The Clock. There was something creepy about the gray cloaked man, something about the way he moved, perhaps, or the way his expression almost never changed. She had a strange feeling that she had seen him somewhere before, but she couldn't quite put her finger on it.

Pilio and Praeses stood for Oded as well, and that was that. "Isn't this decision something the General should take care of?" Willow whispered to Ridi, as the next matter was brought forward. "It is his guard after all."

"Normally yes," Ridi said. "If the woman had come directly to him, likely she would have been granted her request. It was foolish of her to present such a thing to the whole council."

"It was more foolish of us to deny her," Willow said.

Ridi shrugged. He never seemed interested in engaging Willow in any debates.

"Why do they even allow such requests at council?" Willow said. "Do we not have more important things to do?"

"The Seven are the seat of justice in Cairn Meridia," Ridi said. "All men and women have a right to bring a grievance or request to them for judgment, even during the Nightmare."

"But why?" Willow said.

"It is written thus in the Prohibitions," Ridi said, as he often did when she had a question. "This next man is Gryn Silverfeather, chief of the city scribes. He will likely ask for money. The Clock will be apt to give it to him, I think, but he'll not win Pilio's support on it."

And on it went. Ridi nearly always knew what the petitioners would want before they even spoke, and usually he knew how the other members of the council would vote. Most of the decisions were simple and unanimous, others took hours of debate before four of them could agree on a course of action. Willow was silent for most of these, concentrating on the food that was brought to them regularly. After a few days of this, Jair began to look at her with a disquieting stare.

"You've been quiet," he said to her finally, during one of their midday breaks.

"I have nothing to say," Willow replied.

"I find that hard to believe," Jair said. "Considering how insistent you were on being heard when we raised you to Stranger."

"Disappointed, are you?" Willow said. "Well, you all seem to be doing fine without my input."

"Do you think so?" Jair asked. "All of the Seven are given a power, Stranger Willow. The Shepherd feeds us, The Clock keeps the time, the Weaver interprets dreams. Do you want to know what the Stranger's power is?"

"To get tricked by the General?" Willow said.

"To break ties," Jair said. "I suggest you start using your power." And he left her without another word, lighting his pipe.

Willow stared at his retreating back, annoyed. *What does he care what I say?*

she thought. *I never asked for this.* She should have been in the marketplace, selling seeds and gloves to the highest bidder, filling her pockets with gemstones and silver, not listening to a bunch of old men make stupid decisions. Well, five old men and Jair. What did she care if that mother didn't get to visit her son, or if some fat scribe got more money for ink? This wasn't her city. These weren't her people.

Well, she had grown fond of Bryndon and Robin, at least. The council sessions ended everyday before supper, and Bryndon was always waiting for her outside the council room, ready with a sack full of food and a new place to take her. He would ask her about the south, and tell her stories of his parents and siblings. Robin was his only true sister, Willow discovered on one of these hikes. The other children at Claybrook he referred to as "house brothers and sisters," and they didn't seem related to him at all, or to one another.

"There are only one hundred named houses," he explained. "One for each Prohibition, named after the first one hundred families who settled here. So often times children are born to parents without a house. When this happens, they're presented to the house Masters, who decide whether or not to take in the child. It's a great honor, to be a part of a house, even a small one like ours. Some of the great houses have forty or fifty house brothers and sisters."

"And if no one takes them in, what then?" Willow asked.

"They go to back to the common houses with their parents," Bryndon said. "And hope that their own children might be accepted one day."

"That seems harsh," Willow said.

"It's no shame to belong to a common house," Bryndon said. "Just like there's no shame in belonging to a small house, like ours. Come, I'll take you to one."

And so she had found herself outside a square, slant-roofed house later that night, as Bryndon introduced her to a seemingly endless stream of solemn children, women, and men, each of whom insisted on bowing to her with a murmured, "An honor, Stranger Willow." They seemed little different from any of the other Meridians—their clothes perhaps a bit plainer, a bit more worn—but with the same rigid sense of propriety and ceremony that she had found in all the Free Cities. Bryndon had told her all the Masters of the named houses were men, unmarried true-born sons of the house. But the Master here was a woman named Deborah, a strong, pretty woman a bit older than Willow. Deborah asked her to stay for the evening meal, which Willow was happy to do. And as the night wore on they all sat up together, and she listened to stories of the founding of Meridia, and of the great deeds that had been done in her defense during the Nightmares that followed.

"How do you know all those people?" Willow asked Bryndon, as they walked back to House Claybrook.

"Kian's mother lives there," Bryndon said. "He visits as often as he can, and sometimes I go with him."

"What about his father?" Willow asked. "There seemed to be precious few men there."

"They're all in the guard," Bryndon said. Then he added, "Like my father."

And so it went. Willow learned much about the city, most of it from Bryndon rather than Ridi, and she tried to answer Bryndon's questions about the south in return. He asked about seeds and plants, about sheep and cows, and he seemed amazed that southron goats never got much bigger than dogs.

"How do you ride them, then?" he had asked, when she had told him this.

"We don't," Willow said. "Most people have *kalos* for hauling and carrying, and if you're really rich, you can afford a pony."

"What's a *kalo?*" Bryndon asked.

And so it went, two people learning about one another's lives. But mostly Bryndon wanted to know about the creatures of the Nightmare, what they were like. But in that, Willow had precious little to say.

"I have never seen most of the creatures you speak of," Willow said, as they sat on the mountainside one day, sharing a bottle of wine. "No one in Pratum has."

"But how?" Bryndon said. "Surely the Nightmare is too big to hide?"

"We know of the Nightmare, Bryndon, it's just that…" She struggled to find the right words. She did not want explain to him that most southrons believed the mountain people to be a backwards, superstitious people. "Most of Tjabo's army in the south are regular men and women, just like me and you. And they call themselves the Free Army, not the Nightmare. So we know of the war, of course, the endless assault on the mountains. We watch our sons and daughters taken from us to feed its relentless call. But these darkstones and giant wyrms you northerners speak of, the shrieks and milidreads, they are more legend than reality to my people. Most don't think they even exist."

"I think I would be glad," Bryndon said. "If I could live somewhere that the Nightmare never comes."

"It comes, Bryndon," Willow said. She looked out over the valley below them, where the city lay, wrapped in a few wisps of smoke. Even from a distance it was beautiful, with its red and white stone. "The war comes to us all. Only my people never receive seventy years of peace. Tjabo's pressmen take the best of our sons and daughters, the strongest and bravest and smartest, and they turn them into soldiers. The children leave us bright and free, and when they come back—if they ever come back—they are little more than cogs in Tjabo's wheel, thinking nothing for themselves, caring only for the Order."

"The order?" Bryndon asked. "What order?"

"Order with a capital 'O,'" Willow said. "It's a book, the Nightmare's book. Every soldier in the army is given a copy of it, and you will never find one without a copy on her person."

"I didn't know southrons had books," Bryndon said, taking another swig of wine. His face was a little flushed from the spirit. "What's in it?"

"I do not know," Willow said. "I have tried many years to find a copy of one, but they are guarded by a powerful magic, a spell that will destroy the book if it is ever taken from the soldier it belongs to. And it will kill the soldier too. So they guard it fiercely, for their lives depend on it. But whatever is in it, the Order changes them, makes them...It is hard to explain. Faceless. Every soldier in the Nightmare is exactly the same. They say the same things, chant the same songs, think the same thoughts, for all I know. You can always predict what every soldier in the Nightmare will do, because they always do the same things. They stop making decisions for themselves. Order makes their decisions for them."

Bryndon had seen her expression, then, and they passed the rest of that evening in silence, drinking until the bottle of wine was empty.

A small silver bell rang seven times, and Willow shook off her reverie and took her seat again at the table for another round of jack-in-the-box. The next petitioner was a young woman, fifteen at most, wide-eyed and clearly terrified to be in front of the Seven, wearing a dress of white and yellow that had been carefully stitched to look as new and bright as possible. It did not quite manage. She pleaded for justice for her sister, tears standing in her eyes, for she had been attacked and raped by a pair of house-brothers who refused Unshaming.

She asked The Clock to send a Timekeeper to investigate, and talk to her sister in private. Since the request was directed at The Clock, he spoke first.

"A sad tale," he murmured, when she had finished. "One hates to hear stories of such things in our city. It happens that I know the Master of your house, child, Master Kynon is it not?" He waited briefly for her nod. "Master Kynon is an honorable man. Have you not told him this story?"

The young woman said that she had, indeed, told Master Kynon, but Master Kynon, in spite of his reputed honor, had not deemed the accusation credible.

"I'm afraid the Timekeepers have many duties to attend to," The Clock said. "Surely the Master of her house would know best?" This last was directed to Oded, who was next in line to speak.

"Ah, indeed, we rely on the Masters greatly," Oded said, coughing sympathetically in his frail hand. "And we would not want to trouble the Timekeepers from their duties without cause. But I wonder if you might tell us, child, why Master Kynon did not find your accusation credible."

The girl flushed a slow, deep shade of red, and told them that Master Kynon had claimed her sister was always wanton, and that she had likely gotten in bed with a stranger, and tried to blame it on those as were innocent. That Master Kynon did not like to think the natural sons of his house capable of such things, and that he always hated the house daughters, and favored the sons in everything. Willow could see from the reactions of the others that this was exactly the wrong thing to say.

"Troubling, troubling," Oded murmured. "I shall let the General have his say."

Willow looked at Jair, expecting him to say something in the woman's favor. But he sat silently, hands folded in front of him. Finally, he looked up.

"I have nothing to say on this," Jair said, and then he looked directly at Willow, and fixed her with a steady stare.

Willow's mouth dropped open an inch. *What is he doing?* she thought. He was clearly this woman's only hope. No one else was going to speak up for...

And then, with a sickening feeling, Willow knew exactly what he was doing.

Tarius looked as surprised as Willow, and he sputtered through a few questions. "I am sorry about what happened, daughter," he finally managed to say to the girl. "I think a bit more investigation on our part is warranted."

"Unless you have any proof to bring us," Pilio said, when the turn passed to him. "No? Just her word against theirs is it?" He shrugged. "Not much to be done about that, is there."

"I agree," Praeses said. "*Not less than two witnesses shall be required to shame a man, for one witness is like a single stone, and no tower can be built upon a single stone.* The Prohibitions themselves teach us caution in this." He turned to Willow. "Stranger Willow, do you have anything to say?"

Willow looked from Praeses to the young woman standing before them to Jair, who was still staring at her intently. *That damnable man*, she thought. *Alright Jair Thorndike. You want me to speak? Listen up.*

"I do have something to say," Willow said, standing up. "The fact that we are even considering this question disgusts me."

"Now Stranger Willow—" The Clock began to protest.

"It is still my turn to speak," Willow said, cutting him off. "By your own Prohibitions, I am a member of this council, and I have a right to speak. It is clear I have been silent far too long. Your attitude is despicable, your treatment of this woman—What is your name?" Willow asked.

"Keira, madam," she said.

"Keira," Willow repeated. "Keira, I apologize for these men, some of whom I thought knew better." She looked at Jair with her most withering glare, but his face was as still as The Clock's. "As for the rest of you, this woman comes to us begging with tears in her eyes for justice, and you all have the audacity to sit here and claim that she is making the whole thing up, that it would be too burdensome to send someone to check the truth of her claim. If the crime is so clear as she says, it would not take long for someone to get to the truth of it. When I first entered this city, I passed through a gate with three Timekeepers, two of whom were snoring at the top of the gate so loudly I could hear them three stories down."

There were a few scatterings of laughter from the crowd of scribes and petitioners, though most seemed too much in shock at Willow's speaking to do much more than stare.

"No doubt their snoring is of vital importance to the order and welfare of the city," Willow went on. "But perhaps they might spare a morning to insure that the innocent are being protected. And if you will not do it for that reason, then do it to help the General's gunners. Take this shame from these men and use it to fight the Nightmare. Then put these men naked on the front line, and let the southron army deal with them. If you are too craven to do it yourselves, that is."

She sat down. There was a thunderous silence. Oded looked at Willow like she had defecated on the floor, or grown a pair of horns. Even The

Clock was showing visible emotion, a feat Willow would not have thought possible. Willow kept her face rigid and stern. They would not see her resolve break first.

Finally, Jair rose from his chair. "I stand in favor of Keira's plea," he said. "Let a Timekeeper be dispatched to investigate."

Tarius rose right after. And then, to Willow's surprise, Pilio did the same, "You make a good point about the weapons," he said. "We should not turn down any opportunity to strengthen ourselves for the coming Nightmare."

Willow thought that was the worst possible reason to agree with her, but she said nothing, just stood with them.

"Four have stood," Praeses said. "The plea is carried. The Clock, I expect you to carry out your duty vigorously. Let this daughter's accusation be investigated thoroughly."

"As you say, High Defender," The Clock said, looking at Willow like a snake might look at a mouse that had the audacity to bite it.

"Thank you, madam, sirs," Keira said, dropping a curtsy nearly to the floor. "You don't know what this means."

When the bell was rung that evening, ending the day's council, Willow stood, calmly. She walked over to Jair, calmly. She looked him right in the eye. Utterly calm.

And slapped him in the face as hard as she could.

There was a gasp of shock from the servants and soldiers around them, and one of his guards made a motion to draw his sword. But Jair held up his hand.

"Peace," he said to the others. "I deserved that. Stranger Willow has corrected me like a mother correcting her child."

"How dare you play a game with that woman's life," Willow said. She was not calm any more. "You would have sat there and let a few rapists break your precious Prohibitions, let that poor girl go unheard and defenseless, without making a sound, without so much as a word, just to force me to say something?"

"Would you have done the same, if I had spoken?" Jair asked. "I wanted to see what kind of person you were, deep down. I thought perhaps I had misjudged you. I am pleased to see I have not."

"So you would risk a woman's life as some sort of game?" Willow said. "I had thought better of you, Jair." She swung her palm at him again, but this time he slipped away from it easily, faster than she could blink. One moment her hand was poised above his reddening cheek, and the next it was swinging through empty air, and he was holding her shoulders to keep her from falling over. *What was that?* Willow thought with shock. *He's faster than the wind.* And then, close on the heels of that, she thought, *He let me hit him the first time.*

"And I still hope to prove worthy of your thinking," Jair said, straightening her up. "Do not believe I would have left the matter alone, had you not spoken. The woman came to petition the Timekeepers, and she could have been denied that, it is true, without my saying a word. But I have soldiers of my own, men who know how to find the truth of a thing. And I can assure you, I would not have abandoned her. But I would have learned a great deal about you."

Willow blinked. "You tricked me," she said. "You made me think—"

"As I said, it was not well done," Jair said. "But so it is." He smiled, and Willow realized again how beautiful he really was.

"I am glad you have found your voice, Stranger Willow," he said, pulling on his gloves. "There are too many in this city who do not have one." And with that, he strode away.

CHAPTER SIXTEEN
Unwanted

Every tower Shem went to, the answer was the same. The answer was *No.*

"We already have two lambs," the captain of Thirteen told him, a swarthy man with intelligent eyes. "The General made that a priority even before this madness started. You'll find the same in all the other towers, I wager."

"Some towers have been known to keep three at times," Shem said, as he had to ten other captains before this one. "I am the best sabre you'll ever see. Did you go to the Golden Games?"

"I was on duty," the captain said, as the ten other captains had also said. "I'm sorry, but even if we wanted to, you're over the age limit."

"I'm sure if you talked to the General—"

"I'm sorry," he said. At least he sounded like he meant it. Not all of them had. "I've got business to take care of."

And so Shem had moved on to the next tower, and the next after that, riding Betsy down the road in his old guard uniform, his wooden sabre strapped to his belt, thanking Ior for hands to hold the reins, and the opportunity to offer his service. The General's scouts had returned, confirming the Nightmare's approach. The enemy vanguard was ten days away, and Shem intended to meet them when they arrived. If he could convince anyone else to let him.

The captain of Twenty had laughed in his face; the Twenty-Eighth had threatened to have him thrown from the building. He thought he might have a better shot at Thirty-Six, his old deployment, but the captain there had never heard of him, and brushed him off like all the others. He spent a night shivering on the cold floor of Thirty-Eight, a privilege the captain seemed loath to grant him, until Shem offered payment in the form of a bone-handled dinner knife. He woke that morning stiff and sore, his old bones cracking like burning wood, feeling like there was a small child sitting on his chest. He had almost turned around then, gone back to House Haeland with his tail between his legs. But when he had saddled Betsy up, he found himself pointing her south, and then he was at the Thirty-Ninth tower, listening to the captain tell him *No*.

By noon of the second day, he had come to Meridia's Eye. Here the path split in two directions, the roads circling nearly four miles out away from each other at their widest point, before coming back together again about six or seven miles away. A massive canyon separated the two paths, dropping thousands of feet to a crystal blue lake at the bottom. Shem had climbed down to the lake many times in his youth, to swim and fish and explore the network of subterranean caves that surrounded it. They were beautiful caves, fantastical and mysterious, the wet rocks glittering from the light of the lantern, shining off the underground rivers that wound their way through the heart of the mountains. Some caves even went all the way to Cairn Meridia itself, their natural paths widened and marked by men in stages over the centuries. All were abandoned now, though, save for the occasional youth with nothing better to do in the heat of the summer. Shem took the left hand path around the Eye, deciding he would leave the right hand for the return trip, if he made it all the way out to Century Tower without finding a place to serve.

He was thinking of that decision now, facing the Ninety-Sixth. It was a middling-size tower, about sixty feet at the highest point, and it straddled the path, which ran beneath it here. A full-size gate stood at the top of a steep slope on the north side, though the firing turrets only faced south. Shem was hailed by a watchman and asked to speak to the captain, if it wouldn't trouble him greatly. The watchman took in his old lamb's uniform, raised an eyebrow at the wooden sabre, and went to get the captain.

"Captain Truman Granite," the captain said, returning with the watchman. He held out a firm hand. "Always good to see a former lamb. What can I do for you, Shem?"

"Well met," Shem said. "To be honest with you, Captain, I'm here to volunteer."

"Volunteer for what?" Captain Truman asked.

"For acting lamb of the Ninety-Sixth," Shem said.

Truman blinked at him for a moment, and then burst out laughing. The watchman frowned, giving Shem a sympathetic look. Shem was used to the laughter by now.

"Ah, you're serious, are you?" Truman said, when he finally saw Shem's face. "Forgive me for laughing, it's just that—well, there's a reason you're out here at the Ninety-Sixth, I wager."

"I need no training," Shem said. "And if you need a second, I'm the best swordsman you'll see."

"I don't need a swordsman," Truman said. "And I don't need a lamb either, so if you'll excuse me..."

"Sir, a moment," the watchman said. He drew the captain aside and exchanged a few words. Shem edged a bit closer to them.

"—still hasn't returned," the watchman was saying. "When are we going to find time to train someone else?"

"I'll put one of the crossbowmen with him," the Captain said. "Harn's a good lad, he'll do fine."

"Still, we ought to have a backup," the watchman said.

"What was that?" Shem interrupted. "Forgive me, my old ears didn't catch all of that. Did you say you were missing your second?"

"No I did not," Truman said. "I was just speaking *privately* to Private Heryn."

"Our second lamb has been missing for a few days," Heryn offered, earning a glare from Captain Truman. "I was just suggesting to the Captain that we might make use of a man like you, at least until our second returns. If he returns."

"Luckily the guard need not make use of the *suggestions* of common watchmen," Captain Truman said. "The answer is no," he said to Shem. "Now if you'll excuse me."

He turned to go, and then Shem found himself holding the man by the shoulder. "I will not excuse you," he heard himself say. "If you have need of a second, let me serve."

"Unhand me," Truman said, brushing him off. "You are too old."

"Tarn Harrick was over a hundred years old when the first Nightmare came, and he could still swing a sword and draw a bow as well as any man," Shem said. "And when he could not, he laid himself down for his city, as the first lamb."

"Would you name yourself Tarn Harrick then, and be a hero?" Truman scoffed. "I don't need to stand here getting a history lesson from an old man with a boy's dreams of glory."

"I have been champion of the lists three years running," Shem said, desperate to keep the man there, to make him see reason.

"The elders' lists," the captain said dismissively.

"They wouldn't let me fight in the others," Shem replied. "They thought I was too old as well."

"They were right," the captain said. It was clear his patience was wearing thin. "Be off with you now. If you want to help, go to the House of Salt. Tend the fires. Care for the wounded. Leave the fighting to—"

"I'll fight *you*," Shem said.

That got his attention. He glowered up at Shem from underneath his bushy eyebrows, the hairy things quivering like caterpillars.

"You'll do what?" he said.

"Take up a blade," Shem said, pulling his wooden sabre free of his belt. "And face me. If I defeat you, I will be your acting second lamb until your other one returns."

"If he returns," Heryn said.

"And if I lose, I'll give you...I'll give you the book of House Haeland," Shem said.

The Captain's mouth dropped, and Shem wondered if he was going mad. The book was House Haeland's most precious possession, containing much healing wisdom of Meridia, spoken from her own mouth. If he lost it to this idiot over a stupid bet...

"I'll even let you use a steel blade," Shem said, not really believing the words he was saying. "What have you got to lose? Except being humiliated by an old man?"

Truman's face turned bright red, and Shem knew he had him. "Gather all the men not on duty," Truman told Heryn. "I'd like them to watch me beat this fool senseless."

"With pleasure, sir," Heryn said, darting away.

An hour later, Shem was in the small armory getting fitted for his new uniform. It felt even better than the old one.

CHAPTER SEVENTEEN
The Wizard Oded in His Youth

It was twenty-seven years since the last Nightmare, still forty-three before the next, and the Wizard Oded sat at his desk, reading a scroll of the Prohibitions by the light of a candle. Full night had fallen, and the fire had burned down to little more than coals in the fireplace, filling the dark study with pulsing red and yellow light. Oded had always been able to read easily in the dark, and he liked to do so before bed, filling himself with the Prohibitions as he prepared for sleep. He had memorized all of them long ago, of course; such a thing was expected of every child in Meridia. The youngest acolytes were required to memorize at least two commentaries besides, and the final test for a brother to take his full vows included an original commentary on each of the Prohibitions and their practical application in Meridian history. Yet still Oded found the actual reading of the full one hundred refreshing, the plain words on the page, the commands simple enough for a child to understand. It was good to be reminded of simple things, when life was often so complicated.

He heard a knock at the door of his study, and an acolyte entered at his command, a young man with hair the color of coal.

"Begging your pardon, Wizard Oded," the acolyte said. "The High Defender asks for an audience."

"Thank you...Raul is it?" Oded said. The young man nodded, clearly pleased that Oded had remembered his name. He had been Wizard for close to thirty years now, and the last fifteen of those he had stopped teaching. He didn't always know who the newest acolytes were. "You may send the High Defender in."

Raul bowed and left, and Oded rolled up his scroll, rising to his feet as Praeses entered. They greeted each other with a kiss, and Oded bade his friend to sit.

"Shall I send for something to eat or drink?" Oded asked, taking a second chair.

"No, thank you, Oded," Praeses said. He looked wan and tired. This winter the white hairs in his beard had finally won the battle against the dark ones, and for the first time that Oded could remember, there were wrinkles creasing the dark skin of his forehead. *What must I look like?* Oded thought. *If time can catch up to Praeses High Tower?* He had always thought of Praeses as more like a piece of stone than a man, strong as the mountain roots.

"It is late to be meeting," Oded said.

"Forgive me for that," Praeses said. "It could not be helped. I—" He stopped abruptly, and his hands tightened on the arms of the chair. Oded could hear the wood groan slightly in protest. "Something terrible has happened, my friend," Praeses continued. "I need your help."

"For an Unshaming?" Oded asked, confused. The High Defender had the power to Unshame, same as any brother of the House of Summerflower. He would not need Oded's help to do it. *Unless...* Oded dropped his voice to a whisper. "Is it for you, Praeses?" Oded said. "Have you done something—"

"No," Praeses said quickly. "It is not that. It is—"

He stopped again, as if a hand had gripped his throat, dark eyes staring into the dancing colors of the fireplace. And then, all at once, Praeses's voice broke, and the massive hulk of a man put his head in his hands, and began to weep like a small child.

Oded could not have been more surprised if the High Defender had turned into a goat. He looked around awkwardly, wondering what to do. He couldn't pat the High Defender of Cairn Meridia on the shoulder and offer him a warm cup of milk, like he was a little boy who missed his mother. He settled for scooting his chair a bit closer, and offering him a handkerchief.

"Forgive me, forgive me," Praeses said, taking the handkerchief. "I do not know why I—Weaver Anita is dead," he finished abruptly.

"Annie's dead?" Oded said, surprised. And saddened too. Anita hadn't quite been a friend—Oded didn't have friends anymore—but she had been the closest thing to it. "I had thought her illness was getting better."

"It was," Praeses said. "But then…" He trailed off, and his tears seemed to dry up like an empty bucket. Another expression settled down onto his face, the expression of a man about to face a mountain lion. "She had a dream this evening, a death dream. It took her as the sun was setting, and broke her life in its hands. And when she woke she sent for me at once, to tell me of it before Ior took her to the heights."

"A death dream," Oded said. The death dreams were the last visions of every Dreamer, and usually the most powerful. The House of Moonlight often claimed that it was a death dream that had inspired Meridia to write the books of the Great Houses, though there was no proof of it in the histories, unless it was contained only in the Dreamers' book. "She was certain of this?"

"Beyond a doubt," Praeses said. "For the death dream signals the loss of the Dreamer's power, and from what the Dreamers say, there is no mistaking it. It is like losing one's hand or eye."

"What was the dream?" Oded asked, leaning forward.

"She was in a field, blackened and destroyed as if by lightning," Praeses said, staring again into the shifting coals. "And she looked, and the city was below her, and dark storm clouds rolled above it. The storm broke, and lightning flashed to the ground, blasting the city to bits, setting fires that roared to the sky. Then she turned, and saw a woman standing next to her, with a mask on her face and a whip in her hand and seven braids on her head. And the mask was not really a mask, but her real face. And every time the masked woman cracked her whip, the lightning struck down on the city. More women came behind her, hundreds and hundreds of them, and all wore masks, and all carried weapons of shame in their hands. And when they had finished destroying the city, they turned, and the masked one put on a second mask, a mask of black, and walked into the High Tower. The gate slammed shut behind her, and Anita heard the black bell ring out from the House of Time, and the High Tower blew away like ash. And behind it came the Nightmare, screaming and bellowing, with Tjabo's black banner raised high."

There was silence.

The coals in the fireplace cracked.

Oded felt his throat dry up, and he coughed an old man's cough. "Did she know what it meant?" Oded asked, his voice barely above a whisper.

"Yes," Praeses said. "It means our doom. Our doom if we do not act."

"Act how?" Oded said.

Praeses stood and began pacing, like a bear stalking in its den. "It is the women, Oded, the women are the key to this," he said. "Every figure Anita saw was a woman. She was very clear about it, and very clear about the answer. Tell me, why did Meridia write the Prohibitions, why did she teach the people how to remove the power of shame?"

"Every child knows the answer," Oded said, frowning. "Tarn Harrick came to her and asked her for it. 'Show us how to remove the power of shame,' he said, 'So that none can rise up to burn us with fire.'"

"So it is written," Praeses said, nodding. "That is the original and first purpose of the Unshamers, to keep the city free from the danger of shame."

"You tell me of my own house," Oded said. "I have studied scroll upon scroll about such things."

"Then you must see, Oded, as Anita did, that her dream foretells your greatest failure," Praeses said, turning to stare at him.

Oded realized his mouth was hanging open, and closed it with a click. "My failure?" he asked.

"She saw hundreds of women, Oded, *hundreds*," Praeses said, his voice stern. "Women of the city, every one. And all of them had shame objects, powerful ones, strong enough to lay Meridia to waste. How could such a thing happen, unless the Unshamers fail to do what Tarn intended for them to do? Unless the shame of these women is allowed to fester and rot, unchallenged?"

"We have done what our house has always done—" Oded began.

"So you have," Praeses interrupted, looming over him. "And so far the city is safe. Yet this is a vision of the future, Oded, of what will come if we do not act."

"I…" Oded began, licking his lips. "I've always done my best, High Defender. You know I was not meant for this, to be Wizard. Our house was broken by the last Nightmare, most of the brothers killed. I was the only one left, the only one to rebuild."

"And you have done so admirably," Praeses said. "But you must do more, now, you must turn your gaze outward, toward the city that needs your protection. You must keep our women clean and protected, to keep this dream from coming true. Anita was sure of it."

"But what can I do, Praeses?" Oded asked. He knew his voice sounded pleading, but he could not stop it. "We cannot turn people out of their homes, Unshame them night and day, death dream or no."

"No, you cannot," Praeses said. "And Anita did not suggest it. Nor do I ask it of you now."

"Then what?" Oded said. "What did she think I could do?"

Praeses was silent for a long while, as if contemplating this question. Indeed, it was a hard question, for only in extreme cases were people Unshamed against their will.

Finally, Praeses said, "The rules allow for leeway, of course, in determining epitimia."

"They do," Oded said, confused.

"And there are some kinds of epitimia, more painful than others, that deter future shame."

"So it seems," Oded said. "What do you mean?"

Praeses did not answer, simply stood with his hands behind his back, looking Oded in the eye. Oded stared back, confused for a moment, and then, slowly, a thought occurred to him. He did not like the thought. He felt himself start to sweat. Praeses still said nothing, the expression on his face a mix of grief and determination, and just below that, the smallest hint of pleading. Oded saw a choice approach him, pass him, and fade into the distance. He looked down at his hands, and realized how old and spotted they had become.

"Have courage," Praeses said, putting his heavy hand on Oded's shoulder. "We have been given a difficult time to live in. It will take brave men, now, to keep the city safe. To do what must be done." With that, he turned, and strode out the door, and the place where his hand had been felt cold.

Afterward, when Oded was alone in his study, he found himself reading the Prohibitions again, over and over, long into the night. Clinging to simple things.

CHAPTER EIGHTEEN

One Refused, One Accepted

At the touch of Brother Raul's hand, Oded woke with a start. It took him a moment to remember where he was, that he had fallen asleep in his chair again.

"It is just and merciful," he said, hoping they were at that part of the ceremony.

"*It is just and merciful,*" Raul repeated, looking relieved. He had gotten it right, then. He hadn't always. Oded would have sworn before this that he could have done the Rite of Unshaming in his sleep, but that was proving to be false. Raul continued the ritual, drawing the shame out of the young man kneeling in front of them.

There were twenty other brothers in the Room of Unshaming with them, working in pairs at the unending river of Meridians that had flooded the House of Summerflower since the Seven had declared the approach of the twenty-ninth Nightmare. The room was full of groans and painful cries. Oded had told the others that shame would increase dramatically in the wake of the announcement, and he had been right. The histories all spoke of the phenomenon; the threat of death brought out the most foolish and most noble in humanity. Many threw caution to the wind, and indulged their passions with abandon. Others sought out Unshaming for old crimes, long secret, and these Oded was happy to free. But it was exhausting work, and he was too old for it.

When the young man had been freed and sent on his way—the man had stolen three bottles of summerflower wine from a common house cellar and drunk himself into a drooling stupor—Raul told Oded once again to take a rest.

"You need to save your strength," Raul said. "There are others who can take your place."

"We are all tired," Oded said.

"We are not all the Wizard of the House of Summerflower," Raul replied. "We cannot afford to have you sick or worse at a time like this." He leaned closer and dropped his voice. "I thought you had decided to delay that foolish decision until the Nightmare is passed."

"So I have," Oded grumbled. It had seemed selfish to take the Heights with the enemy at the gates, when he could still be of use. That, and Raul had practically chained him to his bed until he had promised to stay.

"Then don't work yourself to death instead," Raul said. "Come, I will walk you to your room."

Oded was about to assent when a young acolyte came running up. "The Clock is here to see you, Wizard Oded," he said. "He awaits you in the Red Room."

"Thank you, my son," Oded said. "Stay here," he told Raul. "Help the other brothers as you can. Some of them look dead on their feet."

He walked the halls slowly, leaning heavily on a polished stonewood cane Raul had found somewhere. Luckily, the Red Room was fairly close to the Room of Unshaming. Each of the seven graces of Ior had a room dedicated to it in the House of Summerflower, decorated to inspire the grace in whoever should enter the room. The Red Room was dedicated to bravery. Battle scenes took up most of the walls—men locked in combat with hulking black darkstones, shepherd's striking huge bears, muscled women fighting off evil-looking men with rape on their faces. Tarn Harrick took up a wall to himself, blood weeping from the arrows in his eyes and arms.

The Clock was sitting in a stout wooden chair, contemplating Tarn's face, when Oded entered. The man looked the same as always, gray and meticulous, his features like a composite of other men's.

"You look on death's door," The Clock said, rising to greet Oded, concern on his face. "Sit, sit. I have taken the liberty of sending for refreshments."

"You are well within your rights to do so," Oded said, sinking heavily into a chair. Another acolyte entered behind him, carrying a tray of red veined cheese and chilled wine. Oded left the cheese alone, but allowed The Clock to pour him a glass of wine.

"I have never seen so many at the House of Summerflower," The Clock said, taking a sip from his own glass. "Ah, that is a lovely vintage. You know I was quite the connoisseur, before I became The Clock."

"We all make mistakes in our youth," Oded said.

The Clock chuckled as if Oded had made some great joke. "But alas, some things must be given up, in exchange for leadership. It changes a man. It gave me a new name, a new cloak, new responsibilities. But one's nature stays the same, you know."

"It is honorable work," Oded said.

"Quite so," The Clock said, nodding and smiling. "Still, I can't help but feel a bit helpless at a time like this. The Timekeepers are not warriors or healers; we have no visions, make no weapons, feed no hungry children. We watch our clocks and chime out the hour, and keep the city gates well oiled."

Oded blinked, not sure what The Clock was getting at. Hadn't he already acknowledged it was honorable work?

"The truth is, Wizard Oded, that I have failed this city," The Clock said. "I'm supposed to be the one that marks the coming of the Nightmare. I'm supposed to be the watcher in the night, the clock that never sleeps, but waits patiently, minute by minute, for the return of our enemy. And yet, here they come, nine days away, sneaking in twenty years early. And me without a word to say."

"We all missed the signs," Oded said. "Only Jair suspected anything, and even he was not sure."

"You are kind to make excuses for me," The Clock said, taking another long, delicate sip. "Tell me, how is your own work going?"

"The brothers are being sorely taxed," Oded said. "I have them working nearly all hours in pairs and shifts, but there are many who need freedom, and Unshaming is tiring work, especially when the object of shame must be preserved for the guard rather than destroyed."

"An ironic situation, don't you think?" The Clock asked. "We spur men to follow the Prohibitions and pursue the graces of Ior; we even build rooms for the purpose," he said, gesturing to the various murals of bravery. "Yet when our lives are at risk, what we need is men who have done shameful things, the more shameful the better. For their shame becomes the power by which we defend ourselves."

"Shame is a precious commodity right now," Oded agreed, sighing. "Fire and lightning are quicker, more reliable ways to defend ourselves than trying to empower people with Ior's graces, and speed is of the essence at the moment. Yet it saddens me all the same."

"How many weapons do you think the guard has as of this moment?" The Clock asked.

"A question better answered by General Thorndike or the High Defender," Oded said. "That is not my business."

"But it is all of our business," The Clock said. "For our very survival depends on it. In truth, I know the answer, I was simply wondering if you did."

"Than why did you ask it in such a strange way?" Oded said. The Clock started laughing again. "What is so humorous?" Oded asked.

"Forgive me," The Clock said. "I sometimes forget how charming plain speech is. I hear so precious little of it these days." He drained his glass and poured another, swirling it around in idle circles. "Since you do not deem it your business to ask after the defense of your city, let me inform you. At last count, the Tower Guard had six hundred and three gunners, nearly half as many as during the last Nightmare. Yet even of those, only half have a weapon ready in their hands. And the ones that they do have are not as powerful as they'll need to be. There are precious few firebrands of wrath and even fewer wind-wands of pride. Of lightning and lust there is more, but still not enough."

"Every shame that is powerful enough to make a weapon is being sent to the towers," Oded said. "We must rely on Ior to provide. That is all we can do."

"Is it?" The Clock said, still staring at his wine. "I wonder."

Oded waited for a moment for The Clock to go on. "What do you mean?" Oded finally said, when he remained silent. "Surely you're not suggesting...*encouraging* shame among the people."

"Of course not," The Clock said, waving that horrible suggestion away. "But why wait for them to come to us? Ior will provide, you say, yet Ior will not come down from the Heights to defend us if the Towers fall, to strengthen our lambs on the crucible. He did not protect Cairn Jarth, or Cairn Creta. He leaves men to work his will in the valleys, and it is men who must do something if we are to survive."

"You have a proposition for me," Oded said. It was not a question.

"I do," The Clock said, leaning forward. "There is shame aplenty in our city. You know it, I know it, enough shame to fill our weaponry to the brim, and then some. But many, if not most, will never come here, for they fear the ridicule of their fellows and the pain of epitimia, the good of the city and their souls be damned. We must not give them that chance. I have men. Trusted by the people, eager to help. Lend us some of your brothers, and let us go together to the people. The Heartspell can see what is hidden, it can find us the weapons we need."

Oded coughed in disbelief. "You would drive the city to fury," he said. "This must not be done. A man must choose to free himself from shame, else it will return stronger in him again."

"We have forced Unshaming in the past," The Clock said. "You have done it yourself."

"Only for the most horrible of crimes," Oded said. "Those deserving death. And only then because we already knew the man was guilty. What you're suggesting..."

"This is not about one man's freedom any more," The Clock said. "Open your eyes, Oded. Two cities have been destroyed already. Fair Meridia is next. We *must* have those weapons."

"I will not do it," Oded said. The Clock opened his mouth, but Oded raised a wrinkled hand. "No, do not say any more. I know our need, but what you suggest is not possible."

The Clock sighed and settled back in his chair, setting his glass of wine on the table. They sat in silence for a moment, and Oded struggled to keep his eyes open. By Ior's gentle hands, he just wanted to sleep. A younger man would know what to do, would have the strength to see it done. He should have taken the Heights years ago.

"You know I have always been fascinated with this story," The Clock said, and Oded realized the hazel-eyed man was staring at the painting of bloody Tarn Harrick again. "There is great depth to it. A man standing before arrows, unflinching, knowing that his pain will bring others peace. A hundred years old and still braver than all the others."

"The Mysteries never say his age," Oded said. "That has always been no more than our best guess. And the older I get, the less inclined I am to believe that."

"Ior graces whom he wills," The Clock said. "Though, in truth, it is not Tarn Harrick whom I think of the most. The true mystery to me is not the man who is filled with arrows, but the ones who draw the bows."

"His sons," Oded said, taking another small sip of wine. He turned away from the painting, not wanting to fill his eyes with blood.

"And Meridia herself," The Clock added, running a finger over his lip in thought. "Killing their beloved father, her last true uncle. Did their hands tremble, do you think, when they pulled back the strings? Did they hesitate, as they looked upon the face of the last great captain of men, the one who had led our people across the endless sea, through the howling storms and the darkness of the grass? Here was a man they respected, a man they honored, a man they loved. And they were going to kill him."

"He laid himself down for the good of all," Oded said. "It was his choice."

"Oh, it is easy enough to see that now," The Clock agreed. "But in that moment, when his sons took aim, when wise Meridia drew back the bow…How could they not have felt fear, hesitation, even disgust at what they were doing? Yet they did not flinch. They did what had to be done. For though it appeared evil, it was really for the good of all."

The Clock turned back to Oded, and he looked sad, careworn. "In truth, I have a second request for you Wizard Oded," he said. "One I dread asking even more than the first."

"Speak it," Oded said, coughing in impatience.

"I would ask you to give me two Unshamers, just for the night," The Clock said.

"To what purpose?" Oded asked.

"To Unshame Stranger Willow."

Oded's weariness melted away for a moment from shock. "Stranger Willow?" he said.

"I know how often we disagree in council, and how much this may look like a petty personal feud to you," The Clock said hurriedly. "But I can assure you that it is not. Examine my heart yourself, if you wish to know for sure."

"That will not be necessary," Oded said. *Not that I could have managed it right now anyway*, he added to himself. "But why Stranger Willow? What do you suspect her of?"

"You remember the dream Weaver Anita had, the death dream," The Clock said. "She saw a woman with seven braids in her hair, and a mask on her face, leading a host of other women against our city."

"I remember it well," Oded said. *I have dreamed of it this very night, in fact.*

"And now, when our hour is dire, this trader from the south shows up at our doorstep," The Clock said. "With seven braids in her hair and a mask of green and brown for her face."

"You think Stranger Willow is the one foretold?" Oded asked. "The one who will attempt to destroy Meridia?"

"I do not think it," The Clock said. "But I fear it. Does it not parallel the dream so closely?"

"Much has been sacrificed for the sake of that dream," Oded said. "Too much, I sometimes think."

"Yet we have come this far," The Clock said, leaning forward. "We have drawn back the bow. Will we hesitate, now, to loose it? Your men are weary, I know, and you say you will not grant me Unshamers to examine the hearts of all the people, despite my urging, and our dire need. Very well. But send them, at least, to examine her, to give us assurance, once and for all, that she may be trusted. Else I fear your work for these many years, the pain that our women have endured, all will be in vain."

Oded cleared his throat, thinking. He suspected, whatever The Clock said, that there was more than a little anger at Willow behind this request. The southron complexion was no more a mask than the northern one. Yet the seven braids...

He sighed. The Clock spoke the truth. They needed to be sure. "I will send word to Brother Halat," he said. Halat was a fair man, and proper. He would see the Unshaming done with the right amount of respect. "And one other brother of his choosing. They will go with you this night, and this night only."

Relief washed across The Clock's plain face. "Thank you, Wizard. You will not regret this."

"I do not think of regrets," Oded said, rising wearily from the chair. "I think of forgiveness." And he called for an acolyte, and a piece of paper.

CHAPTER NINETEEN

Farewell

Robin sat on the fence, kicking the post with her heel. Sounds of laughter came from the window of House Claybrook, bright lights and warm smells, but she turned away resolutely. She was not going inside. They could all celebrate Father's impending death if they really wanted to, but *she* wasn't going to be part of it. She kicked the post again, grunting.

Bumble looked up briefly from where she lay in the straw, but she put her head down again when she saw nothing was amiss. She was near birth, and moving slower than ever, spending most of her time lying in the grass, or eating oats. Robin wished she would give birth tonight. Then maybe Father would stay for a little longer, to make sure the kids were healthy and safe. Bryndon said it would be another couple of days, though.

"He won't stay for me, that's for sure," Robin said to Bumble. "And you're just a goat. So I doubt he would stay for you, either."

Bumble bleated back at her. She always seemed to like Robin the best.

For a moment, Bumble's body seemed to blur, and Robin saw her up on her hind legs, pawing the air, a look of rage on her face. She gripped the edge of the fence, feeling dizzy, as if she might tumble off. Then slowly her head cleared, she looked again, and it was just plain old Bumble, fat and pregnant.

That had been happening a lot lately. She had always seen things, had strange dreams and feelings. Often they were just hunches, the knowledge that a certain person was going to get sick or hurt, an awareness of who would be coming to visit them, before they arrived. But lately they had become more acute, and more visual. And, more troubling. They were nearly all horrible, visions of fire and pain, violence and tears.

The back door opened, letting out a flood of red and yellow light. Robin quickly turned away, crossing her arms over her chest and hunching down as low as possible. It was him. She could tell by the sound of his boots on the bare dirt.

He didn't say anything, just sat on the fence next to her, and put his arm around her shoulder. He smelled like woodsmoke and hay and the honeyed chicken Mother had made for supper. Robin hugged herself tighter.

"Bumble's about ready, isn't she?" her father said. His voice was so much like Bryndon's, only a little deeper, a little harsher with age. "You'll have to help Bryn with it this time. Mind what he tells you, and pay close attention. The herd trusts you."

Robin said nothing, her face buried in her knees. She wanted him to go away. Forever. Or stay forever. One or the other. She just didn't want to have to say goodbye anymore.

"This will be her fourth birth," he went on. "All strong and healthy, so far. Sunstar was hers, you know, the only one we kept. Sent the others off to different houses for one thing or another. Sometimes I wonder if she misses them, if she even remembers them."

"She's just a stupid goat," Robin mumbled into her knees.

"That she is," he said, pulling her in closer. "You know, one of those kids saved your mother's life?" He waited for her response, and then went on when she stayed silent. "This was, oh, eight years ago now. Your mother was pregnant with you, and Bumble was pregnant for her first time. They used to sit together in the yard sometimes, and watch Bryn and Kian and Rhys play at quindo. My two pregnant ladies, I used to call them," he chuckled. "Your mother really hated that.

"Anyway, the time came for you to be born, and you were a strong willed child, even in the womb. Didn't want to come out. And when you did, you didn't want to come out right, kept trying to be born all twisted up and turned about. The midwife got you alright in the end, but your mother...well, she was in a bad spot, you know, from all the bleeding. Couldn't get it stopped. So I sent Bryn running for a humble-healer, and the humble-healers, they can do amazing things. But they make no promises. 'Ior does what he wills,' they always say. 'And sometimes he uses a man to save another, and sometimes we can only send them softly to the Heights.' Anyway, that's what they always say."

He stopped briefly, and Robin felt his arm leave her shoulder as he lit his pipe. She felt cold without it, and scooted closer to him.

"Now Bryn comes back with the woman, the humble-healer," he went on. "Alla's her name. And she's an old lady, mind, but she's still got Ior's fire. You could see it on her face, hear it in her voice. And she herself was saved on the birthing bed by another woman, when she was a lass. And she tells us all to circle up and start praying, just to call out to Ior and ask for his help. And then, well, I felt something, something strange and powerful. It was like…like something in the air or—I don't know. It was Ior. And the old woman lays her hands on your mother and asks Ior to close up her wounds, to stop the bleeding and keep her safe. And so he did. And I still had a wife."

He took a few puffs on his pipe, breathing out into the night air. Robin lifted her head from her knees and looked up at him. "What has that got to do with the goat?" she asked. "You said the goat saved mother's life."

"Oh, well, it happened that Bumble gave birth the same night as your mother, a male and a female. Big and healthy buck, the male. Can't recall his name, though I doubt I gave him one. Humble-healers, they don't expect payment. That's why they can do what they do, you see. But I gave Alla that first-born, as a thank you for what she'd done. Happiest I've ever been to give up a goat. Sunstar was the other, the second-born. They're a good herd," he added, almost as an afterthought.

He took Robin's hand in his own, and she held it to her cheek. Her father's hand.

"You've grown into quite the little girl since then," he said.

"I'm not a little girl," Robin replied, taking the hand away.

"You are," he said, putting it back. "You're my little girl, and you always will be."

He lifted her chin up, so that their eyes met. "I want you to know I'm sorry, Robin," he said. "Sorry I haven't been here for you. Sorry I have to leave again. I thought I would have time, you see, when my service with the Guard was over. And now…" He sighed and trailed off. "You'll have to be brave again, Robin. For me."

Robin started to cry. They were little, quiet cries, wet cries, and she leaned into her father's chest. Bumble heaved herself off the ground and stuck her muzzle in Robin's back, licking.

"Can't you stay?" Robin asked. "They don't need you, not just one person."

"I'm afraid they need a lot more than me," he said. "I know it's hard to see it right now, but I'm going for your sake. And your mother's, and Bryn's, and Teagan and Rhys and Kian. Even Master Florian, if you can believe that. I'm going cause that's the only way to save them, keep 'em safe."

"And Bumble?" Robin asked, drying her face on her skirt. "You'll keep her safe too?"

"And Bumble," he agreed.

"Just promise you'll come back," Robin said. "Just promise, and I'll believe you."

"I promise," he said at once. Robin mostly believed him.

"Now come inside and eat," he told her, picking her up and lifting her off the fence. "Everyone misses you."

They walked inside, hand-in-hand. The others were gathered around the fireplace, Kian and Digon playing dibstones, Teagan and Rhys betting peppermints on the winning throw, Gran giving criticism on it all. She could hear the sounds of Master Florian in the kitchen, cleaning up after the night's meal, while Mother sat in her chair by the fire, mending one of Digon's shirts. Willow sat next to Bryndon, who was reading aloud their copy of the Mysteries, the part about love.

"You're back," Willow said when she saw Robin. "How were the goats?"

"Mostly sleeping," Robin said. "Bumble was awake."

"I missed you," Willow said. "I was hoping—"

"Robin, dear," Mother called across the room, a little too loudly. "Come sit here with me."

Robin made a face at Willow, but she did as Mother asked. She knew Mother didn't like Willow, but she wasn't sure why. Gran liked her, and she never got along with anybody. Maybe it was her face. Robin hadn't liked that at first either. It was like a patchwork cloak when you first looked. Only, if you kept looking, it started to seem prettier. *I should get her to show Mother one of the dream bells*, Robin thought. *She'll like her then.* Robin made up her mind to mention it to Willow after Father was gone.

There was a knock at the door.

"Hail House Claybrook!" came a distant call from outside. "Hail the house!"

"Who's come calling at this hour?" Gran said, frowning. "Do they think us bats, to be receiving visitors in the dead of night?"

"Master Florian," Father called to the kitchen.

"I heard them, Abryn," Master Florian said, emerging with his apron wrapped around his waist. "I'll go see what they want."

He vanished down the hall, and everyone grew rather quiet, listening as he opened the door. All but Digon, anyway, who used the occasion to swipe an extra stone when he thought no one was looking. Gran swatted him across the back of the head until he put it back.

"What's this?" Master Florian said, his voice floating back to them. "Do you know what time—"

There was a muffled murmuring of voices, though Robin couldn't make out the words.

"Out of the question," Master Florian said. "We're in the middle of a house farewell."

Another voice broke in, deeper than the first, and spoke for some length. Robin caught the words "unfortunate" and "necessary."

"I...I did not see you, sir," Mastery Florian said. And Robin thought he sounded a little scared. "Forgive me. But is there no way this could be done at another time?"

The second voice spoke again, this time in a much less pleasant tone.

"Very well, very well," Master Florian said. "If you simply *must* speak to her now. But be quick about it. And take your boots off at the door."

A minute later, Master Florian came back in, leading a small troop of men. Two of them were tired looking brothers in the red and white robes of the Unshamers, and behind them came a pair of tall, strong looking Timekeepers, stout wooden cudgels hanging from their belts. And last of all, in gray and silver, came The Clock. There was a general shuffling and standing as he entered, the Claybrooks rising to their feet. All except Gran, who never got up for anybody. And Willow, who had crossed her arms across her chest.

"Forgive my intrusion," The Clock said, as he entered, though Robin didn't think he looked like he was sorry. "Anwir, would you be kind enough to get the door?" One of the men strode to the back door, ignoring the rest of them, and took up a position in front of it, his hand on his cudgel.

Father looked for a moment at the Timekeeper, his face blank. "Can I ask how we may be of service to you, The Clock?" he finally said.

"I'm here to speak to Stranger Willow," The Clock said.

"I'm right here," Willow said, still sitting. "Speak."

"It would be best to speak to her alone," The Clock said, still directing his words at Father. "This is a small house, of course, but perhaps if you would all retire to the upper level…"

"I don't climb stairs any more than I have to," Gran broke in. "Why can't we just go outside?"

"It would be best for everyone to stay in the house," The Clock said, still talking to Father. "Anwir is here to insure that no one—"

The Clock's words cut off in surprise. Gran had shuffled right in front of Father and was vigorously waving her wrinkled arms at the gray-robed man.

"Oh, you can see me, can you?" Gran said. She planted her hands on her hips. "Thought perhaps you were blind as well as deaf."

"Gran!" Master Florian said.

"Don't you scold me, son," Gran said. "I've a right to speak in my own house. I'm old, not invisible."

"I want everyone to stay here," Willow said loudly. They all turned to look at her, hand resting lightly on the open *Mysteries*. "This family has taken me in, made me their own. Whatever you have to say, you can say it to all of us."

The Clock hesitated for a moment, looking at Digon and the other house children. Robin shivered as his gaze swept over her.

"Very well," he said, turning back to Willow, mouth tight. "I had hoped to spare the little ones this, but let it be on your head, then." He gestured to the two brothers of the House of Summerflower. "I am here to Unshame you."

Shocked silence for a moment.

Then Master Florian sputtered, "But that's absurd. For what shame?"

"Treason," The Clock said, his voice dead and cold.

Robin looked at Bryndon, who had gone dead white. She knew what the word *treason* meant. It meant you pretended to love people, but you really hated them.

"I see," Willow said, voice calm. "Abryn, perhaps you should take your family upstairs after all."

"No, you were quite right," Father said. "We should all be here." He turned to The Clock. "This is very serious, and very unusual. It is the Master's province, is it not, to determine if a member of his house is shamed?"

Master Florian stepped forward eagerly. "It is indeed," he said. "And I have found no evidence of shame of any kind in Stranger Willow, none at all, much less anything to support such a serious, horrible accusation.

House Claybrook does not tolerate such disgrace. What proof do you have of this?"

"The evidence is not for the ears of all," The Clock said. "But it is certainly true. And at any rate, I have the support of the Wizard Oded and the High Defender, who sent me here tonight. But there is, first, something to ask you Bryndon Claybrook," the Clock said, turning to her brother. "A choice."

The Clock held out his hand to the Keeper behind him, who pulled out a short length of rope. "I do not wish to see an innocent boy harmed," The Clock said, taking the cord. He held it out to Bryndon. "This is the sign of your status as Shield to this woman, left with Keeper Loric when she entered the city. I beg you take it and burn it, before the Unshaming takes place. For if you are still her Shield when her shame is uncovered, you will suffer the same consequence as she. Death."

Robin felt a ball of ice form in her stomach. *Death?*

Bryndon looked at the cord like it was snake. He was trembling a little. "But if I burn it, she'll have to leave," he said.

"Indeed she will," The Clock said. "But you will both live. My men will see her safely to the West Gate, where she will be allowed to depart for her own home, by way of Cairn Doxia. This is my offer to you. Burn the cords, and both of you will live. Or else don't, and when the Heartspell uncovers the truth of her shame, both of you will die. Of this I am certain."

Bryndon looked from The Clock to Willow, and back again. Robin waited for him to tell The Clock that his offer was stupid, that of course Willow was not a traitor, that she was lovely and kind and grumpy and strange, that she was the best thing that had ever happened to them. But Bryndon looked at Father, instead, who had a stricken look on his face.

"I do not know," Father said to Bryndon, voice quiet and sad. "Stranger Willow has been good to us."

Bryndon looked around at the rest of them, but everyone was silent, even Gran. Robin waited for a few long moments, confused. She stomped her foot in frustration. No one looked at her, so she stomped it again, harder.

"What's wrong with all of you?" she said, when they finally took notice. "You know Willow's not evil."

"The Nightbringer, you called her, when we first met," Bryndon replied. "The braids and the knife..."

"There is much truth to that story," The Clock added quickly. "More than most know."

"But we *know* her now," Robin said. "Who cares about silly braids?"

She felt The Clock looking at her, frowning, and again she felt like shivering. But she did not return The Clock's gaze, keeping her eyes fixed on Bryndon. They stared at one another for a long moment, and Robin pushed down the tears she felt coming up. They'd all think she was just a silly little girl, if she started crying.

Willow stood. "Enough of this," she said. "Bryndon, you have two people in the room telling you different things. And, in truth, a week ago I would have told you to burn the cord, and gladly would I have left, fleeing this city like a deer from a wildfire. But I do not tell you that now. I am your friend, Bryndon. You have gotten to know me. Only a little, yes; there is much more to my life than a few weeks can tell. The Clock tells you I am a traitor. I say I am not. You must bet your life on the outcome. You must choose who you believe."

Bryndon took a deep breath, and nodded. "Test her heart," he said to the Unshamers. "She is no traitor."

"Child, do not do such a foolish thing," The Clock said. "If she is your friend, why risk both your lives?"

"He made his decision," Willow said, rising next to Bryndon. She took his hand in hers. "And he is no child. You, what's your name?" she said to one of the Unshamers. "Halat, isn't it? You were in the Grove with us that first night."

"I was, Stranger Willow," the Unshamer replied, bowing slightly. He looked a little younger than Father, with light brown hair and a nose that was just a little too big. "And yes, I am Halat. And this is Brother Garis," he said, indicating the rather fat, balding man with him. Garis bowed as well. They both looked like they hadn't slept in days. "We will see that justice and mercy are done for you."

"Indeed they will," The Clock said softly. He looked angry, now, where before he had only seemed stern. Robin wished that he would leave. "You will regret this decision, Bryndon Claybrook."

"You be quiet," Gran said. "This is Unshamer business now."

Master Florian made more horrified shushing sounds in Gran's direction, and The Clock clenched his teeth. But he said nothing, nodding to the brothers to begin.

"If you'll kneel here, Stranger Willow," Brother Garis said, gesturing to the floor in front of him. "And you as well, Shield Bryndon."

They knelt, and Garis put his hand on Willow's shoulder, while Halat did the same on Bryndon's. "This is a forced Unshaming," Garis said, as if he was telling them they were about to begin a game of dibstones. "So we'll skip all the stuff about seeking forgiveness."

"Oh good," Willow said.

"And I'm afraid you can't hold hands," he said. "Physical contact can have odd effects on the spell." He waited until they had let go, and then nodded, smiling. "Very well, very well. We will begin." He cleared his throat, gaze resting on Willow, and began to sing.

Robin had never heard such a song before. Bryndon had told her of it, once, when he had come back from his first Unshaming. *It's like the wind around your face when you run*, he had said, and Robin thought, hearing it, that he was almost right. Only to her it was more hushed than that, more still, the way the house sounded in the morning hours, when everyone was still asleep, and there was a faint tinkle of goat bells outside, and the old stone creaked as it settled a little more on its foundation. A soft blue light began to glow around Willow. The light was in her and seemed to come from her, and she looked to Robin as if she had somehow grown younger.

Then Brother Halat joined in, and his song was different than the first, tumbling and rolling, where Garis's glided. But yet it was of the same kind, too, and the jumps of the second seemed to meet the falls of the first, so that the two interwove with one another seamlessly, and Robin thought not of the house in the morning, but the windswept rocks of the climbing path to Trader's Pass, the old white paving stones worn smooth with age, and the wild blue sky above, chased with sunlit clouds. Bryndon, too, began to glow, and the two lights met and joined into one, growing and growing, until it was brighter than the red and yellow of the flickering firelight.

"Stranger Willow Peeke," Garis said. His voice sounded a little distant, as if it came from far away. "You are now under the eye of the Heartspell, which knows all. I will ask you three questions. One lie and your Shield will die." Mother stepped forward a little, and Father put a hand on her arm. She gripped his hand tightly.

"Do you serve the Nightmare?" Garis asked.

"I do not," Willow said. The glow grew brighter, but nothing else happened. Willow had spoken truly.

"Do you wish the men and women of Cairn Meridia harm?" Garis asked.

"I do not," Willow said again. And again the light grew.

"Have you, since the moment you were raised to Stranger, endeavored always to do what was best for the people of Meridia?"

"I have not," Willow said.

A strangled cry came out of Mother's throat.

"I told you, foolish boy," The Clock said, though there was a kind of fierce triumph in his voice. "A traitor." Robin wondered what the big men with cudgels would do if she tried to hit him.

"Perhaps," Garis said. There was no change in Bryndon. He knelt still on the floor, eyes closed, alive. He seemed not to know what was happening. "In what way have you failed to labor for the good of Meridia?" Garis asked.

"I was angry at Jair, for tricking me into coming here," Willow said, her voice calm. "So I stayed silent during many of the council meetings, trying to prove that he couldn't make me do something I didn't want to do. It was foolish of me."

Garis nodded. "She speaks truly," he said. "This one is no traitor, The Clock."

"But she admitted it from her own mouth," The Clock protested. "She has not sought the best interests of the people."

"She spoke of an animosity toward General Thorndike," Garis said. "Not toward the city as a whole. I see only good intentions to Meridia in her heart. Many conflicted feelings, perhaps, but only good intentions."

The Clock's mouth worked in anger for a moment. Then he said, "Wrath and sloth, then. Unshame her for those."

"Now come, this is highly irregular," Master Florian broke in. "They have tested her for treason and she has been found innocent, must we really go looking for—"

"I also lied to Master Florian about giving thanks to Ior," Willow said. "Though I'm pretty sure he knows that."

Master Florian turned bright red, and began to sputter something incomprehensible.

"Always it is that one," Halat murmured. "Very well, daughter. Brother Garis, what epitimia do you prescribe?"

"But she's not a traitor," Robin said. "She didn't do anything wrong!"

"She did, child," Brother Garis said. "She broke the Prohibitions, and must be Unshamed."

Robin was about to tell Garis that she wasn't a child—and that he was an idiot—when she felt Father's hand on her shoulder. He shook his head, holding one finger to his lips. He stepped forward. "You have your answer," he said to The Clock. "She is not a traitor. It would be best, now, if you were to leave."

Robin saw Anwir, the guard at the door, step behind Father, and the other cudgel wielding Timekeeper moved to The Clock's side. Father gave no sign that he noticed them.

"You are not one to order me anywhere Sergeant Claybrook," The Clock said, and Robin wanted to hit him again.

"You're right," Father said. "But Unshaming is not a public spectacle. This is a family matter."

"He is quite right," Brother Halat said. "Forgive us, The Clock, but you all have no more business here."

The Clock looked at Halat for a moment, grimacing, and then signaled to his men. "Very well," he said. "We will go. I fear we have made a grave mistake here, but so be it." His gaze moved for a moment to Robin, and she felt a sudden urge to slip behind Father's legs. But then he looked away, and the moment passed.

"Fare you well, House Claybrook," The Clock said at last. And he turned and swept from the room, striding away without a backwards glance.

Brother Halat smiled at his back until he was out of sight, and they heard the sound of the door swinging shut behind them. "That man gives one many opportunities to perfect one's love and patience," he said.

"That's one way of saying it," Gran snorted.

"All things may be seen two ways," Halat agreed. He turned back to Willow and Bryndon. "Brother Garis, what epitimia do you prescribe?"

"There is much precedent here," Brother Garis said. "In labor and wrath has she failed, so let her feel the wrath of labor. The sun has set behind the mountains. Until it rises again, this one will feel the pangs of childbirth."

"You mean I will feel them," Bryndon said, his eyes still closed.

Brother Garis blinked. "Oh yes, I had forgotten…" he said. "I suppose I could lessen…" he looked at Brother Halat, who shook his head. "No, of course, it should not be changed simply because—"

"And what is the object of her shame?" Brother Halat broke in.

Garis cleared his throat. "I'm not sure I know what—"

"Take two of my braids," Willow said. "They've caused enough trouble already." Then she added, a bit sadly, "Besides, there are only five cities now that live free."

"So be it," Brother Halat said. He slipped his knife from his belt and sawed through two of Willow's braids. She looked strange without them, as if she was under dressed. Robin wondered if she was cold. Halat handed the braids to Bryndon.

"Bryndon Claybrook," Halat said. "As Shield of this shamed woman, you must undergo an epitimia of pain. While you hold these braids in your hand, you will feel the pangs of childbirth. They will last until the sun rises over the eastern mountains. Then she will be free."

"Witnessed," Brother Garis said. "It is just and merciful."

"It is just and merciful," Brother Halat repeated. They both stepped away, and the blue light flowed from Bryndon into the braids he held in his hand. He stared at them for a moment, a strange expression on his face. And then, his face crumpled, and he slumped to the ground with a low moan.

He wept and screamed and held the braids tight against his side, full of blue light.

Then Willow took his right hand in hers. And a moment later, Mother was at his other side, holding his left, their hands holding the braids together. The blue light spread from Bryndon to both of them, and both cried out at the same time.

"What is that?" Willow asked, gasping.

"I feel it, too," Mother said. "The pain of labor…"

"As I said," Brother Garis said. "Physical contact can sometimes do strange things with the magic. Now we return to the House of Summerflower. Shame not."

The Unshamers shuffled out, and the Claybrooks gathered around their brother, their son. Then Father sat next to Mother, and took her hand, and the light passed to him as well, making him grunt. Robin was shocked to see tears sliding down his face. And then Gran joined him, and Teagan and Kian. Kian held his rough hand out to Robin, and she took it. She watched the blue light climb over her fingers and across her arm, and as it did, she felt a slow twisting deep in her gut, a dull ache that made it hard to stand. So she sat. And felt Rhys take her other hand. And the pain lessened a little as he did so, though the blue light grew brighter. And finally Master Florian, too, wiping the sweat off his forehead, joined the circle. Little Digon sat next to Bryndon, patting his head softly.

The night wore on. The blue light grew and grew, and the pain rose with it, getting brighter and brighter, until it was almost white. Robin fell asleep a few times, dozing on the floor, but always when the twisting woke her, she felt the hands of her family holding hers. And so they passed their last night, sharing each other's pain, together.

CHAPTER TWENTY

Blood Milk and Needlework

Saerin worked by the light of a single candle, sharpening her needles on a small piece of dark pumice stone. They were not dull, but she was bored and nervous, and the needles kept her hands busy. She had already sharpened and oiled every one she had three times over, and was starting on a fourth round. Outside her window, the city street was lit by the pale light of a half-moon and a scattering of houselights, keeping watch on the night while their inhabitants slept.

A small brass kettle hung above the fireplace, simmering with a pale, white liquid that looked a bit like thin goat's milk. It was very specifically simmering. It was not bubbling or frothing, it was not boiling or burning or otherwise doing anything but simmering, just as it was supposed to. She had been tending it all night, raking the coals a bit this way, a bit that way. Adding a few small sticks, a few green leaves, even splashing a bit of water on it from time to time from her wash basin. The heat had to stay nearly constant for three hours for the poison to separate properly. Too little heat and the mixture would be tainted, impure. It might not kill at all, and if it did it would be too slow, take too long to incapacitate. Too *much* heat, and the smoke would fill her lungs with death in a few minutes, and likely hang around long enough to kill whoever came in to check on her later. She did not let it get too hot.

The House of Time rang out the hour, two slow, muted booms that drifted into her small bedroom. Second mare. Tjabo's hour, men called it, when the power of the Nightmare was at its highest. She checked the kettle again, pressing a cloth to her mouth. The cloth had been soaked in a mixture of vinegar and cloves, but even so, the smell coming off the kettle made her gag, like rotting blood and sour milk, burnt hair and fever sweat. Saerin took a small spoon of stonewood from where it had been resting beside the fire and slowly lowered it into the kettle. The wood seemed to *twist* somehow in her hand, as if resisting her, fleeing from the simmering milk. She held on firmly and forced it down, till the spoon hit the bottom of the kettle.

When she pulled it free, the spoon looked like it had been painted, red on the bottom half and white on the top, with a line sharp as a razor between them. It was ready.

Carefully, she took another spoon from where it lay beside the fire, this one made of silver. The blood milk made a faint hissing sound as the spoon slipped in, and the smell coming off the pot shifted to something not altogether unpleasant, copper and peppermint. Saerin let the cloth over her mouth drop, and picked up one of the needles she had been so carefully polishing. It was the biggest she had, a six inch chenille of gleaming steel. The steel was well-forged, but paper thin and hollow in the center. A good sharp twist would snap it in half.

Saerin lifted a spoonful of blood milk from the kettle, red and white liquids swirling together without mixing. Carefully, she poured the spoonful into the open top of the needle, filling it nearly to the brim. Then she plugged the open end with a blob of soft wax from her candle.

A succession of additional needles followed, each smaller than the others, so that by the end she was funneling the poison into a thin, two-inch sharp, drop by drop. This amount of poison would be useless against anyone with any significant power—really it would struggle to kill a particularly large man. But a normal person would probably succumb, or at least be violently sick for a few days, depending on where the poison went in.

When she was finished, the kettle was still mostly full, and Saerin dropped the spoon of stonewood inside. By morning, the purifying properties of the wood would render the mixture little more potent than sour wine, which is what it would look and smell like to anyone who might be curious enough to see what Saerin liked to cook at night. Not that she intended on giving anyone a chance to examine it before she poured the mixture into the drains, but still. It paid to be cautious.

She stood then, putting a hand to her back to knead out the knots. The night was almost half gone, and she was tired. She slipped the largest needle into the sleeve of her shirt, to a special hiding place she had sewn into the lining. Then she faced the window overlooking the street and took a few deep breaths. It would have to seem natural, clumsy, a stumble of weariness and ineptitude. She turned from the window. The floor of her room was smooth and clean, but she stumbled unexpectedly, arms spinning, and fell against her high-backed chair.

Then the needle was out, stabbing, as she buried it in the chest of her imaginary foe.

Too slow, she thought. Speed was life and death. One snag on the fabric of her shirt, one fumble between her fingers, and she was dead.

And long after the coals had died down and the House of Time was striking second lauds in the hour before dawn, Saerin was awake in the dark, practicing her needlework.

CHAPTER TWENTY ONE

The Creation of a Coward

It was forty-four years since the last Nightmare, still twenty-six before the next, and fourteen year old Saerin Blackwing sat on the ground, her legs tucked underneath her, and picked idly at the grass. She was in a small hollow, hidden on the eastern slope of the valley, the ground covered with a soft carpet of clover and blooming summerflowers. Trees rose in a ring around her, hiding the city from view. They weren't stone trees, of course, not this far away from the Grove; Aspen and cedar grew here, squat poplar and red pine, leaves full and green with the height of summer. A full moon rode overhead, filling the little clearing with silver light, but Saerin had lit her lantern anyway. Likely she shouldn't have. A lantern might attract attention, and she would be in major trouble if someone found her out here. She had told Master Usper she was going to be at the Grove all night, praying and fasting in preparation for the mid-summer festivals, and he would tear off her hide if he discovered where she was, and who she was waiting for. But she liked the little yellow light, liked the way its flames danced off the facets of her polished green gemstone. And anyway, there was little chance of someone stumbling upon her here.

A merlin's cry drifted through the night air.

Saerin sat up, listening intently. A second cry wafted through the hollow, and then a third. Saerin called back, hooting her best imitation of a pygmy owl. The bird noises had been her idea, something she had pulled from some of her favorite stories. Saerin heard the sound of something moving in the dark, rustling the tree branches as it approached the clearing, and she stood up, slipping the stone into her pocket, and feeling her hair to make sure it was still in place. He'd want her to look beautiful.

A few moments later, Wynn emerged from the darkness, hooded and cloaked in a robe of green so dark it was almost black. He pushed back his hood when he saw her, revealing his liquid brown eyes and thin, honest face. He seemed a little frightened—but excited too, flush from his climb up the mountainside.

"Did you get it?" she whispered. Then added quickly, "Are you alright?"

"I'm fine, dearest," Wynn whispered back, taking her in a hurried embrace. "Did anyone see you come here?"

"Nobody," she said, pushing Wynn away a little. "Did you get it?"

"Right here," Wynn said, holding out a slim, rectangular bundle.

"Oh, Wynn," she said, taking the bundle with trembling fingers. She turned at once to the lantern, trying to get a better look at what he had brought. "Here, hold this up for me," she said, shoving the lantern at Wynn. "I need to see better."

He opened the shutter a little, letting more of the golden light spill out. Saerin felt her heart pounding as she gently turned the object over in her hands. It was no bigger than a chalk slate, light and thin, wrapped tightly in burlap and tied with twine. The symbol of House Blackwing was emblazoned on the back, a black swift wing over a high tower; it looked like it had been burned into the fabric. Below the symbol, in tiny, cramped letters, were written two words:

On Cowardice

"Do you really have to read it?" Wynn asked.

"We've gone over this," she said, picking at the knots. They were tight and small, hard to see. "I overheard Master Vestus himself. It's not going to hurt anyone. It's just been sitting up in the library for decades, collecting dust. Books are meant to be read, and this one was written by Meridia herself. Here, help me undo this," she said, seizing the lantern. "I can't get the wrapping off."

"But it's against the Prohibitions to read—" Wynn began.

"Taking it from the library was against the Prohibitions," she interrupted, pressing the bundle on him impatiently. "And you've done that already. Don't turn craven on me now."

His face fell, and Saerin realized she had said the wrong thing. He was still a sensitive boy at heart, Wynn, in spite of how tall he had gotten.

"Oh, darling, don't look at me like that," Saerin said quickly. She went up on her tiptoes, giving him a kiss on his bony cheek. *Please let him not start crying*, she thought. It'd take forever to get him to help her if he started crying.

"You know I only do this for you," Wynn said, holding her close. His eyes were clear; the kiss seemed to have kept the tears in check for the moment. "So that we can be together, so you know how I feel about you."

"You've proven how you feel a hundred times," Saerin said, forcing herself to smile. "Come, just help me with the knots. I just want one quick peek at it, and then we'll put it right back where we found it, no harm done."

He leaned down to kiss her, and Saerin endured it with as much patience as she could, her neck straining from being tilted back so far. It wasn't unpleasant, but he was far too tall to kiss comfortably.

When he finally broke away, Saerin took a step back, trying not to look too hurried, and pressed the package on him again. It took a few minutes of picking and pulling, but finally the knot pulled free, and Saerin unlaced the fabric carefully, settling down once again on the soft grass. Wynn knelt behind her, still holding the lantern. Once the ties were undone, the burlap slid off easily, with a soft whisper of fabric, revealing a small book, bound in black leather. There was no decoration or title, no sign of stitching or wear. The leather felt strange, smooth and warm, like living skin. Saerin suppressed a shudder of happiness.

Finally. She had waited weeks for this moment, since eavesdropping on old Master Vestus in his room. He was near death, Master Vestus—the cough in his chest had spread and thickened, and he could barely speak much above a whisper. The new house master, Master Usper, had been at his side for much of his sickness, spoon-feeding him soup and soggy bread, changing his bed linens, talking with the old man when the old man felt like talking. Saerin hadn't meant to overhear them. She'd come in late from a game of quindo, splattered with mud and aching from a well placed blow she'd taken to the ribs.

"—a dangerous thing to keep in the house," she'd overheard Usper saying as she walked by, the sound spilling through a crack in Master Vestus's door. "Why is it not with the House of Summerflower?"

"They have their own copy," Master Vestus croaked out. "I traded for this one, some years ago…who was it now…?" he trailed off. There was silence for a time, and Saerin found herself waiting motionless outside the room, not making a sound. She could not have said why she stopped. She did not think about the action at all.

"Joshua," Master Vestus wheezed, finally. "That was his name. And his brother too, though I don't remember... Peculiar names they have, in Cairn Creta. There had been a fire in their city, and many books were lost. They wanted a tome on tower building, had heard we had a fine one."

"You made a copy, of course, before you made the trade?" Master Usper said.

"Of course, of course," Master Vestus said. And then, "Did I? Yes, I'm sure I would have, only reasonable thing to do. I don't know why I did it, though. As you said, there's nothing we can do with such a book. I've always been curious about cowardice, you know, the common master's worry. At some point we all wonder if we become masters so we don't have to fight on the towers. And to have a book written by Meridia herself..." He trailed off with a sigh, followed by a bout of wet coughing. Usper made soothing noises, settling Master Vestus back on the bed.

"Where is it now?" Usper asked, when the coughing had subsided.

"The library," Master Vestus whispered. His voice was so low that Saerin risked putting her ear to the door, straining to hear him. "Behind the north shelf there's a loose stone...or is it the west shelf? No the north, I'm sure of it. The third stone up from the floor is loose. It's behind there somewhere..."

...And now it was in Saerin's hands. The Whip would be pleased. Saerin had only been to a few meetings with the other masked women, but they were terribly exciting. The Whip was so beautiful, with her red mask and lustrous hair. She'd probably give Saerin one of those green masks, when Saerin brought her this book. But first, Saerin was going to learn about it herself.

She took a deep breath and eased open the cover, holding the book up in the flickering light of the lantern. The first page held no words, just a rough sketch of a man, crouching on the ground, peering into a small stone that he held in his hand. She turned the page again, and read:

The Words of Meridia, as spoken from her own Mouth, concerning the Shame of Cowardice, so named by her Mother Tani's Book, that which has come to us from the Land of the Burning Sky, containing its Applications and Dangers, its Relationship with other Shames, its Use in the Creation of Shame Objects, and such Objects' Utility in the Vision of One's Present and Future Enemies.

Saerin read the last part again, trying to contain her excitement. *The creation of Shame Objects...* A power only the Unshamers had, and this book would teach it to her. She pressed a hand to her side, feeling the stone in her pocket. Then she began to leaf through the pages, turning each one carefully, for fear of ripping or breaking one. The book was thousands of years old, after all, though it seemed as solid as if it had been penned yesterday, the pages flexible and strong, the ink dark. Everything was written in the same hand, clear and flowing, with the peculiar capitalizations and phrasing throughout. Most of it seemed to be theory and commentary, detailed explorations of various examples of cowardice, and their relationship to other examples. Saerin scanned each page rather quickly, looking for the explanations of shame objects.

Finally, on the very last page, there was a single column of text under the heading: *Cowardice Objects*.

"Here it is," Saerin said, pulling the stone from her pocket.

"What is that?" Wynn asked.

"A gem off of the house goblet," she said, without thinking. As soon as the words left her mouth, she wanted them back.

"You stole it," Wynn said, sounding shocked.

"No, not really," Saerin said quickly, cursing herself for a fool. She should have known Wynn wasn't going to like this part. She should have sent him away, waited until she was alone. "I was cleaning it a few weeks ago, and, well, it popped out on accident."

"Didn't anyone notice?" Wynn asked.

Saerin cleared her throat, searching for something to say. "Well Master Usper thought…I mean, Zoe is always so clumsy about those sort of things, he just kind of assumed—"

"You let Zoe take the blame for it," Wynn said, his expression stern. "Saerin, how could you?"

Saerin felt herself flush red, and cursed herself again for speaking. "I…I'm sorry, Wynn. I promise I'll tell him the truth soon. It's just that, I knew that I'd need an object, you know, something that could carry the power."

She watched Wynn's face closely as he understood what she was saying, his eyes going wide. "You mean, you're going to—to *make* a shame object?"

"Just one," Saerin said. "And I promise I'll destroy it right afterward."

"But that's—that's—" Wynn sputtered, trying to find the words. "Saerin, you're better than that."

"Please, dearest," Saerin said, putting her hand on Wynn's bony cheek. "I know we're not supposed to, but who is it going to hurt? We'll be the only ones who ever know." She paused for a moment, hesitating over the next sentence she had formed in her head. And then it came out as, "The bond of marriage will seal it between us forever."

The look on his face was heartbreaking. "Marriage?" he said. "You mean it? You want to marry me?"

"Of course," Saerin said. This time the words came out easily, clearly. "I love you."

"I love you, too," Wynn whispered.

She leaned forward, kissing him deeply, the stone clutched in her fist. There was no telling what storm of emotions was behind that kiss, no way to separate what was good from what was shameful. All were mixed up together in a tangled mess. When at last she pulled away, they were both flushed and sweating, and Saerin's hair was tangled. She straightened it briefly, and turned to the book once again, letting Wynn hold one of her hands.

Like all Shame Objects, the Coward Object must be associated with an Act of Cowardice, the book read. *However, unlike the other Shames, the Power of the Object is derived from the Soul of the Shamed One, rather than the Severity of the Act of Cowardice.*

Saerin skipped down to the heading labeled "*Creation.*"

Hold the Shame Object in your Hand, the book said. *And recite the following Words, careful to be precise in each Syllable.*

Below this was a spell, written in a language that she had never seen before. Yet, as she looked at it, the words seemed to flow out of the page and into her mouth, so that she found herself reading them one moment and speaking them the next. They felt strange on her tongue—rushing, whispering words that ran together like drops of water in a flowing stream. In some ways it seemed like she only really spoke one word, or the same word over and over again. There was no sensation of fear or anxiety, no pain or pleasure. It was more like a release, as if she had been bottling the spell up inside herself this whole time, and was finally letting it free. She let the words carry her along, let them rush out in one great wave, and then it was done.

And the stone in her hand began to glow with a pale light of its own.

They were both silent for a long time, watching the stone pulse. A chill wind stirred the trees around them, but she barely felt it. Then, finally, Wynn squeezed her hand and asked, "What is it, Saerin?"

"It's a shame object," she whispered back, awed. It had worked. It had actually *worked*. "A coward stone. It will show me my enemies, present and future, near and far."

"Enemies?" Wynn said. "What enemies do you have?"

"Let us find out," Saerin said. She looked deep within the stone, and something happened, something difficult to describe. Like an opening up of herself. The glow inside the stone brightened, filling her vision, until the whole world seemed to be tinged with a bright green…

…and then the little hollow vanished, and a flood of images rushed by her, fire and lightning and flood, howling storms and screaming men, demons in masks of blood. She saw a whip and a mace, an axe and a hatchet, gripped by disembodied hands, all of them searching, searching, looking for her tender throat. She saw a blond man in the uniform of the Tower Guard, the pin of generalship on his shoulder. The General beckoned to her, telling her to shelter behind a wall made of stone, and she rushed to it, trying to get away from the horrible hands and their weapons. But when she reached the wall, it shifted and changed, moved and cracked, until it became the High Defender, Praeses High Tower, massive as a small mountain, his skin the color of rock and his beard the color of snow. And he raised his fist to smash her into powder, and she screamed in terror and begged for her life, but the fist came down, down, and crushed her to the ground.

And then she saw Wynn, dressed in the black and violet of the High Defender's guard, with a sword in hand. She reached out for him, weak and helpless, and he raised the sword, and Saerin thought with relief that here, finally, was her protector, her savior. And then the sword came down, and it pierced Saerin in the eye, and pain exploded within her. The sword came down again, and again, and again, thrusting into her, opening her up, spilling her blood, until the pain overwhelmed her, and she slipped into darkness…

And found herself back in the hollow of trees, screaming at the top of her lungs, Wynn's arms wrapped tightly around her.

She collapsed, sobbing. She felt sick, dirty; her skin still felt like it was sticky with blood.

"Saerin, are you alright?" Wynn said. "Love of my heart, what happened?"

She looked up into his eyes—his pretty, brown eyes—but she did not see him. She could not. It was as if a green fog had buried itself within her, and all she could see was the sword that had been in his hand, a sword covered with her blood. Terror rose up in her like bile.

"You!" she said, pushing away from him and scrambling to her feet. "It was *you*."

"What was me?" Wynn asked, concern plain on his face. "Saerin, what did you see?"

"Get away from me!" she screamed, clutching the book to her chest like a shield. She started backing up quickly, shivering in the night air, air that had grown suddenly cold. The stone was like a piece of ice in her fist. "Stay away!"

"Saerin, keep your voice down," Wynn said, looking around nervously. "What happened? What did you see?"

"I saw *you*," she whispered, continuing to back up. Fear pulsed through her, jagged edges of fear that made her want to turn and run away as fast as she could. "Enemies present and future, the book said. You're going to kill me."

Wynn's mouth dropped open. "Kill you?" he said. "A man does not kill his wife."

"I will never be your wife," Saerin said. There was something else with the fear now, something black and slick and hard. "You stupid, foolish... Get away from me."

"Dearest, you're not thinking clearly," Wynn said. He shook his head. "Tor damn me, I never should have brought you that book."

"You killed me with a sword," Saerin said, and she could see it all again in her mind, the black uniform, the bright sword, the pain that ripped her apart. "The stone has shown me."

"Saerin, *I love you*," Wynn said. "How can you not understand that, after everything I have done? Don't you love me, too?"

"I hate you," Saerin snapped, and she felt the black thing inside her pulse with fierce satisfaction. "You're pathetic and weak and small, a little dog begging at the table for scraps. You call that love?"

"Saerin—" Wynn said, the tears flowing down his cheeks.

"Don't you ever come near me again," Saerin said. "Do you hear me? Don't let me see your face around House Blackwing ever again. Or I swear I'll kill you myself."

And then she turned, and sprinted away into the dark of the night, moving as fast as her legs could carry her, fleeing Wynn and his love. And the moonlight was silver and green, and the wind was cold.

CHAPTER TWENTY TWO

Lack of Commitment

Saerin followed the black-haired woman at a distance, a shopping basket under her arm. A few small items were piled on top, but mostly it held her spare linens, arranged to make the basket look full. She had been following the woman for over an hour now, and the basket was growing damnably heavy.

The streets were busier than normal, for the Nightmare had been declared, and that meant everyone had a role to play—supplies to rush out to the towers, uniforms to make or clean or mend, bolts to fletch, pikes to sharpen, pitch to barrel and ship. It was easy enough to stay unnoticed in the crowds, moving among the street vendors, looking at a few needles here, a length of thread there. They were in the Salt District, on Wool Street, where the largest markets were, among the hustle and movement of the morning. Here the buildings were as grand and beautiful as elsewhere, but most were places of business, fronted with temporary wooden stalls and storefronts, displaying the wares of weavers and clothiers and tanners. The day was hot already, quite unseasonable for this time of year. Madge said it was a blessing sent from Ior; one last stretch of warmth and sun before the cold of the Nightmare. Saerin would have preferred one last stretch of reasonably comfortable temperatures, but she supposed Ior had no cause to answer her prayers.

She had arisen well before first light, slipping out the second floor window and climbing down while the rest of the house slept. Without Zoe in her room, she could largely come and go as she pleased, as long as she avoided the stairs past Master Usper's quarters. She was convinced he intentionally kept them creaky and loud so that no one could sneak past him at night, and he had ears like a mountain hare. He'd likely set her to washing for a week if he caught her trying to wander off in the small hours of the morning.

But the window was easy enough if you had a head for heights. And then it was simply a matter of finding a proper place to watch House Whitelimb without being seen. The black-haired woman had emerged at second lauds, a shopping basket of her own over her arm, and then the game had begun, Saerin staying well back, keeping her attention mostly fixed on the vendors and their wares, and stealing enough glances ahead to keep the woman in sight. She bought little, and Saerin suspected the woman's basket was being used for the same thing as Saerin's, as a mask to hide what she was really doing.

That was a good sign. It had been five days already since the ringing of the black bells, and this was the first opportunity Saerin had gotten to follow the black-haired woman, the first morning she was free from chores, and would not be missed. She'd been unable to discover the black-haired woman's name so far—House Whitelimb and House Blackwing did not have many ties to each other—so she still called her "Axe" in her head. She'd figure out who she was soon enough. The man named Shem would have known, but when she'd gone calling, the under-castellan at House Haeland told her the foolish old Master had *rejoined the Guard* of all things, somehow finding a post at the Ninety-Sixth. *He'll get himself killed sooner than the rest of us*, Saerin thought. It was sad, really. Though she suspected the old man would take a few darkstones with him before he went.

Across the street, Axe had stopped to have a few words with a white-haired cobbler. The cobbler said something Saerin couldn't hear, and Axe threw her head back and laughed musically, her hand lingering on the cobbler's arm. The grin on the cobbler's face could have lit up a dark room. Men were so stupid sometimes. She wondered how Wynn would react to a woman like that. Probably profess his undying love her. Saerin relaxed her grip on the basket.

Axe moved on, and Saerin left the leather glove stand she had been standing at. Just as well. She'd been pretending to examine gloves for five minutes, and the man keeping stock had started giving her suspicious looks. Axe walked ahead of her with a more purposeful stride now, no longer wandering from shop to stall. Saerin quickened her strides to keep up, crossing over to the near side of the street, putting Axe directly in front of her. That was the safest way to follow someone on the move. They rarely looked directly behind them, afraid that someone might *notice* them looking and begin to wonder why they seemed so paranoid.

Axe left Wool Street, and Saerin dropped back further as the crowds began to thin. She had turned onto Iron Street, and the sound of hammer on steel echoed from every gray-stoned building, the forges all hard at work arming the Tower Guard. Saerin started to worry a bit. This was not a place for women. Axe would pick her out immediately if she looked back.

They came to a small, dingy looking smithy. It looked nearly abandoned. Only a single hammer could be heard coming from the forge. Axe stopped at the smithy door and knocked, two long taps, and then five short ones. Saerin slipped behind a cart, overladen with what looked like boxes of round helmets, and watched through a small crack between the boxes. The door to the smithy opened, and Axe walked in.

Saerin hurried forward, hugging the wall, cursing under her breath. She felt stupid. What was she thinking? She should have expected this to happen. It's not like the Masked Ones were likely to have a nice open air meeting in the Sacred Grove, where she could watch them like a bird in a tree. She walked past the door and found the alleyway on the far side of the building. Heaps of coal dust and slag metal were piled against the walls. A massive wooden cart with a broken axle leaned drunkenly against one of the piles. Above the cart, recessed deeply into the smithy wall, was a small window of opaque glass.

Saerin looked at the street behind her. Then back up to the window. *That's the stupidest idea you've ever had*, she thought. The window did seem to be in arm's reach of the cart, though. If she could balance on the top of it and pull herself up...why, she'd be just high enough to be in full view of anyone who happened to walk by and wonder why she was trying to break into someone's smithy, just high enough to break her neck when the cart rolled out from under her. She eyed the wood, giving it an experimental kick. It looked rotted, but it felt sturdy enough. Even if she did get up, how could she know what was on the other side of the glass? She might be stumbling into the Whip's bedchamber for all she knew. Saerin looked from the cart to the street, and back again. The Nightmare was only a week away. She would not have another chance at this.

Cursing herself for a fool, she jammed a couple pieces of slag metal under the wheels to keep the cart from rolling and started to climb, swiftly as she dared, shifting her weight carefully, testing each step. She did not look at the street behind her, fearing to lose her nerve. The wood creaked and bent a little, but it held until she reached the top. She reached up with one hand, and felt her fingertips overlap the edge of the sill. Not enough to pull herself up. Saerin pressed herself against the wall and went up on her toes, reaching up blindly, feeling for more stone. This time she was able to get most of her fingers over the edge. Taking a deep breath, she bent her legs and jumped, pulling, the stone edge digging into her palms. She felt the cart shift as she jumped, but then she was up, one elbow draped over the edge, then the other, and then her head was level with the window, and she was panting heavily, trying to see through the smoked glass. It was impossible. There was no way of knowing what was on the other side. Taking a deep breath, she reached out for the bottom edge…

…and the window began to open from the inside.

"—too damn hot in here," a woman's voice was saying from inside the room.

Saerin bit back a scream and dropped down below the window, holding to the ledge with her fingertips, feeling desperately for the cart with her foot.

"Damn. Don't you ever open this thing?" the voice asked again, and Saerin recognized it as belonging to Axe. "It's all rusted. Won't hardly move." There was a loud screeching noise as the window opened little by little. *Don't look down,* she thought. *It's open wide enough, just go back inside.*

"That's good enough," another voice said, and Saerin felt like crying. It was the Whip. She twisted her ankles wildly, but her foot felt nothing but empty air beneath her.

"I'm *hot*," Axe said.

"You're annoying," the Whip said. "Sit down. *He* will be here soon enough, and then it'll be as cold as you like."

"I don't see why we have to keep meeting with him," Axe said, her voice retreating from the window. "Always slithering and sniveling, the half-man, like a sick dog."

"I'd not say that in his hearing," the Whip said. "Unless you want a trip to the pits."

"It'd be cool underground at least," Axe said sullenly.

"Fires can be lit beneath the earth as well as they can above it," the Whip said, her voice cold.

Saerin craned her neck slowly and looked down. The cart was still beneath her, but her jump had tipped it askew, and now the top edge of it was three or four feet below her and to her right. If she let go now she'd likely bounce off the side of it and fall to the alleyway. It wasn't a long fall, but there would be a lot of noise.

"What is the current count?" the Whip was asking.

"One hundred and thirty as of last night," Axe said. "All of strong magic, capable of killing."

"We must have more," the Whip said. "That still leaves half our number unarmed. Everyone must have a weapon before we strike."

"Tell that to the dagger twins," Axe grunted. "My force is ready."

"Then you shall gather weapons for the others," the Whip said.

"Why should I do their work for them?" Axe said, whining.

"Because I said so," the Whip said. "Keep them busy, and keep them afraid. When they have done the deed, they are to drop the shame object into the normal place. You will collect it and bring it to me, that I might bring its power forth. The quicker the better. Than you will return it to the owner, along with their orders for the attack."

Saerin could no longer feel her fingers. Sweat poured out of her in waves. Slowly, slowly, she started to inch to her right, moving her hands a little at a time, bringing her swinging feet closer and closer to the lip of the wagon. If she could just get a toehold on it...

"The lightning should be easy enough to obtain," the Whip said. "Young men who are about to die often think less of consequences, and I know our own kind will not lack for spirit. They are to be sure to make the moment as shameful as possible for both of them. Incest, especially, produces strong weapons. But make your assignments carefully. Nothing must come to light before we make our move."

"What of the firebrands?" Axe asked. "We will need many if the plan is to work."

"Pick out a few of the weaker ones, and get rid of them," the Whip said. "There are dozens fleeing the city everyday. Most will simply assume they turned coward, and ran."

"That still won't be enough, if you want to have much of an army left," Axe said.

"We will make up for any sss-sthortcoming," a new voice hissed.

A chill went through Saerin at the sound of the new voice. She stuck her right foot out and grazed the edge of the cart, taking silent, gulping breaths. Almost there. The air had turned foul, smelling of rot and decay.

"Why are you here?" the Whip said. "I thought I was meeting with the half-man."

"He issth delayed," the voice said. Saerin had trouble understanding the words. They came out of the speaker like he had a mouth full of flies. "Hissth human dutiess interfere. I have your inssstructionsth." Saerin heard a snuffling sound, as if someone was taking in great gulps of air.

"He has missed too many meetings already," the Whip said. "There are only seven days until the Nightmare arrives. If he thinks to take credit for our victory—"

"Who elsthe isthe here?" the voice cut her off. "I sthmell warm blood."

"It is just us," the Whip said. "The house is empty."

More of the great huffing sounds. Saerin felt her right boot finally get a firm grip on the wood, but that was all. There was nothing else for it. She would have to jump, keep her knees bent as she fell and try to catch herself without making too much noise.

She took once last deep breath, swung to the left a bit, and then swung back to right, letting her momentum carry her as she let go…

…when something seized her hair from above with an iron grip, and white hot pain blossomed in her scalp as she felt pieces of it tear away. A gut wrenching screech welled up out of her, but an icy cold hand clamped itself over her mouth, a hand that smelled like that of a corpse, and the sound wouldn't come. She felt herself being pulled upward, through the window, and she bit down as hard as she could on the hand over her mouth. It was like biting frozen wood, and she felt one of her teeth chip. Then she was on the floor, looking up at the red mask of the Whip and the green mask of Axe. And holding her, one hand still wrapped tightly in her hair, was a thin figure wrapped in a cloak the color of midnight and wearing a demon mask. And in its other hand was a slim dagger that gleamed with drops of blood.

A horror.

"Yessth, that issth what your kind call me," the horror said, and Saerin realized she had spoken aloud. "And who are you, to come sthneaking around windowsss in the daylight."

"I recognize her," Axe said. "She's the house sister of that runaway, Zoe of House Blackwing."

"I think, rather, she is the runaway," the Whip said, kneeling to look closer at Saerin's face. Her hair was as perfect and shimmering as ever. "One smart enough to wear another's cloak to meetings." She sniffed and made a face. "She's soiled herself," she said, drawing away disgusted.

"Mercy," Saerin whispered, gagging on the smell of the horror. She let the fear overwhelm her, etch itself on her face. "Mercy, please, I meant no ill toward you."

"You lie," the horror said, waving the knife under her chin. "Your blood will feed my power."

"How did you find us?" the Whip demanded.

Saerin looked from mask to mask, mind racing. She could feel the cold of the horror seeping into her, a horrible, sucking cold, that seemed to steal her very breath away. *I'm going to die*, she thought. And then, strangely: *Forgive me, Wynn.*

"Answer me," the Whip said, kicking her. "Or the blood knife will be a pleasant end to what we will do to you."

"I followed her," Saerin said, pointing to Axe, letting her voice break. "I recognized her when she came looking for Zoe, and I thought…"

"You thought you would listen to a few of our plans and then go scurrying off to the High Defender," Axe said. "Let me kill her, my lady."

"Her blood issth mine," the horror said, shaking Saerin by the head. The pain ripped through her neck and back.

"Please, I only wanted to rejoin you," Saerin said, tears streaming down her face. "I thought maybe if I heard what you were planning, I could join in somehow, help you. Please don't kill me, please…" she whispered. "Please don't drain my blood."

"But I'm confused," the Whip said. "Why run away from our lovely party last week if you really want to be a part of our sisterhood? That shows a real lack of commitment, don't you think?"

"I didn't…I couldn't," Saerin fought to keep her thoughts straight. They seemed to freeze in her brain the way her sweat was starting to freeze on her scalp. "I'm a coward," she blurted out, finally. "I was afraid to kill anyone or have—have *sex* with them." She shuddered. "I got scared and ran away."

"You should have stayed away," Axe said.

"Please don't kill me," Saerin said. "I—I can be useful."

"But you just admitted you are a coward," the Whip said. "Who cannot kill, or even, Ior forbid, have *sex* with someone and get us a weapon for someone braver. What use are you to us?" She shook her head. "I'm afraid you're most useful as a light snack for my associate here."

The horror made a horrible wet hissing sound of pleasure.

"Burn the body in the forge with the others when you're done," the Whip said to Axe, turning to go. "And send someone to House Blackwing later tonight to tell them that this one was seen fleeing the city. If she really is a coward, they should have no trouble believing that."

"I have a coward stone!" Saerin blurted out.

The Whip paused at the door. "You lie," she said. But she did not leave.

"I do not," Saerin said. "I've had it for some years. I can see my enemies from afar, watch their movements and listen to their conversations, see who will attack me in the future. I can tell you what the Seven are planning, where they will put their forces, who they meet with and talk to."

"That magic was not given to the city of Meridia," the Whip said, but Saerin could tell she had her attention. "Save for the book of the Unshamers, which is protected far too well for someone such as you to steal it."

"But it was given to the city of Cairn Creta," Saerin said. "And traded for by Master Vestus of my house, some sixty years ago. Only a few were told of it, to keep others from trying to steal it. It rests in the library of House Blackwing now."

"She's lying," Axe said.

"I can prove it!" Saerin said.

"Keep your voice down," the Whip said, putting a booted toe in her ribcage again. "If you are lying to me…"

"There's a basket downstairs in the alleyway," Saerin said eagerly. "The talisman is inside."

The Whip eyed her for a moment. "Bring it up," she said, finally, to Axe.

"You can't be serious," Axe said, incredulous.

The Whip turned without a word and slapped Axe so hard she staggered to the ground, her mask askew. "You'll do it now," she said. "And count yourself lucky I don't give you a taste of the lash for letting yourself be found out by this fool."

Axe went.

The horror reluctantly let go of Saerin's hair and drew back, standing in the darkest corner of the room. The sucking cold faded. It did not sheath the knife. The wooden floor of the room they were in was stained and splotched with hundreds of dark spots, drops of blood from previous meetings, no doubt. Saerin remained huddled on the ground, touching her ruined scalp gingerly.

Less than a minute had passed before Axe came stomping up the stairs again, basket in hand. The Whip set it in front of Saerin.

"Now," she said. "You have exactly sixty seconds to prove to me that you are too useful to kill."

Saerin gulped and began digging through the linens at once. She picked out a small, blue blanket and began to rip at one of the seams, unraveling the pocket hidden in one of the corners. And then the little green stone came tumbling out into her hand, and she was holding it up for the others to see.

"My seeing stone," she said. "Shame object of cowardice."

"Pretty," the Whip said. "You have thirty seconds."

Saerin took a deep breath and concentrated, trying to block out the pain in her mouth and scalp and side, the chill in her bones, the sight of the demon mask and the bloody knife. She looked deep into the facets of the green stone, and the words of the book came to her again like a rushing wind, and she was speaking the tongue of the book, opening herself to the stone, and it lit up as if a fire burned within it.

"Very interesting," the Whip said.

"It isth the language of sssshame," the horror agreed. "Though I do not recognisth it."

"You have earned yourself another minute of life," the Whip said to Saerin. "So tell me, what is the High Defender doing at this very moment?"

Saerin took another breath and concentrated, calling to mind an image of the High Defender, his dark eyes and white beard, shoulders hulking with power. It was not difficult; she was always afraid of him. The image filled her mind until all else faded, the pain and fear, the room and the gem, until slowly, slowly, it resolved, and moved, and Saerin knew she was looking at him at that very moment.

"He is in his room in the High Tower," Saerin said. She could hear her own voice, but faintly, as if from a great distance. The sounds of the High Defender's room seemed much more real. "He is reading a book, and he is nervous about something. There is a secret of some kind that he is keeping, but that will soon come to light."

"How do you know that?" the Whip said. "You can read his thoughts?"

"It's not like that," Saerin said, shaking her head. "Not directly. It's just…it's just something I can tell about him, something the magic tells me. The book says the coward objects work much like the Dreamers."

"She's bluffing," Axe said. "How are we to know if this is true?"

"Find The Clock," the Whip said. "What is The Clock doing at this moment?"

Saerin pulled away from the High Defender and shifted her gaze. It was much easier now that she was already doing it; the gem worked better with practice.

"He's speaking with a woman," Saerin said. "She has straight brown hair and freckles. They are in the doorway of a common house, and he is asking her permission to speak with the members of the house. He is happy about something. I do not know what."

There was a slight pause. Then the Whip said, "That will be enough." Saerin brought her gaze back to the room. The Whip had turned to the horror. "Forgive me, friend," she said. "But I will have to deprive you of your meal. No doubt you and the others will have plenty to feast on in a week or so."

"My lady—" Axe began.

"I would say nothing, if I were you," the Whip said, caressing the coiled rope at her belt. It sparked and snapped with energy, and Axe shut her mouth. Saerin realized the Whip had turned her namesake into a shame object. It crackled with the lightning of lust.

"Take her to the pit," the Whip told Axe. "Leave her unharmed." She turned to Saerin. "Congratulations. You have earned yourself a few more days of living."

"Thank you, my lady," Saerin said, pressing her face to the floor. "I will serve you faithfully."

"You will," the Whip agreed. "When I want information, you will give it to me, and when the time is right, you will lead me to this book. And you will never, ever think about running away again."

"No, my lady," Saerin said. "Thank you, my lady." And Saerin wished, very deeply, that Wynn was with her.

CHAPTER TWENTY THREE

Straps

The evening session at the House of Salt was ending, as servants came scurrying in to clear away plates and cups and uneaten food. Willow stood and stretched, cracking her spine. She understood, now, what Jair had done in getting her to speak. But now that she was speaking, she found it almost impossible to stop. She was tired, but she had the rest of the evening free to herself, and Bryndon had promised to show her some of the upper passes, where there were clear views of the Insurmountable Heights to the north.

She stepped back as The Clock brushed by her without a glance, a few Timekeepers behind him, elbows stuck out a bit more than strictly necessary. Willow stuck her tongue out at their backs. Since the Unshaming at House Claybrook, The Clock hadn't said a single word to her, except to disagree strongly with anything she said during council. Willow was more than happy to reciprocate. The man was as pitiless as they come. She wondered if he had gears in his chest where his heart should be.

When she turned around, she found High Defender Praeses waiting for her, his big hands clasped behind his back. She stifled a noise of surprise. For all his size, the man could move like a fox.

"Stranger Willow," he said. "Might I have a word?"

"Of course," Willow said, wondering what he wanted. "What is it?"

"It would be better to discuss the matter in private," Praeses said. "Come to the High Tower this evening, after you have supped." He turned and left without waiting to hear an answer. Willow supposed there weren't many people in Meridia who would ever deny a request of his anyway.

Across the room, Jair gave her a quizzical look. Willow shrugged. She wasn't going to deny the High Defender either. This ought to be interesting.

"The High Tower is the largest and last defense of Cairn Meridia," Ridi informed her in his dry voice as they rode towards it that evening. Every once in a while, the sun shone through his spectacles at odd angles, flashing with light. "And the home of the High Defender. It rises over two hundred feet above Tarn's Gap, built of dressed granite and marble. It is also the oldest of the towers, except for perhaps the Low Tower, its humble southern twin, which stands an arrow shot to the south, hidden from this side."

"It doesn't look particularly strong," Willow said, craning her neck up. "There are so many windows."

"The south facing side of the Tower is much different than this side," Ridi said. "It has a strong gate and smooth walls, broken only by half a hundred narrow firing ports, set in staggered rows some thirty feet above the pass. Very defensible. On this side, however, the tower walls are graced with a myriad of windows, dressed in fine wood carvings and paintings, commanding the best views over the valley below. So men know what they are fighting for, Praeses always says, and because no enemy would ever make it to the north side of the tower unless the city was lost, and defense hopeless anyway. It is a vivid symbol of the High Defender himself, strong as stone towards our enemies, peaceful and beautiful to our people."

"Does Jair live here?" Willow asked.

Ridi shook his head. "The General's quarters are in the Low Tower. It has certain…peculiarities that he finds beneficial." And he spurred his goat forward, clearly wanting to leave the matter there.

They crossed a broad, grassy field that lay at the base of the High Tower, dotted here and there with pink turtleheads and blue butterfly weed. Bees hummed from flower to flower, gathering the last nectar of the day. A pair of tower guardsmen met them at the gate, and passed them through with little hassle. Everyone knew the patch-faced southron trader who had become Stranger, and most seemed to know Bryndon as well. Ridi, of course, was dressed in the guard uniform himself, and carried the proper pass keys and seals.

A young servant boy was charged with leading them to the High Defender's rooms. Up and up they went, climbing a seemingly endless series of staircases and ladders, up and up until Willow began to feel a sharp pain under her ribs, and wished she had eaten a smaller supper. Many of the stairs showed the wear of many years and the tread of many feet, and Willow had to take care where she stepped, for fear of tumbling down a flight and breaking her neck.

Finally, they reached a wide, circular landing, perhaps fifty feet across, paved with black marble. Alcoves dotted the stone walls, and in each of them stood a white statue—busts of stern-faced men, lone soldiers battling hulking creatures of the Nightmare—even one statue of a tree that was so lifelike, it looked like it had taken root in the stone.

There were seven guardsmen waiting for them, dressed in uniforms identical to Ridi's, except black where his was white, and purple where his was gold.

"The Defender's Guard," Ridi said, always ready in her ear to explain. "Chosen for their grace, fighting ability, and loyalty. You can see the graces on their breastplates."

Willow nodded. That part she understood, after her conversations with Bryndon. The uniforms of the Tower guard were etched with the emblem of the summerflower, seven petals for the seven graces that Ior blessed them with. A man who possessed the powerful magic of a grace was allowed to color in one of the petals. Gold for chastity, blue for humility, silver for faith, and so on. These seven men were quite colorful. Most had five graces, and one had all but the purple petal of patience. It was that one who approached them, a thin man with shaggy brown hair that matched the color of his eyes.

"Well met," he said, saluting. "I am Wynn Silverfeather, head guardsman here."

"Willow Peeke," Willow said, bowing slightly. "This is my Shield, Bryndon Claybrook, and my ever present shadow, Ridi Greenvallem."

"Defender Praeses wishes to speak with Stranger Willow alone," Wynn said, after the greetings were over.

"Ridi can stay," Willow said. *And good riddance*, she added in her head. "But I don't go anywhere without Bryndon."

Wynn hesitated, and Willow could see the wheels spinning in his head, weighing the potential consequences of disobeying the High Defender. Finally he nodded and gestured for them to follow, leaving Ridi in the care of the other guardsmen. They passed through a doorway, and Willow suppressed a groan when they came to several more flights of stairs, these narrower and in better repair than the ones below, cut out of red marble. Thankfully, however, they had only to climb a few more stories, and then Wynn was knocking at a large, plain, white door.

"Enter," said a deep voice from within.

Wynn turned the latch and led them inside. They were in a small, wood paneled room. A broad window looked out over the city to the north, while the south wall was broken only by a single, narrow arrow slit. The furnishings were plain and sturdy looking, less ostentatious than Willow expected. A number of mountain lion pelts were spread across the stone floor, heads still attached, open and snarling, as if ready to bite the ankles of whoever was foolish enough to walk by. In the corner of the room, a number of blankets were thrown over the top of some hulking thing. Willow had no idea what it was. It looked to be about the size of a small cart, but a bit taller and narrower.

"Stranger Willow," Praeses said. "Thank you for coming. And you Bryndon Claybrook. I did not expect to see you, but you are welcome all the same."

"Thank you, High Defender," Bryndon said, bowing low. "Forgive me if I am intruding."

"Done," Praeses said. "Wynn, we shan't need anything for a while, I think."

"Of course, sir," Wynn said, bowing. He shut the door behind him with a hollow bang.

"Would you like some tea?" Praeses said, pointing to a kettle on the table. "It is still quite hot."

"That would be lovely, thank you," Willow said.

"Bryndon, if you would be of service…" but Bryndon was already moving, as if knowing what was expected of him. There were only two cups, so he poured one for each of them and took none for himself.

"I'm pleased to see you taking an active part in the proceedings, Stranger Willow," Praeses said, as he sipped his tea. The cup looked like a toy in his massive hands.

"Are you?" Willow said, surprised to hear him sound like he meant it. "We do not seem to agree on much."

"Wise Meridia instituted the position of Stranger for a reason," Praeses said. "I am glad you found your voice. There are many in this city who do not have one."

She looked at Praeses in surprise. "That's what Jair said to me," she said.

"Did he?" Praeses said, a small smile appearing on his dark face. "I'm always amazed what sons take from their fathers. And what they leave behind."

"Sons?" Willow said. "You don't mean, you and Jair…"

"Is that so surprising?" Praeses asked.

"Of course it is," Willow said. "You two look nothing alike."

"Ah, as to that—he is not my natural son," Praeses admitted. "He had no house of his own, and his mother died before she could find a place for him. So I took him in instead, raised him as my son, gave him the name of my old house. I am sure Bryndon knows the story, do you not?"

Bryndon nodded. "It was before I was born, Defender, but my Gran told me the tale."

"And what did she tell you?" Praeses asked. "I am always curious about how much truth gets passed down to the people."

"Well, I don't clearly remember all of it, my lord," Bryndon said. He looked decidedly uncomfortable, and ran a nervous hand through his hair. "The General's mother, she was—well, Gran told me she was soft-headed."

"Soft-headed?" Willow asked.

"Wit-sick, is the term your people use," Praeses said. "She was a child her whole life, never learned more than a few words, and most of those were names of food. Her mother took care of her until she was near twenty, but after her mother died…well, go on Bryndon, what happened next?"

"Gran told me that the master of her common house took over for her mother, but that he…" Bryndon trailed off, but Willow could guess the next part.

"Raped her," Praeses said, nodding. "Though I suspect that was going on to some extent even before her mother died."

"That's what Gran thought too," Bryndon said. "And she got with child. And the master, he knew that should she begin to show, he would have to face the House of Summerflower and the Unshamers. So he led her out into the wilderness, on the path to the Insurmountable Heights, and abandoned her there. Some time she spent on the mountain, wailing and crying, for she did not know what had happened, or why the master had left there. And then, on the third day, when she had laid down in a puddle to die, the High Defender found her, picked her up, and carried her back to the High Tower in his arms."

"She was a pitiful thing," Praeses said sipping his tea. "I don't think she stopped shivering for three weeks." Willow was having trouble seeing Praeses in this new light. It seemed there was far more to him than she had thought.

"But she survived," Bryndon said. "And gave birth to the General in her due time, dying on the birthing bed. There was a twin girl, as well, but she followed her mother to the Heights a few weeks later, dead from sickness. And the General was left without house mother, father, or sister. And so the High Defender raised him as a son. The High Tower was his house, and the soldiers were his house brothers."

"What happened to the master?" Willow asked.

Bryndon glanced at Praeses, who nodded for him to go on. "The High Defender Unshamed him," he said. "He set him no epitimia, no penance or sacrifice for what he had done. But he named the master's own body as his object of shame. And then...he destroyed the object."

"An end all together too good for him," Praeses said. "Had I my way, I would have sent him to the lowest pits of the whispering things. Yes, that was well told, Bryndon. Your Gran was well informed."

"Thank you, High Defender," Bryndon said, bowing again.

"It was good of you to take him in," Willow said. "You raised him well."

"He is far better than me, you mean," Praeses said. "And you would be right. He has the gentleness of his mother, a quality I have ever lacked. And it is no surprise to me that we are often at odds with one another. For I am often at odds with myself." He sighed and set down his tea cup. "But come, I did not bring you here to discuss Jair."

"Why did you bring me here?" Willow asked.

"To plead with you," Praeses answered, to Willow's surprise. "I wonder, Willow, if you know what room you are in right now."

Willow shook her head. "Is this room special? It seems far more plain than others I have seen."

"Bryndon, do you know?" Praeses asked.

"It looks like a lamb's nest, my lord," he said, nodding toward the corner, where the cart-sized object was hiding under the blankets. "That's the crucible I wager."

"It was, once," Praeses said. "But a few centuries ago, High Defender Darius thought this location too remote from the main defenses, and moved it to a different location, much lower. The new nest is more exposed than this one, but Darius was fearful that a lamb here would not know how the battle fared below, and so would not know when to trigger the crucible.

A fair point, I think, though other options could likely have been found." He waved his hand, brushing aside Darius and his military tactics. "Do you know, Willow, how the crucible works?"

"Ridi has mentioned something about it," Willow said. "But Ridi speaks far more than the capacity of my ears to listen."

Praeses laughed, a rich, low timbre. "He is quite thorough in everything he does, that is for sure," he said. "But the crucible is a fascinating piece of magic, and worth hearing about."

He held his cup out for a fresh cup of tea and went on. "Two millennia ago, Tarn Harrick and his niece Meridia led a group of people to this valley, fleeing the whispering things of the grass and Tjabo's dark men. And Meridia set them to build towers along the southern road, that they might defend themselves from Tjabo when he inevitably came for them. Soon after, Tjabo did indeed come, leading the first Nightmare with the cold at his back. Long they fought among the towers, and though Tarn and his sons were great warriors, still they were being pushed back, tower to tower, by the Nightmare. For they found that their enemy grew more powerful with every soldier they killed, stronger and faster, able to shrug off wounds that would kill any normal man. Finally, exhausted, they were driven back to the last tower, and the enemy was at their gate. So Tarn sent for Meridia, and begged her to use her magic to save them."

"I remember this part of the story," Willow said. "She filled him with arrows."

"Indeed," Praeses said. "But Tarn took them willingly, sacrificing himself that Meridia might have the power to defeat their enemy. And at his death, the last tower shone like a burning star, and all who saw it among the enemy were killed, save for Tjabo himself, who was and ever will be blind.

"And so after the Nightmare had passed, before Meridia took the Heights, the people begged her to teach them how to use this magic, for they knew they would have need of it again. And so Meridia built the first crucible, and showed the people how to link it to the towers, so that its magic would work properly. Here, let me show you."

He stood and walked to the far wall, where the old crucible stood in the corner, and pulled the blanket free. It looked to Willow like an instrument of torture. A low table of granite stood up from the ground about one and a half feet, the stone rough and uneven. Four steel posts rose up from the corners of the table, supporting two iron bars that ran from corner to corner in the shape of an X. And hanging from those bars, pointing down toward the table, were a multitude of blades, some over a foot long, others little bigger than thorns.

"This is an old crucible," Praeses said. "Very different from the ones we have now. Modern crucibles have only four blades, two each for the eyes, and two each for the pits of the elbows, the same places that Tarn was struck with his son's arrows. But it was thought that more blades would produce more powerful magic, an idea proven demonstrably false in the twelfth Nightmare. You can see the way it works. When the tower is nearly lost, the lamb climbs onto the table, holding the trigger in his right hand." Praeses pointed to a small lever that Willow had missed at first glance. "Then, when he is prepared to give himself up for his brothers, the Captain of the tower gives the signal. And he pulls the trigger."

There was a screeching of metal, and the blades dropped toward the table, stopping with a loud boom a few inches above the stone.

"And the Nightmare is driven back," Praeses said. "For a time."

He cranked the blades back up, locking them back into place. "How long a time depends on the lamb himself," Praeses continued. "For when the blades pierce a man, the magic of the crucible seizes his life, and puts it into his hands. It is written in the Mysteries that the spikes will never actually kill him. Rather, they will stay lodged in his flesh, causing extreme pain, pain beyond what a normal blade would inflict. This pain will last for as long as the man is willing to withstand it for the sake of his brothers. No one knows how that works, really. Meridia did not reveal it to us, and of course no one has ever survived to tell us. But sooner or later the pain will be too great, and when that time comes, the man will choose to die, and the magic will wink out. And then the Nightmare will come forward again."

"Why does it—" Bryndon began, then cut off with a choking sound. "What are *those*?"

"Ah, yes," Praeses said quietly. "And now we come to my plea."

Willow looked at Bryndon, and saw his face was as pale as milk. "What is it?" she asked.

"It has *straps*," Bryndon said, sounding strangled. "*Straps.*"

Willow looked at the stone table again, confused. Of course it had straps. How else would you expect a man to—

Then Willow understood. The crucible was supposed to be willing, an act of sacrifice for the good of others. Straps were not necessary for that. In fact, they were detrimental to it.

This machine was made for murder.

"Do you know why the Nightmare grows stronger with every man it kills?" Praeses asked. "There are three kinds of magic, Stranger Willow. The graces of Ior, that strengthen a man's body. The objects of shame, that come from the land of the blackened sky, and strike with fire and lightning. Both of these we have long used in defense of our city. But the third kind of magic, we have never taken up."

"What is this magic?" Willow asked.

"It is the magic of the whispering things," Praeses said. "The blood magic, Meridia called it, that steals the power in a man's blood and uses it to strengthen another. All of the minions of the Nightmare are imbued with it. Indeed, it creates them. The blood magic twists and shapes men and beasts into unnatural, horrid forms, creatures built only for killing and dying. Meridia thought it an abominable form of power, and wrote no books on it, wishing the knowledge of it to die with her on the Heights."

"Because it is Prohibited," Bryndon said. "It is a terrible shame to use it."

"Ah, but she did not destroy it fully," Praeses said. "Indeed, she left us with one hundred monuments to it, sitting at the top of every tower."

"The crucibles?" Bryndon said, sounding incredulous. "The crucible is not blood magic. It is the magic of love, of one life laid down for another."

"So I thought, at first," Praeses said. "Long years I searched, to find the books that would let me unlock the secrets of the blood magic. There were times when I despaired of their very existence, for the whispering things guard them well. But they have allied themselves with men, and the magic of men must be held in books. They hid their secrets among many books, a bit of knowledge in one, a small spell in another. From before even the last Nightmare, I made it my work to find them and study them, delving deep into the heart of the Nightmare's power. And I have lived long, and learned much. And what I learned, I used to make this."

He ran a finger along the edge of one blade, and Willow saw a thin sheen of wetness remain where his finger passed over it. The blade began to glow with a strange light, somehow white and red and black all at once. It cast strange shadows over the Defender's face, and then faded, letting the light of the setting sun reign once again. And then there was no more blood on the blade.

"The greatest work of magic that this city has ever known," Praeses said, his voice almost loving. "For you see, I have done what Meridia could not. I have combined all three kinds of magic in this machine: grace, shame, and blood. When used, it will turn the very stones of this tower into a weapon, an object of shame with phenomenal power. But where Meridia's crucible lasts only as long as the lamb is willing to suffer, this magic—this magic will last forever."

"Forever?" Bryndon asked. There was a strange expression on his face. The disgust was still there, yes, but there was something else, too. Something like hope.

"You see the importance of this, now," Praeses said. "A power that lasts forever, a defense that the lamb cannot lay down. We need only pull our soldiers back, and wait for the Nightmare to come to us. The power of the High Tower will fall upon them as an unquenchable inferno. No one need die. No brothers and sons. No husbands and fathers. No longer will we need to fear the Nightmare, no longer will our people need to perish every seventy years. We shall have a Golden Generation forever, and live in peace. And yet, to do it we must be willing to commit one murder. To take one life in our defense, that ten thousand may not have to be given."

"You want me to support this," Willow said. "You need my vote in the council."

"I wish only for the authority to use it in the most dire circumstances, with the Nightmare knocking on the door," Praeses said. "It will not work, otherwise. Like a normal crucible, the minions of the Nightmare must see the tower for its magic to destroy them. For this authority, if our need is dire, I ask for your support. The Clock saw the power of it early, and he has worked to help me create it, using some of his own power and knowledge to solve some of my early difficulties. He is fully behind it. Pilio could be swayed as well. I was once sure of Oded, but now...age has hardened me like seasoned wood, but it has softened him. There is little left but dry rot in his heart, and he cannot be relied on, especially to support something new, and against the Prohibitions besides. He already regrets other favors he has granted me, I think. And Jair and Tarius will oppose it at once, of course. They care more for their own nobility than their people's safety." He turned to Willow and locked into her with his dark eyes. "And that leaves you."

"But are you not asking me to condemn a man to ten thousand years of torture?" Willow asked. "Who could deserve such a thing? How would you even begin to choose who to...."

Praeses shrugged. Somehow the shrug was more troubling than the machine itself. "I do not claim any man deserves it," he said. "But like all shame objects, the worse the shame of the victim, the more powerful the magic would be. Scores flock to the House of Summerflower every day.

We might have our pick. But I think, rather, it would be better to go house to house, and test every person we can, starting with the eldest. For the very worst shames will not come into the light on their own."

Willow did not know what to say. She realized again that she did not belong here, that it should be someone else making this decision, someone from the Free Cities, someone who was used to authority, to holding others' lives in their hands. The whole idea of the crucible made her shiver, even when the death was willing. And this...

"So Willow Peeke," Praeses said, covering the machine once again with the blanket. "This is your burden, as wise Meridia decreed that it would be. What will you decide?"

CHAPTER TWENTY FOUR

No

"And what did you decide?" Jair asked, a small smile on his face.

"What do you think?" Willow said. "I told him he could take his 'greatest magic in Meridia' and choke on it."

Jair laughed. They were in a private study in the Low Tower, where Willow had commanded Ridi to take her after the meeting with Praeses had come to its uncomfortable end. She had to tell Jair at once.

"I imagine he took that about as well as he did when I said it to him," Jair said. "Though I was more respectful about it, I wager," he added.

"You knew about this?" Bryndon asked, sounding surprised. He sat in a stout wooden chair, carved with spears and arrows. Willow thought it looked like the most uncomfortable chair in the world. She much preferred to stand.

"Of course," Jair replied. "Many years ago, when I first became General. He was afraid he would be dead by the time the next Nightmare came, and wanted to be sure I knew what kind of power he had created. He wished me to order our outer towers abandoned, to let the Nightmare come unimpeded to the High Tower, so that we could defeat them without losing a man. I understand the draw, of course, to never have to worry about the Nightmare again." He shook his head. "But that is not the way."

"This is why I am here, isn't it," Willow said, understanding dawning on her. "To keep this thing from being used."

"He is a fool to trust the defense of the city to a weapon we've never used before, especially one that is so shameful," Jair said. "The guard has used the power of shame for generations, but this is something altogether different, and more wretched. The shame objects free those from whom they are made, purify them of their wrongdoing. But the blood magic is simply evil. It serves the whispering things, and them alone. Even Meridia was afraid to use it. To murder a person with it, to embrace this endless torture—" His face grew serious, and troubled. "I do not know what this thing will do, Willow, if it is used. But I know that it must not be used. I would do everything I could to keep it from being used, simply because of its evil, but I also fear it would be disastrous. There were other traders I spoke with, others that might have served as Stranger. But when I met you… I knew you would never agree to it."

"You were right about that," Willow said. "I should have been on this council years ago, when we could have done something to keep this thing from being built. Far too much of the power here is in the hands of men. Did not Meridia teach you of the wisdom of women?"

"Of people, Meridia said much. Of men and women, she said far less," Jair said. "We have filled in her silence with foolishness."

"Then you should have forced some sense into everyone's thick skulls," Willow said.

Jair did not answer right away, pulling out his pipe, and tamping down a wad of tobacco into the bowl. He struck a match, and drew deeply, filling the air with the smell of smoke. "That would prove more difficult than you think, Willow Peeke," he said. "Tell me, Bryndon, how did the pain of childbirth feel to you?" At Bryndon's look of surprise, Jair shrugged and smiled. "I have some eyes and ears in the city," he said.

"It was horrible, General," Bryndon said. "If my family had not been there, to help take some of the burden away from me…" He shuddered.

"Yet this epitimia is prescribed everyday," Willow said. "And worse besides."

"The House of Summerflower has been dark for many years now," Jair said, nodding. "Dark with the cries of women in pain. It saddens me to see it so."

"Not enough for you to do anything about it," Willow said, not bothering to try to hide the anger in her voice. She still remembered the pain that had washed over her, when she had first taken Bryndon's hand.

"Why ever do you think I have done nothing about it?" Jair said. "I have spoken out many times, tried to show them the truth. Praeses, Oded, The Clock—they are all terrified of a prophecy made long ago, the death dream of Weaver Anita Moonlight, which foretold the destruction of Meridia through a masked woman."

"The Nightbringer," Bryndon said.

Jair nodded, puffing idly. "That is how she is known among the people. The Six at the time did their best to keep the dream a secret, but the worst things always have a way of slipping out, while the best things often stay hidden for years. The Clock thought you were the Nightbringer, Willow. Even after the Unshaming, I still think he half believes it."

"He is insane," Willow said. "Him and Praeses and Oded and all of them."

"Insane?" Jair said, looking at her with his sharp blue eyes. "They believe that these epitimia will save us, will keep this Nightbringer from ever rising to power. In other words, Willow, they are doing exactly what they think is best for this city. And in that way, they are as insane as you and I."

"Perhaps evil would be a better word then," Willow said fiercely. "For that is what they have done at the House of Summerflower, and that is what they propose to do with this crucible."

"Take care not to speak too hastily of those of whom you know almost nothing," Jair said. There was no hint of anger in his voice, but there was rebuke. "You think this machine is evil, these epitimia unjust, and I agree. The one rips the Prohibitions to shreds, and the other twists them into knots. Yet there is much of Praeses you do not know, many years spent in service for this city, for this people, for the man sitting before you."

"But we cannot afford to wait any longer," Willow said. "Whatever you want to call the men who built it, this crucible is dangerous and evil. We cannot allow it to hang over our heads like an axe, ready to fall."

"It is guarded day and night," Jair said. "By at least three of Praeses's guards, formidable men all."

"Surely they would be no match for you, if it came to swords?" Willow said.

"Aye, that is true," Jair said. "And what would I do then, once the machine was destroyed? Should I drive Praeses from this city by force of arms, seize his post for myself, and set myself up as king? Only Ior himself could claim that right, and what he has forborne to do, I would be foolish and proud to attempt. Goodness is not something that can be ordered or forced, Willow Peeke. Goodness is a choice—No, it is a thousand choices, a million, made every day. I cannot make those choices for Praeses, nor The Clock, nor Oded. I cannot force them to grace at the point of a sword. Swords are for the Nightmare, and their servants. Swords are made to keep chaos at bay, and to give men time to choose the good for themselves. For there is always hope for a fallen man while he is alive. But if he dies, his hope dies with him."

"You will do nothing, then," Willow said.

"I have brought you here," Jair said. "We have spoken out against it, and so we have stopped it."

"But will not Praeses use it anyway, even without the support of the Seven?" Willow asked. "He is already willing to murder in order to use it. What does the vote of a council mean to him?"

"As to that, I think you are right," Jair admitted. "But it will only work if the council agrees to pull back the soldiers, bringing the Nightmare to us. Otherwise he cannot use it, not unless the Nightmare is knocking on our door."

"So there is still a danger," Willow said. "If the Nightmare breaks through, he will use it."

"The Nightmare will not break through," Jair said.

"How can you be sure?" Willow asked.

The look on Jair's face was a fierceness approaching joy. He flexed the fingers on his right hand. Willow thought he had never looked more dangerous.

"You leave that to me," he said.

CHAPTER TWENTY FIVE
Kids

Bumble shifted and pawed at the straw, changing positions once again. Robin stopped pacing long enough to watch her settle back down.

"You're not going to speed it up walking around like that," Bryndon said.

"I know," Robin said. "I'm not stupid, mud head." Bryndon had helped Father with three other births, and was making a big show of his superior knowledge. He claimed everything was going fine, but Robin wasn't so sure. The vision of Bumble screaming in rage and pain had not faded from her memory.

"She seems close," Willow said, leaning against the inside of the fence. "Though it is long since I had a herd of goats to care for."

"Very soon," Bryndon agreed.

They waited on one end of the pen, away from the rest of the herd. The other goats seemed to respect the birthing process, remaining in a tight group on the far side. Lunker was stalking from one end to the other, snorting and butting his head on the fence every few steps.

A few minutes later, Bumble shifted again, and began to moan, low and urgent. Robin patted her on the head, making soothing noises, and the she-goat licked her hands, nuzzling into her leg.

"You're sure everything is alright?" Robin asked again.

Bryndon checked Bumble's hindquarters. "She's doing fine," he said. "Here, come around to this side. You can see for yourself."

Robin moved next to Bryndon, and he set her in front of him.

"There, you see that," he said, pointing. "The birthing sac is coming out. If all is well, we should see a front hoof next."

As her labor moved, Bumble switched from a low moan to a kind of barking howl. Bryndon took up a position at Bumble's head, leaving Robin alone to watch for the hoof. It came out slowly—a black, polished stone.

"I can see it!" she said. "It's the front right hoof."

The barking howls rose higher and higher, and Robin could see a second hoof. The birthing sac was nearly all the way out now, full and white, like a wet egg, and it pulsed forward and back, forward and back, slowly working its way free.

"There's the head," Bryndon said. "Do you see it?"

Robin could, small and black behind the white sac, resting between the hooves.

"Pull it out now," Bryndon said. "Help her."

"But it's so small," Robin said, hesitating. "I'll hurt it."

"It's tougher than it looks," Bryndon said. "Small but strong. Like you. Go on and pull it out, smooth and straight."

Robin shuffled forward on her knees and grabbed the little kid by both hooves. They were slick and warm and hard. Leaning back, she used her weight to pull the kid forward smoothly. There was resistance at first, as the head slowly cleared the birth canal. Then a pair of little wet ears slipped free, and she pulled the kid the rest of the way out easily.

"Well done!" Bryndon said, smiling. "Quick now, wipe its mouth and nose clean so it can breathe."

He tossed her a clean rag, and Robin bent to wipe away the mucus and fluid covering the little kid's face. The birth seemed to have broken whatever silent agreement held between the goats, and Lunker and Clover were the first to crowd around, licking and sniffing. Robin elbowed them out of the way, avoiding Lunker's peevish snips, continuing to wipe the kid clean. A dark birth mark decorated its forehead, but otherwise it was white and pink. It smelled of blood and spit, acrid and hot and gamy.

"A girl," Bryndon said, lifting the kid's leg. "That's good. Leave her for the others. There's another to come."

Robin saw that Bryndon was right. Bumble was lying on her side again, shifting back and forth, though she was not calling yet. A small pool of red stained the straw beneath her, but there was less blood than Robin expected. The rest of the herd gathered around to investigate when she left the kid alone, and Sunstar began to clean the newcomer vigorously.

The second kid came much easier, and this time Robin didn't need to be told what to do, pulling the little goat free as soon as its head was clear, cleaning its face for its first breaths in the free air. Its fur was a deep brown, like bark on a tree. It was a little smaller than the first.

"And a boy," Bryndon said, examining him. "Father will be pleased."

"They're beautiful," Willow said, a smile on her mossy face. "Well done, Robin."

"Fetch the bucket now, red bird," Bryndon said. "And don't be stingy with the molasses, no matter what Master Florian says. She needs to recover her strength."

Robin rushed to the trough for a bucket, filling it with cool, clear water. The molasses jug hung from a hook in the kitchen, and she poured in a generous portion, mixing them together with a wooden spoon.

"It's done then?" Master Florian said, when he saw her in the kitchen. "How many?"

"A girl and a boy," Robin said. "Willow says they're beautiful."

"I'm sure," Master Florian said. "Be sure to clean this floor up before bed tonight, you hear. You've tracked in enough mud to grow a stone tree. And that's quite enough on the molasses, girl. You're not trying to sweeten her for supper."

Robin poured in a bit more anyway, and slipped back outside. Bryndon and Willow were busy wiping the kids clean with a pair of damp towels. Robin took the bucket to Bumble, pushing the other goats away, who swarmed around hoping to get a few mouthfuls as well.

"Good girl, Bumble," Robin said, petting her head as she drank eagerly from the bucket. "You're going to be a good mother, I bet." She felt like she had passed some kind of test, like she knew something she hadn't known before. She had seen life come forth, and it was smelly and strong and beautiful. Bumble pulled her head from the bucket and licked Robin across the face. Her tongue was wet, and it smelled of molasses.

CHAPTER TWENTY SIX

The Shadow of the High Tower

The High Defender's rooms were at the very top of the High Tower, where the lambs nest would have been in any other tower. Here though, it was a living quarters for Praeses and his dogs—richly ornamented furniture and linens, a separate privy and bath, a massive hearth, and three tall shelves full of books, a library larger than any save that of the House of Summerflower. Wynn had often wondered what was in some of those books; many of them did not have titles, or were in languages he did not understand.

It was the Defender's habit to retire to his rooms for an hour of reading in the evening, after the day's business was done. The Nightmare was a few days away, now, but Praeses had not changed his habit. He sat by the window with a book on his lap, his dogs Patience and Diligence at his feet, and read but little, often pausing to think. The books always looked small in his big hands. Sometimes he would ask Wynn a question, as if testing a thought in the air.

"Did you have a girl in your sights before you joined the guard, Wynn?" he asked.

Wynn shifted his grip on his spear. "Many guardsmen do, Defender," he said.

The Defender smiled. "As good a non-answer as any," he said. "Come, there must have been someone. Tell me of her."

Wynn paused a moment before answering. "She is a Blackwing, sir," he said finally.

"Ah…" Praeses said, understanding. He seemed to expect more, so Wynn went on.

"We met at the Flying Ball," he said. "That's the dance the Blackwings throw every year, sir, where they bring all their friends from the lesser houses. Give us a taste of their superiority." It was hard to keep the bitterness out of his voice. Some things were hard to let go of. "I remember it well, the roaring fires and the summer wine, the music and dancing. There was every kind of bird you could think of roasting on a spit somewhere, chickens and merlins and geese, hawks and owls and eagles, dripping with fat and honey. They'd even managed to get some kind of strange southron animal, a pig I think it was called, stuffed full of mushrooms and gravy. Marvelous to see and smell, though the taste was strange."

"I have been to the Flying Ball, when I was still a boy myself," Praeses said, to Wynn's surprise. It was strange to think of Praeses as a boy, as something less than the force of nature he was now. "It was still much as you describe, then."

"Then you know of the games they play in Blackwing Tower," Wynn said. "The jumps and dives from the central spiral staircase, the net of ropes on which they swing and balance, like spiders on a web, or squirrels upon a tree. They say that only a true Blackwing can play the flying games without fear of falling. And she…she was the best of them all."

"Your lass?" Praeses asked.

"She was never mine," Wynn answered. It was hard to admit that, even now. "I watched her for hours, dancing on the ropes over fifty feet of empty air, and nothing but stone at the bottom. She was fearless, breathtaking. She made leaps no one else would attempt, her yellow hair flying out behind her like wings. She was still a child, then, no more than ten. But you could see the beautiful woman that was to come, and I—I did not guard my heart as I should have."

"How old were you at the time?" Praeses asked.

"Fourteen," Wynn said. "Old enough to know better, to know she was too far above my station. The Blackwings sometimes honor our daughters with a match, if they are particularly beautiful or charitable. But their own daughters are reserved for others of their station, and she was a natural daughter, a pure blooded Blackwing. If I had set my mind on one of her house sisters perhaps, an orphan who could be given away without polluting the bloodline…but I did not. I followed her around the rest of the night, fetching her candies and sweetbreads and the choicest meats, dancing only with her, seeing only her, lost. When I left, I wept and told her I would do whatever she wanted of me, as long as I could see her again."

"The Master of House Blackwing was not pleased, I would guess," Praeses said.

"He was a kind man," Wynn said. "And that proved ill for me, for he let me see her often over the next few years. We played games and shared secrets. I helped her with her chores, and in return she let me stay with her and bring her presents. And sometimes she would kiss my cheek or my hand. And she grew ever more beautiful with each passing year, fine and delicate as a summerflower."

"When did you propose?" Praeses said.

"When she was fourteen," Wynn said, coloring. "I feared she might have other suitors, and I thought—we knew each other so well. And I had worked so hard to be worthy of her. Ior had graced me with diligence, bravery, faith. Three graces at nineteen, more than some men earn in a lifetime. And, well…"

"You had been offered a place in my guard," Praeses finished. "Do not worry. It is not the first time a young man has been attracted to the prestige of the Defender's guard. You have served me well, and faithfully."

"Thank you for saying so, sir," Wynn said, bowing. "Yes, I thought, perhaps, having brought much honor to myself… But mostly, I was foolish in love. Master Vestus was old and dying, then, and the new Master laughed in my face, and then told me I was forbidden from seeing her again. I should have stopped there. But I went to her instead, and asked her to be with me, without the blessing of her house. And she said—" Wynn stopped abruptly, realizing he was treading on dangerous ground.

"Yes?" Praeses said. "What did she say?"

"I—she asked me to do something shameful, Defender, something— It is not something I wish to recall. I have since been freed of it, but the memory is hard. I did what she asked, and it caused both of us much pain."

"And when it was done, she did not do as was promised," Praeses said. It was not a question.

She thought I was going to kill her, Wynn thought, but he said nothing. He could feel a stinging behind his eyes, and prayed desperately to Ior that he would not break down in tears in front of the High Defender.

"We still spoke occasionally," Wynn said. "But I gave up hope."

"A sad tale," Praeses said. "Though not uncommon. Do you ever miss her? Ever wonder what your life might have been with a woman by your side, children to raise?"

Every day, Wynn thought.

"I think of many things," he said. "This is the life I chose." Saerin had never really loved him anyway, even before the book. In spite of everything he had done for her. Or perhaps because of it.

Praeses nodded and returned to his reading. The sun crept below the western peaks, and Wynn lit a number of lanterns, angling the mirrors so they shone on the Defender and his book. His eyes were not as strong as they used to be, he claimed, and the light helped them.

Soon however, the Defender put his reading away with a sigh, and sat long in thought. Flickers of emotion flashed across his face, and several times it seemed as if he was speaking to someone else, arguing with his shadow. He put his head in his hands, and Patience reached up to lick him for a little while. Praeses didn't seem to notice.

"Will you be wanting supper brought up soon, Defender?" Wynn asked.

The High Defender didn't answer, except to raise his head and look out over the valley. Woodsmoke rose above it in a lazy haze; from here, the Grove was a dark smudge of green on the horizon. As he looked, the last rays of the sun slipped through a break in the ring wall, and the shadow of the High Tower thrust itself across the city like a black sword. Wynn was about to repeat the question when the Defender finally spoke.

"Do you know your history, Wynn?" he said.

"Defender?"

"The story of the Free Cities," Praeses said. "Of Tarn and Tani and the one whose name is forgotten. You know it well?"

"Every child in Meridia knows that story, Defender."

"Just so," Praeses said. Diligence nuzzled her head under the Defender's hand, and he petted her absentmindedly. "And do you think it has a happy ending, or a sad one?"

"I..." Wynn hesitated, confused. "Happy, I suppose," he said. "Though, as the Unshamers say, all things may be seen two ways. I've never thought about it before."

"Few do," Praeses said. "Everyone knows the story, but few think about how it ends. The dark men of the grasses spread, and their greatness is lower than the grass, and their freedom is lived in chains."

"*And the men of the valleys kept watch, and endured*," Wynn finished.

"But that is merely the end of the book, not the end of the story," Praeses said. "You understand, of course, that the story goes on in us, every day."

"You mean we keep watch, and we endure."

"We do. And that is all we do," Praeses said. "The Nightmare comes and breaks our towers, kills our brothers and fathers. Kills our sons." He turned away from the window and began pacing the chamber, shooing Diligence away. The dog settled down in front of the fireplace. "We keep watch, and we die. Then we rebuild, so that we may die again. For what, Wynn?"

"For our wives and sisters and daughters," Wynn said.

Praeses laughed—a harsh, grating sound. "You have a lot of wives and daughters, Wynn? You need more Unshaming than I can give, then, if you have been so untrue to your oaths. Or perhaps this girl that you do not name is still very important to you. Answer me truly, when the Nightmare comes for you, why will you die?"

Indeed, Wynn thought of Saerin, but instead he said, "I will die for other men's wives," he said. "For the Golden Generation, that can live in peace."

"Life, yes, it is precious," Praeses said. "But it is not a life of peace. It is a life of grief. A life of watching nearly all the people you love die for you."

"A life of gratitude, then," Wynn said.

"All things may be seen two ways," Praeses agreed. "We keep watch, and we endure. But we do not triumph."

He stood up and began to pace, arms clasped behind his back. "Tell me, Wynn," he said. "What do you know of the House of Moonlight?"

Wynn shrugged. The Defender was changing topics quickly, as he sometimes did. "The same as all others, sir. It is the home of the Dreamers, the ones who Ior graces with the gift of seeing with other eyes."

"The future, the present, the past," Praeses said, nodding. "And all of them women, of course. Prophecy was one of the few things Meridia was not able to teach to men. Tarius is there only to watch and protect them, to control and interpret what could undo a city. And he is good enough in that capacity. He's been Weaver as long as you've been alive, but there were others before him, of course. Weaver Anita was the last, a Dreamer herself. Rare that, but not unprecedented. And before her was Weaver Edwyn, a young man, only thirty when he came to power. And ambitious, too, always making the right friends, doing favors for the right people. I think he aspired to High Defender some day. And then, quite suddenly, he vanished, taking the Heights and leaving Anita in charge."

"At thirty?" Wynn asked, dumbfounded. "But why?"

"Because he had learned how the story ends," Praeses said. "A Dreamer had come to him, a woman known for the clarity and power of her visions. And when he heard what she had to say, he saw a horror he could not stand, and his plans for power turned to dust and vanity. He came to me, the night before he left, with the sight of his own death in his eyes, and told me what he had learned."

He stopped pacing and stared at Wynn intently. Wynn did his best not to shuffle his feet. The Defender's full stare could pin a man to the floor.

"So let me tell you how the story ends," Praeses said. His voice was flat and cold, seemingly devoid of emotion. "The story ends with you dead on the floor, half-frozen blood leaking out of you in a slow ooze, while the darkness of the Nightmare rolls over your city like a black flood. It ends with your sweetheart in a steel collar, cast into the deepest pits of the whispering things, to scream and suffer the rest of her miserable life away. It ends with our people dead and our way of life shattered, with the Prohibitions trampled underfoot and the golden palaces of the dark men filling the fair valley, living their lives in chains. She had seen it, Wynn. She knew. Not a time or day. She knew not if it would be this Nightmare, or the next, or if another hundred generations would pass before the end. But the end itself is inevitable. Like a seeping wound, like an iron hot poker slowly cooling in the winter snow. The cold and death will triumph. We will sit in our towers and die nobly on our walls with faith in our hearts, a sword in our hands, and the Prohibitions on our lips. We will die and die and die. And blessed Ior will sit on the Heights, and he will do *nothing*."

He stopped, looking at Wynn with his dark, fiery gaze, as if waiting for a response. Wynn groped for something, anything to say, but all he could see was Saerin, with a chain around her neck and shadows in her eyes.

"Nothing to say," Praeses said quietly, sounding disappointed. He turned to the window once again. "You know the General and I have many disagreements. He likes to speak of the time before we came to this land. Before we had the Prohibitions to govern us, and we were still a people of the sea, setting our sails to go where the winds blew. He would go back to that time, I think, if he could. Back to the time when shame was allowed to fester like rotting meat, instead of being seared out of our flesh before it had the chance to destroy us. But such a time is two thousand years past and gone. We are a people of the stones now, high and strong. And so we have endured. But ice is stronger than stone, Wynn. Ice and time. It comes season after season, weakening, cracking, until the cornerstone shatters, and the tower built upon it falls.

"We can keep watch, and endure, yes. And rule by the Prohibitions as we ought to. But it is not enough."

"What else is there?" Wynn said. *They'll not take her,* he thought. *Whatever else, she will not feel the cold hand of despair.*

Again, the Defender was silent for a long time, hands held behind his back. Then he said, "When Tarn and his sons struck Tjabo down, Meridia commanded her uncle to take up the staff of flame, to burn a path through the grass to freedom."

"*Now see, Tjabo's shame will be our salvation,*" Wynn said.

"Take up the weapon of our enemy," Praeses said. "And we will triumph."

"But...we have hundreds of firebrands," Wynn said, confused. "We have lightning wands and bows of wind, all taken from the power of our people's shame."

"Yes, *our* people," Praeses said. "It is the weapon of the enemy I speak of, the source of *their* power. Tell me, Wynn, why does the Nightmare grow stronger as the battle goes on?"

Wynn felt a hot sweat break out under his white wool, but he was suddenly very cold. "The blood magic?" he asked. "But we know nothing of it."

"Once that was true," Praeses said. "But no more. There is a way, Wynn, another path we might take, our only hope of saving this city, of saving the people we love. But it will take courage. It will take a man willing to do what is best for the city no matter what. To make a hard choice."

And then there was a look on the Defender's face that Wynn had seen only once before, a hard, dark, wild look, and a memory of Saerin came to him unbidden, of Saerin and a green stone and black book.

"Make that choice with me, Wynn, and we will crush the Nightmare under their own boot," Praeses said. "And when they are destroyed, the General will finally have the power to form our own army. An army of right and justice. An army of light. And with the weapon of the enemy we will melt the golden palaces of the dark men and burn the grasses to ash. And our children will live to see the day when Tjabo's blind eyes crack in the heat of our flames."

The two men stood facing one another, with only the sound of the wind sighing through the windows. Wynn hardly dared to breathe. Diligence trotted towards him and stuck his head beneath his hand, licking.

The act seemed to break some sort of spell, and Praeses looked himself again, old and powerful.

"I have commanded you for five years, now, Wynn," the Defender said. "But what I ask now, I do not command. Do you understand? For this must be done in secret and in the darkness of shame. But it *must* be done."

Wynn thought of Saerin, and nodded. "I am your man, Defender. To the last."

The Defender took one last look at him, and smiled. "Very well," he said. "Then bring up my supper. And then I shall show you what we must do."

CHAPTER TWENTY SEVEN
Trust with Your Life

Garrett lay alone on his bunk, playing with Lena's black stones, rolling them over his knuckles. It had taken him months to learn that trick, to pop the three polished rocks back and forth like jumping fish, but he enjoyed the skill involved, the simultaneous concentration and mindlessness that it took. He flexed his toes and stretched, kneading the muscles in his leg with his other hand. They had nearly healed completely from his journey over the mountains; nothing remained of the bruising but a few faint yellow splotches around his knee. It had been horrifying, that first time he had woken up, and had seen how bad they were, like they belonged to a dead man, bloated and black beyond recognition. The healers had told him he likely would have died, had he not reached Century Tower when he did. As it was, it had been a near thing.

There was a knock on his door.

"Come in," Garrett said. "I'll be down for supper in a minute, I was just—"

It was General Thorndike.

"Sir!" Garrett said, scrambling to his feet. The black stones went flying, skittering across the floor like drops of water on a hot pan. "Forgive me, sir, I thought perhaps Sergeant Floramel—"

"At ease," the General said. "I don't mean to disturb your rest."

"Not disturbing anything, sir," Garrett said. "Just sitting here thinking is all."

"One of my favorite activities," the General said, pulling up a pair of chairs. "Sit with me. I want to talk to you about something."

"Thank you, sir," Garrett said, taking the chair and wondering what the General could possibly want to talk to *him* about. He had a whole army to run, and death at the doorstep. Sergent Floramel said the Nightmare would be at Century Tower by sunset tomorrow.

"Do you have an assignment for the battle?" Jair asked.

"Not yet," Garrett said. "Though I suppose I'll probably get a crossbow, and protect one of the gunners. That's what most of the scouts are doing I think. Not much need for scouting when the enemy is charging you full speed."

"And you are content with that?" Jair said.

"Crossbow work's not bad," Garret said, shrugging. "And begging your pardon, General, but a common house man like me has got to learn to be content with bread and a bed, if you take my meaning."

"I do," Jair said, tapping his finger softly on his knee. "There is little else a man needs, in truth. Do you mind if I smoke?" He waited for Garrett's nod, then pulled out his pipe, lighting it from Garrett's candle. He sat puffing on it for a moment, the smell of tobacco filling the air.

"I never properly thanked you, Garrett," Jair said. "You showed great courage, risking your life to come so quickly and warn us."

"Any man would have done the same in my place," Garrett said.

"But few would have succeeded," Jair said. "I saw you a day after you came in, did you know that? You were still unconscious and feverish, so I let the healers do Ior's work. But I saw what you put yourself through, to get here in time."

"Thank you, General," Garrett said. "It was Crack and Cringe, though, that ought to get our thanks."

"The first casualties of this war," Jair said, nodding. "They will be remembered."

"It's strange living in this room now, without them here to fill it up," Garrett said. "Always did want a room of my own, every since I was a kid. Now that I got it though…" He shook his head. "They were good men, General. Brothers to the end."

"You knew them well, then?" Jair asked, looking at him with a strange intensity.

"'Course," Garrett said. "Knew near everything about them, I'd say, and they knew everything about me."

"What of the other scouts," Jair asked. "How well do you know them?"

"We're pretty tightly knit, I suppose," Garret said. "Crack and Cringe were the closest with me, of course, seeing as how we ran the most missions together. But you go on missions with near everybody at one point or another, if you've been around a little while like me."

"And how many of them would you trust with your life?" the General asked.

"Sir?" Garret asked, unsure of what Jair was asking.

"There is something wrong in this city, Garrett," he said, standing and pacing back and forth, smoke puffing up around him. "Something I can't quite put my finger on yet. But I have reason to suspect that some of our very own men are in league with the foe."

"Working for the Nightmare, sir?" Garrett asked, surprised. It was hard to imagine a man of the Tower Guard betraying his city like that. "Our own men?"

"Perhaps I am wrong," Jair said. "Yet little else makes sense. And there are other pieces at play here as well, forces still hidden in the shadows. Soon enough they must step into the light, and we must be prepared to meet them when they do. I need men I can trust. And I have a better use for your skills than bottling you up in a tower."

Garrett stood and gave a firm salute. "I'm your man, General. Just say the word."

Jair nodded in approval. "Then sit, and pay attention. You must move swiftly, and as silently as possible." And he began to explain to him what he had in mind.

CHAPTER TWENTY EIGHT
The Nightmare Comes

Jair stood on the observation deck of Century Tower, dressed in the white and gold of the Tower Guard, hands clasped behind his back. Below him, Tarn's Pass clung to the mountains, winding its way round the steep slopes of Mount Widower and out of sight to the south. Century Tower stood solidly in the middle of the pass, rising a hundred feet up and spanning less than four paces at the base, the first defense of Cairn Meridia against the Nightmare to come. From below, Jair knew it looked imposing, like a giant stone sword ready to fall on whoever might be foolish enough to attack it. But from the top he felt like he was teetering on the butt of a pike, trying to keep his balance.

Behind him, a loose assemblage of men waited with Willow and Bryndon, the tower men sweating profusely. The Nightmare was coming, and that meant full battle dress and cold gear, a double wool doublet, fur-lined trousers and boots, wool gloves and hoods. Everyone was baking in the sunlight, red faced and shining. He'd need to remind Captain Nils to have the men towel off before the first wave hit them, when the sweat would freeze on their skin. There was still another hour until sunset, however, when the first attack would come. The Nightmare's power waxed in the night, and so they would wait until then to strike.

Nils would likely remember to tell the men himself though, truth be told. He had taken command of Century Tower before Jair had even been born, and knew what he was about. His Sergeants were good men too, Daned of House Floramel and Nicolas of Stonepillar, both with long experience in command. Very soon, they would fight, and likely they would die. It was odd to stand with them, knowing that. Daned had a blunt and honest face, and bore the golden mark of chastity and the orange of diligence, proper graces for a Sergeant, at least in times of peace. Now, however, Jair wished Century Tower had a proper humble-healer; there were precious few of them in the guard these days. *I should have been raising them up,* Jair thought. *Spent too much time on tactics and weapons when I should have been fanning Ior's graces into flame.* Nicolas, at least, was graced with the red petal of bravery. His strength would be needed.

"Have all the scouts reported back, Ridi?" Jair asked, turning at last from the window and striding inside.

"All we expect to, General," Ridi said. He looked strange in a breastplate and helm, with sword and dagger belted to his side, though he still carried his papers. "Eighty-six have reported for duty to their respective Towers; six others have failed to report for some time and are presumed lost. The rest, as you know, are out on the General's orders."

"Excellent," Jair said. "Be sure that every man of them is given an extra ration and an extra hour of sleep if possible. We have worked them hard."

"As you say," Ridi said. Jair took a moment to look at him. He had seemed more reserved of late, and there were odd moments when it seemed like he was about to say something, and then his jaw would tighten, and he would stay silent. Jair decided he'd have to keep an eye on him. The approach of death affected every man differently, and everyone in the guard knew Ridi Greenvallem. They would look to him for courage.

"General, I wonder again if you might reconsider telling us what you intend for these scouts," Captain Nils said. Jair suppressed a frown. Ridi had done his best to keep the matter quiet, but there were near thirty men involved, from as many different towers, and that was hard to hide. So far, however, no one seemed to know what Jair had sent them out to do. All for the better. But that had not stopped the captains from asking. And asking. And asking some more.

"A man who does not know a plan cannot betray it to our enemy," Jair said, as he had before. "They have their orders and you have yours, Captain. In any case, our job here remains the same, as I am sure you have not forgotten."

"No, sir," Nils said, stiffening.

"Very well," Jair said. "I would speak with your men. Bryn, Willow, stay here and keep watch for us, if you would. Ring out at the first sign of the enemy."

"Yes, General," Bryndon said, stepping eagerly back out on the observation deck. Willow snorted at his eagerness and followed without a word. There was no question why she was going, and it was not to obey an order of Jair Thorndike. Jair wondered again whether it had been a good idea to bring them here. The boy had heart, certainly, but he was a boy still, and hadn't the benefit of a single grace. This wasn't a place for him. But he wanted Willow here. So far, he felt like this was a bit of a game to her, an annoyance, and perhaps a chance to teach a bunch of northern men that there were good people in the south. She didn't understand, really, what was facing them. And he wanted her to see.

Captain Nils gave orders to gather the men and then led the way out, down the spiraling wooden staircase that dropped to the gatehouse below. It was a long way down, past the lamb's nest and the gunner ports. The ports were stacked on top of one another in Century Tower, two landings per ten feet, all covering the pass below, for a total of eighteen. Most were firebrands, though the upper four gunners would be fighting with lightning. Fire was more effective against the massed hordes of the Nightmare, but lightning was better from such a height, strong enough to reach the ground below with full potency. Two crossbowmen stood with each gunner, short swords belted to their hips. If the Nightmare breached the gate, their job was to protect the gunners from the flying shrieks and crawling milidreads, with their poison stings.

And if *they* failed…well then waiting above, at the very top of the tower, the lambs stood ready with their crucible.

Jair had already spoken with both of them, the lambs, enfolding them in a quiet embrace, asking if they had any message to send to loved ones. Neither of them had, so he left them to their prayers. Later, he realized that he had never asked for their names. They would not be the only men to die for him that day that he did not know.

The pikemen were drawn up for him when he reached the stone floor of the gatehouse, standing at ease in loose ranks, their pikes glimmering above them in the light of the setting sun. It came streaming through the open firing ports in visible golden shafts, sparkling on the dust motes that floated through the air. There were eighty pikemen in all, the max that Century Tower could hold, led by Sergeant Daned. Together with the gunners and crossbowmen, they were no more than seven score strong, the first to stand against the legions of the Nightmare. This was the way of the Tower Guard; each tower stood alone against the full might of the enemy, until either they or the enemy broke. Hundreds of years ago, during the coming of the eighth Nightmare, the General had tried massing the guard together and fighting in the passes. The tactic had proved so disastrous that all mention of his name had been stricken from the histories, most of them burned out with fire. No one had dared try it since.

Jair examined the crude barricade that had been raised to either side of the gate. It stood near seven feet high, built of rough stone and wood, supply barrels and casks, crates of spare cloth and pike heads, even the mess table and chairs, all drenched with water. When the Nightmare came, the water would freeze solid, creating a barrier of ice, formidable even to the massive strength of the darkstones. The barricade was only there in case they lost the gate; its purpose was to funnel the enemy together, making them an easy target for the gunners above and keeping them from surrounding the pikemen and overwhelming them.

If they lost the gate.

Jair did not intend to lose the gate.

He picked a spot on the barricade where the sun shone brightly and leapt easily atop it, throwing back his cloak, so that the seven-colored flower on his breastplate glittered in the light. Sergeant Daned took up a cheer, his voice echoing from the tower heights as the other men joined him. Jair looked out over their faces, young and old, dark and fair of skin and hair, sweating in their abundance of clothing, and raised his hand for silence.

"Men of the Tower Guard!" he said. "We are not supposed to be here."

The cheers died away, and Jair heard his words echo back to him, weak and faint, as if spoken by a shadow.

"Long years have we lived in these mountains, since wise Meridia herself led us here, and mighty Tarn Harrick stood against blind Tjabo, with the first Nightmare at his back. And from that time until ours we have stood here every seventy years to defend what is ours, to keep ourselves free from King Tjabo and the Nightmare. It is fifty years since the last time we threw the Nightmare from our lands, twenty years before they should have come again. I say again, we are not supposed to be here.

"We were supposed to have twenty more years, twenty years of peace. Time to rest and train, time to prepare and strengthen, time to armor ourselves in the strength of Ior's grace.

"You have been denied that time. You must fight now, and you must fight with courage, whether you have the grace of bravery upon your chest or not. For the foe comes. They come with swords and axes, sharp teeth and claws, knives that drink blood and poisons that drive men mad. They come with cold and corruption, storms and darkness. They come with fell creatures from the deep pits of the dark things, twisted and engorged with their cruelty. You will face all these things and more, yet remember, the greatest enemy is despair. My brothers, do not despair.

"Fight!"

"Thorndike!" came the cry from the ranks. "Thorndike and the Guard!"

Then others said, "Meridia! Meridia and the Free Cities!"

The noise swelled and grew like a mighty tree, and Jair let it have its way, knowing the men needed to hear it, to hear the sound of their own power, to see their general in a shaft of golden sunlight, with the seven graces of Ior upon his chest. To have this one moment free from fear.

How long it went on, he did not mark, but the time came when another sound broke through the voices of men, a harsh, high clanging, the sound of Bryndon Claybrook ringing the bell of Century Tower high above them, the sound of approaching dusk, and the first sight of the Nightmare in the pass.

Jair drew his sword and held it aloft. "They come!" he said "Be strong and courageous. Love is one life laid down for another."

"And such love will always prevail!" they cried.

"To your posts!" called Captain Nils, giving the General a final salute. It was his command now.

Jair leapt down from the barricade and took the steps again, climbing up to the observation deck. He had time still, before nightfall, and he wanted to see the enemy for himself in the light of the sun. The sound of the bell reverberated around him, drowning out the scrape and clink of metal on stone below, the beating of his own heart.

When Bryndon saw him crest the last stair, he finally let the bell rope fall, and the quiet that followed was deafening by comparison. "Show me," was all he said, and Bryndon led him back out onto the observation deck without a word, where Willow waited.

She turned to him, braids swinging. "Jair, I—I am sorry." Her face broke, and she turned away. Jair reached out a hand, but she did not see it, and she strode from the deck without another word.

"Go with her," he told Bryndon. "Private Yaren has mounts waiting for you below. Your time here is finished now. Pray for us."

Bryndon nodded and turned to go. Then at the last moment, he turned back and wrapped Jair in a fierce hug. Then he was gone.

Jair took a deep breath and turned. He strode to the very edge of the platform, and there he looked out on his enemy, the foe he had waited his entire life to see, the creatures he had read about in countless books and histories, the Nightmare of Tjabo the Blind and Nameless, come at last. He looked out, and saw.

The Nightmare stretched out below him like a river of darkness, rounding Mount Widower in dense waves of black and red, packed shoulder to shoulder on the pass, from one end to the other. Hundreds of banners rippled in the wind, fierce wolves and red eyes, bloody pitchforks and flaming whips, burnt trees and severed heads, the emblems of the lords of the Chained Cities. And outnumbering them all was Tjabo's own banner, three tears of white on a black field. Rank upon rank of darkstones marched toward him, each of them eight feet tall and as wide as three grown men, draped in massive armor, black as pitch, carrying their giant axes and scythes and spiked hammers. Some rode on the backs of giant wyrms, long and thick as tree trunks, crawling along the ground on hundreds of legs, bent at impossible angles, massive ram's horns curling back from their heads. Above the teeming hordes, the air was thick with flying shrieks, flapping their bat-like wings, talons dark and gleaming, crying their terrible hunt. And leading them all were the stooped, shuffling figures of the horrors, who seemed somehow even more deadly than the rest of them. They sounded their horns, and the black echo of that noise reverberated off the mountain stone, and filled the air with their hatred.

And General Jair Thorndike, with the seven graces of Ior gleaming on his chest, felt the first touch of cold, and watched a single snowflake drift quietly to earth.

Part Three

No masks shall you make or wear. For a mask hides the shame of him who wears it, until the shame consumes the soul, and the mask becomes the man.
—The One Hundredth Prohibition

The coward is all things to all people, for the coward does not have the courage to be himself.
—From *On Cowardice*, by the wise and blessed Meridia

CHAPTER TWENTY NINE

Fire Flung, Shaken Stone

Jair lost the gate within an hour.

He did everything right. When the first wave of darkstones came forward, the gunners tore into them with fire and lightning, pounding them from above. Jair watched from the observation deck as they rushed forward, snarling and howling, and littered the ground with their dead. The front ranks fell like wheat to a scythe, and the men cheered and shouted encouragement to the gunners above them.

More darkstones rushed forward, seizing the fallen and hoisting them up over their heads as if the massive bodies weighed nothing. The lightning and fire continue to fall, but they did less damage now, and soon there were darkstones within range of the crossbows. Then came the shrieks, narrow bodied and wide winged, like massive, hideous bats, flinging themselves at the gunner ports, trying to worm their way inside. Only one shriek actually made it in, quickly cut down by the sword, but their purpose was more to distract then kill. To keep the gunners occupied while the first wyrm surged forward, massive and long, with black scales and a gaping, fanged maw. It came with incredible speed, like a striking snake, far faster than Jair would have thought such a large creature could move.

And with the wyrm came the storm.

He had read of the storm, of course; it had been a part of the

Nightmare since the beginning. The storm was the reason his men wore their wool and fur, the reason they littered the walkways with crushed salt, kept fires roaring in the braziers. Then the storm came, and within minutes Jair abandoned his place on the observation deck, fleeing the howling wind and stinging hail, the lightning that never seemed to stop flashing. But most of all, fleeing the cold. A bone crushing, hideous cold, that seemed to steal the very breath from his lungs.

Then the wyrm reached the gate, its thick scales burnt with fire, lightning holes smoking in its sides. It let loose a fell cry, terrible to hear, and battered at the stout wooden beams with its massive curled horns. Captain Nils drew the pikemen up in ranks in front of the gate, and then Jair was walking from man to man, reminding them of their training, where to aim for the soft spots in the darkstones armor, how to listen for the Sergeant's calls over the noise of battle, how to set their feet to absorb the impact of a charging foe. And most of all, he told them to be courageous, to remember that Ior was with them, that they were men of the guard, over whom the Nightmare would never prevail.

The gate shattered and fell, and the darkstones came pouring through, with their clubs and axes, their spiked maces and flails and swords thick as a man's leg. Jair put himself where the fighting was fiercest, moving from one opponent to the next, and his sword was soon dark with blood, his arms aching from constantly striking the darkstones looming above him. Then the horrors came, slippery and quick, flinging their knives ahead of them. The line bent. Men died. Sergeant Nicolas roared and swung his battle axes, cutting three darkstones down by himself before a shriek latched onto him from behind, and sent him to the Heights.

Then they lost.

And Captain Nils rang the lamb bell.

And the tower filled with silver light.

The Nightmare cried out and died, the cold left, and Jair led the survivors away, making for the next tower, ordering the remaining men to carry the wounded. The first lamb gave them a ten minute head start before the light winked out. And the men paused and turned and saluted their brother, who had laid his life down for them.

"What was his name, the lamb?" Jair asked Captain Nils. They were carrying a wounded soldier between them, his right leg missing from the knee down, a tourniquet twisted above the wound to stop the bleeding.

"Berwin," Nils said. "May Ior take him graciously to the Heights."

And then the Nightmare came again.

They were smart. That's what Jair was the most surprised about. He had thought of them as little more than mindless beasts, a force of nature to be weathered and withstood. But they were incredibly cunning, sending their forces forward in waves, so that only a portion of their army was within sight of the tower when the power of the crucible was unleashed. And they seemed to know exactly how to attack each tower. Nothing escaped their notice—the smallest idiosyncrasies in design, the places in the pass that were most difficult for the gunners to hit, the weakest parts of the gates—they exploited them all without hesitation, screaming their chilling and inhuman cries.

Ninety-Nine was smaller then Century Tower, its gate thinner and unreinforced. It fell in half an hour. Ninety-Eight did better, mostly thanks to its lamb, who gave them near twenty-five minutes before he gave in. His name was Hywell. The Ninety-Seventh was one of their strongest towers, with three dozen firing ports and close to two hundred men. It lasted almost two hours, until a few dozen milidreads managed to bore through the solid granite of the outer wall, and sting half the gunners to death before they could be cut down. Their poison was horrible, a blackness that spread through the veins and caused incredible pain. The humble healers made it to a few of the men, but most of them died screaming.

Jair fought and killed and shouted, meeting the Nightmare in the front ranks. He called out enemies to the gunners, directing fire at the wyrms first, thrusting a pike through the ports to keep the shrieks at bay. He carried the wounded, putting them in carts to send back to Meridia, stacking them like cargo. The soldiers from the first three towers who were still strong enough to fight were sent back as well, to towers near the back lines that had room for more men. Jair had stacked the first towers to the brim.

And so he fell back to the Ninety-Sixth.

The blue stone shivered and cracked, a horrible sound, as if the mute rocks were screaming in pain under the assault of the Nightmare. Shem gripped the leather thongs of his shield. Though fires still roared in the braziers, his hands were numb, and he had lost feeling in his nose. Frost coated the walls in great furry patches, like white moss.

Captain Truman shouted orders over the pounding at the gate, moving the pikemen into position. From his lofty perch in the lamb's nest, Shem could see little more than the tops of their helmets, polished and shining. Many of those men would be dead soon. The General was among them, and Shem could see him moving from man to man, saying a few words to each. Every man he spoke to stood up a little straighter as he passed.

The last firing port closed, and the gunners turned around, shame objects glowing in their hands. All firebrands. The next chance they had to shoot, the enemy would be inside the tower. Ninety-Six was built as a hollow column, with clear lines of sight from the gunner platforms to the gate. A wide ramp rose from the gate, switchbacking upward toward the gunners and the ladder to the lamb's nest, where Shem waited. There was very little protection up in the lamb's nest; the first few shrieks that managed to squirm past the crossbowmen would be on them in moments. Shem squeezed the grip of his sword.

Harn clapped a hand to his shoulder. "Pray with me, will you Shem?" he said. "I want my heart to be strong enough to get everyone out."

"We may beat them back yet," Shem said. "The new pikemen—"

"Let us work at our task, and leave the others to theirs," Harn said. He looked at Shem, unblinking. He was very young. Shem nodded, and the two men joined hands, heads bent close together, so that they could hear one another over the shouting orders, the pounding at the gate.

"Front ranks at charge!" Captain Truman said. "Gunners lock!"

"What is the first mystery?" Shem asked.

"The first mystery is love," Harn said. "Love is a bridge, an open gate, a free city. Love is the last summerflower in a burned field. Love is a warm hand on a cheek gone cold."

The stone screamed, and the gate splintered and snapped at last, sundered into pieces on the tower floor. The first darkstone roared through, bent nearly double, just small enough to fit. A ribbon of flame took it in the face, and it went down gurgling, trampled over by the next in line. Captain Truman shouted another command, and the rest of the guns opened up, spraying death on the Nightmare below. The pikemen stood patiently on the top of the ramp's first landing, weapons pointed forward, ready to take the first enemy to break through the fire wall. They would almost certainly break through.

"Love is a fire softly flickering," Shem said.

"Love is a candle's light in the darkness," Harn said.

"Love is a spark on a bed of dry grass."

Fires burned the darkstones as they came, and soon the air was swirling with ash. In the confined air of the tower, the heat built quickly, and the cold strained and cracked, loosening its grip, becoming the chill of winter rather than death. A few shrieks slipped through the gateway and flew like arrows at the gunners, claws reaching. But the crossbowmen were waiting for them, weapons cocked. They filled the creatures with bolts, dropping them to the ground, where they were trampled underfoot. The stones surrounding the gate were soon ripped out by huge manacled hands, widening the entrance, and the Nightmare increased from a trickle to a steady stream, darkstones rolling through in twos and threes, snarling and slobbering in their black armor, dying in the flames.

Shem and Harn fell into an easy back and forth, repeating the mysteries they had learned from years of training, the truths said so often they had become something like a song, the rhythm of a mother's croon to her child, the tuneless melody of love.

"Love is a river that always flows."

"Love is a well that never runs dry."

"Love is rain on the withered leaf."

The first darkstone broke through the fire wall, charging up the ramp with a massive hammer raised above its head. Captain Truman cried havoc and the pikemen rushed forward, ranks tight and straight. Halfway down the ramp they crashed together, and five steel points took the stone at once, in the neck and chest and frozen face. The sixth man missed his mark, striking the shoulder an inch or two higher than he should have, his pike turned to the side. The hammer came down, and the man died. Another stepped into his place.

"Love is a shield against the flying arrow."

"Love is an arm raised to block the blow."

"Love is a child held above the flood."

The gunners had stopped aiming. They pumped flames into the doorway as steadily as they could, sure of hitting a target, any target. The mossy white ice was melting off the walls, running in steady streams to the floor, where it mixed with the ash to form a kind of dark paste. Stone's blood, men called it. Captain Truman belted out the location of shrieks to the crossbowmen, who fired as fast as they could reload now. Some had drawn swords; they hacked at the shrieks like they were cutting tree branches, forming small rings around each gunner to keep the raking talons at bay. The gunners had to stay alive for as long as possible; their fire was all that kept the Nightmare from ripping through the pikes like linen. A few were pale and bleeding, gashes on their legs and guts, their protectors holding them upright so that they could see their foe. Until they bled to death, anyway.

Shem was calm as he helped Harn into position. There would be shrieks up in the nest soon, and they would both need to be ready before that happened. The younger man's face was both afraid and strong. The crucible was a swinging gate, and so Harn stood upright instead of lying down, legs together, arms held out to the sides, like an arrow pointing toward the heavens. They spoke the words in unison.

"Love is a head bowed low and humble."

"Love is a moment spent in silence together."

"Love is a kiss on a tear-stained face."

Shem moved the lamb spikes into position. Two thick nails for the bare creases of Harn's elbows, two smaller, needle-like spikes for his eyes. Harn himself held the triggering lever in his right hand. Shem saluted, still whispering the mysteries, and turned away from Harn for the last time.

Men died below him. And as men died, the Nightmare waxed ever stronger. Darkstones passed through the wall of fire with little more than a snarl, and the pikemen began to retreat up the ramp, giving ground slowly, bloodily, pikes stabbing and thrusting, white and gold flowers straining to hold back a flood of tar.

Then suddenly the front ranks of the Nightmare collapsed. Shem saw half-a-dozen darkstones stumble back, a few missing arms and legs. And after them came the General, sword a blur, moving faster than Shem would have thought possible. Two horrors snaked forward, knives reaching, and Jair split between then, dropping low while his blade spun high in a short arc above his head. The horrors fell back, clutching their ruined throats, and he was on to the next foe, fighting alone on the the ramp, keeping the Nightmare at bay by the strength of his arm.

There was a rush of wings and blackness, and then claws reaching out for Shem's throat. He stumbled and nearly fell, throwing his arm up to block the blow. He felt a hot line of pain rip across his face, and then he was screaming and hacking, using the sword like a club, smashing the shriek to the ground. *Stupid old man,* Shem thought. Watching the fight below instead of protecting Harn's back, like he was supposed to. When the next shriek came over the edge of the nest, Shem was ready, and skewered it with one thrust. He continued to whisper the mysteries, blood pouring down his cheek, and heard Harn doing the same behind him.

"Love is a brother welcomed home."

"Love is a meal joyfully given."

"Love is faith in love itself."

The General had given the pikemen the respite they needed, and they had closed ranks again, winning back some of the ground they lost. But many of the gunners were down, and the Nightmare continued to pour through the rent gate, bringing more of the storm inside. The General was still fighting, but it was defensive now, desperate, cutting down the enemies who slipped through the pikes, a frantic movement from one foe to the other, impossible to keep up. Captain Truman looked up, and Shem crossed his hands over his chest. Ready.

"Love is one life laid down for another."

The captain swung his hammer against the bell, and its sound rose pure and sweet over the screams of men, killing and dying. Behind him, Shem heard Harn take a deep breath.

Then he heard the sound of the lever being pulled, the squeak of the gate swinging shut, and the soft thud of spikes sinking into flesh.

The world went white.

Jair heard the sound of the lamb bell echoing off the tower walls and growled in frustration. It was too soon. They could have held out a little longer, another ten minutes at least. A milidread leapt at him, poison sting reaching for his throat, and Jair skewered it on the point of his sword. He flung it off contemptuously. They needed to find a better way to deal with the nasty things. Too many men had their eyes up, focusing on the massive darkstones and the shrieks, while the little milidreads slipped under their feet and stuck them full of venom. Perhaps the third rank could take their pikes low, keep the creatures off. They'd need to widen ranks a little to give them line of sight, but—

His thoughts cut off as the crucible activated above. The stones of the tower turned brilliant white, and there was a sudden cessation of noise. The sounds of the Nightmare disappeared completely, the storm outside was driven back. Darkstones fell dead to the floor without a word; the horrors disintegrated into dust. Jair held his shield above his head as the shrieks came tumbling down like black hail. And as warm air flooded back into the tower, there were only the sounds of his men, panting with exhaustion, crying out with pain.

Jair sheathed his sword and slung his shield over his back. "Captain Truman, get them moving out," Jair called out.

"Captain's dead sir," said another voice. It was a tall, dark haired sergeant that spoke. He looked vaguely familiar, but Jair didn't know his name. "Blood knife caught him right before the crucible activated."

"Ior take him graciously to the Heights," Jair said. "Whose command is it now?"

"Mine, sire," the man said. "Sergeant Claybrook, sir."

Claybrook? Jair thought. He realized now why he looked familiar. He was the older, rougher version of his son. Jair seemed destined to meet the whole house.

"Very well, Sergeant," Jair said. "Get the wounded on whatever stretchers you have and get the men moving. Triple time on the march, you hear?"

"Yes sir," Claybrook said, saluting.

Jair headed up to the stairs at the top of the ramp, passing a few gunners and crossbowmen on their way down. He counted half-a-dozen who were on their feet and able-bodied, the others were either bleeding from injuries or waiting silently for him at the top of the ramp. Jair climbed to the highest port and flung open the hatch, looking out on the south pass. The light of the tower illuminated the bodies of hundreds of darkstones, lying dead within steps of the gate, a wyrm in their midst. They were laid out in marching ranks, with no sign of injury, all felled by the power of the crucible. So the Captain had made the right call after all, timing the bell perfectly to take out a whole battalion. Jair wondered whether they might be able to do that every time. A single man at a discrete observation point perhaps. They could signal the approach of a new wave of troops, let the Captains know whether to hold out for a little longer or release the magic. He'd have to talk to Captain Fane at Ninety-Five and see what was available.

The rest of the pass was littered with more dead, a stretch of road that wound a quarter mile south before rounding a spur that dropped away to the now overrun Ninety-Seventh. Jair knew the rest of the Nightmare was just behind that spur, waiting for the light of the tower to go out.

It was time to leave.

As he turned to go, another man's feet appeared on a ladder above him, the lamb's second, climbing down. Jair gave him hand with his sword, which had gotten caught on the ladder.

"Thank you, sir," the second said. He was an older man, short and brown and wrinkled, long past retirement. A long, thin scratch ran across his forehead, dripping blood slowly down his face. "How many did we get, sir?" the man asked.

"A few hundred with the crucible," Jair said, moving swiftly down the stairs. It was surreal to see them so bright, as if lit from within. He wondered if he would ever get used to it. "Probably killed twice that with the rest."

"I got three up in the nest," the old man said, following close behind.

"Harn will hold for a good long while, I think. He's got a good heart."

"Harn Floramel?" Jair said, surprised. This tower was full of ghosts, it seemed.

"You know him, sir?" the man said.

"He served as my squire for a day," Jair said. "How did you come to be his second? You must have retired twenty years ago."

"A mere fifteen," the man said, smiling ruefully. "Captain Truman was kind enough to take me in. Their second had gone missing, and, well, I challenged him to a sabre duel, sir, to prove I was up for the job. Rather foolish of me, I know, but…I have some strength left."

"You protected your lamb," Jair told him. "That is all the guard could ask from you." They had reached the ramp. Most of the men were gone already, marching for the Ninety-Fifth, but a few remained behind with Sergeant Claybrook, gathering the silver pins of the fallen for their families back home.

"What's the count?" Jair asked the sergeant.

"Fifty-two dead, another twenty or so wounded," Claybrook answered. "Most of those look to live, I think."

"Very well," Jair said. "Let us finish quickly and go."

Two minutes later, they slung two remaining wounded men among them and left the Ninety-Sixth to the dead, all but Harn Floramel, whose life was still shining with splendorous light. The pass rose steeply here, climbing up some five hundred feet in a series of switchbacks, twisting along a spiny ridge that crumbled away into cliffs on either side. When they reached the top of the ridge, Jair stopped.

"Take your men ahead," he told Sergeant Claybrook. "I want to see how quickly they can move through a tower once the crucible fails. I need to get a sense of the timing here. I don't want to get caught with a squadron on the pass." Any battle on the slopes would be disastrous, especially with the storm raging around them.

Claybrook hesitated. "You shouldn't be here by yourself, General," he said. "What if they send shrieks—"

"I'll stay with him, Sergeant," said the old second lamb. "I'm not much good carrying injured men up the slopes, but I can fight with a sword well enough."

"That'll do," Jair said, before Claybrook could offer him more men. "Get to it, Sergeant."

Claybrook looked like he wanted to insist, but he read the look on Jair's face and turned without another word. Jair turned to face the Ninety-Sixth below, as the sound of their booted feet and tinkling armor faded behind him.

"What's your name?" he asked the old man.

"Shem Haeland, sir," he said.

"Well met, Shem Haeland," Jair said. He looked Shem up and down. He was small, and wrinkled, but there seemed to be strength in his shoulders, and he did not seem afraid. "How good are you with that sword?" Jair asked.

"Better than most," Shem said. He did not sound boastful. "I reached the finals of the sabre at the games this year, before the bells rang, though it was a near thing. Tomos would have beaten me, I think."

"The Defender's guard?" Jair asked, surprised. "He's the finest swordsmen in the city."

"Begging your pardon, sir," Shem said. "But that's you."

Jair shrugged. He had never crossed blades with Tomos, though he had seen him spar often enough. The matches rarely lasted more than a few minutes. If this Shem was really near his equal...

"I have something rather foolish in mind," Jair said. "It seems the Nightmare sends four or so horrors in advance of the main force whenever a tower falls to take out stragglers. They caught a few of us after Ninety-Nine fell."

"Four is it?" Shem said. He looked around, examining the terrain. "Might be a good place to teach them some caution you think?"

"Good man," Jair said. "Every man is a tower that stands in a narrow pass. You see that col below us, where the pass splits around that old rockfall? I'll take the bottom leg, where the path is a little wider. You take the high trail, and make sure nothing swings around behind me. Fall back if you can't handle it, and give a shout. I'll be close behind."

"Yes, sir," Shem said. "I'm your—"

His last word faded as the light below them winked out. The tower was down.

"Love is one life laid down for another," Jair said quietly, putting fist to heart. It was the traditional salute to the lambs, when they finally died. Harn had done well.

"Come, let us go," Jair said, after a moment of silence. "The advance force will be coming swiftly."

They started down the slope, stepping carefully in the darkness of the night. Jair's internal clock told him it was around midnight, a spare four hours since the Nightmare began. Four towers in four hours. There had been worse starts to a Defense before, but not many. Jair thought again of Cairn Jarth and Cairn Creta, gone forever, destroyed by the relentless might of Tjabo's dark army after nearly two thousand years. *That will not happen to my city*, Jair thought. *Come Nightmare, and you will not find me easy prey.* When they reached the split in the trail, Shem saluted and stalked up the higher pass, vanishing out of sight in moments. There was little chance the horrors would try the upper pass first. It was narrower and far more difficult, rocky and unstable. They would try to swing round the lower pass instead, looking for the wounded or stragglers.

Jair could see the Nightmare flooding around the turn below Ninety-Six, the lightning of the storm illuminating the mass of creatures. They came forward slowly but inexorably, a black glacier crawling its way up the mountain side. Jair wondered whether he was doing the right thing. There had only been four horrors last time, yes, but what if they sent ten this time, or twenty? Jair would still be able to see them before they reached the split. He could whistle Shem down and take them back up the slope. Shem looked like he was swift enough to make it to the shelter of Ninety-Five's gunners. He would have to—

Jair heard something behind him, the sound of multiple sets of boots on stone. He turned, wondering how a force could possibly have slipped behind them, when a small group of men emerged from the darkness, carrying a pair of shuttered lanterns.

"Ridi," Jair said, surprised. "What are you doing here?"

"Well met, General," Ridi said. The castellan had brought four others with him, their hoods raised against the coming storm. "Sergeant Claybrook said you stayed behind to observe, and I feared you were going to do something foolish. I see I was correct."

"Just teaching the Nightmare a little caution," Jair said, smiling. "Come, your swords will be welcome. I sent Shem up the high split. He could use some help."

Ridi nodded and dispatched two of the others to support Shem. "You'll wear yourself to the bone fighting like this," Ridi cautioned. The same nervousness that Jair had seen earlier was back. "The men would be devastated if you were lost."

"I'm feeling strong yet," Jair said. "The men need me to fight. The Nightmare is…proving stronger than I had hoped." The storm clouds had reached Ninety-Six, and Jair could see the tide of black break around the tower like water round a stone in a stream bed. The cold was already beginning to return in advance of them.

"At least take some summerflower wine," Ridi said, offering him a leather bottle. "Fortify yourself a bit."

Jair sighed and took the bottle. Ridi could be like an old aunt sometimes. The wine was sweet and well chilled, tasting of apples. He thanked Ridi and handed it back.

"You'd best fall back a bit now, Ridi," Jair said. "The horrors will be here shortly, I think." Ridi was no fighter, and Jair suspected he would be more at ease toward the rear of the line.

"Of course, sir," he said, "As long as you're feeling alright."

"I feel strong," Jair said. The cold was coming back with a vengeance. It seemed to move ahead of the Nightmare much more rapidly than any of its minions. Jair suppressed a shiver.

"Are you sure?" Ridi asked. "You look pale, sir."

"I'm fine," Jair said. The cold seemed to be inside him; the chill of the summerflower wine had turned his guts to ice. He looked down slope again, scanning the path for a sign of movement, but his eyes didn't seem to want to focus properly. Purple splotches kept marring his vision. Jair shook his head to clear it, but the action made him dizzy, and he put a hand on one of the tumble stones to steady himself. It was ice cold.

"Sir?" Ridi said, opening the lantern a bit more to look at him in the light. "Is everything alright?"

"Cold…" Jair muttered. "Why is…that wine of yours. Making me cold."

"Ah…" Ridi said, putting a hand on Jair's shoulder. "Sorry about that, General."

Jair felt Ridi push him to the ground, and he fell heavily, knees banging on the hard stone. The world was twisting and fading strangely. Everything was cold. So cold. And as consciousness slipped away, he realized something was horribly wrong.

Shem waited at the head of the upper trail, sword in one hand, shield strapped to his forearm. He gave thanks for his weapons, and for the strength of the General protecting the path below. He had chosen a spot with large rocks to either side, the narrowest point he had found, and the best ground. The footing on this ridge was treacherous, and he had never fought a horror before. There were training exercises in the guard, of course, bouts where the best knife fighters would go up against the others, and one touch with the knife was enough to lose the bout. Shem had never been touched. The reach of the knife was too short to be effective against a careful opponent. Still, if there was more than one of them, he'd likely have to go on the offensive. They were quick and deadly creatures, likely better than the knife fighters had been. The practice bouts had always had an air of relaxation about them. Most of the participants never expected to meet a real horror, after all.

He heard the sound of boots behind him, and he turned swiftly, backing up against the narrow west wall of the mountainside. Had they slipped by the General already?

But it was two men, dressed in the uniform of the guard. One carried a shuttered lantern, and both carried drawn swords.

"Hail, men of the guard," Shem said, stepping back out onto the path where they could see him. "Where did you come from?"

"Ridi Greenvallem brought us down, looking for the general," the one with the lantern said. "He sent us up here for you."

"Glad to have some support," Shem said. "I'll take point if you—"

He barely got his shield up in time, blocking a blow that would have taken off his head. The man with the lantern swore and struck again, sharp point digging for Shem's unprotected elbow. Acting on instinct, Shem slipped forward, right into the man's chest, letting the point slip past him. He slammed his shield upwards and heard his opponent cry out as his nose crunched under the steel blow. Then Shem was spinning, dropping low and turning to face the second man.

Treachery. The thought floated across Shem's mind like scum on a pond. *What in Ior's name could have possessed them...* He had no time to think about it. The two men were coming forward again, the second bleeding profusely from his swollen and broken nose. They moved to opposite sides of him, as wide as the path would go, trying to force him to turn and expose himself on one side. Shem backed slowly, feinting to both sides, watching their approach. They were both tall men, but not particularly big, perhaps if he could get them close to the edge of the path...

With a sudden movement, the man with the broken nose stepped and flung the lantern at Shem's face. Shem raised his shield to block it, then realized his mistake.

A moment too late. The lantern shattered on impact, spraying oil over Shem's shield and clothes. The flame caught the fine spray and flared up, fire burning on his shield, clawing at his face. Shem flung the shield away immediately to keep the fire from spreading, and then the two men were on him, hacking at his exposed body. He retreated rapidly, giving up the high ground, his sword a blur, raking back and forth to turn his opponents' blades. They were average swordsmen at best, but there were two of them, and one had a shield. Shem soon found himself fighting desperately just to keep from getting skewered. He had to do something different, and he had to do it quickly.

Shem charged.

The tactic took the two men completely by surprise, and Shem split between them. He swung at the man with no shield with a wide, arcing blow, a poor strike under normal circumstances, but it had the desired effect. The man jumped backward to avoid the overreach, and Shem pivoted and followed close behind, digging a shoulder into the man's chest. His momentum carried him back...and over the edge of the path. The man dropped out of sight, falling down to the rocks below.

Shem slipped to the left, and felt the wind of the second man's blade pass by his ear. He thanked Ior for guessing right. And turned to face the man, sword flashing...

...and a rotten stone dropped out from underneath his foot.

Shem felt himself falling, his feet clawing at a ground that slowly tilted away from him. A shower of rocks fell with him, and there was an endless moment of weightlessness as he drifted through the thin air.

Then something rose up and hit him in the back, and Shem knew no more.

CHAPTER THIRTY

The Cold Deepens

Ridi hurried toward Ninety-Five as fast as he could. His three remaining men struggled along behind him, carrying a shrouded body. Ridi was sweating profusely. They were approaching the most dangerous part of the game, now, where one stray glance could get them all killed.

"Remember the plan," Ridi said to his men for what felt like the hundredth time. "I talk; you carry. Get the body to the carts at once, and start for the Low Tower as soon as you can."

They grunted acknowledgment. They knew the plan as well as he did. Ridi was glad that Shem fellow had managed to kill one of them, so Ridi didn't have to. It wouldn't have looked right coming back with the same four men and an extra body. He'd have needed to kill one of them for the story to be believable. Killing was always so unpleasant, so uncontrolled. People did surprising things when they were about to die. Ridi hated surprises.

The lookout on Ninety-Five hailed them, and Ridi called back, telling them to open the gates. Captain Fane met them in the gatehouse, his shock of white hair squashed beneath a short half-helm. "What happened?" Fane asked, seeing the shrouded body. "Where's the General?"

"It was as I feared, Captain," Ridi said. The words came out in a rush, and Ridi forced himself to slow down. He had practiced the speech so many times in his head, it was difficult to make the words seem natural. "Jair had stayed behind to fight some of the advance scouts on his own. We thought there were likely to be no more than four, but we found twenty instead, horrors all."

"*Twenty,*" Fane said, looking worried. "Against seven?"

"We fought them off, sir," Ridi said. "The General is worth ten men by himself. I'm afraid poor Alwyn didn't make it though," Ridi said, looking at the body sorrowfully. That wasn't his real name. Ridi had forgotten his real name. "Jair sent us on ahead. He and the second lamb from Ninety-Six, Shem I think his name is, are delaying the remaining horrors. They should be along shortly, sir."

He waved to the men to carry the body through, and they trotted by, two at the General's head, the other at his feet.

"How close is the bulk of the Nightmare behind them?" Fane asked.

"Still a half-mile off at least," Ridi said. "It's slow going for a large army over the ridge line."

"I'll dispatch a squad to help them," Fane said.

"A wise decision," Ridi said. "The General takes too much upon himself. Is the injured and deceased wain ready to go?"

"Aye, all loaded. Your man Alwyn will be the last," Fane said. "You'll be taking them yourself, then?"

"I'm no fighter, Captain," Ridi said, meaning it. "I can be of more use with the wounded. And I want to get them out of here before the storm hits."

"Go, and Ior bless you," Fane said, and he began to shout for the twelfth squadron to form up for a sortie.

Ridi hurried away, wiping sweat surreptitiously from his brow. He pushed down the sickness boiling in his stomach. The wain was waiting for him outside, two carts of injured and one of corpses, the few they had spare hands to carry out. The General was on the top of the corpse cart. One pale hand had slipped free of the shawl. It made Ridi shiver, but the thought of trying to tuck it back in to the shroud was more than he could stand. Ridi climbed aboard the driver's seat and signaled to the other carts to follow. It was a long journey back to the city, with a dark room waiting for him at the end of it. He was very aware of the pale hand behind him, and scooted as far forward on the seat as he could manage.

Ridi heard a distant boom of approaching thunder. He snapped the goats' reins, and did not look back.

The trio of wagons moved more swiftly than a man could travel on foot, pulled along by teams of four goats each, massive pack animals with broad shoulders and strong backs, animals who had made this journey their whole lives, animals who knew the path as well in the dark as in the light. The sound of thunder and war faded away, and only the occasional moan from an injured man interrupted the steady clip-clop of the goat's feet. Every mile or so they were hailed by another tower, but Ridi had all the proper seals and keys, knew all the pass codes and half the watchmen besides. And who would want to slow a wagon of wounded men, when speed was of the essence for many of them? They stopped only for a brief moment to rest the goats, a few quick words to some of the soldiers who wandered near, wondering how the battle was going ahead, scanning the cart of dead men for familiar faces.

And when the carts moved on, their came a whispering, whispering, of a rumor, that Jair Thorndike was missing. That he was dead. Or worse, that he had abandoned them. And the Captains were keeping it quiet, for fear of the men losing heart. Where this rumor started, or what information it was based on, none knew, and in truth many of the men scoffed and thought it nonsense. But it stayed in the back of their minds anyway, in the darkest places where men thought the worst of others and the best of themselves. And every man in the tower stood a little closer to the braziers, as if to fight off a sudden chill.

And so the wagons moved on, all through the night. And the dawn brought bad news, and the threat of storms.

Incense filled the council room in the House of Salt. Willow couldn't decide if it was a pleasant smell or not. It tickled the back of her throat and made her want to cough, but there was something relaxing about it too, and something powerful. Tarius tended the flame with care, adding a pinch of one spice, a slow handful of the next, whispering back and forth with the Dreamer. She was a small woman, the Dreamer, with thick, dark hair and pale, hazel eyes, wrapped in a purple robe a few sizes too big for her, with baggy sleeves that seemed always in danger of catching fire from the burning incense. Her name was Milena.

Willow turned to ask Ridi what the incense was for, but there was no one behind her except Jair's silent guards. Ridi hadn't been with her since last night, when they had left him with Jair. It was strange not to have him around, and Willow was surprised to find that she missed him. Willow knew he had returned earlier that morning, riding at the head of wagons full of the dead and dying, and was taking care of them in the Low Tower. The news had followed closely behind him, carried by a harried looking messenger on a weary mount.

Jair was missing.

Somewhere on the path between Ninety-Six and Ninety-Five, he had simply disappeared, along with some common soldier from Ninety-Six, a man by the name of Shem. Bryndon knew him, though Willow soon found that was not unusual. The castellan of House Haeland was well known, and all agreed he was a good swordsman, a kind Master, and the best of men. A sortie by Captain Fane had found no bodies, either on the path or on the slopes below, though in the dark of night, they could not see very far down. Nor had they found traces of any enemy, living or dead, though they had not been able to search long, having to flee ahead of the approaching Nightmare. Ninety-Five had held out a long time, almost three hours, hoping that the General would somehow appear, would find a way to sneak or cut through the Nightmare and rejoin his brothers. But finally, exhausted and facing total annihilation, Captain Fane had activated the crucible, and Ninety-Five had been abandoned. And now with every tower that became overrun, hope faded, and the whispers of Jair's death began to grow louder.

Within hours of the news, a messenger from the High Tower was knocking on the door of House Claybrook, calling for a meeting of the council in the House of Salt. When Willow and Bryndon arrived, the others were already present, Jair's seat conspicuously empty, and Milena seated before them, the slender form of Tarius Moonlight beside her, lighting the incense. A few servants and guards stood in the council room as well, but otherwise the meeting was closed, open only to the Seven. Bryndon was one of the few exceptions, waiting silently in the corner. Willow was glad that he was there.

Praeses stood, calling the meeting to order, a haggard look on his white-bearded face. "A meeting of the Seven has been called, yet there are only six here," Praeses said. "We have reports from Captain Fane of the Ninety-Fifth that General Jair Thorndike has gone missing, lost somewhere on the southern pass. Many fear him dead."

"A grievous loss for the Tower Guard, if true," The Clock said.

"If true," Praeses repeated. "It is a grievous loss for us all." For a moment, Willow could see the pain hiding behind Praeses's stern eyes, Praeses the father, the man who had raised Jair Thorndike like his own son. But only for a moment. Then it was gone, and only the High Defender remained.

"Yet the Nightmare stands between us and learning the truth of this news," the Defender continued, voice hardening. "We have need of Ior's eyes, that see all and know all from the Insurmountable Heights. Tarius, can the House of Moonlight help us?"

"We see only what Ior gives us to see," Tarius said, sadness cracking the normal misty quality of his voice. There seemed to be more lines on his face than Willow remembered. "But Milena is our most powerful Dreamer. If there is a truth that Ior is willing to give us, she will see it."

"Very well," Praeses said. "Begin."

Milena curtsied to the council and sat cross legged on the stone floor, resting her hands in her lap. Softly, slowly, she began to chant, a rhythmic sing-song that seemed to come from a great distance, as if her voice was producing only an echo of an echo. Tarius began to chant back to her in reply, the same song in a different key, and soon their voices had merged into one. The harsh note of the incense faded away, and it smelled to Willow like the tall cedars of her home, the rolling forests of Pratum after a rain, when the leaves muttered softly underfoot, and the breeze from the mountains blew clear and clean through the tree trunks, carrying the chill of spring snow and the promise of warm bread waiting on the hearth.

"The dream is dark." Milena's voice came floating out in a rich alto, and Willow realized with a start that she had fallen asleep. She sat up, blinking, and saw Pilio rubbing his eyes, as well, Bryndon slumping against the wall, Oded leaning back in his chair. Only Tarius, Praeses, and The Clock seemed fully awake, Tarius continuing to chant, feeding a few more spices into the flames.

"It is a clear dream," Milena said, her eyes still closed. "But what it shows me clearly is darkness, an impenetrable black, as if all light has been sucked from the world."

"Is the General alive?" Tarius asked. "Is it the blackness of death?"

Milena didn't answer, continuing to breathe deeply. Willow fought to keep her own eyes open. She couldn't shake the smell of cedars, the feeling of home. Whatever magic this was, it seemed to want to drag her down into sleep. She jerked her head up from the table. *He must be alive*, she thought. And then, for the first time in her life, *Ior send that he is alive*.

"He is not dead," Milena said, and it was as if a giant breath had been let out of the room. There was hope yet.

"He is not dead?" The Clock demanded, his voice harsh. "You are certain of this? Jair Thorndike is alive?"

"He is not dead," Milena repeated, running her fingers absently through her hair. "Though he is not yet alive. He hovers on the border between death and life, the valley and the Heights. He does not move or speak, he does not think or feel. He breathes, and his heart beats. I can hear it, like a pounding drum in the darkness."

"Where is he?" Tarius asked, his voice much gentler than The Clock's. He shot the gray-cloaked man a look, as if to silence him from asking any further questions. It was the most confrontational Willow had ever seen Tarius.

"In the darkness," Milena said again. Then she frowned, and Willow could see her eyelids twitching. "I do not want to see..." she said. Her hands flexed and pain rippled across her face, and soon she was twitching uncontrollably, her fingers wrapped in her hair.

"Tarius..." Willow said, worried.

"The dream will not let her go," Tarius said, raising a hand. "She will be alright. Milena, what do you see?"

There was a long pause, and then she whispered a single word.

"Masks."

Ridi sat on the stairs, huffing for air, eyes bleary and exhausted. Every part of him hurt, his legs and arms and back, all of them sore from the long night spent sitting in the hard wagon seat and on fire from the work of hauling Jair's body through the inner passages of the Low Tower. He had trusted his men only so far as to get Jair to a safe place inside the tower, away from any prying eyes. But he was determined to haul the body up himself, that only he might know where it was. And now he was wishing that he had brought them along, and just killed them afterward instead. Not that he likely could have managed. They weren't apt to drink from his wine bottle anytime soon.

He wanted to cry. The shroud had slipped free a little more during his climb up the stairs, and the tip of Jair's nose was poking out. It was worse than the hand. Ridi thought for sure that every once in a while the nostrils twitched with breath, that Jair was just playing with him, that very soon he would sit up, and wrap his pale hand around Ridi's throat, and then he would squeeze...

"You great stupid bastard!" Ridi screamed. He stood and kicked the body as hard as he could, then did it again for good measure. "You damnable, shameful—"

His voice cut out with a strangled moan. The hand had moved.

But it was just dislodged from the kick, and it dropped slowly to the stairs with a soft thud. Ridi almost cried with relief, then realized he had been screaming at the top of his lungs. Sound traveled poorly in the muffled, close quarters of the Low Tower, but still—it was a foolish thing to do. Any man who saw him now would want to know what he was doing dragging a body up the staircase, far from the temporary mortuary that had been set up on the ground floor.

In a sudden panic, Ridi seized Jair by the boots and began to drag him up the stair again, his head bumping softly on each step. Soon he had left the candles behind, and darkness enveloped them. He had to use two hands to handle the body, so he carried no lantern, and moved through pitch black. All those years of meeting Jair in the morning, of walking through the dark until he knew it as well as the General—and now he was carrying his body through that same darkness. It was almost enough to make Ridi laugh. It was more than enough to make him cry.

But he had promises to keep. The Whip was not kind to people who disappointed her. Ridi shivered at the thought of what she had done to him when the Willow woman had showed up without his knowledge. The shiver was half pleasure and half pain. He knew there would be far less pleasure if he failed her this time.

Grunting with effort, he pulled the last few feet up the stairs, and started down the hallway, his calves burning as he shuffled backwards. He felt the wall with his foot, kicking it until he felt the softer resistance of wood. Then he pulled the latch down, cursed his weak body under his breath, and finally, mercifully, hauled Jair the last few feet in, and dropped him to the floor. Into the one place that no one would think to find the missing General—

His own room.

Shem woke, shivering. Every part of him hurt, especially his head, which felt like someone was beating it from the inside with a hammer. It was hard to think.

He should be dead. He knew he was not dead. The tiny hammer told him he was not dead.

He saw again the second man coming toward him, sword raised. Felt the stone slip out from under him. The moment of mindless panic as he fell. And then...

He should be dead.

It was difficult to think.

He groaned and tried moving his arms. His legs. They seemed to work. Why was it so cold?

He tried opening his eyes, but they did not seem to move. Slowly, he worked his hand up to his face. It felt like he was dragging it through mud. He fumbled at his eyes, pulling at the lids, until finally something gave way, and they snapped open.

The world was white. Snow was all he could see, deep and thick and shining with a thin veneer of ice. The light was unbearable, and Shem closed his eyes almost at once. A little knife joined the hammer inside his skull.

For awhile, all he could think about was the pain. Then he thought, *Thank Ior I am alive.* That seemed to help. He started thanking him for other things, his hands and feet that could move, his eyes that could open. The pain did not lessen, but the ritual helped a little, cleared a bit of the fog in his mind. Carefully, he opened his eye a tiny crack, and began to take stock of his surroundings.

He was lying on his back. He moved his hands all over his body, touching his ribs and chest, hips and shoulders. A thick layer of snow was mounded up over his right side, a small drift that the wind had piled up above him another three feet. His left side was pressed against a rock wall. He shifted, opened his eyes a bit more, and tried to sit up.

He should be dead.

He was lying on a small spur of rock, not three feet wide, that jutted out from the cliff face a mere ten to fifteen feet below the edge. He had fallen directly on top of it, and somehow Ior's hand had held him there, kept him from rolling off the edge. The mountains around him were covered in snow, dark, brooding hulks of stone wrapped in white, though the cliff face that he was perched on was largely blown clear. He put his hand down and felt something that was not rock, squishy and hard at the same time. He looked down, and saw dark, sightless eyes staring back up at him, a face that was frozen in a strange, bewildered expression.

He was lying on top of a dead man.

It was the first man who had attacked him. The man with the lantern. The one Shem had sent tumbling over the edge, right before he himself had slipped and fallen. His body must have cushioned Shem's fall. A double miracle then.

Shem tried to close the man's eyes, but they were frozen open. Tiny ice crystals clung to everything, and the wind moaned through the rocks. It was a stiff wind, cold and piercing. But it was a regular mountain wind, without the fury of a storm. Shem looked, and saw the sun hanging behind gray clouds, high in the southwestern sky. He had spent the whole night and most of the day on the mountainside. The Nightmare had come, and gone, and passed him by. And Shem realized that the whole might of Tjabo's army now stood between him and Meridia.

A few minutes later, he began to climb, thanking Ior for every painful step.

CHAPTER THIRTY ONE

The Masks Move

The House of Time rang second lauds, the eighth hour after midnight on the second day of the twenty-ninth Nightmare. The sun rose over the mountains as it always did, shining on the beautiful stone houses and their painted windows, the wives and mothers and Masters of Meridia, going about their morning business. But the light was dim, and the warmth of the spring was gone. The news from the towers was woe and horror, for the General had gone missing, and without him the Captains of the Guard struggled to hold the Nightmare at bay. Whispers spread from house to house, of lambs who refused to sacrifice themselves in the crucible, gunners turning their weapons on their own brothers, towers lost with all defenders. The High Defender himself had sent out word this morning, that he intended to take up command of the guard, and fight alongside the common soldiers. In solidarity with the soldiers, certain honorable, well known women of means had called for a general outpouring of prayer and supplication to Ior, to strengthen the High Defender and the men of the guard. And all throughout the city, columns of women gathered at the ringing of the bell, dressed in robes of mourning, black and gray, with their hoods pulled low across their faces.

Across the city, the columns spread, winding through the cobblestone streets, singing a mournful dirge, a hymn to the sadness of wives and mothers, sisters and daughters.

Robin was asleep in House Claybrook. She tossed fitfully on her mat, muttering and whispering. She wanted to wake up. Every part of her that was aware of the dream wanted to wake up. Because it was not just a dream, it was the Nightmare. The Nightmare had come to Meridia. Not through the front gate, but through the hearts of its people. Robin slept on, watching the women wind their way through the streets, singing and hiding their faces beneath their hoods. Something horrible was about to happen. Something she did not want to see. But the dream held her in its grip, and would not let go.

Weaver Tarius walked through the House of Moonlight, apprehensive, hands clasped behind his back. It was usually a calming experience, the morning walk, something Tarius did to relax. The Dreamers were often awake at night and asleep during the day, so the halls were always quiet and peaceful, lit by the soft sunlight filtering through the clouded glass skylights and the silver candles that graced the walls.

But this morning the walk was unsettling. The Dreamers were in a frenzy of tears and terror of late, fearing to ask Ior for his dreams, fearing even to sleep on a regular basis. Many had gone to bed only hours before, and as he strode the halls, Tarius could hear the sounds of the women moaning and crying, their sleep fitful and frantic. He supposed he should have expected it. The Dreamers always took it terribly when the Nightmare came; the Book of Moonlight said so often. Death and destruction visited them every night, the dreams forcing their gaze onto the worst horrors of battle, sights not fit for hardened men, let alone women.

Tarius completed his circuit of the sleeping quarters and found himself wandering into the entry hall, where the servants had laid a fire in the hearth. Milena was sitting by the fire, holding a steaming mug of what smelled like cider in her hands. Tarius always thought she looked like a child, wrapped up in her too big robe, though she was old enough to have grown children of her own.

"Do you hear the singing?" Milena said when he entered, staring into the fire.

Tarius stopped and listened. Very faint, filtering through the stone walls, he could indeed hear it, a low song in a minor key.

"The mourning women," Tarius said. "I had not thought they would come to this part of the city."

"They come for us," Milena said. She was paler than usual, looking worn and drawn around the eyes. "Go and see."

Tarius went to the window. He threw open the shutters, and poked his head out, into the morning air. It was fresh and clean, and smelled of snow. Colder than he expected. A few gray clouds were gathering around the western slopes. The Nightmare must be affecting the city already.

He looked south, along Moon Street, and saw the head of the column of women just coming into view. There weren't very many in this group, only fifteen, perhaps, led by a tall, stately looking woman in a fine black robe. Her head was lowered, and her hood pulled up, so that her face was hidden, but her brown hair hung down in long braids in front of her, which swung from side to side as she walked.

"Do you see the flames?" Milena asked.

Tarius jumped. He had not heard her walk up behind him. "What flames?" he said, looking back at the fireplace. It looked like Milena had spilled her cider. There was a small puddle next to her chair. "The flames on the hearth, you mean?"

"In their *hands*," Milena said, looking at the women. The song was growing louder.

"In the hands of the praying women?" Tarius asked. The Dreamers would speak like this sometimes, as if staring at something just past the visible world. Tarius had learned from experience not to dismiss it as fancy. "Milena, what do you mean?"

She put a hand on his shoulder, gripping it as if she was about to fall. "The *flames*," she said. All of the color seemed to have drained from her face. "They're holding the flames in their hands."

Tarius felt something warm drip on his leg. "Milena?" he whispered. There was a puddle around their feet now, one that stretched back to the chair by the fire. "Good Ior, what have you done?"

"Not going to burn," Milena whispered, holding up her thin wrist, slick and red with her blood. "I'm sorry Tarius." She pointed out the window, where the women were singing, nearly right outside the House of Moonlight.

The House of Time rang terce.

And the tall woman with the long brown braids raised her head, and Tarius Moonlight locked eyes with her, a pair of shining eyes in the red face of a demon, and saw her horrible smile as she drew out a long, coiled whip from beneath her robe, crackling with blue lightning.

She snapped the whip at Tarius.

Shepherd Pilio signed another expense authorization and set it aside to dry, moving on to the next one. There was a stack on his desk three feet high, most of them the accumulation of the weeks before the Nightmare had arrived. The money was already spent and gone, but Pilio took the time to read them all anyway. More than a few merchants had tried to earn themselves a bit of extra coin by charging more for their products in the name of war. Pilio did not stand for that sort of thing in his city. And so here he was, going over bits of paper line by line, while miles away, men fought and died to keep the Nightmare at bay. He felt a fool, and he felt useless, and he did not know what else to do, except move on to the next line.

There was a knock on the door of his study.

"Enter," Pilio said, putting his quill down.

It was Cedrik, his eldest, every hair on his head perfectly in place, as always. "The mourning women are here," Cedrik said. "You wished to be notified."

"Thank you, Cedrik," Pilio said, pushing back from the desk. "I will say a few words of encouragement to them. The Seven must lead by example."

"Very good, father." Always serious, Cedrik. Pilio hoped he would meet a girl with a sense of humor soon, somebody that could give Pilio some laughing grandchildren. His son led the way, down the spiral staircase and through the council room, out onto the wide stone dais that stood at the top of the broad steps leading up to the House of Salt. The women stood in rows on the street below, perhaps twenty-five of them or so, hoods drawn up, singing "Meridia Takes the Heights." A sad song, for certain, a song about a woman facing her own death. Pilio put a hand on his son's shoulder and listened to them sing. He was a good lad, Cedrik.

The House of Time rang terce.

The women fell silent. Pilio stepped forward to thank them for their prayers and their support of the brave men of the Tower Guard. Then, as one, the women drew their hoods back, and raised their heads, and Pilio found himself staring at twenty-five masks of polished black, and one of bright green. The woman with the green mask pulled a silver mace from the belt beneath her robe, and it glowed a fiery red in her hand.

Pilio jumped in front of his son, and the flame took him in the back.

Oded woke. Early morning light filtered through his window. It was past time to be up, past time to be making his way to the Room of

Unshaming for his morning shift. Raul had been letting him sleep in, taking longer shifts himself, insisting that Oded get more rest. He was acting like a Wizard already, Raul. Oded supposed that was a good thing.

He sat up and dressed for the day, putting on a few simple clothes and splashing water on his face from the washbasin. He could hear the muffled sound of the House of Time, ringing terce. Far too late to still be abed. He took his walking stick from its place beside the door and hobbled out, stiff and tired. The wood clicked on the stone floor.

There was a dull, rolling thud of thunder.

Oded stopped, frowning. Hadn't the sunlight been coming through his window?

Down the hall, a small, blue moth came fluttering toward him. Oded held out his finger, but the moth passed by. There was another roll of thunder. And another. And then Oded was walking as fast as he could toward his room, as a river of blue crooks flew around him, thousands of the things, fleeing whatever was happening elsewhere in the House of Summerflower. And Oded could hear the sound of screams, coming from somewhere nearby.

He stumbled back into his room and slammed the door shut, a few crooks following him in, fluttering toward the window and the safety of the open skies. Oded knelt over a locked chest at the foot of his bed, sweeping aside a jumbled stack of scrolls and coins and broken quills. He fumbled at his neck for the key, and tried to fit it to the lock on the chest's lid, but his fingers were shaking too badly. He took a deep breath and tried again, finally feeling the silver key slide in. The lock was sticky from lack of use, and it squealed a little as the rust broke free. But it opened.

Oded flung a set of linens to the floor, digging for the bottom until he found them.

The knives were a twin set, made of black hilts, with blades of sharpened bone. He had taken them from a house master, almost fifty years ago now, a man who had been executed after his Unshaming. He picked them up, one in each hand, and as he did, the yellow blades began to glow with blue fire, and Oded felt a surge of raw energy and rage flow into him, the magic of the man's shame, still as strong as ever after all these years. He muttered the Prohibitions to himself, letting the familiar words calm the storm of emotion, mastering the flow. Long ago, Oded had learned that Ior would never grace him with his power, that he was a man undeserving of such gifts. He had no strength of body, no power to heal. But he was the Wizard of the House of Summerflower, and his house was under attack.

He thrust the knives forward, and a azure spear of flame flew forth from them, blasting his wall and blackening the stone with ash. He would use the weapons that Ior had given him.

Oded strode from the room, leaving his walking stick behind. Dozens of crooks still fluttered about in the hall, drifting through the air like bright blue snow flakes, and a massive column of ants scurried along the north wall, glossy black against the gray stone. The thunder echoed and boomed strangely, both inside and outside all at once, so Oded followed the sounds of screaming instead, and found himself heading toward the Room of Unshaming.

He passed into the interior halls. All of the candles were out here, and the only light came from the fire in his hands. He felt the wet crunch of beetles and other things beneath his boots. The air smelled burnt. He rounded the corner, and saw another light, a flickering white on the stone walls ahead, and felt hot air rush past him, and the boom of thunder. The rage of the knives burned through him, and Oded realized that he was running, somehow, and his old knees screamed inside him, and he burst round the corner and saw a man in a black cloak, with a black mask upon his face and a length of black wool wrapped around his fist, flinging lightning at a crumbling stone door. The man caught a glimpse of him and turned, but Oded did not stop. He rushed forward and plunged the bone daggers into the masked one's neck, and the fire flowed out of him and through the bone daggers and into the masked one, and when the man opened his mouth to scream, only flames came out. He dropped to the ground, blackened and smoking, and Oded found himself on his knees, shaking and sweating, his stomach boiling. The smell was horrible. He put an arm over his face to block it out.

"Wizard Oded!" a voice said. Oded looked up and saw Brother Raul, looking at him through the hole the masked one had blasted in the stone door. Raul threw open the latch and hurried to Oded's side, a look of concern on his kind face.

"Are you alright, Wizard?" Raul asked. Small bits of ash rested on his shoulders and forehead.

"Not at all," Oded said, coughing, as Raul lifted him to his feet. "What is happening?"

"We are under attack," Raul said. "I do not know who these people are, but they have many—"

There was a concussive shock, and Raul's last words were lost, along with the rest of the world.

Oded looked up at blue sky, broken with dark gray clouds, and realized that he was on his back, and that the roof was missing. He could hear nothing but silence, and a kind of buzzing, trembling pressure.

He sat up and saw the south wall was gone as well, blasted through, the brick jagged and broken, the ivy aflame, spilling out onto the green grass of Summerflower Hill. A handful of masked ones stood outside, perhaps twenty yards away, shame objects in hand. One of them pointed to another part of the wall, and as one they unleashed a blinding array of bolts. Oded felt the press of hot air from their passing, but heard nothing, and saw more of the wall crumble from the onslaught.

The power of the knives filled him, and Oded rose shakily to his feet. The group of masked ones did not see him, and twin arrows of blue fire took one in the head, blasting him to the ground. The others turned, and scattered, as more threads of fire ripped through them. Oded limped forward, pressing the attack. He caught a flash of movement out of the corner of his eye, and turned to see a pair of masked ones charging down the hallway at him, thick daggers in each of their hands, glowing with flame. Oded turned, but his foot rolled on a loose brick, and he fell, dropping his knives. The power in him vanished, and Oded felt nothing but crushing pain, in his knees and ears and back. The dagger-wielding masked ones pointed their weapons at him, and Oded knew that he was going to die, and the thought was a relief. And then Raul was standing in front of him, and the fire ripped through his chest like a sword. And as he fell, Oded felt a rush of tiny wings around him, a river of blue crooks, thousands upon thousands, and the crooks flowed and crashed into the masked ones, engulfing them, drowning them, the moths heedless of the tongues of fire. The masked ones fell and writhed on the ground, flinging fire indiscriminately, burning themselves. And then they were still, and the river of crooks moved on, flowing down the hallway and out of sight.

And the Wizard Oded held his dead Brother Raul in his old, wrinkled hands, and wept for his friend. And he wondered why he was still alive.

Praeses waited in the morning sunlight, his seven guardsmen standing behind, The Clock at his side. They stood on the broad grass field directly north of the High Tower, dotted with wildflowers. The city lay below them in the valley, its red and marble roofs glittering a little in the sunlight, the smoke from early morning cook fires rising lazily into the sky. Storm clouds were gathering above the West Gate, dark gray and moving slowly in the wind, and Praeses tried his best not to appear impatient.

They were losing the battle.

The messages from the front were universally bad. Too many men had been lost, too much blood spilled, and the Nightmare was getting stronger and stronger with every tower they destroyed. The last messenger this morning had reported the shame weapons were starting to become almost useless, their enemy breaking through the fire walls with ease. Only the General's pikes seemed to be holding well, especially in Towers that had a few red-petaled soldiers. And the crucibles, of course, they were doing their job.

But he was anxious to be away. The soldiers needed him and his guards; their powers would be of great use. But even more, they needed leadership. The Captains knew what they were about in their own towers, but no one was capable of seeing the larger battle unfold, and no one had the authority to command even if he did. It was time for Praeses to do his job. But he had promised The Clock that he would wait until the women had blessed him with their prayers and songs, and so here he was, drawn up with his guardsman in front of the High Tower, listening to fifty or so women sing "Meridia Takes the Heights." They were all kneeling, heads pressed to the ground, facing away from him toward the Insurmountable Heights, where Ior looked on.

Far across the city, the House of Time rang terce.

The women stood, and turned. And Praeses looked on as fifty masked faces looked back at him, fifty masked women in black and gray robes, and before him, a woman with a mask the color of emeralds, pulling forth a wide-bladed knife that glowed with a red flame, and letting forth a cry of triumph as she pointed the knife at Praeses, and an arrow of fire hurtled toward his chest...

...And the High Defender raised his hand, and the red arrow broke around him like water around a rock, leaving him unharmed, without so much as a speck of ash to mar the white of his cloak.

"Defender!" The Clock said, and behind him, Praeses heard the cries of his guardsmen and the sound of seven steel blades being drawn. "What—?"

A ball of flame flew toward The Clock, and this time Praeses did not bother to swat it aside. He just stepped in front of the Clock and let it hit him, and the fire flashed around his face and was gone, like nothing more than an illusion. The woman with the knife lowered her weapon, shock plain on her face.

"You fools," Praeses said. "You damn fools. What in Ior's name are you doing?"

"We are going to kill you," the green mask said. Another weapon glowed behind her, and another, and another, blue lightning and red fire, knives and clubs and strips of sheets, meat hooks and roasting spits, even a rolling pin—shame gripped by every hand.

"No, traitors," Praeses said. "You are all going to die."

Then the real battle began.

Willow rang out another cloth, soaked with blood, and plunged it back into the steaming water. It was a never ending task, the linens, keeping enough of them clean and dry to change the soldiers' dressings regularly. The mess hall was the largest room in the Low Tower, and nearly every inch of it was covered with injured men, the healers moving from soldier to soldier, tending their wounds. There were four other rooms in the Low Tower exactly like this one.

She had not expected to be playing nurse. Not playing, even, she *was* a nurse, though she had no training in healing. But one visit to Ridi in the Low Tower, and she had helped one of the healers carry a man to a new bed. Then the same healer had sent her for a fresh bunch of herbs right afterward and...well, soon enough she and Bryndon were scurrying around like everyone else, trying to keep up with the unending stream of injured and dying men. Most of them were being sent on to the House of Salt or other places in the city, but their wagons couldn't carry very many at a time, so they had to wait in the Low Tower until their turn came. Ridi seemed grateful for their help. The last couple days had taken a heavy toll on him; he looked thinner and bonier than normal, his eyes were bleary and dark, and he looked utterly strange without his papers.

Willow suspected that Jair's absence was hitting him hard. In spite of the Dreamer's assurance that he was alive, the search for the missing General had yielded nothing. Praeses assumed he was being held prisoner somewhere by the Nightmare, and Willow was inclined to agree. If that was the case, however, he was certainly behind enemy lines, and out of reach of any of their forces. Praeses kept most of that information to himself, but Willow could tell by the carts coming back that the battle was not going well. They couldn't hold the line, much less push the Nightmare back. Right now they were just focused on surviving.

She hung another rag on the line. Bryndon came up beside her, pulling some of the dry linens into a small basket. He looked as tired as she felt; somehow his hair had gotten impossibly tangled again.

"Healer Carys needs some more bandages," he said. "The gunner from Sixty-Five is soaking through them too fast." He paused, looking at her. "Are you alright?" he asked.

"Are you?" Willow replied. "Is anyone here? All this—" Willow gestured around the room. "This is horrible, Bryndon. I just wish there was something more I could do."

"I think—" Bryndon began, but whatever he thought, Willow would never know, because at that moment a loud crack of thunder boomed overhead.

"What was that?" Willow said.

There was another boom, and then another. They seemed very close, like the Low Tower had been plunged into the middle of a raging storm. Willow looked out the window, confused. The sun was still out, the skies mostly clear. The other healers looked as puzzled as her.

The thunder came again, and this time it didn't stop, rolling along with a continuous crack and rumble. She rushed outside with Bryndon, joining a small group of healers and other servants. The sky was blue and clear over the rough stone of the Low Tower, the wind mild, with a faint hint of cold. Yet the thunder continued to roll.

"Bryndon?" Willow said, looking at her Shield. He looked as confused as she was, and afraid. "Is this some kind of weird valley storm I don't know about?"

"There's no storm," he said. "Those are…That must be shame weapons. A *lot* of shame weapons."

"This close to the city?" Willow said. "But the Nightmare can't possibly have come this far yet."

"Look!" a healer cried. Willow turned and looked. He was pointing *north*.

Toward the High Tower.

It stood in the narrow pass a few hundred yards away, blocking their view of the city behind. White light sprang up around the base, popping flashes silhouetting the tower against a rising column of black smoke. Willow had never seen lightning in the full light of day, and the effect was strange, especially on the shadow of the High Tower, which flipped from north to south with eye-wrenching speed.

The High Tower was under attack.

"Ridi!" Willow called out. The castellan stood a bit away from the rest of them, looking at the lightning with a sickly expression. "How many soldiers are here in the Low Tower?"

"Two hundred and thirty-one at the moment," Ridi said, keeping his eyes on the High Tower. "Though there are a few more carts leaving for the city soon."

"No, I mean, able-bodied, fighting soldiers," Willow said. "How many of those do we have?"

"Thirty, Stranger Willow," Ridi said. "Normally there is more, but they were sent forward early in the battle, to fill vacancies in some of the other towers."

"Gather them up," Willow said. "Somebody is attacking the High Tower from the north, and we're going to find out who it is."

Willow waited long enough for fifteen of the thirty guards to join her before she set off, unable to stay still any longer. The lightning flashes were growing less frequent, and she feared that meant there were fewer targets left for the lightning to hit. She snagged a crossbow and a quiver full of bolts from the armory on her way out; Bryndon did the same. Hand weapons wouldn't be any use against an enemy with lightning bolts. And fire, too, if the smoke was an indication.

"Crossbows ready," Willow said. "And stay spread out. We don't want to all get taken out with one bolt. If you see someone try to shoot you, shoot them first."

They did as she said, obeying without question. *I guess being a Stranger comes in handy sometimes,* Willow thought. *Hopefully, I don't get us all killed.* It seemed highly likely that she would. She was no warrior, and there were only fifteen of them, seventeen counting herself and Bryndon, against who knew how many enemies.

They covered the ground to the High Tower quickly, moving at a near run. The gate was open and unguarded, a bad sign, but not surprising, given what was happening on the other side of the tower. Willow moved into the gatehouse cautiously, thunder pounding in her ears. A narrow tunnel wound beneath the tower to the other side, with numerous stairwells and ramps shooting off toward other places higher up. The tunnel was built to be a killing ground, the walls thick and set close together, murder holes spaced above them at regular intervals. Willow moved ahead, her gut a giant ball of ice, her hands gripping the crossbow. It was wide enough for two to walk abreast, so Bryndon stayed at her side. Willow had a moment to think about what his mother would do to her if she got her son killed, and then the thunder grew to deafening levels, and they burst out on the other side of the tower, and all other thought was driven from Willow's head.

The field in front of the High Tower was destroyed, ripped up in massive chunks from repeated lightning blasts, scorched and black and ashy from fires that burned everywhere. Black-cloaked bodies were strewn about the field, some moving feebly, most still as death. The battle had moved away from the northern gatehouse, and a clump of standing figures in black cloaks were about a hundred yards in front of Willow, turned away from her. Most of the lightning was coming from them, though Willow couldn't see what they were attacking.

Then she saw black-cloaked body rise twenty feet in the air, as if lifted by a giant hand. He hung for a moment, kicking feebly at the emptiness below him. And then whatever power was holding him reversed direction, slamming him to the ground with bone crushing force. A couple of men plunged into the right flank of the group, swords out, through the gap that the man's body had created in the group of black cloaks, and Willow recognized the uniforms of the Defender's guards. She expected the others to turn and burn them to cinder with fire or lightning, but instead they broke apart like a hornets' nest, scattering in all directions to get away. Then a small clump of black cloaks turned and sent a ball of flame at the guards that was the size of a small house, and Willow's breath caught as they were enveloped in fire.

But the guardsmen burst out a moment later, seemingly unharmed, and began chasing down those that had scattered, cutting them down with the sword.

Willow hurried forward, dropping into a small hole that had been blown out by a bolt of lightning, and waved to her men to do the same. This was no battle for them. Soon, it became clear that this was no battle at all.

It was a rout.

The black cloaks were losing, badly. Every half minute another of their members was sent flying through the air by some invisible force, smashed to the ground or slammed against the side of the High Tower and let to fall. Willow looked in vain to see where the blows were coming from. Then there was a break in the wall of bodies standing between them and the city, and Willow saw what was happening.

The High Defender was ripping the black cloaks apart.

He stood calmly in the midst of the storm, his white cloak thrown off, his golden breastplate flashing in the light of the fire and lightning being thrown at him in continuous waves. He knocked the magical attacks aside like they were flies, and whenever there was a slight lull, he thrust his hand forward, seized another black cloak in his invisible grip, and flung him away. Nearly twenty yards separated him from the black cloaks, and he made no contact with them. But it was as if the reach of his arm had been magically extended, and his blows crossed the gap between them easily.

"What is happening?" Willow said to Bryndon.

"The High Defender's power," Bryndon said, not taking his eyes off the battle. He seemed to be talking to himself more than Willow. "We never knew what it was."

Willow turned back and watched a black cloak smashed to the ground as if by a boulder, and another swatted through the air like a bug. He landed not five feet from where Willow crouched in the lightning hole, landing with a horrible snapping of bones.

"That one's a woman," Bryndon said, looking sick, and Willow saw that he was right. The figure's hood had fallen back on impact, revealing long black hair beneath, pinned with a silver encased emerald. For some reason, Willow was more disturbed by the fact that her hair was done than by the unnatural angle of her neck.

She shuddered and returned her gaze to the battle. Praeses was stalking forward now, needing to defend himself less often, walking straight toward the heart of the enemy formation, crushing and smashing with his fists. The last small clump of black cloaks broke and ran, heading for the city gates, and four more of the Defender's guards streaked after them, swords in hand, gaining quickly. Willow looked away, not wanting to see what happened next. She heard a few piercing screams, and then there was silence.

"It's over," Bryndon whispered. "He's coming this way."

She did not have to ask who "he" was. The High Defender walked toward them, and Willow thought she had never seen him, not really, until now. Once, long ago, Willow had seen a whirlwind rip through the forests of Pratum, a twisting, howling storm that had torn hundred-year-old trees up by the roots and flung them around like twigs. The High Defender was like that whirlwind, wrapped in the broad shoulders and dazzling armor of a soldier, and the white beard of an old man. Willow was terrified of him.

He paused and reached down to the ground, hauling up a small man in a rich, silver-gray cloak.

"The Clock," Willow said, hurrying forward. "Is he alright?"

"Quite alright, Stranger Willow," The Clock answered her, brushing dust off his costly clothes. "Terrified and deafened, nearly, but alive.

Thanks to the High Defender."

"I saw," Willow said, looking at Praeses. "How did you…I mean, what was that?"

"Wise Meridia gave the Six powers to rule and protect," Praeses said. "The Wizard Unshames, the General fights, the Weaver dreams, the Shepherd makes. The High Defender defends. I am not without power of my own. So Meridia decreed when she gave our ancestors the books, that the High Defender and his guard would be given the strength to defeat those who wield the power of shame. Long have my predecessors guarded this power, kept it secret. Fifty women with crossbows would have ended me. Fifty women with shame objects…" He shook his head. "This is a grievous day. How so many turned against us—"

He cut off at the sound of more thunder, and everyone looked around, expecting to see another masked figure. Then Bryndon pointed to the city below and said, "Look!"

Smoke was rising, great massive plumes of black, spread out in four columns from east to west. From the west, low, dark clouds were rolling slowly in, as if wanting to meet their smoky cousins, casting a shadow over the city.

"The great houses!" The Clock exclaimed. "They are under attack."

"So these were not the only traitors in our midst," Praeses said. He growled in frustration, and Willow felt as if the earth around them moved a little at the sound. "They have timed their attack well. I cannot leave the city undefended, yet the Nightmare approaches from the south, and our men need me. By the time I deal with these masked creatures, they may be at our doorstep. This is a matter for the Seven, yet one is missing, and smoke now rises from the homes of three others." He turned to look at Willow and The Clock. "We must decide this."

"The city is under attack now," The Clock said. "What is our guard protecting if we let these, these *traitors*, destroy their homes and families."

"For once we agree," Willow said. She shrugged at The Clock's look of surprise. "I only hate your bad ideas," she said. "If these others have as many shame weapons as this group, no one else can handle them but the High Defender."

Praeses watched the smoke rise from the city for a moment, listening to the sound of thunder. It was growing colder, and Willow shivered as an icy blast of wind moaned across the field.

"Very well," Praeses said, finally. "The council has spoken. Mahel, Matthias, Tomos," he called out. Three of the guardsmen stepped forward, two with the broad shoulders and thick limbs of blacksmiths, the third whip-thin and graceful. "I am sending you in my stead. Head toward the front as we planned, and give Captain Ryna of the Twenty-Fifth the command. He is to keep a close eye out for suspicious behavior and possible traitors. Anyone suspected of such behavior is to be cast out in front of the Nightmare with a sword and shield. Alone. Understood?"

"Yes, sir," they said, and set off at once.

"General, there are a lot of people down there that will be in a panic soon," The Clock said. "Might not something be done to get them to safety?"

"What do you suggest?" Praeses said.

"I shall send word to my Timekeepers," The Clock said. "People trust them. They will be able to calm the panic. We can lead some to safety, the outer houses at least."

"Where will you take them that is safe?" Willow said. "These rebels look to be everywhere."

"There is a small force of guardsmen at the West Gate," The Clock said. "Guarding Trader's Pass. Only a few shame weapons among them, but even that is better than nothing. Besides which, the High Defender can keep these rebels occupied here. We must only get them away from the fighting, where they can't be targeted or hurt."

"There's a storm coming in," Bryndon said, pointing to the thickening black clouds. "The West Gate's not big enough to hold the whole city. They'd be perched on the mountainside with no shelter."

"Better some cold and snow than fire and lightning," The Clock said. "It is our only option."

They looked to the High Defender, who thought a moment and then nodded. "Do as you say," he told The Clock. "Take the people west. I shall go to the House of Summerflower and work my way east, across the city, driving them toward the Grove. There is magic in that place that few know of."

"What shall we do?" Willow asked. "House Claybrook—"

"The Timekeepers shall get Bryndon's family out," The Clock said. "Leave that to me." He strode off toward the High Tower, calling for messengers.

"Stay here with the rest of the guard." Praeses said, glancing at the men behind her. "You seem to be giving them orders already. We cannot risk a force of these rebels coming on our soldiers from the rear, and we cannot lose another member of the Seven. I put you in command of the

High Tower, Stranger Willow. Protect it with your life." After a moment, he added, "It is my home."

And with that, he stalked off, his guards following close behind.

CHAPTER THIRTY TWO

A Fire in Meridia

It was nearly an hour's journey to the House of Summerflower for Wynn and the rest of the guard, moving at a steady trot through the city streets, following the broad back of the High Defender. Throngs of confused people called out as they passed, looking with fear to the columns of smoke rising up over the city, hearing the sound of thunder close by, feeling the chill wind that drove the dark clouds overhead and rattled the glass windows. Every hundred yards or so, Wynn stopped and answered, calling out to the onlookers that the city was under attack, that they should take warm clothing and food for one day's journey and go at once to the West Gate at the head of Trader's Pass. They cried out questions, wondering what kind of attack, what was going on, why they should go west, but Wynn stopped only long enough to command them again to leave, to take warm clothing and food, and then he was off again, hurrying to catch the High Defender and the rest of his brothers.

Then at last they rounded the curve of Summerflower Street, and looked, and Wynn felt a cry of anguish rising to his lips at what he saw.

The House of Summerflower was no more. Where the rambling structure had once stood there was now little more than rubble, broken and burnt bricks, blackened ivy and ashes. A single, crumbling inner wall remained upright, sagging drunkenly, its top jagged and broken. Several thick columns of smoke rose from the ruins, signs of fires still burning. And there were bodies, most in red and white cloaks, a few in black masks. And dozens of other women were lying still as well, no mask on their face but the mask of death. Apparently not all of the women in the prayer lines were traitors, then. Some must have been caught up in the event, thinking to do their duty as faithful servants of Ior. They had been cruelly rewarded for their piety.

The other masked ones had spread out in a rough arc around the ruins, blasting a large pile of rubble on the northwest corner. A few arrows of fire answered from behind the rubble, signs of life from the Unshamers.

Praeses roared—a thick, guttural bellow of rage, drawing the attention of the masked ones. Wynn drew his sword with the others, and charged.

Robin cried with relief as the dream lifted her away from the House of Summerflower, away from the blood and screams of dying women. She felt the dream shift and change, trying to take her somewhere else, and she struggled toward wakefulness, wanting it to be over, for the visions to stop. She clawed and reached for the surface like a drowning girl through water. But the current pulled her under, and dragged her into darkness.

Total, utter darkness.

She waited for the dream to change, to show her something different. But there was only darkness. Silent and impenetrable.

No, not completely silent, Robin thought. There was something…the sound of shallow breathing, and a scuffling of leather on stone.

There was a harsh squeal of metal, and then a burst of bright yellow light, and Robin saw that she was in a rather large, simple bedroom, and a man was walking into the room, spectacles perched on the end of his nose, swinging a hooded lantern in his hand. And on the floor, moving feebly, was a tall, blond man with seven colored petals on his golden breastplate.

General Jair Thorndike.

The man with the lantern gasped when he saw Jair and pulled something hurriedly from his pocket. It was a small glass bottle, tinted a dark blue, and wrapped in leather. He pressed the bottle to Jair's lips and tipped it in, holding the General's nose. Jair coughed and sputtered, and some of the red liquid dripped down his chin onto the floor, but he seemed to swallow most of it. And the spectacled man let Jair's head drop back to the ground, and Jair moved no more.

"Sleep," the spectacled man said, and it sounded to Robin like he was about to cry. "Sleep, General. It will be over soon enough. And then we will not have to worry anymore." He patted Jair on the hand and then stood and left, taking his lantern with him, and the room was plunged once again into darkness.

Robin crawled along the floor on her knees, moving slowly until she felt the warm body of the General beneath her hands.

"Wake up, Jair," Robin said, shaking him. "You have to wake up."

Jair made no movement.

"Wake up!" she yelled, shaking him again. And it was as if the dream trembled, and threatened to crack.

"Wake up."

Robin was being pulled away, drawn upward as if by an invisible hand. She passed through the ceiling, rising rapidly through a series of rooms and hallways, higher and higher until she rose up through the roof, and saw below her a squat, gray tower, that looked as if it was a part of the mountain itself.

"Wake up, Robin," a voice said.

Robin opened her eyes. Kian's broad, plain face was above her, looking scared.

"Hurry up and get dressed," he said. "Something's gone wrong."

"What?" Robin said, blinking. "What do you mean?"

"I don't know," Kian said, sitting back and wringing his hands. "There's a Timekeeper come to the door, and he says we've got to leave, that the city is under attack. And then he left for House Stoneshoulder."

"The Masked Ones," Robin said, suddenly, remembering the name from her dream.

"How'd you know that?" Kian asked. "That's what the Keeper said, that we were under attack, and that the one's attacking us'd be in masks."

"I saw them," Robin said.

"Where? How?" Kian asked.

"In my dreams," Robin said. Kian could be so slow sometimes. She looked around, realizing the house was very quiet, the fire low and glowing. "Where is everyone?"

"In the city," came Master Florian's voice, as he strode in from the yard. He had a blanket wrapped up under one arm and a basket of food in his hand. "Bryndon is still at the Low Tower with Willow, and Gran and your mother went to the market with Teagan and Rhys. We're headed for the West Gate as soon as possible. I've already got Digon mounted."

"But there's fighting in the city," Robin said. "They've got fire and lightning and terrible masks and—"

"That's why we're getting out of here now," Master Florian said. "So get up and get moving. And dress warm. There's a storm moving in."

"I've got to get to Bryndon," Robin said, scrambling to get her clothes on. "He'll know what to do."

"I've told you what you're to do," Master Florian said sternly. "You mind me, Robin Claybrook."

"You don't understand," Robin said, pulling at her boots. They were getting too small for her, and she had to squeeze her feet in. "I know where the General is. I saw him. And a man with spectacles came in and made him drink something that kept him asleep, and then I started rising up and up, like I was flying—And I saw where it was."

"I don't want to hear about your dreams," Master Florian said. "This is what comes of Gran filling your head with delusions and—You come back here right now!"

Robin was already walking away, heading for the back door. They had two mounts now, with Willow's still in the barn. She could take one and let Digon ride the other up to the West Gate. Master Florian and Kian were old enough to walk. Then Master Florian stepped in front of her, interrupting her thoughts.

"Now you listen to me," Master Florian said, seizing her by the shoulders. "You are going to come with us right now, or I swear by the Prohibitions that I will bundle you up and tie you to the back of my saddle."

Robin stuck her tongue out at him and broke away, racing for the open door. He couldn't stop her. She had to get to Bryndon, had to tell him where Jair was, had to—

A pair of hands lifted her up off the ground, and Robin started to kick and punch, wriggling with all her strength. She felt her foot connect solidly with Master Florian's gut, and then she was on the ground, ears ringing, colors flashing before her eyes, dazed from a blow to her face.

"You foolish little girl," Master Florian said. "Why won't you ever mind me?"

She ran at him screaming, arms pinwheeling, and then the world went muffled and white, and when she regained consciousness, she was bundled up in an old quilt, tied up with rope, and draped like a sack of potatoes across the back of Willow's goat. And snow was beginning to fall.

The path was littered with corpses. Horrors and shrieks, hulking darkstones in shattered armor, giant wyrms with their guts frozen solid around them. And men, hundreds and hundreds of men, shrunken from blood knives and torn apart beyond recognition, all being slowly buried in the snow that fell softly to the earth, unified in death. Shem picked his way through the mounds, trying to keep to the clear parts of the trail. Around the towers, however, the bodies were packed so close together that he was forced to climb over the top of them, trying not to look at the faces of his dead brothers. It was hard to think of things to be thankful for.

As he traveled north, he could read the progress of the battle in the corpses. Ninety-Five had stood for a long time, piling up the dead Nightmare around its base in massive numbers. No less than three wyrms had fallen trying to take it, the last dying with its head inside the tower, pierced by half a hundred pike thrusts. Ninety-Four had not fared as well, nor Ninety-Three, which was the smallest and weakest tower of the hundred, barely thirty feet tall. Or at least, it had been thirty feet at one time. When Shem found it, it was nothing but a pile of rubble strewn across the path, knocked down like a child's toy by the power of the Nightmare.

The battle worsened as he trudged north, with fewer enemy dead and more men of guard. The crucible at Eighth-Five had failed almost immediately, or perhaps hadn't even been used; every man of the garrison lay motionless inside, trapped and slaughtered. Shem walked through it without a backward glance, putting one foot in front of the other, looking neither to the left, nor the right. He found some frozen apples in a wooden barrel in Eighty-One, and carried them next to his body until they had thawed out enough to eat. The taste was sweet, and cloying. Shem forced himself to choke three of them down, at least to fill the gnawing emptiness he was feeling after a full night and day without food. He washed the taste out with a few mouthfuls of snow, scooped as far away from the corpses as he could get. That wasn't very far.

He had to get back to the city. It was the one thing he cared about, the one thing he knew would make the wretched journey meaningful. He would get back to the city, and he would find Ridi Greenvallem, and ask him why two of his men tried to kill him. His memory of the events were a little confused and fuzzy from the blow to his head, but he remembered Ridi's name. It still baffled Shem, how the castellan could have turned on the guard like that. He'd been a brother for years, serving the General faithfully in everything. To suddenly try to kill him, when the Nightmare was come, and the very survival of the city was at stake…it was beyond anything Shem could understand. He prayed often that Jair was alright, that he had managed to escape Ridi's treachery unharmed. But he did not like the cold wind he got in answer.

And he did not know how he was going to get back. The Nightmare had obviously moved on far enough that their whole army was between him and the city. Indeed, the only reason he was able to move along the mountain road at all was because the Nightmare had gone before him, pushing most of the bodies to the side of the path or dumping them off a convenient cliff, though there were plenty that they simply trudged over, smashing the corpses to the ground with the weight of thousands of booted feet. He could not fight his way through, and he did not think he could sneak through either. Even with a horror's cloak around his shoulder and a blood knife in his hand, he wouldn't pass for a horror for very long. For many miles, he could think of no better option. He'd expected to die for his city, of course, but he had never thought he would die fighting. Lambs had a different fate.

Then he came upon the shattered gate of Seventy-Five, the southern point of Meridia's Eye, where the east and west roads came together again, and he had another idea. It was fairly stupid. He saw that at once. More than likely he would break his neck before the end of the first hour, and die needlessly on the mountainside, far away from the battle. He stood in the gatehouse of Seventy-Five for what felt like a long time, fighting through the fog that still gripped his mind, staring at the frozen blue lake below him, trying to think, trying to remember.

Then at last he gave it up. He would likely die. But it was the only way.

Decided, he found a pike, broken in half, and used it to pry open the door of the tower's supply room. Inside it was dark and jumbled, but after his eyes had adjusted from the white glare of the mountainside, he found what he needed: a small, iron lantern made to hang on a backpack. He filled the backpack with extra bags of oil, and a few more apples and cakes of honey bread. A little more searching revealed a set of climbing spikes, leather gloves, a length of rope, and a gleaming sword. After a few moments thought, Shem hung the sword belt across his chest, scabbard resting beneath his backpack.

And then he walked back outside, into the falling snow, and started a slow climb down the cliff side to the frozen lake below.

Cairn Meridia burned. Black smoke rose above the city in massive plumes, hanging above the rooftops like a dark crown. Above this, the thundersnow storm still whirled and moaned, smoke and cloud, fire and ice, meeting and mixing, so that hot ash and cold snow fell to the ground together. And over everything was the sound of shouting and screaming.

Every few streets, Praeses found a group more or less organized under the auspices of a Timekeeper, leading the people to the West Gate. But the Timekeepers were few, the people many, and much of the city was in chaos, old men and boys shouting orders, young women running through the streets in groups, scarfs pressed over their mouths, mothers carrying their daughters on their backs, the hems of their dresses near half-burnt off. The mothers were the wisest, moving quickly and silently toward wherever the smoke seemed thinnest, the sound of thunder less.

Praeses walked in the opposite direction. Power walked with him. It thrummed through his bones like liquor, love, and lightning all at once. He was no longer angry. He had gone beyond anger, into something else, something black and hard and strong. Every step of his booted feet cracked the cobblestones beneath him, so that he moved like a massive boulder, crushing and smashing. He did not feel the cold. He did not feel the heat. All he felt was power.

The remainder of his guardsmen were with him: Amhar, Mercher, Simon, Wynn. He could feel the power radiating off of them as well, like an echo of his own. There were hundreds of shame objects being used in the city, and with every blast of fire and bolt of lightning, Praeses could feel himself grow a little stronger, a little more powerful. He was the High Defender of Cairn Meridia, and the city strengthened him as it cried out for help, the ancient protection of Meridia still as strong now as it had been when Meridia spoke the spell.

The screaming sounded a bit louder to the east, so Praeses led the company toward it. He had moved through half the city that way, killing the masked ones as he went, following the sound of screaming to the Salt District. Here the fires burned hottest and highest, for there was much to burn: grain and wood and wine, furniture and lamp oil and wool. Most of the roofs were shingled instead of bricked, and in the tight quarters and narrow alleys, the fire had spread quickly from roof to roof. How many were still trapped inside? Likely a good many, with no one to protect them, no one to tell them want to do. But there was no time to stop. No time to help. In the hard blackness, Praeses thought little of them anyway. His power was for killing, not saving.

They rounded a corner. Two masked rebels stood in the street, flinging fire at a butcher's shop, shame objects glowing in their hands. Praeses signaled charge and rushed forward through the falling snow, bare-handed. His men kept pace behind him, steel and stone, rolling through the street like a small avalanche, ready to help if necessary. So far it hadn't been necessary.

The masked ones turned. One broke and ran at once, wisely, booted heels flying. The other, foolish in her power, flung red fire in Praeses's face. Praeses passed through the flames like so much wind. He seized her by the neck and wrist and ripped the shame object away. It was a knife, blade stained red with blood. It seemed most of them had committed murder to gain their power—the more brutal and cruel, the hotter the flames would burn. This knife was very small. It would have taken many thrusts to kill.

One squeeze and it broke apart in Praeses's hand. Another squeeze, and the woman's neck snapped like a dry twig. Just another dead traitor. Praeses dropped her without a word.

The second one was fast, very fast, and was well down the street already, moving with sure feet on the slick paving stones. Not fast enough.

Praeses reached out. The immense power inside of him reached out with him, and a haze formed in the air above the running woman's head.

Praeses swung his fist down.

The haze fell like a hammer, and she collapsed, arms and legs flying, smashed to the ground.

Praeses reached out again, and wrapped his power around the woman's legs, dragging her closer. He could feel the black wool of her pants, the soft flesh of her calf underneath, as if his hands were physically gripping them. Panicked, the woman turned and lashed out with fire, but it was faint and weak, and Praeses paid it as much heed as he had the first. He pulled the woman's throat beneath his booted foot. Ending her.

And they set off again, through the falling ash and snow, heading for the nearest black plume of smoke.

Saerin was alive. That was all she cared about, really, the continued beating of her heart. Long days she had spent, after the Whip had decided to spare her life, locking her up in the darkness of the smithy's cellar. The cellar was damp and dirty and cold, and she had developed a wet cough within a few days of her imprisonment, spitting up yellow phlegm threaded with blood. The Whip had taken her seeing stone, depriving her of knowledge of the outside world, but once a day, she would come to the cellar and ask to see what certain people were doing, usually the High Defender or the General, sometimes one of the other Seven, Pilio or Tarius or the southron Stranger, Willow Peeke. Other times she would ask after people Saerin had never heard of, Timekeepers and Unshamers, certain members of the tower guard.

"I can't see those people," Saerin told her the first time. "That's not how the magic works."

"Is it not?" the Whip had said, voice dropping dangerously low. "Perhaps you should try it anyway."

"But there's nothing—" And then the butt end of the whip had crashed into her face, cracking two of her front teeth, and Saerin had fallen to her hands and knees, coughing uncontrollably.

"Your continued survival depends on your continued usefulness to me," the Whip said, as if nothing had happened. "If this power of yours cannot do even the simplest things—"

"Cowardice," Saerin choked out, wheezing. "Cowardice is centered on the self, threats to me. I can only see people who are my direct enemies. But once I show you where the book is, you can learn it for yourself."

The Whip had seemed satisfied with that. Or at least as satisfied as she ever got. She continued to ask after people Saerin didn't know, whipping her for every person she couldn't give information on, little bits of lightning licking Saerin's back until the smell of burning flesh filled the cellar. Axe would always come down after the Whip left, to give Saerin a bowl of thin soup and a few stale heels of oat bread. She only ever brought heels, and Saerin wondered how she got so many. Probably going door-to-door, asking the house masters: *Excuse me, sir, but I'm keeping a prisoner in a cellar near here and I was wondering if you had any spare bread heels?*

Axe had plenty of kicks and taunts, too, and wasn't shy about sharing them with Saerin, who soon had a motley of bruises on her chest and stomach to match the scarring on her back. Saerin fought back only once, throwing the bucket she used as a toilet in Axe's masked face. She'd not brought food for three days after that, and Saerin suspected Axe only relented because she became too weak to answer the Whip during their daily meetings.

Only the House of Time allowed Saerin to maintain some level of sanity. The sound of the massive bells drifted in every hour, breaking the long, painful monotony of her imprisonment, the steadily worsening cough. A week passed with Saerin still alive, and then she knew by the gem visions that the Nightmare had come. The first night she lost sight of the General, seeing only blackness when she cast her gaze toward him. The Whip seemed pleased with this, and hardly whipped her at all that day. And afterward, Axe had come down with a bucket of fresh water and a rough bar of soap.

"Clean yourself up," she said, setting the bucket on the floor. "You've got places to be tomorrow, and we can't have you smelling up the city with your filth."

"Where are we going?" Saerin said. "Are we going to attack?"

"You keep your mouth shut and your questions to yourself," Axe said. "And strip. Those clothes are barely worth burning. I'll bring you some others."

"I want to keep my boots," Saerin said. "I can never find boots that fit me."

"Fine," Axe said. "Just get rid of the rest of it. And shut your mouth."

Saerin did as she was told, scrubbing off a week's worth of accumulated filth as best she could. The clothes Axe brought her were warm and of good quality: linen undergarments, a wool dress, leather gloves. The cloak was gray and thick, made for winter. When she was dressed, Axe took her to a small, windowless storage room on the ground floor. It was dusty and dim, with an assortment of broken smithy tools and slag metal on the floor, lit by a bit of light that leaked in through the locked door. Saerin thought it luxurious. She even got her hopes up that Axe might bring her a slice of real bread, but, alas, the house masters seemed to be keeping her well supplied with heels.

And then this morning, before the dawn, she'd been awakened by the Whip, dressed much as Saerin was, except in a black cloak where Saerin's was gray. A small crossbow was on her left hip, the diamond-tipped whip on her right.

"Take this," the Whip said, handing her a familiar, black mask. "Keep it under your cloak until I say otherwise."

"Where are we going?" Saerin asked.

"To destroy the city," the Whip said, grinning behind her demon mask. "Certain well respected women have called for an outpouring of prayer and supplication for our noble soldiers. There has been a considerable response."

"How many of them are ours?" Saerin asked.

The Whip smiled. "You see, Axe, she's not stupid," she said. "Cowards rarely are. Though she should have learned by now, at least, that she shouldn't ask questions that don't concern her."

"Forgive me, my lady—" Saerin began.

"Save it," the Whip said. "I'll be pleased to listen to you beg for mercy later. For now, we must go. You will follow close behind me. You will do exactly what I say, when I say it. And if you take one step away from me trying to flee, I will blast a hole in your back big enough to drive a cart through. Understand?"

"Yes, my lady," Saerin said, meaning it.

The rest of the morning was a haze of blood and smoke. They'd gathered with a small group of the Whip's deputies, six fierce women in green masks, and one man, pale and thin. Two had stayed with the Whip: a short, thick woman with white hair and a stained wood hatchet, and Axe. And when the House of Time rang third lauds, they'd started their slow march, hoods down, singing the old hymns every one of the traitors knew by heart. The Whip and the green masks stayed in the center of their small group, their heads bent and hoods up, to hide their masks. The other women with them did the same, though they wore no masks. Saerin kept looking at them, wondering which ones were traitors, which ones were just women, unlucky enough to be walking with the most shameful woman in Meridia.

Then they had come to the Moonlight District, winding their way through a deserted side street, and the Whip had raised one hand in the air. As one, every woman with them reached into their cloak, and fashioned a mask upon their face. And so Saerin had her answer. There were no innocents with them. In this group, at least, everyone was guilty.

She stayed close to the Whip's side as they walked the city streets, all of their heads down now. She sang with the rest as they came to the House of Moonlight. She heard the House of Time ring terce. And she watched as the Whip blasted Weaver Tarius to death with one crack of her whip.

And then the haze had descended, and the fires started to burn, and the blood started to flow. The House of Moonlight turned into a slaughter house, Dreamers crying out as they were burned and shocked, as the beautiful marble columns of their house were brought down around their ears. Bystanders came running at the sounds of pain, and the masked ones cut them to the ground with flame. Soon enough the House of Moonlight was no more, and then the group had scattered, moving through the district in pairs, setting fire to everything they could and killing whoever was unlucky enough to cross their path. Cairn Meridia was a city of stone, but they found things to burn all the same, shutters and doors and carts and furniture.

Saerin stayed with the Whip and her lieutenants, scurrying along behind, defenseless and terrified, wondering when a bout of flame was going to catch her unawares, or a brave man with a crossbow was going to stick a bolt in her gut. There were a handful who tried, mostly men and a few women, leaning out from the second story windows of their homes.

Three of them managed to hit the Whip, twice in the shoulder and once in the back, but she simply laughed and blasted the attackers to bits, pulling the bolts free without so much as a grunt of pain. Smoke leaked out of her along with blood. It was if she had become a shame object herself, so saturated with the power of shame was she.

The storm clouds moved in, massive rolling thunderheads of lightning and snow. For the Nightmare had revealed itself to be in the city, and wherever the Nightmare was, the storm followed. An hour after the attack began, second terce rang, and Saerin found herself huddled on the ground, her cloak over her face, trying to shield herself from the bits of shattered stone that flew through the air as the Whip tore apart a cartwright's shop.

Third terce. Saerin watched as Axe buried her weapon in the throat of a charging butcher. He managed to slash her shoulder before he died. Saerin was relived to see that she, at least, bled normally, and cursed exceptionally.

Sext rang out as they were leaving the Moonlight District, taking their fire and blood to the Clock District. The House of Time dominated this part of the city, the clock tower rising high over the tops of the workshops and houses, built of the same white marble as the other great houses.

Second sext. Third. Somehow, by the time the clock struck none, six hours after the attack began, Saerin was hungry. She didn't know how she could possibly want food, but she did, and managed to swipe a half loaf of bread from a dead scribe in a silver jacket. She ate everything but the heel.

At second none, they began to meet other masked ones, women in singed robes and cracked masks, some with blood on their bodies, some with blood on their hands.

"The High Defender is fighting," one black mask with a kitchen knife reported. "Nothing seems to effect him. I saw him walk through three bolts of lightning and smash one of ours to pieces."

"And you ran away like a coward," Axe growled at her.

"Orders were to burn and destroy," Kitchen Knife snapped back. "Not get killed trying to fight a man who don't even notice lightning."

"You've done well," the Whip said. "Come with us. I've got special plans for the High Defender." She patted the crossbow at her side.

They added slowly to their group over the next hour, until nearly fifty women were behind them, every one of them telling the same story. The High Defender was moving, and he was unstoppable, driving the rebels north and east. The Timekeepers seemed to be moving the people in the opposite direction, and many of the streets they came to were abandoned now, devoid of all but animal life. Strangely, the Whip ordered Axe to kill every goat who had been left behind in the evacuation. The screams they made as they burned sounded disturbingly human.

And finally, as the House of Time rang third none, eight hours after the Nightmare in the city had began, Saerin realized where they were going. And she knew her time was almost up.

"Cry mercy!" the masked one screamed from the ground, her flames vanishing.

Wynn saw the High Defender hesitate, his foot hovering, ready to crush. None of the others had spoken. Just fought and screamed and died like they were supposed to. Like evil always did.

"I beg Unshaming!" the woman continued, her voice high and frightened behind the expressionless black mask. It sounded vaguely familiar to Wynn. "High Defender, by the Prohibitions, I repent of what I have done and beg Unshaming."

"How dare you," Praeses whispered, bent low, his face inches from the woman's mask. "You worthless cur."

"I am less than worthless," she said, hands covering her face. "I am Shamed and broken. I am lost and weary. I am reeling in the depths."

"You quote the Mysteries to me?" Praeses roared. He seized her by the shirt and lifted her to eye level, as if her slight body was no heavier than a doll. "You ask Unshaming behind a mask, with a weapon of murder in your hands? You cry mercy while my city burns! What kind of woman are you, to change heart in an instant?"

"I am Alessia of House Blackwing!"

Wynn nearly dropped his sword in shock. *Alessia? It can't be...*

But it was. Gloved hands pulled the mask free, and behind it, indeed, was pretty little Alessia, her beautiful face filthy with ash and soot, her clear blue eyes welling with tears. She looked completely terrified. "Please, High Defender, have pity on me," she wept. "I didn't mean to—Cael said he was going to marry me, and Master Usper wouldn't let him. He should have let him!" She dropped a small glass phial, filled with a black liquid. It shattered into a thousand fragments on the stone below, its flames flaring up one last time as it was destroyed.

Poison, Wynn thought, as the black liquid stained the snowy ground. And Master Usper, the man who had laughed in his face when he had asked for Saerin's hand in marriage, dead. At the hand of this child. Wynn did not know how to separate the storm of emotions inside of him. Many of them were not honorable.

"You are a traitor," Praeses said. "And you will die a traitor's death."

And before he knew what he was doing, Wynn found himself stepping forward and putting a hand on the High Defender's shoulder. It was like touching a rock. Every muscle in Praeses body was as tense as a charging bull.

"Defender," Wynn said. "This one is a child."

Praeses hesitated, looking back at Wynn. He could see the black hardness of power pulsing in the Defender's eyes.

"A child," Praeses said, as if he didn't recognize the word. His voice sounded far away.

"Wynn, is that you?" Alessia said, recognizing him. "Have mercy on me, Wynn, please. You are all bound by the Prohibitions. I cry mercy to the High Defender, who must hear my plea. You must test my heart, and Unshame me."

"I must?" Praeses said, turning back to her, his voice quiet. "I must? You are nothing but evil to the core, and seek only to save your own worthless life."

"You must test me."

"I will end you!" Praeses said, snarling, hesitation overwhelmed by rage.

"She begs for testing," Wynn broke in. He kept his voice cautious, soft. The Defender was liable to snap her in two at any moment. "Let her be tested."

"You would beg mercy alongside her?" Praeses asked. He turned and looked at the others, Mercher, Amhar, Simon. They all nodded, silent, agreeing with Wynn. He had never loved his brothers more than in that moment of silent support. "Girl she may be, and one who knows you it seems," Praeses said. "But her heart is as black as any man's, and deserves no Unshaming. She must die like all the others."

"The High Defender must not violate the Prohibitions," Wynn said. "Else your power to protect the city will wane. She has cried mercy and begged to be tested. Her death would be an injustice. Our city is nearly lost. Defender, you must remain strong."

The High Defender looked back at Alessia's terrified face, and Wynn could see a bit of the old Praeses breaking through. He knew Wynn was right. The city was lost without him. They needed him to crush the rest of these rebels to powder in his hand, and then they needed him to turn and do the same to the Nightmare in the passes, coming for their city. The city needed him, and his power.

Fires burned around them, but otherwise it was silent, only the low rumble of thunder overhead and a few hoarse cries in the distance.

"So be it," Praeses said. "Alessia of House Blackwing. You are guilty of grave crimes against the Prohibitions of Cairn Meridia. You have thrown yourself at the mercy of the High Defender, and begged to be tested in the presence of witnesses."

Praeses placed his hand on her heart and spoke the Heartspell. The pale blue glow flowed out from his fingers into her chest, and settled into her skin. Her eyes grew wide as Praeses opened a window on her soul, and beheld her shame, feeling her anger, her fear. The regret too, and the self-hatred, the shame that gave her weapon its power. Wynn prayed Praeses would find repentance, as well, real repentance, shining like a tiny firefly in a dark field.

"The High Defender will hear you, as written in the Prohibitions," Praeses said. "Remember that the magic of the Heartspell will know your mind. One lie and you will die. Do you understand?"

Alessia nodded, her mouth hanging open in shock. She hadn't expected him to agree. Well, let her heart be tested. Wynn had done everything he could for her. For Saerin.

"Witnessed," Wynn said. "It is just and merciful."

"It is just and merciful," Praeses said, dropping Alessia to the ground. She shuffled back, clutching her throat.

"Who leads this band of masked fools?" he asked.

"I do not know," she said at once, looking at the blue shine on her skin. She was wise in that, at least. Wynn knew it was best to answer quickly, without thinking. The mind needed time to formulate lies. "I knew only the one who recruited me, and one other. Otherwise we met only in masks. We called her the Whip, a tall woman with a deep voice and brown hair. She wore a red mask that had the face of a demon."

"What are the names of the ones you know?"

"My friend Gwendolyn of House Haeland brought me to the others and gave me my mask. She was in another group, and I do not know what has become of her. This other was a girl from Whitelimb." She nodded toward the body of her former companion, lying huddled and still on the ground. The snow and ash fell on her head in soft waves.

"How many masked ones are there?" Praeses asked, a question that was on Wynn's mind as well. They had killed too many to count so far, slicked the streets of Meridia with blood, but still they kept coming, in endless waves.

"I do not know," Alessia said. "A few hundred, maybe, or as many as a thousand. We never met all together, but it seemed like many."

"What was the plan?" Praeses asked. "What does this Whip intend?"

"I do not know the whole plan," Alessia said. "They were careful of how they spoke. Some were set to attack the Great Houses: the High Tower, Moonlight, Summerflower, and Salt. The House of Time was to be left alone, so that we could hear the ringing of the bells. Most of us were meant to spread throughout the city, starting as many fires as possible, and killing any that tried to stand against us. But when the clock tower rang second none we were to make for the Stone Gate. I know not why."

The Stone Gate was the entrance to the Grove Road, on the north side of the city, where most of the biggest and wealthiest houses were. Praeses had been driving the Masked Ones in that direction all day, though apparently it had been part of the plan all along.

"When did second none ring?" Praeses asked Wynn.

"A quarter hour past, I guess," Wynn said. "But there are guards on the Stone Gate, and they will not go easily. And even after the rebels break through..."

"It will take time to set up a proper defense," Praeses agreed, seeing the possibilities. There was no way out of that part of the city, except back through the Stone Gate. If they could pin them in a narrow area...

"Very well, Alessia," Praeses said. "Your heart has proved true. Go now from here, and help those who are suffering and in danger. As for the magic, I leave it on you. Yes, even so. Women can still set fires with their hands, even when they have no other power. And if the city survives, you will be Unshamed. Go."

"Please, my Lord—" Alessia said.

"Go now, or I fear your heart may betray you, to your death," Praeses warned. "Leave us."

Alessia took one last look at Praeses, a horrified expression on her face, and fled, vanishing quickly over the crest of a hill. *If the city survived,* Wynn thought, watching her run. If it did not, the Heartspell would grow stronger and stronger, searing the shame out of Alessia's flesh until she died. *Someone just switched sides.*

"Come, my brothers," Praeses said, turning north. "We head for the Stone Gate. Wynn, with me. Simon, take the others on ahead and scout. Wait for me outside the south side of the square."

He turned to Wynn as the others saluted and jogged off, swords out. Wynn could not read the expression on the High Defender's face. It seemed equal parts anger and sadness.

Praeses sighed and looked around. The street was in shambles, stones strewn across the path, houses blackened and burning. "I have failed this city, Wynn," Praeses said, taking in the destruction. "We have found and killed many foes, yet this...this is not victory."

"We have done what we could, sir," Wynn said. "There was no way of knowing—"

"Do not try to lessen the evil of what has been done," Praeses said. "What we have long feared has come to pass." He looked as if he was about to say more, but then waved his hand, as if brushing the matter aside. "I want to thank you, Wynn," he said quietly.

"Defender?" Wynn said, confused.

"I had forgotten myself," Praeses said. "I was so filled with vengeance... thank you for reminding me of mercy."

"Of course, sir," Wynn said, taken aback. Praeses really was a good man at heart. "It is my privilege, sir."

"I have another task for you," Praeses said. "One that will take courage, of the kind we spoke about in the High Tower. The enemy is in our homes, and it will soon be at our gates. The cold is coming, Wynn; it cracks the cornerstone even now."

Wynn straightened and nodded. He knew what the High Defender meant. "I stand ready to do what must be done," he said. *For Saerin*, he thought. "For the good of the city," he said.

"Remember how the magic of the crucible works," Praeses said. "The greater the shame, the greater the power to destroy the Nightmare."

"I remember, sir, but, I don't understand what you mean," Wynn said.

"This 'Whip' the girl spoke of," Praeses said. "The leader of this rebellion, the cause of this murder and destruction. There is no one else whose shame runs so deep, no one who is more deserving."

"You would use her..." Wynn began.

"Find her for me, Wynn," the High Defender said. "Find her, and get her back to the High Tower as soon as you can. Get her back, and get her back alive. The fate of our city depends on it."

"I will not fail you," Wynn said. "One act of bravery. One shame to save many."

"Good man," Praeses said, clapping him on the shoulder. And they set off toward the Stone Gate, through the falling snow.

They walked down the center of the Grove Road, in plain view of every window, masks in place, weapons in hand. The street looked deserted, as the Whip had expected it to be. Doors stood abandoned and ajar, and a few scattered belongings littered the street, blankets and food and random pieces of clothing, even a small doll, nearly buried in the snow. The black marble facades of the great houses rose around them, dark, hulking shapes, with the mountains behind, tops obscured by the storm. Snow fell in steady waves, parting frequently as the wind pushed it to and fro, destroying the tracks they made toward House Blackwing.

And what will happen to me when we get there? Saerin thought. A coward good for nothing but her eyes, and easily disposed of once those were no longer needed. And once she showed her where the book on cowardice was, the Whip would have everything she needed to make a seeing stone for herself.

They had broken through the Stone Gate easily enough, though the guardsmen had killed three of their number before the Whip had smashed them down. Once through, she had split the group up again, leaving a strong force to hold the gate while others moved to the great houses, setting fires and killing anyone foolish or weak enough to have stayed behind.

The Whip stopped, and called a halt. Saerin stumbled and looked up. They had reached House Blackwing, and its stone tower loomed above them, a dark finger pointing to the sky.

"The coward and I are going up," she told the green masks. "I want you two to stay here and bring a few of the houses down into the street. House Haeland and House Greenvallem should do."

"Bring down a whole house?" white-haired Hatchet asked. "What for?"

"Because I said so," the Whip said. "Two houses. House Haeland and House Greenvallem. The rear guard will get pushed off the Stone Gate eventually, and when they do I want a barricade here for them to fall behind. Our work here may take time. You have power. Use it."

She turned and strode into Blackwing without another word, and Saerin shuffled after as fast as she could, trying to keep pace with the taller woman's strides.

Inside, the house was dark and quiet, the storm a muted murmur outside the walls. It wasn't warm, but the cold was less intense, less painful. The general aura of hurried abandon they had encountered elsewhere lay thickly on House Blackwing, chairs knocked to the floor, possessions abandoned, a few plates and cups in the kitchen, half-full of food and grape wine. In the dining room they found Master Usper, black-faced and cold, a cup of wine spilled on the table next to him. To her surprise, Saerin nearly started crying at the sight of him.

House Blackwing was massive and labyrinth, filled with odd doors and twisting staircases, even a few ceiling hatches that were only accessible by ladder. The Whip gestured to Saerin to lead the way, and Saerin crept forward, hunched over, trying her best to look broken. The lamps were out, and the only light filtered through a few mismatched windows of smoky glass. Saerin could hear the moan of the wind outside, carrying the muffled sounds of rolling thunder. Every inch of her skin felt stretched thin with tension.

Finally, they came to a high, arching door made of polished black stone. Saerin pushed it open, and they found themselves at the base of Blackwing tower, staring up at a narrow spiral staircase. It climbed through the center of the tower without railing or wall, just bare stone steps carved from a solid central pillar. Narrow window slits were cut into the wall periodically, and the storm had blown through them, covering the walls and steps with a thin and slippery sheen of half-melted snow. The spiral seemed to go up forever, and Saerin swallowed audibly as she looked at it.

"Up you go, coward," the Whip said.

"I don't like heights," Saerin said, shivering. "All the others made fun of me because I could never—"

The Whip slapped her across the face. It felt like getting hit with a quarterstaff. Green and purple lights exploded in her head, and she could feel her face immediately start to swell.

"You'll like me a lot less if you don't start climbing," the Whip said.

Saerin started climbing.

The steps were rough and narrow and horribly uneven in height, and the dusting of snow was as slick as she feared. Saerin was soon acting dizzy and sick, her eyes blurry from concentration. She kept one hand stuck fast to the central pillar, and the other out in front of her like a blind woman, ready to reach out in case of a fall. Her legs began to shake, and somewhere in a far corner of her mind some part of her wondered how long it had been since she had last slept.

She was half-way up when she fell the first time, stubbing her toe on a step that was just a quarter-inch higher than the others. The stairs rose up to meet her, but she caught herself mostly on her hands, teeth clicking down on her lip at the impact. She tasted blood. Behind her, the Whip cursed and whacked her a few times with the butt of the whip. But there was more desperation in her voice than anger. *She hates this,* Saerin thought. *One of us really is afraid of heights.* The thought gave her little comfort. She rose as shakily to her feet as she could manage and stumbled forward again, hands out, ignoring the empty space that groped for her with cold hands.

She fell twice more before they had climbed another quarter of the staircase; the second time she smacked her knee against the stone so hard she cried out, and her eyes welled up with tears. The Whip hit her again and growled something Saerin did not hear. There was little the woman could really do to her, suspended in the air as they were. Unless she wanted to send Saerin down to the stones below. *Soon enough,* Saerin thought, putting one foot in front of the other, blinking back tears. *She has need of me now, but soon enough she'll try to smash me like a clay pot.*

The fourth time she fell, it took the Whip five minutes to get her going again, threatening all manner of horrible pain while Saerin clung to the steps and wept. When she finally started forward, it was on her hands and knees, groping for the steps above her blindly, wrapping her robe around her neck like a scarf to keep it from tripping her up.

Finally, she tumbled out onto a wide landing, and felt solid ground beneath her. They had come to a wide, airy room. Graceful wooden shelves lined the walls, filled with dozens and dozens of scrolls, of all shapes and bindings, the history House Blackwing, as written by every master since the founding of Meridia. The earliest scrolls had long since crumbled to dust, but copies were always made first, so that the history lived on. Between the bookshelves were a number of broad, high windows, a few of which had swung open in the storm, and drifts of snow were piled around them. The snow was streaked with black, and Saerin realized that it was stained with ash from the fires. She wondered vaguely what the ash used to be, before it was burned. A fence post maybe. Or a bed.

"Get up," the Whip said, sticking a booted foot in her stomach. "You've wasted too much time already." She seized Saerin by the collar and hauled her to her feet, shoving the green seeing stone in her hand. "Find the High Defender," the Whip said. "Tell me of him."

Saerin held herself up on the window frame, and looked out, down Grove Street and past the Stone Gate, where the fires burned and people fled. She took a deep breath, letting the cold of the storm sink into her, clear her mind. Then she looked at the stone and thought of the High Defender, let his presence sharpen before her. The dark eyes and white beard. The broad shoulders and arms. The way he radiated power with every step. The words rushed out of her and the stone began to glow.

And then she saw him, stalking down a cobblestone street, smashing the stones underfoot with each footfall. Relief flooded through her when she saw Wynn at his side. There was blood on his uniform, but he showed no other signs of injury. They were somewhere in the Clock District, judging from the abandoned houses and Keeper buildings.

"Is he dead?" the Whip demanded, the urgency plain in her voice. Urgency and something close to hope. "Is the High Defender dead?"

Saerin shook her head. "He lives. Six of his guardsmen are missing." She saw Praeses walk through a wave of fire and snap the necks of two women, one in either hand, and suppressed a shudder. "He is on None Street somewhere, fighting our fire starters." Crushing them to fine powder was more accurate than "fighting," but Saerin didn't think the Whip would want to hear that. "He is coming this way."

"What of the House of Summerflower?"

Reluctantly, Saerin pulled her gaze from Wynn and cast it toward Oded and the home of the Unshamers. Saerin felt a great deal of resistance to her eye, like she was trying to push her way upstream through swift mountain rapids. When the image finally swam before her, she saw why.

The House of Summerflower was no more. It lay in pieces, scattered across the width of Summerflower Hill, the snow slowly burying the red brick and burned ivy. Oded lay beneath a stout wooden desk, the top of which was covered in rubble. He seemed to be breathing, but that was all. Other than the shifting smoke, there was no movement.

"Well?" the Whip demanded.

"It's gone," Saerin said. The feeling was strange, surreal. She realized that somewhere in the back of her mind she had expected the attack to fail, had thought the real destruction of the Unshamers impossible. "A few walls are still standing, but most are thrown down. I see many dead Unshamers, and a few of ours. I do not think Oded will survive."

The smile beneath the red demon mask was hideous. "The first of our victories," the demon said. "Come, we have lingered here too long. When we reach the Grove Gate you shall look again. Show me this book."

Saerin turned from the window. The stone floor beneath her feet was smooth and clean, but the hem of her robe tangled between her legs, and Saerin stumbled, arms pinwheeling, falling headlong into the Whip's body. Saerin's little weight did not move the bigger woman an inch, and Saerin's neck snapped back at the impact.

"Off me you clumsy fool," the Whip said, pushing Saerin to arm's length. "Watch where you—"

The Whip saw the needle then, the one Saerin had slipped out of her sleeve, the one she had carried in her boots through her capture and imprisonment, the one filled with blood milk, enough poison to kill even one as powerful as the Whip.

The Whip jerked back with a hiss.

She almost escaped.

She was cunning and fast and cruel, and she was always on the lookout for treachery, always sleeping with one eye half open. There was a moment when Saerin and the Whip locked eyes, and each saw the other's death, and the moment seemed in doubt, and Saerin's hope shrunk within her as the old cowardice wailed for her soon to be broken body, the silent emptiness that awaited her.

And then the needle slipped between the Whip's ribs with ease, and Saerin pushed it in as far she could, stopping when she felt the point grind against bone. It snapped as easily as a twig, and the blood milk flooded the Whip's chest with death. Her weapon fell from nerveless fingers, diamonds clicking against the stone, and this time when Saerin pushed her, the other woman toppled to the ground as easily as a child.

"No," the Whip said, reaching for her namesake. Blood dripped out of her mouth, blood and a sickening white foam. It frothed around her lips like soap. "No-no-no-no. Not you."

"Me," Saerin said, knocking the Whip's hands away. The demon had no more strength than a babe. "Die quietly now. And quickly. It'll be the nicest thing you've ever done for the world."

"They'll kill you," the Whip said, her voice thick and wet and no more than a whisper. The white foam was leaking out of her eyes now, weeping slow milky tears down her cheeks. "You'll die... die screaming."

"We shall see," Saerin said.

The Whip opened her mouth to say something else, but only pink foam came out. It smelled of peppermint and iron.

She died quietly, but not quickly, spewing blood and water on the floor until Saerin thought she must surely be nearly empty, drawing ragged breaths and clutching at her throat. Saerin had thought her death would be sweet, triumphant, but the reality was hideous. Death was ugly no matter who was doing the dying.

When it was finally over, Saerin took off the Whip's red mask and studied her for a moment. She was a plain faced woman, handsome rather than pretty, her mouth twisted in frozen agony, a small scar marring her chin. Saerin did not recognize her, and amazingly, felt a bit disappointed. She was nobody special, then. Just another dead woman.

Wynn caught the bolt of lightning on his sword and darted forward, steel flashing, opening the masked one's throat. That one had been a man, a man in a green mask, armed with a stout cudgel. He felt a little better about killing the men, but only a little.

Praeses was crushing his way through the gatehouse, driving the masked ones back. Wynn entered the battle where he could, but mostly he was searching, looking for a woman in a red mask, with a whip at her side. *For Saerin*, he thought, driving the point of his blade into a fat woman with a length of sheet clutched in her fist. *May Ior keep you safe.*

Working quickly, Saerin removed her formless black mask and hung it from her belt, putting the Whip's in its place. The Whip's robes were far too big for her, and soiled with blood and phlegm besides, but she sawed five inches off the bottom hem with her knife, scrubbed it with snow as best she could, and put it on anyway, keeping her own cloak on beneath it. In the gloom of the storm no one would be able to tell. Not until it was too late, anyway. The hair was the bigger problem; the Whip's was a shimmering brown, Saerin's a pale blonde. She decided to keep hers tied up and tucked it underneath the gray hood. She left the body where it was. No one would ever come up here to look for her. And even if they did, it would likely take time for any of them to work out what had happened, or how to find the impostor when they did. Half of them would be probably celebrate, anyway.

Then Saerin took a deep breath, and eyed the whip on the ground. It looked much smaller, somehow, as if the death of its wielder had diminished it, reduced its power. Taking the glove from her right hand, she reached out, and took hold of the bone handle. Power flooded into her in an instant, a raging tide of sweetness and energy, and Saerin fell to her knees, gasping for air, fighting to keep herself from being carried away by the storm. She felt herself grow flushed and wet. Her limbs felt stronger, faster, colors looked brighter. *Was this how the Whip felt all the time?* she thought. *This rush of power and longing?*

No wonder she always wanted more. This was sweeter than summerflower wine, sweeter than dancing, sweeter than life. This was life, and this was death, too. For there was an urgency along with the sweetness, a pounding need that Saerin had never felt before. Desperation and anger.

And fear, that soft, sickening welling of fear that Saerin knew well.

She touched the diamonds along the tip, felt the polished bone of the grip. It had remarkable balance and weight, and she could feel the power that filled her thrumming through it, like an extension of herself. So much cruelty and destruction wrought through such a beautiful thing.

Squaring herself toward an unbroken window, she gave it a test snap. Blue lightning flashed and struck, shattering stone and glass and sending fragments of the wall flying in all directions. The sound of the thunder was almost deafening in such a tight place, and the heat from the bolt immediately drenched Saerin in sweat beneath the overabundance of the Whip's robes.

Well. That wasn't so hard. The lightning was just like the whip, light and balanced. *Now let's see how long it will take me to die.*

Saerin took the steps down two at a time, moving easily. The Whip may not have been from House Blackwing, but Saerin was, and she had climbed those steps a hundred times. When she reached the front door, Saerin straightened up to her full height and stalked out into the storm, snow falling around her in white bursts. Anyone who saw her would be expecting confidence and strength, so she strode as straight and purposefully as she could. The Whip did not cringe or cower. The Whip was bold and strong, a force of nature, master of lightning and fire, cruel and implacable. She found the green masks hard at work where she had left them, tearing up the foundations of the buildings with lightning and fire, tumbling them out into a rough barricade across the road.

"Haven't you finished with that yet," Saerin snapped as she approached.

"Almost finished, exalted one," Hatchet said. "What happened to the coward?"

"The fool tried to knife me," Saerin growled, shaking the whip. "She got her reward early."

They laughed, Axe clapping her hands, Hatchet sending a tongue of flame up into the sky to celebrate.

"Glad you're so thrilled," Saerin said, a horrible smile frozen on her face. She snapped the whip again, easily, like moving her own arm. The bolt struck Hatchet full in the chest, blasting her back to the pavement, where she landed with a hard crack. Her robe caught fire at once.

"What...?" Axe said, confused, her weapon still hanging uselessly at her side. "Exalted one, why—"

The second bolt struck her in the shoulder, a glancing blow, and Axe shrieked in pain. She thrust her axe forward, but Saerin was already moving, ducking behind a shattered corner of the smithy. Rock exploded around her, showering her back with shards of brick and stone. Saerin crawled forward, hiding behind the broken walls, hiking her robe up around her waist. Axe was screaming obscenities at the top of her lungs, hurling flame after flame.

Saerin fired her second bolt from the other corner of the smithy, twenty feet away from the rubble where Axe's attacks continued to pound. This time Saerin hit her in the abdomen, and she dropped without a word.

And then the power in the whip surged with triumph, and Saerin cried out in pleasure and pain and...

...and then Saerin was screaming in blind rage, and she found herself standing over Axe's body, the whip beating the dead woman into a blackened mess. She fell to the ground and dropped the whip, putting her head in her hands as racking sobs took her. Somewhere in the back of her mind, she knew she should get up, that this was madness, that any masked one who saw her now would know her for an impostor in an instant—but she couldn't seem to stop sobbing and shaking, huddled beneath the falling snow. She had never been so cold, so terrified.

"Wynn," she said, rocking back and forth. "Wynn, where are you?"

But Wynn could not hear her. He was coming toward her, fighting somewhere with the High Defender, or dead maybe, and if he saw her now he would cut her to pieces without hesitation. Yet even so, she heard his voice, whispering to her as he had when she was little, when she had sat with him after mother died, and let him cradle her in his warm arms. *Hush, Saerin,* he always said. *Don't be scared. You were made to fly.*

"To fly," Saerin whispered, looking at Axe's burnt corpse. The sight of it made her sick, and she looked away, hearing again the sounds of fire and destruction, heading her way. Death made no woman great. Death kept all the honor for herself.

Saerin stood and made herself look again at the corpse. Tentatively, she picked up the whip again. But whatever black surge had come over her was sated now, and she felt only the sweetness of it, the power and hunger. She struck the axe with her whip, then did the same with the hatchet, breaking them and the power inside them. That made her feel a little better. She needed to move. The wind blew her the sound of fighting, approaching from the south. Likely the rear guard, catching up with her. Most of the others would already be at the Grove, or finishing their fires on the way. They would expect the Whip to meet them at the Grove, as well, to lead the final attack on the High Defender.

She couldn't pass for the Whip under close scrutiny. Better to put her black mask back on, and blend in with the rest of them. Better to keep the whip hidden at her side, until it was time to start praising death again.

So Saerin walked down the street with her back straight, wondering if she would get to see Wynn again before she died.

CHAPTER THIRTY THREE
Cold in Trader's Pass

Bryndon hated standing still, so he paced, back and forth, back and forth, across the little room in the High Tower that he and Willow waited in, watching the fires spread in the city below. The room was full of maps, small and big, old and new, some vibrant with color and paintings of fantastical beasts and some no more than a few spare black lines on a sheet of parchment. It was a room that normally would have fascinated Bryndon, but he could watch little else but the smoke, and think of little else but his mother, and Gran, and Kian and Rhys and Teagan and Digon and Master Florian. And his father on the front line, alive or dead, he did not know. And Robin most of all. He half expected to see her come riding up the road to the High Tower, hair flying out in the wind, red faced and wondering why Bryndon hadn't sent for her. But she must have minded Master Florian for once, because the road stayed deserted all day long, save for a few refugees fleeing the carnage below. These refugees were greeted with the sight of two dozen crossbows from the High Tower windows, and a loud hail from the soldiers holding them, to come forward slowly, with their arms raised high above their heads. They were searched thoroughly for shame objects before they were allowed to pass through the gate. None had turned out to be rebels.

"You're driving me crazy with that pacing," Willow said, for what was probably the fifth or sixth time that hour. They had been in the map room since the attacks began, and the snowstorm was not as fierce outside their window as it seemed to be in other parts of the valley. "Can't you stay still for ten minutes?"

"We should be out there doing something," Bryndon said. "We can't sit here and watch these people torch everything."

"What do you suggest?" Willow said. "Did you become a powerful warrior when I wasn't looking? Has all that pacing suddenly put a few shame objects and Tjabo's impenetrable armor in your hands?"

Bryndon snorted and paced. "There's got to be *something*," he said. "Has there been any word of Jair?"

Willow shook her head. "The man has vanished, down to whatever blackness that Dreamer Milena saw," she said. "Fat lot of good that did us anyway."

"We know Jair's alive," Bryndon said. "Milena might not be able to say the same."

They both looked out the window, toward the Moonlight District far off in the valley below. The House of Time had struck none, six hours after the attack began, and the storm was still obscuring the view, lacing the sky with snow and filling it with thunder, though Bryndon was sure some of that was coming from the rebels in the city. Every once in a while they would see a bright flash through the houses, and then a rumble would reach them a few seconds later.

"I don't mean to speak ill of the dead," Willow said quietly. "If Milena is dead."

"I know," Bryndon said, waving that away. "Either way she's out of our reach here. I wish we could talk to her again, ask her some more questions. Maybe she would see something different this time."

"Alive in the dark," Willow mused. "It is said that Tjabo's pits are utterly dark, that a man who spends a year in their blackness will go blind, simply from unuse."

"He'd need months and months to be taken to the grasslands," Bryndon said.

"I know that," Willow said. "But there are any number of places that might serve for a dungeon around here. Deep cellars, caves, even interior rooms, if they are deep enough inside a place. All could serve as places to hold the General. Would you *please* stop pacing?"

Bryndon sat down with a growl of frustration. *How can she sit at a time like this?* he thought. Then something she had said struck a chord in him.

"Caves..." he said. "There *are* plenty of caves around here. I wonder—"

He started rifling through the maps, searching. They were organized by region, ranging from the Far Falls in the east near Cairn Jarth to Meridia's own streets. There were even a decent number of maps of the south. After a few minutes, Bryndon found what he was looking for.

"Here," he said, rolling the map out flat on the table. It was an older map, the lines faded a bit with age, some of the notations and depth readings obscured. "Put something on the corner there, to hold it down."

"What is this?" Willow said, setting her knife where Bryndon had pointed.

"A map of the cave system around the southern pass," Bryndon said. "See here? This red line is the pass, and the crosses are the towers, with their number and capacity listed beside. And the black lines here are the caves, running through the mountains."

"There's hundreds," Willow said. "How did they explore all these?"

"Lots of lamp oil I guess," Bryndon said. "There's a few up around Trader's Pass, actually. Kian and I used to play games in them in the summer, when it was hot." Bryndon remembered it well, but it seemed like another time, another Bryndon, the one that had only cared about being the fastest boy in Meridia. "We used to play a game called courage, to see who was the bravest. We would walk to the point in the cave where the light was just about to die, and then we would both take a step forward. And then another. And then another, and another, and another, until we were in pitch blackness, and one of us got too scared to go on." Kian had been surprisingly good at that game. There was something about darkness that Bryndon couldn't stand.

"So you think Jair might be in one of these caves?" Willow said. "If they are as dark as you say, then they would match Milena's description."

"It's possible," Bryndon said. "I'm just not sure..." he traced the road to Ninety-Five, and his hope died a little. "Ah, but I don't know how he could have gotten there," Bryndon said. "He disappeared between Ninety-Six and Ninety-Five, and there are no cave entrances listed that far south."

"Maybe there's something the map maker missed," Willow said, peering at the map.

"Maybe," he said doubtfully. "But if so, I don't know how it helps us. The Nightmare stills stands between us and him, and if it's a new cave, we'd have to spend hours above ground searching for the entrance, days maybe. The Nightmare will be here by then."

The bad news from the front lines had continued. Willow had

commanded the messengers to bring them regular updates, and the updates were getting worse. Praeses guards had become heroes almost at once, holding gates alone, cutting the Nightmare down with astonishing skill. They had rallied the men for a few towers, slowing the Nightmare down to a crawl. But as the day had worn on, they tired, and the black army steadily gained speed again. They needed the High Defender, and they needed him soon.

"There's got to be something we're missing," Bryndon said. "Jair Thorndike would never abandon his men, and he's too strong to let himself be captured by the Nightmare. Besides which, the Nightmare's not really a capturing sort of army. They kill, they destroy, they don't take prisoners."

"Maybe they've got something special planned for him," Willow said.

"Like what?" he asked.

"I don't know," Willow sighed. "This whole thing is way beyond me, Bryndon. The Nightmare was bad enough, but these masked ones…I thought all of you Meridians hated Tjabo. That was the one sensible thing about you."

"I thought so too," Bryndon said. "There have always been a lot of people who didn't like the High Defender, or Oded. Unshaming is a painful process."

"And people don't like being told they're doing something shameful," Willow added.

"But the General—everyone loves Jair," Bryndon said, thinking. "And these masked ones, they're Meridians. If there were some of them in the guard…"

"But they're all women," Willow said. "There are no women in the guard."

"All the ones we've seen are women," Bryndon said, the idea gaining steam in his mind. "But if there are men, it would make sense to put them in the guard, where they could sabotage the towers from within."

"Like kidnapping the General," Willow finished. "But even so, that puts us no closer to figuring out where he is."

"No, it doesn't," Bryndon admitted. "But I think I know someone who might be able to help." He looked west, across the fields, to the snowy slopes beyond. "Get your crossbow, Willow. We're going to see my sister."

The first thing Robin tried was screaming.

When she woke, perhaps a half hour after Master Florian had her trussed up like a sack of grain, her first thought was to wriggle free. But the ropes were tight around her body, and wound around in such a way that any pull she got on one end simply tightened another. Her hands were pinned to her sides, her face to the clouds, and the steady bounce of Willow's goat made her dizzy and sick. So Robin tried screaming, calling up her most bloodcurdling shriek, the one she kept reserved for only the most important of tantrums.

"Stop that this instant," Master Florian said, his head appearing above her.

"Untie me," Robin said.

"So you can run off and get yourself killed?" Master Florian said. "I think not."

"Then I'll keep screaming," Robin said, and proceeded to do just that. Then she saw Master Florian raise his arm and another white fog came over her brain. When she woke again, they were climbing the stone steps, moving slowly on the thick, broken stone, and Robin had snowflakes on her eyelashes and a pounding headache.

"I have to go," she said to the sky.

"You're not going anywhere," Master Florian's voice answered. "Be quiet."

"No, I have to *go*," she repeated.

"You're lying," Master Florian said. "You just want me to untie you."

"I'm going to wet the blanket," she said.

"Too bad for you," he said.

"It's going to smell awful," she said.

"I'm sure the goats won't mind," he said.

"I'm going to throw up," Robin said.

"That's not going—"

But Robin didn't hear the rest of it because she was, indeed, throwing up, puking out a mess of stomach bile with a few remnants of last night's dinner. It dripped down the goat's hindquarters and landed on the snow behind them.

Master Florian muttered in disgust, but he wiped her mouth clean with a handkerchief and gave her a few swallows of water from his leather canteen. It was icy cold, and Robin felt some of her dizziness wash away.

"Please untie me," Robin said. "I won't run away, I promise." *I'll ride away*, she thought. *Or walk very quickly.*

"No, Robin," Master Florian said. "You had your chance to come along freely."

"But I *know* where the General is," Robin said. "I saw it in a dream.

He—"

"Say one more word about that to anyone," Master Florian said. "And I'll stuff this vomit-soaked handkerchief in your mouth, and tie it shut with another."

Robin shut her mouth.

It took them longer than usual to reach Trader's Pass, taking their time because of the snow, and the passengers that the goats were carrying. Master Florian, too, was not used to the climb, and was forced to take breaks every few minutes to catch his breath. When they finally crested the summit and began their descent, Robin heard a man's voice hail them.

"Master Florian of House Claybrook," she heard Master Florian answer. Robin twisted and turned, trying to get a good look at the man he was speaking to, but all she could see was the corner of the goat's saddlebags. "This is Kian and Digon, two of our house brothers."

"What's the girl doing on the goat?" she heard the Timekeeper ask.

"Poor child is crazed with grief," Master Florian said, sounding genuinely concerned. "Started going on and on about how she could fly, how she knew where the General was. She was trying to run off straight into the city, and it was the only thing I could do to get her here where it's safe."

"Is the city really under attack?" the Timekeeper asked.

"I thought you would know," Master Florian said, sounding surprised.

"I was asleep this morning," the Timekeeper said. "And Keeper Loric comes barging in, blaring about masked women and some sort of attack, and before I know what's happening he's got me dressed and out the door, galloping for this pass. I saw some of the smoke and heard the thunder, but none of these masked ones he was rambling on about."

"We haven't seen anything either," Master Florian said. "A Keeper came to our door this morning, telling us the Great Houses were on fire, and that we should come up here."

"Well, you're going to have some company soon, I wager," the Keeper said. "If there really is an attack, I suspect it'll get real crowded up here before the day is through. Find yourself some shelter if you can. And a fire wouldn't be amiss, if you can find enough dry wood. There's a stand of trees on the west end of the pass. We'll have some cold people up here."

"Thank you, Keeper," Master Florian said, and they left the Timekeeper standing at the entrance of the pass.

"There's a cave up there by that rock spur," Kian said. Robin twisted her neck to look again, but another wave of dizziness forced her to close her eyes. "Bryndon and I used to go exploring in it. Not quite enough room to stand up, but the goats would fit, and we'd be out of the snow at least."

Master Florian thought that a splendid idea, and they found the cave without too much trouble, leading the mounts in. The dark gray of the sky was replaced by the dark gray of the cave ceiling, only a foot or so above Robin's head. Master Florian left her with a word of warning about trying to escape, and set off with Kian and Digon to look for firewood.

Robin tried squirming free again, but by the time Master Florian and the others returned with the firewood, she had made almost no progress, and had to stop, frustrated. He kept a close eye on her after that, staying by the goats while he sent the others for more firewood.

The hours rolled steadily on. Robin began to cramp up a little, and started flexing her fingers to keep her hands from falling asleep. The cave was cold. Colder than the air outside had been, and Robin soon lost feeling in her nose, though the rest of her body was fine. The blanket, at least, was a warm prison.

Eventually, Robin started to hear the sounds of other people at the entrance of the cave, more refugees from the city, sharing stories, drawn to the light of their fire. They all had the same tale: terror in the streets, fire everywhere, masked women with shame objects wreaking havoc and destruction. None had seen any of the others from House Claybrook, alive or dead. Some spoke of seeing the High Defender, fighting the masked ones and winning, brushing off their flames like they were no more than flies.

"He's got two shame objects himself," one old man confided to them. "Daggers made of bone, and the fire that comes out of 'em is green as grass."

"No, he's got two swords," another man said an hour later. "Two-handed monsters that he wields with one, and sometimes he uses a whip of lightning."

"It's a masked one as has the whip," a woman said. "I saw her myself. A hideous demon mask on her face. Do you happen to have any food, good Master? A heel of bread even? My boy is hungry, and I can pay."

Master Florian allowed as he might have half a loaf somewhere, and sent the woman on her way with a tinkling of coin and many thanks.

"I'm hungry too, you know," Robin said, when the woman had left.

"Would you care for a handkerchief?" Master Florian said. But he said nothing when Kian cut up an apple for her. She felt like a baby bird as he fed her.

She closed her eyes and pretended to sleep, keeping her breathing regular and deep, her eyes closed, listening for the sound of Master Florian leaving. If she could get alone with Kian, or better yet Digon, she could probably convince one of them to let her out. Kian always liked her, and was clearly uncomfortable whenever he looked at her. And Digon could always be bought with promises of candy. He was such a little kid sometimes...

Robin woke with a start. She really had fallen asleep. She looked around, finding herself on the floor instead of on the goat's back, though still tied up tight. She was closer to the fire, but it was colder than ever, and there was a Timekeeper at the entrance of the cave, talking to Master Florian.

"—on his way," the Timekeeper was saying. "All men of age are to meet at the head of the pass for further instructions. The battle below is nearly finished, and The Clock would like to organize some rescue missions into the city, to find and rescue anyone who may still be trapped or in need of help."

"Are they quite sure it's safe?" Master Florian asked. "We can still hear the thunder..."

"Those are the orders," the Keeper said. "I don't know. Maybe he just wants to organize things first."

"Very well, very well," Master Florian said. "We will be there." He turned back to Robin as the Keeper left.

"Awake, are we?" he said. "Well don't you think about running off again. Digon is playing with the boys from House Granite, and Kian is coming with me, so there's nobody that's going to let you out."

"Where are the others?" Robin asked. "Gran and Mother and Teagan and Rhys?"

"They, haven't returned yet," Master Florian said, looking troubled. "Don't you worry about them. Your mother is smart enough to lie low until the danger has passed over. So you just lie there by the fire and be quiet, and if I hear you screaming or hollering, I swear—"

"The handkerchief," Robin said. "I know. Just go on and leave me then."

Master Florian snorted, but he left, taking Kian with him, who gave Robin an apologetic look as he walked away. Robin wondered if she might be able to wriggle close to the fire. Maybe if she could burn the ropes off... No, that was a stupid idea. Like as not, she'd set herself on fire, and Master Florian would get mad at her for yelling for help.

She heard footsteps behind her.

Robin froze, listening. The sound was faint, but distinct, and growing louder, footsteps in the cave behind her, coming closer.

She twisted and wriggled, turning herself around so that she was facing the other direction, down the black mouth of the cave. It went back a good fifty feet before turning a corner, dimly lit by the reflected light of the snowy brightness behind her.

"Master Florian?" she called out. "Are you still there?"

No response. The noise was a shuffling, squelching kind of sound, and Robin thought of all manner of creatures, horrible monsters from her dreams, creatures of the Nightmare and worse, and the footsteps grew louder, and louder, and closer, and then Robin saw it, bending low beneath the roof of the cave, turning the corner, a black thing holding a lantern, staring at her with sickening white eyes.

Robin started screaming, and thrashing around, praying for someone, anyone to hear her, for Master Florian to come back and check on her, for Kian with his dumb face. The black figure stopped and stared at her, setting its lantern down on the ground, blinking in the sunlight.

"I know I look like a monster," the figure said. "But I promise you I'm just a muddy version of myself."

Something about the tone of his voice made Robin stop squirming.

"What did you say?" Robin asked the thing.

"I'm Shem Haeland, a lamb of the tower guard," he said, and Robin saw that he was telling the truth. Black mud covered him from head to toe, some of it fresh and wet, some of it cracked and dry. But underneath the mud, still recognizable, was the uniform of the tower guard. And he had a sword belted to his side.

"What are you doing in the cave?" Robin asked, still a little unsure of him. "Why are you all covered in mud?"

"That's a long story," the man who called himself Shem said. "And likely not one for young ears. But I was left behind after the Nightmare attacked my tower, and I had no way back to the city, except through these caves. I used to explore them when I was a boy, though I'm surprised I still remembered as much as I did. As it is, I got turned around a time or two—Where have I come out, little one, and what are you doing here, trussed up like a kid for slaughter?"

"Don't call me little one," Robin said. "I'm Robin Claybrook, and I'm here because the rebels are attacking the city and a Keeper told us to come up here and Master Florian wouldn't believe me about the General and he won't feed me either and my nose is cold and I have to *go.*" Robin realized she was crying, and scrubbed her eyes angrily on the blanket.

"What about the General?" the man asked, bending close. His face looked kind of nice, under all that mud. He was terribly old, though.

"He wouldn't believe me," Robin said. "But I know where he is, and I have to tell Willow because she's Stranger and people will listen to her." She started struggling again, pushing at the ropes furiously.

"Stay still, Robin Claybrook, I'll get those," Shem said, slipping a knife under the ropes. A few quick cuts, and suddenly she was free, blessedly free. She kicked off the blankets and tried to stand, legs wobbly from being restricted so long.

"I know your Gran, you know," Shem said, helping her to her feet. "She told me once that you're a Dreamer."

"I have lots of dreams," Robin said. "Bryndon always asked about them."

"And you know where Jair is? He's alive and well?"

"He's asleep," Robin said. "And no one's been able to find him. But I know where he is."

"Well, come on then," Shem said, nodding. "Let's go find this Master Florian of yours. We'll get to the bottom of this soon enough."

"We have to go to *Willow,*" Robin said. *Why wouldn't grownups ever listen?* "Master Florian will try to tie me up again."

"I'm sure I can convince him not to do that," Shem said. "Come on, I need more information—"

"I'm not going with you," Robin said, and then she was darting away, struggling through the snow, fighting her own stiff muscles. The pass was full of cook fires and people, livestock and possessions, even a few tents scattered here and there. Robin passed an ornate, sculpted chair, and wondered what could have possibly possessed someone to haul such a thing up a mountainside. She looked back, and saw Shem following her at a walk, calling out for her to wait, but she plunged on. It was cold. Very cold. And she was soon shivering, snow melting in her boots, the wind pushing against her.

A large group of men stood at the head of the pass in front of her, and Robin slowed down, frustrated. She had forgotten about the meeting with The Clock. The men were blocking her way. She looked behind her again and did not see Shem. She must have lost him. Crouching, she scampered behind a snow drift that had formed a small ridge line, parallel to the canyon side. She crawled through the snow, teeth chattering, until she was directly behind the group of men. Once they left she could slip by, and make her way to the Low Tower, where Willow was. But she would find somewhere to pee first. *Why was it so cold?*

"—don't understand," a man was saying. She couldn't see who it was, but the voice seemed to be coming from the front of the group.

"I'm just waiting for a few more friends to arrive," another voice said. There was a break in the crowd, making way for a man of middling height, dressed in a rich robe of gray wool, trimmed with silver. "Then we can begin," The Clock continued.

"This is all the men of age," a Keeper said, and Robin recognized the man who had greeted them that morning. "Who else are you waiting for?"

"A few friends," The Clock said. He unbelted his robe, in spite of the cold, shrugging it to the ground. The clothes beneath were of thick black wool, fastened with silver buckles. "But I think…yes, I think they have arrived."

"Sir?" the Timekeeper asked, looking confused. "Are you alright, sir?"

"Fine, fine," The Clock said, but he had started twitching, and his face was working, as if in pain. Robin got a whiff of something terrible, rotten and acrid. "Yes, yes, here they are now. My friends are here."

He pointed, past the group of men waiting at the head of the pass, to the top of the slope, where the descent into the valley began. And there, cresting the ridge line, was a group of men, of average height, clad in robes the color of ink, stooped and thin, with demon masks covering their faces. And in their hands, dripping blood…

"Horrors!" the Timekeeper said, as men began to shout in fear. "Sir, what are—"

His voice cut off with a gurgle as The Clock buried a knife in his throat, and Robin watched in dumb shock as the man began to shrink and flatten, his skin stretched tight over his bones as the life drained away, away, and even more terrible was the look on The Clock's face, a horrible rictus grin, and Robin thought, *It looks like a mask, like something made of wood or iron,* and men were screaming as the rest of the horrors descended on them, bringing the deathly cold, and the smell of an open grave, and some fought, and some ran, and Robin crouched behind her snow drift and shivered, and she saw Kian run by her and stumble to his knees, and she watched as a horror seized him from behind and raised its dagger, and a small drop of blood fell to the snow…

…and there was a blinding flash of light and a hot blast of wind, as a bolt of lightning took the horror in the chest.

Robin looked around, bewildered. More lightning flashed, coming from behind her, over the top of her head. She turned, and saw a man standing on the slopes above her, a glowing shame object in his hand. And rising around him out of the snow were more men in white cloaks. They charged downslope, crying "Thorndike! Thorndike and the guard!" flinging themselves into battle with the horrors.

"Kian!" Robin yelled, as the horror behind him rose again from the ground. "Look out!"

Kian stumbled away as the horror came after him again, clutching its smoking chest, until another soldier stepped in front of him, wielding a sword and shield, drawing its attention away. Battle was exploding around them. Men ran, trying to get out of the way as the soldiers and horrors clashed. A young man with a flaming hammer fought with The Clock, who seemed to snake away from the flames like oil from water, fighting with a knife in each hand, pressing forward. The soldier slipped on a patch of bad snow, and The Clock's knife grazed his cheek, where it stuck like glue, dropping the man to the ground to finish its deadly work. A bolt of lightning struck The Clock a glancing blow on the shoulder, but the blood magic was in him, and he seemed to barely notice it.

Kian had spotted Robin, and he ran to her, churning through the deep snow.

"We've got to get away from here," Kian panted, pulling her by the shoulder. "Come on, there's—"

"Look out!" Robin screamed, pointing.

The Clock was coming for them. He had seen Kian run by, and grinned his horrible grin at the sight of the two of them.

"Claybrooks!" he whooped, second dagger in hand. "Come feed my knives!"

Robin tried to turn, turn and run, but her legs were cramped from the cold, and the ground seemed to have turned to ice, and she knew he was going to get them, and she was going to shrink and dry out like the soldier with the club.

Then there was a ring of steel on steel, and a mud-stained Shem Haeland was there, standing between them, sword moving with short subtle blows. The Clock hissed and came at him, knives moving like striking snakes. Shem held his ground, keeping The Clock at bay, his blade opening up wounds on The Clock's chest and neck. Red blood poured out of the wounds, more blood than Robin had ever seen, more than seemed possible. But The Clock kept coming, forcing Shem back, points flicking inches from his skin.

"Go Robin Claybrook," Shem said over his shoulder. "Run far from here."

"Come on!" Kian said, dragging her away.

Robin stumbled after him, deafened by the sound of thunder, the sight of blood. Cries of "Thorndike!" still rose from the soldiers. And Robin thought of her father, and his words to her that last night. *You'll have to be brave again, Robin. For me.*

And then she had wrenched free of Kian's grasp, and was running back the other way, toward the battle, ignoring his cries. And there was the dead soldier, no more than a dusty remnant of his old self, and there was the hammer, still aflame at his side, and Robin seized it, and turned and saw Shem fall to one knee, and The Clock's blade raised, and the rage and power of the hammer flowed through her and in her and out of her again as a massive spear of flame, a flame that took The Clock in the back. He screamed and dropped to his knees, and in that moment Shem stepped to the side, and took off The Clock's head with one blow. It bounced away, still grinning.

Robin turned, looking for someone else to burn. But the battle was nearly over, the horrors dead or dying. Nearly all of the soldiers were fighting with lightning or flame, and others fought the horrors in twos and threes, overwhelming them with blows. She felt a hand on her shoulder, and looked up to see Shem.

"You'd best drop that," he said, gently prying the hammer out of her fingers. "It's not good for someone so young to feel such anger."

Robin felt the power of the hammer leave her as it fell to the snow. She started shivering again, and Shem scooped her up in one arm. She clung to him, pressing her head against his muddy shoulder.

"The General," she muttered. "We've got to get to Willow."

"In good time," Shem said. "First I want to know what's going on here."

He carried her through the snow, Kian following closely behind. They were approaching the soldier who Robin had first seen on the ridge line, the one with the lightning. He was coming down to meet them, sliding a little on the snow.

"Hail, soldier of the guard," Shem said, waving. "I am Shem Haeland, lamb of tower Ninety-Six."

"Garrett Common, scout of Century Tower," the man said. "You are far from Ninety-Six, Shem Haeland."

"And you even further from Century Tower," Shem replied. "What are you doing here on this mountainside? And these others, who are they?"

"We're scouts, all of us," Garrett said. "Up here on special orders from the General himself. Been out here for days, since before the Nightmare hit."

"But why?" Shem said. "How did you know these horrors would come? And The Clock?"

"Didn't really," Garrett said, shrugging. "I don't think the General did either. He just said he was worried. If Cairn Jarth and Cairn Creta were really gone, then the western passes have been open to the Nightmare for some time. Not the whole army, of course, but he thought maybe a smaller force of horrors or milidreads might slip by the watch. He just told us to wait, and be ready. And if we saw any creatures of the Nightmare, to destroy them. Didn't expect The Clock, though. What was he doing with a pack of horrors, and a pair of blood knives besides?"

"The blood magic can be used by creatures other than the Nightmare," Shem said grimly. "He moved like one of them, though he did not have the smell, or the cold. But we have been betrayed by more than him. Come, I'll tell you more along the way."

"Along the way to where?" Garrett said. "I've got orders."

"I can guarantee you that if Jair knew what we know, he'd tell you to come with me," Shem said. "We go to the High Tower." He patted Robin on the head. "This one is going to help us settle some matters of justice."

Bryndon found Robin a few miles from Trader's Pass, held in the mud-stained arms of Gran's old friend Shem Haeland, walking along with a scout named Garrett, who carried a lightning wand. It took twenty minutes of reassurances to get Robin to stop hugging him, and twenty more minutes of confused questions before Bryndon understood what was going on.

"So you do know where the General is?" he finally said to Robin.

"Sort of," she said. "It's somewhere in the Low Tower, the one that looks like part of the mountain. It looked like a bedroom in my dream, but it was dark."

"And the man with him," Shem asked. "What did he look like?"

"He was tall and thin, with a bony nose and dark hair," Robin said. "And he had spectacles, and a bunch of papers in his hand."

Bryndon looked at Willow. There was only one man they knew who fit that description, one of the last men to see the General before he disappeared. Bryndon set Robin on his mount and swung up behind her.

"Come on," he said, turning the goat back towards the High Tower. "We're going to ask Ridi Greenvallem some questions."

CHAPTER THIRTY FOUR

The Grove

The bulk of the rear guard reached the Grove Gate a few minutes behind Saerin. Unlike the Stone Gate, the Grove Gate was unguarded and mostly ceremonial. It had only a small gatehouse, with a few locked storage rooms inside the stone walls. They waited inside, out of the snow and wind, and in the fading light Saerin could see the fear in them all, the anxiety over the approaching High Defender and his seemingly unstoppable power.

There were twenty or so masked ones left in the rear guard, along with the two dozen that waited with Saerin. A green mask led them in, a silver mace in her hand.

"Where's the Whip?" Mace said, looking around. "She should be here by now."

"She's not," someone said. "Probably run off, with her whip between her legs."

"Watch your tongue," Mace said, shaking her weapon at the speaker.

"She'd be smart to do it," another woman said. "Our weapons do nothing against the High Defender, or his guards. And she's gone and led us into a dead end here. He's going to smash us to bits."

"He won't do anything of the kind," Mace said. "Happens I know what the Whip was planning here." She swung her mace at a lock on one of the storage rooms, smashing it to bits. "Look and see," Mace said. "That's what we'll have for the High Defender."

There was a general crowding around, as each tried to see what was inside. Saerin stood back, not wanting to get caught in the press of bodies.

"Crossbows?" someone said, the same woman as before. "What bloody good are these?"

"The Whip said they'd do for him," Mace said. "He's protected against our magic. But plain, cold steel—that'll be our answer."

"That's stupid," the woman said. "Why wouldn't she have told us this before?"

"She let all of us get killed!" someone else said.

"She had her reasons," Mace said. "And if you want to keep yourselves from bloody getting killed too, than you'll start handing out those crossbows."

"I'm not doing it," the woman said.

Mace turned and bashed her across the face, sending blood in a fine spray over the rest of the masked ones, most of whom recoiled back in shock.

"Cold steel," Mace said, shaking the dripping weapon at them. "Get the damn crossbows out."

They got them out. They were old, bulky things, but the bolts looked sharp and the hinges well oiled. Saerin took hers along with the others. It was much heavier than she expected, but with two hands she could manage. Not that she planned on using it anyway. Lightning might not be any good against the High Defender, but against these women, it would do better than a crossbow.

"Through the gate," Mace ordered. The sound of the battle was nearly on them. Saerin heard cries of pain and fear. "And spread out through the trees. Any of you who can climb, do it. You hide, and you wait until the Defender comes in a good ways, hear? He'll come after the rest of the rear guard, and that's when you take him down."

There was a murmuring of assent, and then they set out into the storm and the falling night. The wind had picked up, blowing her robe around her in billowing waves, and Saerin clutched it tight, keeping the whip hidden. She let the crowd pass her by, and faded to the back of the group. They were all fixated ahead, looking for places to hide among the trees. It was now or never.

Saerin slipped the red mask off her belt and put it on. The masked ones thought the Whip dead, or fleeing. If they turned and saw the red mask now, it might cause a moment of confusion, a moment Saerin needed to strike. She spotted Mace and fell in behind her a good ways, loosening the whip. The wind was shaking the stone trees like she had never seen before, bending them almost double.

But that wasn't right. *The wind is hardly blowing now.* Something else was moving the trees, something…

She saw Mace ahead of her, her flaming weapon glowing in her fist, and readied her whip to strike. The sweet power and need burned through her, yearning toward her enemy, poised to kill. Then she saw a tree bend down behind Mace's back, and a twig grazed her shoulder.

There was a flurry of movement in the dark.

Mace cried out, and a branch struck her in the mouth with a sharp crack. The blow knocked her backwards, and a web of limbs enveloped her, pressing her against the trunk. The tree began to shake and shiver. Fire flowed out of Mace's weapon in a bright plume, but her hand was pinned against the tree, and the fire did no more than illuminate her own doom. The darkness of the trunk turned blacker than anything Saerin had ever seen, and began to consume Mace's body, swallowing her like an open mouth, and Saerin thought, absurdly, that the trunk wasn't wide enough to fit her body, that the tree would choke on her and spit her out.

Then she was gone. And the tree was bending towards Saerin.

Screams and cries echoed across the Grove, rising above a low, rustling groan, the sound of the trees killing masked ones. *Dear Ior, they are* moving. *The trees are moving on their own…*

Saerin had a moment to realize she had called upon the name of Ior, and then she dropped to the ground, and felt the soft whoosh of a branch swing over her head. She scrambled forward, panting heavily, her face pressed into the snow, looking for a path that might be out of reach of the limbs. The trees were everywhere, behind and in front, to her right and left. She had never realized how many trees were in the Grove until now.

The Flower Fountain. The Flower Fountain was in a clearing, well away from any trees. If she could work her way there…

Another branch reached down to block her path, and Saerin skittered to the right, only to find another tangle of branches in front of her.

"I'm not your enemy," she called, crawling backwards. She hunted desperately for a way through, ducking the swinging limbs, hearing nothing but the beating of her own heart, and the sound of death earning honor for herself. The sweet power of the whip had turned to ash, and she felt nothing but fear now, a blind animal's fear of death. A masked one was fighting off a ring of three trees with a sword of fire, hacking at the branches furiously. One caught her elbow as it raised for a strike, and then it was over quickly, branches carrying sword and woman into its open maw.

"I'm not the one you want," Saerin cried again, as a slim branch laid hold of her shoulder. She snapped it with one powerful strike and rushed forward, panicked now, not watching for the open areas between the trees. More branches scraped across her, and she felt her robe rip and tear, felt blood welling up from cuts on her hands and neck.

Then something caught her foot, and she was down, ankle pinned beneath a branch the size of her calf.

"I'm not the one you want!" she screamed, as the branch began to drag her back. It wasn't fair. She was on their side; she was trying to kill the masked ones, just like them. "Let go! Wynn!"

The branch ignored her, continuing to drag her back, and Wynn did not come. She lashed out with the whip, striking the limb with rage, but the leather seemed to have no more power than an ordinary whip, slapping at the wood uselessly. She sent a lightning bolt hurtling toward the tree, but the blue white brilliance disappeared into the darkness of the trunk and vanished without a sound. Shame had no power here.

There were more branches on her now, thin twigs and heart-shaped leaves. She wrenched her foot as hard as she could, and felt a sharp pop in her ankle, followed by a blooming red wash of pain. Bile rose in her throat, and she felt like screaming and puking and choking all at once, she felt her stomach flip inside out. She thrashed and snapped some of the smaller twigs, sending bolts of agony up her ankle and leg. Through the tangle of branches, the darkness loomed much closer, hungry, waiting eagerly for her. The Whip's red mask slipped and half-blinded her, and in a far corner of her mind she realized that she was going to die.

With a final cry of rage, she threw the whip from her as far as she could, tangling it in the branches. As the last of its power left her, the pain of her ankle came crashing down full force, and she thought, as she was slipping into darkness, that Wynn would think she had betrayed him.

Full night had almost fallen, but the flashes of lightning from the thundersnow above still gave Wynn enough light to see by. The red-masked one lay curled up on the ground, moaning in pain. A leather whip was coiled near her, and Wynn kicked it out of reach. It sparked and crackled as it skittered away, lightning twisting along its length. He was not worried about someone else picking it up. To carry a shame object in the Grove tonight was a death sentence.

Wynn could hear the sound of solid booms echoing from the direction of the Flower Fountain, muffled screams and cracking bones. The High Defender was not taking the chance that the remaining masked ones might beg Unshaming. He was crushing them from afar, or tossing them into the stone trees. They took care of the rest. Wynn shuddered and hunkered down, trying not to look at the silent sentinels rising up around him. They were defending the Grove. The stone trees themselves, sacred to the city of Cairn Meridia, were rising up to destroy the Nightmare that had come to the city. As Meridia had said they would. *Even the trees and animals will come to your defense...* the story said. So it had been foretold long ago, and so it was. Wynn had heard that story a hundred times, but he had not thought of what it would be like to live through it, to see the trees move of their own accord, to feel the dark branches hovering just above you, like a mountain lion ready to pounce.

Wynn tried to put them out of his mind and knelt to examine the red masked woman, the one Alessia had called the Whip. She was conscious, but didn't seem aware of her surroundings, her blue eyes unfocused and roving. It was clear the trees had gotten a hold of her; the rich black robe she wore was ripped and torn in a dozen different places, and her right ankle was broken, hanging off her leg at a sickening angle, swollen with pooling blood. She had made it to a small clearing before falling, out of the reach of the trees' thickest limbs, and Wynn suspected that was the only reason she had survived long enough to drop the whip. He could *see* the trees around them bending towards her, waving as if in a mighty wind, hungry for justice. He could drag her back towards them. Put the whip in her hand and let the trees do the work. The Defender wouldn't be able to blame him for that. He'd never know. And then there would be justice. Simple justice. No survivors. No hard decisions. No opportunity for the Defender to use the weapon of the enemy.

Except Wynn knew he would just be delaying the inevitable. Praeses had made up his mind. If it wasn't this one, it would be someone else. And didn't this one deserve it the most? Wynn brushed a loose strand of blond hair back from the Whip's face and wondered what evil she had done. The mask had slipped a bit, revealing a pale patch of her chin. Wynn grabbed the edge of the mask and settled it back in place. He did not want to know who she was. It was better not to know.

He tore a strip of cloth off of her ragged cloak. The hem looked like it had already been sawed off with a knife. Gently, he wound the cloth around her neck and began to squeeze. She flailed for a few seconds, hands scrabbling at her throat. Then her eyes rolled back, and her hands fell limp to the ground. Wynn kept the pressure up for another slow count to thirty, then he unwound the cloth and pressed his ear to the Whip's chest. The heartbeat was frantic, pulsing, but still strong.

Gently, he scooped her up into his arms, pressing her face against his chest. She smelled like blood and earth. With her hood up, she would look like any other woman, a good woman of Cairn Meridia, being carried to safety by a member of the Defender's guard. Wynn wondered again what she had done in her life, how much shame stained her soul, if some part of her was sorry. He hoped she would die evil and unrepentant. That would make it much easier.

Settling her more comfortably against his chest, he set off towards the High Tower, trotting through the looming trees with evil in his arms. Carrying her to her death. Her body was warm, and she weighed no more than a child.

Praeses tossed another rebel into the trees, watching them swallow her up in an instant. It was old and dangerous, the Grove, the final resting place of Tarn Harrick himself, and the magic of Meridia was laced through every inch of it. The book of the High Defender spoke of it as the final refuge against the Nightmare, the place of the living towers. And tonight the towers were at work.

"High Defender," Simon said, trotting up from the tree line. "The remaining masked ones have holed up around the Flower Fountain, sir. There are a dozen at most, but they have crossbows, and won't be taken without a fight. Mercher nearly took a bolt in the eye."

"Leave them," Praeses said. "They'll not be able to escape. Have you seen the leader?"

"No, sir," Simon said, looking worried. "And Wynn is missing as well. I fear he may have fallen somewhere in the Grove."

Praeses kept his face smooth, bottling up the surge of triumph that welled up in him.

"No need for worry," Praeses said. "I've sent Wynn on a separate mission. Call the others, and take up positions here at the Grove Gate. If they do break through the tree line somehow, no one must be allowed to escape. Understood?"

"Yes, sir," Simon said, saluting. "Where will you be?"

"I must return to the High Tower," Praeses said. "This battle is over. Our true enemy comes for us now." And he left without a backwards glance, the sun peaking one last time through the clouds as it sank into the western sky.

CHAPTER THIRTY FIVE

The General and the Castellan

Ridi Greenvallem was nowhere to be found. Bryndon asked four different healers and a grumpy old guard with a thick black mustache, and their answers were all the same.

"Haven't seen him since the attack this morning," Carys the healer said. She was the fifth. "I thought he was in the High Tower with you." She frowned at the bits of dried mud Shem was dropping on the floor. "You know, there's a washbasin of warm water sitting by the fire," she added.

"Where are all the injured men?" Bryndon asked. The gatehouse of the Low Tower was nearly empty, healers scurrying around with stretchers, picking up the few who were left. Night had fallen, and the fire in the hearth was roaring. Torches burned along the walls.

"Moved them on to the High Tower, along with the couple prisoners up in the high cell," Carys said. "And from there the wagons are headed to the West Gate. The Nightmare is coming, and Captain Goran of Tower Seven told us to make ready. There will be a garrison coming shortly, mostly survivors from the other towers."

"They're at Seven already?" Shem asked, his face troubled.

"Eleven," Carys said. "But he doesn't think it will be too much longer, not unless the High Defender can do something to stop them. He's still fighting in the city, last I heard, though that was some time ago."

"Carys, do you know of a place here in this tower, some interior room away from any light?" Bryndon asked. "It might be a bedroom, or something like it."

"You mean the General's room?" Carys said, frowning.

"The *General's* room?" Bryndon repeated. "How did you know we were asking about the General?"

"That's the only room I know of that would fit your description," Carys said. "It used to be the old prison cell. I would go there sometimes, if the prisoners were sick. Then Jair turned it into a bedroom for himself, said he wanted to get used to the darkness, be able to fight in it, and the like. Foolish idea, I thought, though I was glad I didn't have to go there anymore. Darkness gives me the creeps." She shook her head.

"Which way is it?" Willow said.

Carys gave them directions and bustled off, calling to a few healers to watch how they were moving an injured soldier. Shem led the way, grabbing a torch off the wall, taking the stairs two at a time. Bryndon followed behind with Willow, Robin still clinging to his side, with Garrett taking the rear. Bryndon would have preferred Garrett in the front, where he could have kept an eye on him. The scout seemed sincere enough, and Robin said he had saved a lot of lives in Trader's Pass. But too many people had proven false over the past day for Bryndon to feel comfortable with someone he didn't know.

The torches disappeared off the walls, and soon they were walking through the darkness, following the light held aloft in Shem's hand. No one spoke. There was only the sound of their feet on the stone, their breath in the air. Robin's grip on his hand was like a vise.

Finally, Shem stopped before a small, oaken door, hinged with iron. "Fifth door past the turn," he said quietly. He handed the torch to Willow, and drew his sword with a soft whisper.

Then he turned the latch and shoved the door open.

Jair Thorndike lay on the floor, still dressed in his uniform, his feet splayed out to either side. And sitting with him, holding Jair's head in his lap, was Ridi Greenvallem.

"You'd best not come in," Ridi said, blinking in the light of the torch. He waved something in his hand, and Bryndon saw that it was a black hilted knife, slowly dripping blood. Ridi put the knife to the General's throat, hovering an inch away. "One nick with this, and he'll die."

"We'll stay out here," Shem said calmly.

"Stranger Willow, Bryndon, so good to see you," Ridi said. He sounded exhausted, small, as if it took every ounce of energy in him to speak. A mess of papers was scattered all over the floor, some ripped and torn, others crumpled into tiny balls. "I'm afraid I don't know your friends. I've been meaning to thank you for helping me with the wounded."

"Why don't you put the knife down," Shem said. "That would be best."

"I think this is the only thing keeping me alive right now," Ridi said, looking at the knife. "Really, I think I'll keep it."

"How could you do this?" Willow demanded. "Jair trusted you. You were with him for years. He loved you."

"I loved him, too," Ridi said, and Bryndon, in spite of the knife he was holding to Jair's neck, believed him. "But he was in the way, you see. He would have messed up the plan."

"The plan to destroy your own city?" Willow said, the anger thick in her voice. "The plan to betray us all?"

"Nobody understands," Ridi said, tears rolling down his face. The knife quivered. "I knew that no one would understand."

"Ridi," Shem said softly, as the castellan began to sob. "Listen to me. You know there's no way out of this for you."

"Oh I know, I know," Ridi said, sniffing.

"So just put down the knife," Shem said. "And tell us what you did to the General, so we can help him. There's still time to undo some of what you've done."

"Just a few drops of blood milk, slipped in summerflower wine," Ridi said. "Not difficult to make, if you know how. And not difficult to cure either. Some stone tree sap in clean water. You'll find a bottle in the closet."

"Ridi, please," Shem said. "Just come back. Come back. It's as easy as wandering astray. You don't have to do this."

"But I do," Ridi said. "I'm too far gone now, too far…" He trailed off, and Bryndon saw the knife hand drop a little, as if it was too heavy for Ridi to hold anymore. Then Ridi smiled and straightened, and the knife got steady as bedrock.

"Tell him, I'm sorry," Ridi said.

And he slipped the knife quietly across his own cheek.

Jair Thorndike woke. There was light, a soft, red glow of light, flickering across the walls. So there were walls, too. And a closet. And a bed, that he was lying on. And standing above him, looking down with worried eyes, there were people.

"He's awake," one of them said. She was a strange-looking woman, with mottled skin and five braids of dark hair. Jair thought he knew her from somewhere.

"General Thorndike, are you alright?" an older man said, leaning over him.

"I know you," Jair said.

"It's Shem Haeland, sir," the old man said. "We fought together at Ninety-Six."

"You were with me…" Jair said. He felt like a black, cold fog was lifting off of his brain. "You were with me when—Ridi!" Jair said, remembering. *The man poisoned me*, Jair thought, astonished. *Ridi Greenvallem, a traitor.*

"Ridi is dead, General," Shem said. "Dead by his own hand."

"Willow, is that you?" Jair said, memories flooding back. "And Bryndon, too." He spotted another man behind Bryndon, a shock of red hair on his head. "Scout Garrett," Jair said. "What are you all doing here?"

"*I'm* here, too," said a young girl's voice. She was standing next to Bryndon, arms crossed over her chest.

"Robin is the reason we found you," Willow said. "She's Bryndon's sister, and a Dreamer. Maybe the last one we have left."

"How long have I been asleep?" Jair said, sitting up.

"Almost two days," Willow said, handing him a bottle. Jair looked at it warily. "Don't worry, it's not summerflower wine," she said.

Jair took a drink and tasted cold water, with a slight bitterness. More of the fog burned away, and he downed the rest of the bottle in three great gulps.

"Two days," Jair said. "Where is the Nightmare now?"

There was silence as they all looked at one another, troubled expressions on their faces. "It took you a few hours to wake up," Bryndon said. "So I went below to get the latest messages."

"Where is it?" Jair said again. "How far have they come?"

"When you disappeared, most of the men thought you were dead, or that you had abandoned them in fear," Bryndon said. "They fought as best they could, but the despair…"

"Where?" Jair demanded, seizing Bryndon by the shoulders. "Where is the Nightmare?"

Fear and sadness gripped Bryndon's face. "Five," he whispered. "They are at Five."

"Back, General?" the frazzled looking messenger asked.

"You heard me," Jair said. "Pull them back, all of them but the lambs.

And tell the lambs they are to use the crucible as soon as the Nightmare is in range. I want everyone else split between here and the High Tower. Firebrands here, lightning in the High Tower. Pikes as full up in both towers as possible. Understand?"

"Yes, sir," the messenger said, saluting. "Good to have you back, sir," he added, and then turned his mount and set off at a gallop up the road, spurring his goat on with a leather thong. *Good to be back*, Jair thought.

"Are you sure this is wise?" Willow asked. They stood outside the gatehouse of the Low Tower, the six of them, facing south, where the lightning of the storm flickered, lighting up the mountains in the dark of the night. "It's a lot of ground to give up."

"It's the best we can do," Jair said. "This is our choke point. The path is narrowest here, between the High Tower and the Low, barely wide enough for two darkstones to walk abreast. And we can hit the Nightmare from two towers at once. By now they're too strong for the power of a single tower to slow them for long. Besides which, I can make better use of every man we have left here than anywhere else. The Low Tower is as strong as the mountain itself, and the High Tower will take ages to storm. They'll have to fight their way through every story, and our pikes will make them pay for it in blood."

Jair turned to Shem. The aged lamb had found time to wash a little, and his hands and face were clean and brown, though mud still coated his uniform.

"You showed much courage and wisdom, Shem Haeland," Jair said. "I have an honor to give you as a reward."

"There's no honor needed," Shem said, inclining his head. "I've done what I could do."

"Nonetheless, I will give you one," Jair said. "The Low Tower has not seen battle for millennia, and so I filled it with clerks and healers instead of soldiers. The soldiers are coming back to it now, and with them many who have served as the seconds for the lambs. But I would ask you to be my lamb here."

"No!" exclaimed Robin. She stepped in front of Shem, as if to protect him. "You can't kill him," she said, pointing her finger at Jair. "I won't let you."

"Hush, child," Shem said, trying to draw her away.

"I am not a child," Robin said, stomping her foot. "It's too many, too many people." She started to cry, still pointing her little finger at Jair's chest. "Father and Mother and Gran and Rhys and Teagan and—and he saved my life, and he's kind and I won't let him die too!"

"Robin, my life is not yours to protect," Shem said, kneeling down. He turned her toward him. "It's my life to lay down, my blood to shed for this city."

"But it's not fair," Robin said.

"No, it's not," Shem said. "It's not fair at all. It's love."

He scooped her up in his arms and carried her inside, crying on his shoulder.

"Scout Garrett, you said most of the people are up on Trader's Pass?" Jair said, trying to keep the sadness out of his own voice. There were more young girls crying tonight than Robin Claybrook.

"Yes, sir," Garrett said. "At least, they were when we left this evening."

"Be sure that Robin gets back there safely," he said. "She has had enough grief for one day. This place will be a battlefield soon, and that is no place for a young girl."

"I don't know, General," Garrett said, shaking his head. "If there's a little girl around who's got more fire than Robin, I hope I never meet 'em."

"I'll go with her," Willow put in. "She trusts me."

"No, Willow," Jair sighed. "I have another task for you and Bryndon. Scout Garrett, you are dismissed."

The young man saluted and left, leaving the three of them alone.

"I really think I ought to go with Robin," Willow said again. "Bryndon and I aren't going to be much use to you."

"Not as fighters against the Nightmare," Jair said. "But you have forgotten the second danger we face, the danger from our own High Tower."

Comprehension dawned on Willow's face. "The crucible," she said. "Praeses will want to use it once he sees the Nightmare so close."

Jair nodded. "You must go," he said to them. "You must go, and break the machine before he has a chance to use it."

"How? It's made of solid stone and iron," Bryndon said.

"There's a simple, round pin at the base of the trigger," Jair said. "Take it out, and the crucible won't drop."

"But what if you can't hold the Nightmare back?" Willow asked. "What if you fail, and Praeses's crucible is our only hope?"

"I will not fail," Jair said. He clenched his fist around his sword. "This time I will not fail."

CHAPTER THIRTY SIX

High Tower, Low Tower

Bryndon and Willow climbed the High Tower as fast as they could, up the stairs and ladders, following the path that they had taken once before, seeking the plain white door and the wood-paneled room behind it, where the old crucible waited. Bryndon asked the guards at the gate whether Praeses had yet returned, and they found they were in luck. He was still in the city, or on his way out of it. There was time, still, to make sure that he could not use the crucible when he returned. Bryndon led the way, slower than he would have liked, Willow huffing and puffing behind him. They got turned around twice, finding themselves in unfamiliar hallways that dead ended at firing ports on the south side, forcing them to retrace their steps. Bryndon's mind was focused and calm, the calm that came from moving, going from one place to another, as fast as possible. The same as any race.

Finally, they reached the circular landing of black marble, with its dome ceiling and white statues still standing peacefully in their alcoves. Bryndon took the red stairs two at a time, leaving Willow behind a little. He crested the final step and wrenched the door open, rushing inside.

A bare sword greeted him.

"Bryndon Claybrook?" said the man holding the sword. He was a young man, with shaggy brown hair, dressed in the black and purple of the

Defender's guard, and he seemed utterly shocked to see Bryndon. "What are you doing here?"

Bryndon stared at the man, trying to place his face. Six colored petals decorated his uniform. "Wynn Silverfeather," Bryndon said, the name finally clicking. "You took us up here the first time."

"Bryndon have you—" Willow's voice came up the stairs, cutting off when she saw Wynn, holding the naked sword.

"And Stranger Willow?" Wynn said. "What is going on?"

"I could ask you the same question," Willow said. "Who is that?"

She pointed over Wynn's left shoulder, and Bryndon noticed with surprise that there was a small, slumped woman resting on the ground, clothed in a black cloak. He'd been too focused on the sword to notice her. On the woman's face, framed by her golden hair, was a red, snarling demon mask, fell and hideous.

"She is none of your concern," Wynn said, moving in front of the body.

"That's where you are wrong," Willow said. She strode forward, stepping in front of Bryndon, walking toward Wynn like she didn't notice the sword between them. *She's learned how to be Stranger at last,* Bryndon thought.

"You mean to kill her, don't you," Willow said, not really asking a question. "Use the crucible and doom us all."

"The High Defender ordered me—"

"The High Defender was denied authority to use this machine by the council of Seven," Willow said. "That verdict still stands."

"The Seven are dead," Wynn said flatly. "Only you, the High Defender, and The Clock remain, and two of those have voted for the use of the crucible in dire circumstances."

"The Clock is dead," Willow said. "And a traitor besides. He was killed in Trader's Pass this afternoon, after trying to slaughter the people of Meridia with a pack of horrors. You would trust his judgment on this?"

"You're lying," Wynn said, but there was doubt on his face, and the sword had lowered considerably.

"My sister saw it with her own eyes," Bryndon said. "He had a pair of blood knives himself, and he killed one of his own Timekeepers and a guardsmen before Shem killed him."

"The Clock played Praeses for a fool," Willow said. "He convinced Praeses to stay in the city long enough for his traitor friends to launch their attack. He likely corrupted Ridi Greenvallem to poison and kidnap the General. He had all of the citizens sent away from the city and the protection of the Defender, so he could feast on their blood in the pass. Everything he has done has been pure evil, pure destruction for Meridia. And he *helped Praeses create this monstrous thing.*"

"Then he has done so to his detriment," Wynn said. "The Defender is sure. This will be the weapon that will save us, the weapon that will protect us once and for all from our enemies. If The Clock has planned all of these betrayals, then all his plans have failed, for the rebels are defeated and he is dead." His voice dropped to a whisper. "And this is our only hope."

"The General will save us—" Bryndon began.

"The General will fail!" Wynn said fiercely. "He has already failed. He may hold out for a time, but the Nightmare will win in the end. And the cold will come for us, and your blood will freeze on the stone, and everyone you've ever loved will die."

"It cannot be used, Wynn!" Willow shouted. "I command you, as Stranger of Cairn Meridia, and with the authority of General Jair Thorndike, to stand aside!"

Wynn moved faster than Bryndon would have thought possible, slamming the blunt hilt of his sword into Willow's forehead, dropping her cold.

He stopped and looked down at her with shock. The sword dropped to the floor with a steel clatter. Blood welled out of a gash on Willow's forehead, and her legs twitched in unconsciousness.

And Bryndon ran.

He heard Wynn curse, and the sound of his footsteps behind him. Bryndon ran faster than he had ever run in his life, flying down the stairs at breakneck speed, out of control, on the verge of falling face first at every moment. He could feel Wynn chasing him, hear the sound of his panting breath. But Bryndon Claybrook was the fastest boy in Meridia, and he knew this was a race he had to win.

Bryndon was tumbling out of the High Tower and sprinting for the Low before he thought about where he was going. The first levies of troops had arrived, battered men in torn and bloody clothing, some with bandages wrapped around their foreheads or shoulders. They barely spared a glance for Bryndon as he raced by, haunted looks in their eyes. He almost stopped to ask for assistance from them, to lead them back up to the crucible, but one moment's thought dispelled that idea. These men had no idea who he was, and would be far more likely to listen to a Defender's guard than a random boy from the city. Some even might want to pull the trigger themselves, if it offered the promise of ending the bloodshed. There was only one man who would believe him, only one man who could face down a warrior like Wynn and prevail.

Jair Thorndike.

He flew over the stone, heels kicking up pebbles behind him. There was a press of bodies at the Low Tower gate, men in ranks of four and five, double timing it to their posts.

"Make way!" Bryndon called, trying to struggle through. "Make way! Message for the General!"

A few men stepped aside, but most gave him no more than a glare and an elbow, and Bryndon was forced to push his way in, ignoring the curses of the men he toppled into. Finally, he broke through to the gatehouse, finding a little more breathing room. There were many more soldiers here, some even looked fresh and well polished, levies from the abandoned towers that had not yet seen battle. They were drawing up at the gate, ready to bear the brunt of the Nightmare's power if they broke through. When they broke through. Bryndon leapt onto a barrel of crossbow bolts, scanning the milling crowd for signs of the General. A few Captains called orders over the noise and commotion, a pair of soldiers carried off one of their brothers, who was moaning about the cold, the cold, the terrible cold in his bones.

The observation deck, Bryndon thought. *That's where he'll be.* He darted off, heading for the southern staircase.

Please Ior, make that where he'll be.

He felt a terrible stitch in his side as he began to climb again, and he ignored it, keeping his legs pumping, his lungs breathing. Pain was not going to slow him down. Climbing, climbing. Pain was going to drive him forward. Up and up, higher and higher. Pain was his fuel, his energy, pain and desperation and the image of Willow Peeke, unconscious on the floor, bleeding from the head.

A guard stepped in front of him as he crested the last landing. "Halt!" the man said. "No one—"

Bryndon blew by him without a word, toppling him to the floor, the man cursing as he fell. He wrenched open the door to the observation deck, praying again that the General was there.

Jair turned and looked at him, a lit pipe in his mouth, worry washing over his face when he saw Bryndon alone. "What's wrong?" Jair said. "What's happened?"

"Wynn. Silverfeather," Bryndon heaved out. Black spots swam over his eyes, and he put a hand on the wall to steady himself. "Hit. Willow. In the head. Praeses. Going to use the crucible."

"Now?" Jair asked, the urgency plain in his voice. "Is he going to use it now?"

Bryndon shook his head. "Not there yet. But, he's coming," he said. He had never felt this tired in his life. His lungs felt like they were full of cold acid. "You have to go. Stop him."

Jair said a few choice curses that nearly made Bryndon pass out from surprise. He held up a hand to the soldier Bryndon had knocked over, who had come charging down the hall after him, sword ready.

"The Nightmare is nearly here," Jair said. Bryndon saw that he was right. The storm clouds were rolling forward in the night sky, and they looked to be past Tower Three, making the last half-mile journey to the Low Tower. The last two brigades of men streamed through the gate below, and already a few tongues of fire flamed forth from the firing ports below them, the gunners testing their range and power.

"I cannot abandon my men again," Jair said. "Not when they need me the most."

"There's no one else," Bryndon said, pleading. "Others might join him, might help Praeses use it."

Still Jair said nothing, looking to the south where his enemy lay, hands clenched at his sides.

"He hurt Willow," Bryndon said. "Please, Jair. There's no time."

And at last, with a wolfish howl of rage and frustration, Jair turned to the High Tower, threw his pipe to the ground, and set off at a dead run. And Bryndon, at last, collapsed to the ground, and let the dark spots overwhelm him.

Willow fought through the haze, struggling toward wakefulness. Pain waited for her on the surface, a red ache that throbbed inside her skull. She groaned and opened her eyes, finding herself on the floor, a snarling cougar pelt inches from her face. She tried to push herself up, but her arms wouldn't move. After a moment, she realized that they were tied up, bound together by what felt like strips of fabric torn from a piece of clothing. Her ankles, too, were lashed together, the wool digging painfully into her flesh.

Hands seized her and lifted her off the ground, sending the room into a dizzying whirlpool. Willow choked back the bile that rose to her throat. The hands set her down in a seated position, back against the wall, and

Willow closed her eyes until she felt the room stop flipping. She needed to get up, do something, stop Wynn from using the crucible, but it was all she could do to sit upright. A permanent red haze seemed to blur her vision, and she could feel the blood dripping out of her forehead and down her cheek. Wynn was lifting the red masked woman into position on the stone table, fitting her arms and legs into the thick leather straps. She looked no bigger than a child, her robe ripped and torn in dozens of different places, her ankle a swollen mess. Whatever blow or poison had rendered her unconscious seemed to be wearing off, for she was moving weakly, making small, pathetic noises of pain.

"Stranger Willow," came a deep voice from the door. "I had not expected to see you here."

It was Praeses.

The High Defender looked like a wild, burned version of himself, his clothing covered in ash and soot, his white hair and beard scraggly and unkempt, patches missing from being singed off by flame. There was a strange, feverish look on his face, as if his dark skin had been mixed with a pasty chalk. He was smiling, but the smile didn't seem to reach his eyes.

"You can't—" Willow cut off with a groan as the words caused a fresh wave of pain to wash over her. She gritted her teeth. "You can't do this," she finally finished.

"I do not think you are in a position to stop me," Praeses said. "And where is your Shield tonight?" he asked, glancing around the room.

"He ran off," Wynn answered. "I tried to catch him, but he got away."

"Jair is probably on his way here right now," Willow said. "He won't let you do this."

"You found Jair, did you?" Praeses said. "We'd best move quickly then." He slammed the wooden door shut behind him and slid a thick iron bar across it. Then he turned, and saw the small figure lying on the table, and his calm smile cracked, and it seemed to Willow as if he was staring at his own death.

"High Defender, what's wrong?" Wynn asked.

"Who is this?" Praeses whispered, pointing at the woman on the table. "Wynn, what have you done?"

"It's…it's the Whip, sir, the leader of the masked ones," Wynn said, looking confused.

"This is *not* the Whip," Praeses said. "This is not. Who is this?"

"But it is, sir, it's her," Wynn said. "She had the red mask and the whip right next to her—"

"This is not her!" Praeses screamed. He seized Wynn by the front of his uniform and lifted him straight up into the air. "Who is it? Who?"

The red masked woman groaned, arms straining a little at the straps. "Wynn..." she said faintly. "Wynn."

Wynn looked from Praeses to the masked woman and back again, terrified, heels three inches off the ground. "I did as you commanded, High Defender," he said. "I do not know...I left the mask on. Please, sir."

"Wynn," the woman whispered.

"How does she know your name?" Praeses demanded.

"I don't know," Wynn said, looking as confused and frightened as Willow felt. "You said a red mask, and a lightning whip. She had both."

Praeses hurled Wynn away, tossing him to the floor like he was a sack of flour. Striding to the table, he bent and ripped off the red mask.

The woman beneath looked no more than twenty, with fair skin. She blinked up at Praeses, looking confused and still half-unconscious.

"Wynn?" she mumbled.

"*Saerin?*" Wynn said, the color draining from his face. "It can't be. You're the Whip?"

"Wynn," was all Saerin said, closing her eyes again.

"She is not the Whip," Praeses said. "You have been fooled. Who is this?"

"It's Saerin Blackwing, Defender," Wynn said. "My...the girl I told you about."

Praeses bent down and slapped Saerin lightly on the cheek. She opened her eyes again, and this time when she saw Praeses's face she seemed to recognize him, and recoiled back in fear.

"Not me," she whimpered, the words jumping out of her at once, wrists straining at her bonds as if she sought to put her hands over her face. "You're not looking for me."

"Indeed, I am not," Praeses said. "Where is the Whip, the real Whip, whose clothing and weapon you seem to have stolen?"

"It's not me," Saerin said again, not seeming to understand the question. "I'm not who I am anymore."

Praeses seized her cheeks in one massive hand and forced her to look at him. "Where. Is. The. Whip?" he repeated slowly, emphasizing each word.

Saerin stared at him for a moment, confused. And then said, "I killed her."

"A little thing like you?" Praeses said. "How?"

"Blood milk," Saerin whispered. "I put a needle in her heart."

Willow had watched all this in silent confusion, but now, like a swiftly growing seed, a horrible realization sprung up in her mind.

"How did you know?" she asked Praeses. "How did you know she wasn't the Whip?"

Praeses looked at her for a moment and then stood, wandering over to the tiny arrow slit that faced the pass south. "They are almost here," he said, looking out. Indeed, as he spoke, the wind moaned outside the High Tower, heralding the approaching storm. The anger that had filled him before seemed to have drained out, and he looked calm, at peace. "Just a few more minutes, and they will be in range. And my work will be finished."

"How did you know?" Willow said again. "You recognized that it wasn't the Whip as soon as you saw her. How did you know that?"

"It takes courage to defend a people," Praeses said, and Willow felt like he was only half-talking to her. "Courage to know that sometimes one must do a shameful thing, to protect a greater good."

"Damn it, it was you," Willow whispered. "Ior save us, it was you the whole time."

"The greater the shame, the greater the power of the shame object," the High Defender said, continuing to ignore her. "That is the immutable law of shame magic."

He shook his head. "My life's work it has been, Willow Peeke, to build this crucible, and so I did. Yet without a proper sacrifice, my work was not complete, for the magic could not be used, might not prove strong enough. And then she came, a little girl born of rape, and I saw in her the completion of my work. A woman raised to be saturated with shame from skin to heart, a woman who could die to protect my people forever. So I told everyone she died a few weeks after her half-wit mother, and raised Jair as my son, the best General that the city had ever known. But it was her I really cared about, watching from afar, her that I treasured. My poor, beautiful daughter. Serving her father's will, even as she plotted to kill me."

"But I thought The Clock..." Willow said.

"As I told you before, Willow, The Clock saw the necessity of this path early on," Praeses said. The temperature was dropping, and the wind began to blow little bits of freezing rain and sleet through the arrow slit, coating Praeses's beard and face with dripping water and ice. "He helped me build this machine, helped me see the necessity of it. It was he that raised my daughter, he that shaped her into everything that we needed her to be. I'll admit there were some adverse side effects from our work with the blood magic, some of his…appetites…and friends turned distasteful. The blood magic can have that effect, can change a man into something…less than he was before. But even that served its purpose, for without The Clock we could not have contacted the Nightmare, could not have assured them of success. It was a small price to pay for what we were going to accomplish."

"A small price!" Willow said. "He and his *friends* were going to murder half the people of your city."

"What is a thousand lives for ten thousand years of peace?" the High Defender said, finally turning away from the storm. He sighed behind his coating of ice. "Though I'll admit, I could not bring myself to destroy Jair. He had to be removed, of course, to insure the Nightmare reached the High Tower, and once Ridi saw the necessity of this path, he agreed to do it. But Jair was a son to me still. And a better man than his father."

"But I'm not the Whip," Saerin broke in, struggling to free herself. "I killed her already."

"You did," the High Defender said quietly. "And yet you put on her mask, and took up her weapon. And I think you have plenty of your own shame, Saerin Blackwing. Perhaps you will not make this weapon as strong as she would have, but I think it will be enough."

"You *think*," Willow said. "You *think* it will be enough? You have brought the Nightmare to your doorstep, destroyed your own city, and broken the Prohibitions like so many twigs, and now you *think* this machine of yours will be enough? You are a greater fool than I can imagine."

"And what would you have me do?" he said, tightening in anger. "As you said, the Nightmare is here. It is done. This is our only hope now."

"No."

It was Wynn. He had drawn his sword, and he stalked between Praeses and Saerin, point forward.

"Wynn Silverfeather," the High Defender said. "Don't be a fool."

"I will not let you kill her," Wynn said. "Not her. Put anyone else on it. Put the Stranger on it for all I care. But not Saerin."

"There is no time," the High Defender said fiercely. "Willow will not serve. Her shame is born by her Shield, and you have foolishly let him escape."

"Then put me on it!" Wynn shouted. "Or better yet, throw yourself on. You seem to be the one most suited for it."

"I cannot!" the High Defender roared. The ice distorted his face horribly, reflecting the flickering red light of the torches in strange ways.

"Don't you think I would have done it already, had I the ability? But the magic does not work that way. The victim cannot desire his own death. It must be *murder*, Wynn, not sacrifice. It must be shameful. And it must be now."

"Praeses!"

A faint shout came up the stairs, through the door. And then a second time, closer.

"Praeses don't!"

"Jair!" Willow shouted back. "Jair come quickly!"

"Get out of my way, Wynn," the High Defender said, moving toward his guardian slowly. "Put down the sword."

"Stay back," Wynn said. "I will kill you where you stand."

"Wynn, please, don't let him hurt me," Saerin whimpered.

"Praeses!"

"It is the only way," the High Defender said, continuing to inch forward. The storm was breaking over the top of them now, and thunder boomed beneath them, the gunners in the High Tower opening fire on the Nightmare.

"I mean it!" Wynn said, thrusting the point of the sword forward. Praeses leaned back a little, and then began inching forward again, hands flexing.

Willow struggled to her feet, balancing herself against the wall, as a pounding began on the door, Jair fighting to break his way in.

"Father!" Jair shouted. "Father don't do this!"

Willow hopped towards the door, making it a few feet before she tripped and fell, falling painfully on her shoulder. She struggled to her feet again. The pounding grew more intense. The thunder boomed.

"This is your last chance, Wynn," the High Defender said, shouting now over the noise. "Step aside!"

Wynn darted forward, sword flashing for the High Defender's neck. There was a flurry of movement, too fast for Willow to follow, and then suddenly Wynn was struggling in the High Defender's arms, his sword stuck in the bigger man's gut, and the two of them were stumbling toward the window, and Willow tripped and fell again and smacked her head against the floor, and the thunder came from inside her skull and outside all at once, and she heard the sound of the door cracking as she watched Praeses hurl Wynn bodily through the window, shattering the glass, and the sound of the breaking glass and the breaking wood swirled together, and Wynn opened his mouth to scream but no sound came out, just the howling wind and hail that ripped through the opening like a rushing flood, and then the door finally fell behind her and the High Defender stumbled to the crucible with a sword in his belly, where Saerin struggled and screamed, and his hand reached out for the trigger.

And then Jair Thorndike was leaping over Willow, and there was a screech and crash of metal, and the awful sound of spikes thudding into flesh.

And then the world went black.

CHAPTER THIRTY SEVEN
The Cold Steel Point

The world went black and then white and then red, and all at once the room at the top of the High Tower became deathly cold. The High Defender collapsed to the floor, bleeding uncontrollably from the sword in his belly, face chalky beneath his dark skin. His blood mixed with Saerin's, leaking out from the crucible in a slow puddle. Jair stepped around him and seized the crank, trying to turn it, to raise the spikes back up, to undo what the High Defender had done. But the crank would not turn.

Willow sat up, squirming to her knees. "Jair, what's happening?" she said. The air was painfully cold to breathe. "Is it working?"

"I don't know," Jair said helplessly, tears in his eyes. He bent down to the still body of Praeses, feeling for a pulse in his neck. But after a moment he straightened, and turned away. The High Defender was dead.

"Look, Jair," Willow said. "The stones are changing."

And indeed they were. The walls and floor were slowly turning black, a horrible, unnatural color, like a sucking hole that absorbed all light. Jair ripped the bonds around Willow's hands and feet free, and helped her to the arrow slit, looking out over the battle below.

The Nightmare was drawn up around the Low Tower, fighting to break through the gate. Flames and lightning still fell on them with dizzying speed, all the remaining strength of the tower guard keeping them at bay.

Willow heard the sound of a bell.

She had heard it once before, on a green field in the early spring sun, waiting for Bryndon to run his last race. It was the black bell, wailing with grief, miles away in the city, and yet clear and loud here, as if it swung in the High Tower itself.

"It is midnight," Jair said. "It is ringing out the hour."

"Look!" Willow said, pointing.

An arm of blackness was extending from the High Tower, the same light sucking color as the stones, standing out clearly in the darkness. It arched slowly toward the Nightmare, reaching from the room where they were standing and over the top of the Low Tower like a black rainbow. It settled on the ground past the Low Tower gate, swallowing up the Nightmare's forces where it came to rest.

"It's working," Willow said, shocked. "It's killing them."

Jair looked on, saying nothing. Then he rushed to the other window without a word, and Willow followed after, teeth chattering.

"No," he said, pointing below. "It's bringing them in."

And Willow looked below, shielding her eyes from the pounding wind and rain. And beneath her, pouring out of the very stones of the High Tower itself, was an endless stream of horrors and darkstones, milidreads and shrieks and giant wyrms. They rushed out of the tower and streamed forward, crying victory, nothing now standing between them and the city they were built to destroy.

The High Defender's crucible was not a weapon, or a shield.

It was a gate.

The sound of the black bell broke through Shem's steady recitation of the mysteries of love. He looked up at the man with him, a dark skinned Defender's guard named Mahel, who had spent the last half-hour silently passing a whetstone back and forth over his blade. They were in the lamb's nest, set on the west side of the Low Tower beneath the observation deck. The only way in was a narrow, man sized hole in the floor, which looked down on the gatehouse below, and could only be reached by a small rope ladder, that stood rolled up in a corner of the room. Only the flying shrieks could reach them in this room, and then only one at a time. So far the Nightmare had not breached the gate, and the soldiers waited in ranks below, breath frosting in the air.

"What is that?" Shem said, at the bone-chilling sound. "The black bell?"

"No other bell makes that cry," Mahel said.

The bell rang twelve times, and then Shem felt the cold of the Nightmare deepen, and the lamp in the corner grew dim, as if the light was struggling against some dark hand that tried to snuff it out. When at last the cry of the bell ceased, there was a lessening of the storm outside, and no longer did Shem hear the pounding of enemies at the gate.

"What is happening?" Shem said. "Why have they stopped?"

"I don't know," Mahel said. "But I don't like it."

He stood and sheathed his sword, then threw the rope ladder down the entry hole, unrolling it to the floor below. "Stay here," he said. "I'll be back."

He vanished beneath the floor. Shem stood and began to pace, rubbing his arms to stay warm and reciting the Prohibitions, one by one. Gradually, he heard an increasing amount of noise from below, men talking to one another, their voices confused and frantic. He stopped and looked down. The captains were meeting by the gate, a few of them staring through the view hole outside. Mahel was standing with them, deep in conversation with bearded Captain Ryna.

By the time he had reached the fifty-third Prohibition, Mahel was poking his head into the room again, Ryna following close behind.

"What's going on?" Shem asked as they came in.

"The Nightmare has stopped attacking us," Ryna said, his face grim.

"Why?" Shem asked.

"We don't know," Mahel said. "A few men saw the General sprinting for the High Tower, moments before we engaged. Then the whole High Tower changed color, like it does when a crucible goes off, except this time it's black as pitch. Some kind of black rainbow appeared over our heads, extending from the tower, and fell before the gate. And as soon as it appeared the Nightmare stopped attacking us."

"I'm readying a force of men to go and investigate," Ryna said. "But we need you to stay here, unless the attack on the gate resumes. Close the portal and just listen for the bell. If you hear it, pull the trigger."

"Yes, sir," Shem said. "I won't—"

"Shem!" a voice came floating up through the floor. "Shem!"

"Bryndon?" Shem said, going to the opening and looking down. Sure enough, the young man was below, waving up at him.

"Shem, it's the High Defender!" Bryndon said. "He's used the crucible."

"This isn't the work of a crucible, Bryndon," Shem said.

"Not a normal crucible," Bryndon said. "The High Defender made another one, a horrible one, designed for murder. He thought it would be a weapon, something that would turn the tower into an object of shame powerful enough to wipe the Nightmare away. But something's gone wrong with it, just like the General thought it would. That's where he went, to try and stop it."

"How do you know about this?" Shem said.

"The High Defender showed it to Willow and me, trying to get her support to use it," he said. "Shem, it's a *bridge*, the dark arm is connected to the High Tower somehow. I can see the Nightmare from the observation deck, walking over our heads like they are on solid ground. They're marching right up to the High Tower, and then they just vanish into the stone, like it's made of air. The gunners took a few shots at them, but the bridge just absorbs it."

"They're going around us?" Shem said. "They're going straight into the High Tower?"

"Or worse," Bryndon said. "We've got to do something."

Shem looked back up at Captain Ryna. He knew what he had to do.

"Take every man here and go," Shem said. "If the Nightmare is at our backs, you'll need every sword and lick of flame you can get to fight them off."

"But we'll leave the tower undefended," Captain Ryna said.

"Its defenses are no good to us now," Shem said. "Except maybe one."

It took a moment for Captain Ryna to understand. "Now?" he said. "You want to use it now?"

"Bryndon said he could see them from the observation room," Shem said. "Which means they can see us, too. At the very least I can keep more of them from coming over until you can reestablish defense in the High Tower. It's the only chance we have."

Mahel and Ryna exchanged glances. Finally, Mahel shrugged, and clapped a hand to Shem's shoulder.

"Honor to the lambs," he said, and started back down the rope ladder without a backward glance.

"May Ior give you strength," Ryna said. "Do it when you are ready. And remember, if that boy is telling the truth, this is the last crucible we have." And he, too, slipped down through the floor.

And Shem turned to face his fate at last, the cold steel point of love.

CHAPTER THIRTY EIGHT

A Star in the Storm

"To battle!" Jair called to his soldiers, as he moved through the tower. "Sword and flame, thunder and bow, to me!" He held his sword aloft, charging down the stairs. "The Nightmare is in your city! The Nightmare has come! To battle, to battle! We fight!"

The soldiers left their posts, falling in behind him, and soon he was moving with a small army, triple-timing to the northern gate of the tower. The stones were black, and difficult to see; they seemed to avoid his gaze, and several times Jair nearly tripped at a step that seemed to hit his foot out of nowhere.

"To battle! To battle!" he cried, and others took up the call.

"Thorndike!"

"Meridia! Meridia!"

"We fight!"

"We fight!" Jair repeated.

He came at last to the northern gatehouse, finding nothing but death and chaos. Soldiers expecting to face the Nightmare from the south had suddenly found them at their backs, and the ranks were in disarray, sergeants bellowing confused orders. Jair burst into the fight with a hundred men at his back, crying havoc.

"Forward!" Jair yelled, plunging into the fray. "Push them back! Defend the city!"

Then his vision narrowed to the foe in front of him, and Jair fought like he never had before, not to defend, not to give ground slowly, but to push the Nightmare back, to take the ground by the point of his sword. They rose to meet his blade like so much grass, and he mowed them down, hissing horrors and howling darkstones, mace and sword, fang and sting, all passed him by. Lightning and fire exploded around him, and soon there were others at his side, blond pikemen with empty flowers on their breastplates, dark skinned sergeants swinging double axes, two swordsmen in the black uniforms of the High Defender's guard, their steel moving like the wind. Together they pushed the Nightmare back, together they drove them from their tower, together they killed and died and shouted the name of their city like a curse and a blessing all in one.

They reached the gate and then pushed past it, onto the northern field, churned and blackened, great mounds of dirt frozen solid in the bone breaking cold. The storm raged against them, but Jair led his men forward like a steel fist, punching into the line of enemies streaming out of the tower's blackened stones. He wondered when he would die, how many of the Nightmare his soldiers would kill before they were overwhelmed. He slipped by a horror's knife and split the creature nearly in two. A pair of giant wyrms crashed into the pikemen to his left, trampling them into the ground. The soldiers behind swarmed over the creatures, hacking and stabbing.

Then, rising up over the noise of battle, there came a hollow rumble, a great cracking sound that shook Jair's very bones. He looked up, and he saw the High Tower rocking back and forth, as if it was a tree shifting in the wind. The battle raging around him paused, a deep breath, as every eye turned to look at the mass of black stone looming above them. There was another great boom, and the High Tower swayed north, and then south, and then it was falling, falling, and men and monsters alike ran to escape the crushing weight.

Then there was a sound like a great rushing wind, and the tumbling stones broke apart in the wind like so much dust and ash, spreading across the field in a black snow. And as the High Tower vanished into nothing, Jair could see the Low Tower revealed behind it, like a star in the storm, casting its silver light on them all.

There was a great scream, a single cry of death in a thousand throats, and the creatures of the Nightmare dropped dead to the ground at the sight of the tower, burning with light. And the storm lessened overhead, and the horrible cold broke with the coming of the wind, which was warm and sweet, and smelled of spring.

Shem.

Jair looked around the battlefield, panting. Hundreds of men lay dead, or wounded, their white uniforms overwhelmed by the massive hordes of black figures. Perhaps half of his force was still standing. Beyond the Low Tower, Jair could see the storm clouds still raging, and over the city it was the same, though they looked smaller and weaker there, as if the source of their power had been cut off. His left hand was stinging with pain, and Jair realized with shock that it had been laid open to the bone, and the small finger was gone, down to the second knuckle. He hadn't even felt it.

"General Thorndike!" came a hail across the field. Jair turned to see a long line of soldiers, marching up from the south, Captain Ryna at their head. The levies from the Low Tower. "What in Ior's name just happened?"

"We have been granted a respite, Captain," Jair said, walking to meet him. "Shem Haeland has done with one act what I could not—closed the gate. The High Tower had become a thing of the Nightmare, I think, and like the rest of the Nightmare, it could not abide the light of the crucible."

"Is it over then?" Ryna asked, looking around in awe and fear at the battlefield. "We've won?"

"I think not," Jair said, shaking his head. "Look to the city, see how the storm clouds still boil overhead. Listen and you will hear the sound of buildings being destroyed. We came too late. Many of the Nightmare have already entered the valley, and they are wrecking destruction below. And there," Jair said, turning to the south. The Low Tower was so bright that it almost hurt his eyes to look at it. "The storm has retreated, but it is still there. We have split the Nightmare in two, and dealt them a grievous blow. But the battle is not over yet."

The men looked at him and at each other, and Jair could see the bone weariness in their eyes, the look of men who had seen too much and suffered too much, bloody and dirty, driven past the point of exhaustion. And now enemies on both sides, and their city under attack. And a clock ticking down to the moment their protection to the south would fail.

"What are your orders, sir?" Ryna asked. It was, perhaps, the bravest thing that Jair had ever heard anyone say.

Jair sheathed his sword. "Form up," he said. "We march into the city."

"All of us?" Ryna asked.

"All of us," Jair confirmed. "We must protect our homes and our people first."

"But when the crucible fails," Ryna said. "There will be nothing stopping the Nightmare from pouring in."

"They are already in," Jair said. "We shall deal with the enemy that is in front of us. Right now that is all we can do. That, and pray that Ior grants Shem the strength to endure. We need it."

And he walked off, calling for the men to make ready the march, looking for a bandage for his hand.

Garrett kept to the high side of the valley, staying off the normal trails, as far away from the city as he could get. The going was slow and dangerous in the darkness. One loose stone or false step could break their mount's leg, or send them both tumbling from the saddle. Robin sat in front of him, huddled in Garrett's cloak. She hadn't said a word since they'd left, just sat with her hands gripping the saddle horn, head down. Garrett thought she might be asleep. The sound of thunder echoed behind them; the battle for the Low Tower had begun. Garrett felt foolish walking away from it. He should be with his brothers, not babysitting this little one. She didn't seem to need much babysitting anyway. He'd seen the way she had torched The Clock.

Suddenly, Robin sat up straight. "The bells," she said. "Do you hear the bells?"

"Awake are you?" Garrett said, moving their mount around a bad-looking stretch of ice. "There's no bells ring—"

Then he heard it.

Like any other bell, and yet different, a cry of loss and pain, a cry of lament, a mother wailing over her child. The black bell rang out from the House of Time, and Garrett felt like it was right next to them, loud and close, instead of a few miles away down in the valley below. Twelve times it rang, and then there was silence. A cold wind came blowing over them, and Garrett shivered in his uniform, grateful that Robin's warmth was next to him.

"We have to go back," Robin said.

"To the High Tower?" Garrett said. "No way. The General ordered me to get you safely to Trader's Pass, and that's what I'm going to do."

"We have to go back *now*," Robin said, turning to face him. "Something has gone wrong. There's a gate...I know you can't see it, but it's—it's like a hole ripped in the world, and the Nightmare is coming out of it. We have to help, Garrett."

"What are you talking about?" Garrett said, confused. "We're not going back to help."

"Why won't old people ever *listen*," Robin said, striking him sharply in the stomach.

"Ow!" Garrett said. It felt like he had gotten hit with a tiny hammer. "I'm listening, I'm listening. And I'm not old. You're just not making any sense. Why would we go back?"

"To help," Robin said, her voice indicating how impossibly slow and difficult he was being. "You've got lightning don't you? Bryndon showed me how to shoot a crossbow once. We'll find one of those for me."

"But as soon as we get back to the tower they'll just send us away again," Garrett said. "They're not going to let a little girl fight."

"I'm not—"

"You *are* a little girl, Robin," Garrett said. "My sister Lena is older than you, and she's a little girl, too."

"But don't you want to help?" Robin asked. "Wouldn't you rather be with your brothers, fighting, than here babysitting me?"

Garrett's mouth dropped open. "How did you—?" he began. She had said almost exactly what he had been thinking.

"I'm a Dreamer, Garrett," Robin said. "And I'm telling you, we have to turn around and help."

Garrett looked to the southwest, where Trader's Pass lay on the slopes a few miles away. There were a lot of people up there, people who would be crushed and killed if the Nightmare broke through, people he wouldn't be able to protect on his own, Robin among them. He thought of Crack with a knife in his belly, and Cringe standing alone on Tarn's Bridge, bow in hand, one man in a narrow pass.

"Trust me," Robin said, taking his hand in hers.

Garrett sighed and nodded. "So be it," he said. *And may Ior forgive me if I get this little one hurt*, he thought. "We go back to the High Tower."

"No, not the High Tower," Robin said to his surprise. "The city. We'll fight our battle there."

Jair wrapped his bloody hand in bandages, waiting for the Low Tower to fall. He formed up the remainder of the guard, three columns of pike, supported by shame objects and crossbows, and he looked at the shining brightness to the south, expecting it to fail at any moment. He heard the House of Time ring once to mark second mare, the first hour after midnight, and he found himself in tears, that Shem Haeland had lasted an hour and endured so much pain for his brothers. He set off toward the city below, leading his men toward the Nightmare that waited for them, leaving the warmth of the field and plunging back into the cold. And every second that passed he expected to feel the tower behind him fail, to give the order for his men to turn, and face the enemy that was coming for their backs, and die for his city at last. They marched down the ridge line, and the tower vanished behind them, still shielding them from the Nightmare without.

And as the battle was joined in the streets of the city, and one hour became two, and two became three, and the long night wore on into morning, still the tower burned below the horizon, like a tiny sun, about to rise.

CHAPTER THIRTY NINE

Sharp Horns

Bumble the goat was hungry and thirsty and afraid for her kids. The air was bitter cold, and her kids nestled against her for warmth, half-buried in straw. The straw was old and fouled with droppings, but the gate was shut, and no man had come to lay down fresh straw for some time. The food in their trough had disappeared last night, and the water was low and frozen. Bumble swallowed snow and fed her kids whatever milk would come. It was little enough.

Black smells filled the air, an overwhelming foulness of smoke and ash, blood and rot and the stench of sickness. Her tribe stood around her, silent and close. Snow and ice clung to their bearded chins and sharp horns. The man-roof of dead wood kept the worst off of them, but there was nothing to protect them from the wind, and the wind blew strong, strong enough to cut through even their thick coats. They stood together and licked one another for comfort, rubbing their hides for warmth, taking turns on the outside. All except the buck, the one the man called Lunker.

She knew the buck by smell and touch and sex, a thousand different things that made up his name. He stood at the gate of the pen, as he had for the last two days and nights, since the man had not come, driving his horns into the dead wood over and over again. They curved back from his brow in thick arcs, and sometimes they would get caught beneath the slats of the gate, driving the buck into a frenzy of shaking and pawing until they ripped free. He wanted food and water. He wanted the man. He wanted free. So far all he had done was shower the ground with frozen splinters and snap one of his own horns in half.

Her she-kid tried to suck, pulling at dry udders. A dark birthmark blackened her brow, between her horn buds. It was her fourth she-goat, though Bumble scarce remembered the other three, except as absences. The man had taken them all away from her. The last time she had bit him and lowered her horns, but he had taken the kid anyway, and struck her with the wood-arm. She stood and looked at the gate, but the man did not come. She sniffed the air for his scent. The black smell was stronger, more vile; it made her snort and shake. She looked again for the man, and saw the thing.

The thing was shaped like a man, with a man's covering and a man's stature. But it was not a man. Its face was red and motionless, bobbing above its neck like a dead thing, and the smell that came off it was *wrong*, horribly wrong, sickly sweet corruption—the stench of a thousand corpses. Bear and fox and mountain lion, man and bird and vole, and goat, overpowering the others, the smell of dead, rotting goat. The thing stepped under the roof. Lunker backed away, head lowered, tail wagging in warning, smelling of fear.

The thing opened the gate and then it was in the pen, the pen that was supposed to keep them safe from predators. They bleated for the man, calling, crying. And the thing came on whispering, whispering, and Bumble saw it carried a sharp man-claw, this thing that was not a man. It was coming for her kids. She knew it was coming for her kids. The scent of their death was strongest of all. The kids knew it too. They bleated pitifully and scrambled behind her, pressing themselves between her and the frozen slats of the fence.

Panicked, Clover tried to break around the thing and out the gate, crying in fear—but the thing moved like a snake. Bumble saw the man-claw sink into Clover's throat, and her smell withered and died, drying away into nothing. The tribe shied backward, frenzied and bleating, trying to climb over one another in their haste to get away. But the fence stood behind them as it always did, and there was nowhere to go. The claw found Rose, who fell to the ground and soiled the straw, her eyes rolling in fear until the life drained out of them. Bumble rose to her feet and called, whipping her tail back and forth, showing her horns.

The thing turned for her.

All thought of her kids vanished. She forgot the strength of her body and the edge of her horns, and fear was all she knew or had ever known. Black, rotting fear. Bumble wanted to run away, flee out the open gate into the fields. But the thing stood in her way, holding its claw, which dripped blood on the ground as it walked. For the first time, she knew the cold, really knew it for what it was, the soft bite of despair, the dead frost of sleep without rest. She stood with her head down and trembled, waiting for the claw to find her throat. The thing whispered something to her, and it drove away all other sounds, the terrified screams of her tribe and kids, the thunder and wind, the distant crackle of fire. All seemed to grow quiet as the whispering filled her ears. And she almost understood it, almost knew what the sounds meant, as the claw came for her...

...and the storm above them broke. For a moment, the rising sun slipped between the mountains and the clouds, and cast its light full upon the dead face of the whispering thing. It hesitated, silent and still, as if confused or blind by the sudden yellow glare, and Bumble remembered the smell of her kids and the beating of their hearts. She remember her courage.

She rose up on her hind legs, hooves flashing at the thing's chest. Then the buck was beside her, calling, threatening, his head lowered. The frozen wood of the gate had snapped off part of his right horn, and it shone in the sunlight, sharp and broken. He slammed it into the thing's leg, jerking his head, left and then right, pulling free as the claw slashed down at him. Sunstar charged the thing from behind, slamming into its kneecap, taking a chunk out of its legs with a vicious bite.

And then they were all screaming, the whole tribe, screaming in defiance and rage, screaming their hatred of the whispering thing, screaming for their lives. Now it was the whispering thing that smelled of fear. The dead face hissed and spit at them, swinging its bloody claw from side to side. They came from the flanks and the back, horns and hooves flashing, teeth ripping. Fern sunk his horns deep into the flesh of the thing's hindquarters. He bleated and heaved, lifting the thing up in the air, legs spinning, and slammed it back to earth with a wet crack. Lunker darted in and sunk his teeth into the thing's wrist, wrenching his head from side to side. The claw dropped to the frozen ground, and then they were swarming over it, striking and pawing, burying the thing in a mass of living flesh.

Then at last the thing lay motionless, its body shattered and broken, its dead face rent and unrecognizable. But the smell of death faded with its life, and Bumble could smell good things again—her kids and her birthing, milk from her teats, the musk of buck and tribe. She licked her kids and Lunker's broken horn. He rose up on his hind legs and bleated, calling their victory.

Then the sun slipped behind the clouds, leaving them in twilight once again. Far off, Bumble heard the distant cry of more goats, calling in fear. The others heard them, too, and they milled around, anxious, shuffling and stamping.

Lunker strode out the open gate, then back to the tribe, bleating. Again he walked out, head down as if readying to charge, and again he turned back to the others and called. More sounds of fear floated in on the wind, sounding louder and more frantic. Bumble nudged her kids forward, pushing them out the gate. The others followed, one by one, into the snow and wind.

And Lunker led them toward the sounds of fear, ten goats and two kids who had found their courage, seeking another whispering thing for their sharp horns.

CHAPTER FORTY

Hunting

"To the left," Robin called out. "A darkstone."

"I see it," Garrett said. He raised his hand and slashed, throwing lightning at the thing. It ripped through the darkstone's armor and dropped it to the ground, smoking. They seemed much weaker in the city, the Nightmare, much easier to take down.

"Good shot," Robin said. She sat in front of him in the saddle, holding the reins so Garrett had two hands for fighting. The morning sun was up behind the clouds, though there was only a faint lightening of the gloom to show it. Only a few flurries continued to fall to earth, and the wind had died down to almost nothing, but the clouds were still thick overhead. They were on Goat Street, moving carefully among the burned houses and scattered belongings that dotted the paving stones. A dozen or so other soldiers were spread out along their flanks, most of them pikemen from the High Tower, who had come to the city with the General. They had met up almost an hour ago, and Garrett had the only shame object among them. So now they were wandering the streets, pikemen protecting Garrett and Robin while they hunted for creatures of the Nightmare.

She always seemed to know where to take them, finding their enemies alone or in small numbers, taking them away from the larger pockets of Nightmare that would have overwhelmed them. There were other groups taking care of those, the bravest and best fighters, led by Jair and the Defender's guards. The sound of their battles could be heard in the distance, the thrum of arrows and the roar of flames and men. Garrett's group had dedicated itself to removing the stragglers, the ones who had so far avoided notice.

"This way," Robin said, turning them to the right. "We'll find a pair of horrors."

They trotted down the cobblestones, soldiers jogging to keep pace. Garrett strained his eyes, trying to penetrate the gloom. The power and drive of the shame object was wearing him to the bone; he was using it too much. Perhaps someone else could take over for him soon. Any of the other soldiers might do.

Robin reined up at a dead stop, jarring Garrett out of his reverie.

"What's wrong?" he asked.

"I'm not sure," Robin said. "It feels like…"

There was a low, deep rumble beneath their feet, and the buildings around them began to shake.

"Fall back!" Robin said, turning their mount around "Run! Run!"

The pikemen didn't need to be told twice, backing away as quickly as they could. The rumbling grew louder and more violent, and then there was a tremendous crashing of earth behind them, and Garrett felt a fist-sized paving stone strike his helm and then he was on the ground, scrambling backward.

The wyrm rose above him twenty feet or more, standing on its back legs, raised to its full height. It bellowed and crashed back to earth like a falling tree, rushing toward him, razor sharp teeth bared in its open maw.

There was a loud bleating, and something crashed into the wyrm from the side, a mass of white and brown.

Goats? Garret thought in shock. *What in Ior's name—*

The goats swarmed over the wyrm's head, kicking and slashing with their horns. The fell creature bellowed and turned, snapping at them, but they slipped back. And a second fist of animals charged in from the other side, bloodying the wyrm's flanks.

"The lightning!" Robin yelled. "Garrett, give it the lightning."

Idiot, Garrett said to himself. *Staring at goats like you've never seen them before.* He had dropped the shame object when he fell, but it was lying a few feet away from him, half-buried in the snow. He scrambled forward, seized it, and turned, sending blast after blast into the wyrm. The goats broke and fled at the flashing and thunder, and the wyrm bellowed and writhed and fell, dead on the street.

The creature lay motionless, looking much smaller in death. A few of the goats wandered back toward it, sniffing, giving the corpse a few bites for good measure. One goat with a broken right horn lifted his leg, and marked the corpse for his own.

"Lunker!" Robin said, dismounting. She rushed forward, and at the sound of her voice, many of the goats turned and ran to meet her. "Lunker that is you! And Bumble and Sunstar and Fern. What are you all doing here?"

The goats gave no answer, except to crowd around Robin, licking and bleating and rubbing against her. She laughed, a pure, joyous sound that took Garrett's breath away. And he remembered, at that moment, what they were really fighting for.

He walked over to the reunion, signaling for the rest of the pikemen to spread out and keep watch. Robin turned to look up at him.

"They came to help us," she said, smiling. "My goats. They want to fight too."

"Goats," Garrett said. He threw up his hands. "Great. We can use all the help we can get."

CHAPTER FORTY ONE

Holding Fast on the Sea

Shem pulled the trigger.

The spikes moved slowly, so slowly, inching toward him. Spikes reaching for his eyes, his arms. He thought of Harn and Garrett and Captain Truman. He thought of Gran and Robin and Bryndon. He thought of Jair, and he thought of Willow.

And he did not flinch as the spikes slipped home.

There was pain.
Blossoming within him.
He forgot who he was.
A man screamed.
A man wondered whether he was going insane.

A man saw nothing, and the nothing was worse than the pain. Then he opened his eyes. There were spikes in his eyes, but he opened them anyway, and he saw that he was adrift on the sea, and the sea and sky were black and raging. He had never seen the sea, and he knew that he was not really on the sea. He knew that he was really in the Low Tower, dying for his brothers.

But that knowledge meant nothing. He was on the sea, and he clung desperately to the mast as the storm drove over him. And every drop of water that touched him hurt more than anything had ever hurt in his life, and every flash of lightning was like a thousand drops of water, and every gale of wind drove ten thousand needles into his flesh.

And outside the storm, darkness loomed, above it and beneath it and around it. And the darkness was Nothing, the darkness was Death, the darkness was The End.

The darkness ate the pain and was worse than the pain. It ate the storm, and lessened the pain, and the man knew that he could cast himself into it, and die. That he could let go of the mast, and sink into the water, and let the blackness swallow him up. He wanted to die. His whole world was pain, and he wanted to die.

He clung to the mast.

He heard the sound of his daughter screaming. He was up in an instant, hefting his hoe like it was a spear. Across the field, she lay in the grass, half sitting, a little girl of five, holding her ankle, terrified and crying. The bull stood above her, snorting and pawing the ground, wicked horns gleaming. It darted toward her, and she screamed again, but the creature pulled off at the last moment.

The man was running, already running, burning his lungs with his yells, trying to get the bull's attention. Again, it turned and charged, and again it pulled off just before the girl was impaled. The man knew that there would be no third miss.

The bull reared up on its hind legs and plunged forward, galloping as fast as its massive bulk would allow. The man scooped up his daughter, threw her to the side, and turned to find the bull upon him. The horns moved slowly, so slowly, inching toward his chest. He thought of his daughter, and did not flinch as the horns slipped in, and the bull drove him into the soft grass.

And there was pain.

He felt the pain of the bull's horns in his chest, and the pain of the spikes in his eyes, and the pain of the storm surging around him. And the darkness beckoned, and offered him release from the pain, the blessed release of death.

He clung to the mast, and there was another person there, an old woman, bent and ugly, dressed in strange, ancient clothing.

"Why did you step in front of the bull?" the old woman asked.

He said nothing, for he was incapable of speaking, of thinking, of doing more than enduring, and living in pain.

"Shem," the old woman said, and the man remembered that was his name. "Why did you step in front of the bull?"

And another vision came.

The old man in front of Jonat was walking slowly down the cobblestone street, bent over a twisted oaken walking staff, a full leather bag over his shoulder. The old man had nearly fallen twice, but he had straightened himself before he had lost his balance fully. He was a proud old man, and he would have refused any offer of help. So Jonat kept watch from a distance, making sure that he didn't hurt himself, and followed the old man home. The sun was setting over the western mountains, and the light was growing dim.

My name is Shem, Jonat thought.

No that couldn't be right.

But the old woman had told him his name, and it was Shem. The street blurred and thinned, and Shem felt the pain of the crucible spikes, and Shem clung to the mast in the storm, and Shem lay gasping for air on the grass field, two massive wounds in his chest. And Shem walked with Jonat, and he was Jonat, and he was just worried about the old man, and making sure that he didn't fall, and that he could keep his pride.

The old man turned down an alleyway, and Jonat hurried to keep up, leaving the potato stand he had been pretending to look at. The alley was clean and well swept, as all the alleys were in Cairn Doxia. Jonat ducked behind a wooden cart that leaned drunkenly against the alley wall, one axle broken. The old man clicked his way forward, shifting his bag to another shoulder.

"Need any help?" a voice said to the old man.

A thin young man with shaggy blond hair emerged from the far end of the alley, hands shoved in his pockets.

The old man stopped, clutching his bag. "I'm quite fine," he said, voice scratchy and wet. "I can still walk on my own."

"That bag looks heavy," the blond man said, striding forward. He didn't seem to be looking at the old man at all, eyes scanning up and down the alley instead. "Why don't you let me carry it for you."

"No, thank you," the old man said firmly. "I'll bid you good night."

The blond man look offended. "That's a bit rude, don't you think?" he said. "I was just trying to help."

"I don't want your help," the old man said. "Now if you'll please…" He gestured to the side of the alley.

"It's wide enough for the two of us," the blond man said. "What are you afraid of?"

"I'm not afraid," the old man said.

"Well you should be."

The blond man jumped forward, and the old man stumbled back and fell. The fall probably saved the old man's life, for the small axe aimed for his throat passed over his head. And then Jonat was darting forward, and the blond man looked up and saw him coming, and he threw the axe at him, and it came toward him slowly, slowly, and the man who was Jonat wanted to flinch and run, but the man who was Shem knew that if Jonat flinched he would let go of the mast, and slip into the nothing, and so he ran forward, into the blade, and felt it slice into his neck.

And there was pain.

"Why did you run into the axe?" the old woman asked. The boat shifted and tossed on the waves, but she didn't seem to notice, standing as if on level ground.

Shem didn't know. He felt the wood beneath his fingers and arms, he felt the agony of the spray and the spikes and the horns and the axe, he felt the darkness beckoning to him, pressing in. It had swallowed up more of the storm and the sea, and Shem could see it approaching the boat, slowly, eating up the water.

"You have to answer me," the old woman said, and Shem saw that one of her eyes was as black as pitch, and the other was as bright as a star. "Somehow, you'll have to find a way to answer."

Ash shivered in the darkness with a dozen other young girls, huddled together in their earthen cell. The cell stank of piss and worse, and it was always cold, colder than it should be, the cold of dread things moving in the tunnels outside their cell. They had been sent to the tunnels to become those things. Ash was terrified of this, of the dark magic that would be worked on her, the tainted blood they would force down her throat, to turn her into a darkstone or a horror, to fill her with hatred and loathing and the need to kill.

The cold deepened, and she smelled rotting blood, and heard the whispering, whispering begin. The pale one was coming for them again. The other girls heard it too, and there was a mad scramble. They pressed themselves against the back wall, biting and kicking to be furthest away from the door. The pale one had bad eyes, and it always chose the first girl it could see, or touch with its hideous hands.

The door creaked open, and the pale one came in, holding a glowing green lantern, its empty face partially hidden behind a low hood. It whispered, beckoning, calling for another girl. The others starting shoving and cursing, and there was a scream of pain in the far corner. Then a little girl, the smallest of them, was shoved forward. It was the northerner, the one with the strange accent and the creepy, monotone white skin. She had forgotten the girl's name. Wren or Robin, maybe. Some sort of bird.

The pale thing saw her and wrapped a hand around her wrist. Bird screamed at its touch, and the sound of burning flesh filled the cell. Bird kicked the pale one in the face and scrambled away, and then the knife was in its hand, the cold knife, that stole a person's soul, its blade almost invisible, tinged with blue. The girls screamed and ran, fleeing the horrible blade, though there was nowhere to go, nowhere to escape. The pale one pinned Bird against the corner, and raised the knife to strike.

And then Ash was running, jumping, and the knife was falling, slowly, so slowly, and she held her hands up in a flimsy shield of flesh, and the knife went through both of her palms, and she could feel the cold magic scrabbling at her soul, sucking it away, and the pain was unending and everything.

It was worse than anything, worse than the axe, worse than the spikes, worse than any pain, the feel of his soul draining away, of Ash's soul draining away, the wretched, terrible cold of it, the fear and despair and loss. Shem wept and slammed his head against the mast as hard as he could, wanting more pain, more agony, anything to overwhelm the sucking cold, anything to tell him he was still alive.

"Why?" he screamed at the old woman. The sound rent his ears to pieces, and Shem felt something inside his head pop, and felt blood rolling out of his ears and down his cheeks, and the blood burned like molten steel.

"Yes, exactly," she said, an eager look on her ugly face. "That's it, Shem. Tell me why. Why did you step in front of the knife?"

"Stop pushing!" Taisia said, but Gideon had already brushed her aside, running to the blueberry bush with his long, loping strides.

"Mine!" Gideon said, claiming the bush as his own. His basket was already full near to bursting, and Taisia had little more than a quarter of hers full, and that with pitiful looking berries, shrunken or overripe.

"Gideon, come *on*," Taisia said. "You already have enough. Grimp said I have to get a full basket, too."

"I got here first," Gideon said, stuffing a handful of berries in his mouth. "Come and get it if you want to pick some."

Taisia knew better than that. She had the scars and bruises to remind her what happened when she tried to fight Gideon for something.

"Grimp's going to beat you good," Gideon went on, grinning with blue-stained teeth. "No full basket for you. And I'm going to watch and *laugh*." He demonstrated, cackling with evil mirth. He smashed another handful of berries in his fist and threw the sticky mess at her.

"Just leave me alone," Taisia said. She turned and ran up the path, the tumbled stones of the mountain rising above her.

She heard Gideon yell and start after her, and she ran as fast as she could, basket in one hand, her dress held up with the other. But he was older and taller, and he caught her quickly, shoving her in the back with two hands, so that she went sprawling. Her basket tipped, and her berries scattered all over, many falling off the edge of the path, bouncing down the rocky slopes below.

"Whoops! Spilled your basket," Gideon said. "You should really be more careful, you know, walk like a proper lady instead of running around like a fool."

Taisia sat in the dirt and started to cry, big wet tears running down her cheeks. Her basket had hit a stone and gotten a hole in it. Grimp was going to be furious.

"Oh quit bawling you big baby," Gideon said. "I—"

There was skittering of pebbles over rock, and then a horrible tearing sound, and Taisia looked up, and there was a massive boulder, red-brown and moss covered, tipping over the trail, above Gideon's head, slowly toppling over. And then she had shoved the older boy aside, and looked up in time to see the boulder slowly, slowly coming down on her. The red-brown rock swallowed her up, and then there was crushing pain, and blackness.

It was much closer now, the blackness, it was hovering just outside the boat, and getting closer, closer. And Shem lay crushed under the boulder and held onto the mast. The old woman poked him with her stick, though he could not feel it, could not feel anything in his body but the crushing pain.

"You're getting closer," the old woman said. "That was quite a thing to do. You still haven't told me why though."

"I don't know," Shem said, and he was surprised to hear his own voice, and the air that came out of his ruined throat, though maybe that was just the axe in Jonat's throat. "Who are you?" Shem asked, the words bubbling out through the blood.

"I'm Meridia, of course," the old woman said. "Who else would I be?"

They dragged her into the town square, fifty strong at least, and bound her to the stoning poll, its bottom half stained red and brown with the blood of criminals past.

"Please don't do this," Ofydd pleaded at the mayor's side. "She made a mistake, is all. I've forgiven her."

"She broke the Prohibitions," the mayor said. "That wise Meridia herself gave us, that protect Jarth from the Nightmare and the power of shame. An adulteress cannot be suffered to live."

"But our children," Ofydd said. "You would deprive them of a mother."

"Her own actions deprived them," the mayor said. "She is guilty, and she has no one to blame but herself. Do you deny that she betrayed your marriage bed?"

"I know that she did," Ofydd said, the words paining him even to say. The morning he had walked in on her, tangled together with another man...His rage had nearly burned his home to the ground. "But she has turned away from those ways and set herself on a new path. Please, honorable mayor, have mercy. I still love her."

"This is about justice, not love," the mayor said. "Stand aside, Ofydd."

The mayor brushed past him, and leapt atop the dais, declaiming to the crowd Ana's crimes. Ana was ignoring the mayor, and looking at Ofydd, fear and sadness crushing her face, blood oozing from her lip, her beautiful black hair tumbled down her forehead. *I'm sorry,* she mouthed to him. And then... *Goodbye.*

The crowd cheered at the reading of the sentence, and all bent to the ground, picking up the stones. There were always stones here; the mayor made sure of that—fist-size hunks of the mountains, some stained with the blood of past victims. They lined up around Ana in a half-circle, and the mayor raised his hand, and Ana closed her eyes, and shrunk away from her fate.

And then Ofydd was stepping in front of his wife, and the stones were hurtling toward him slowly, slowly, and he did not flinch as they crashed into him like drops of rain.

And there was pain.

Every drop of rain was like a stone, but there was very little rain now, for the darkness had nearly swallowed the storm, and it was moving in. Shem watched the rudder vanish into it, and now he could feel the cold blackness sucking at him, like the cold of the pale one's knife, trying to drag him away, much stronger than the storm had been.

Meridia had moved a little closer, looking over her shoulder at the blackness. "*Now* surely you can tell me why you did that," she said.

"You killed her," Shem said, stones pelting him, stone crushing him, the horrible cold of the knife draining his soul. "Your Prohibitions."

"Did she die?" Meridia said. "I thought you stepped in front of those stones."

"She would have died," Shem choked out. He had felt Ofydd's grief and fear, his love of his wife. "She will die anyway."

"Perhaps," Meridia said. "Assuming any of this is real, of course. We shall see."

A late summer storm had ended the games early, and so Leuel came home as the bells were ringing second none, an hour before she'd expected. There was something strange about the house when she walked in, some feeling, like the air was wrong. She heard the sound of people in the kitchen, and she walked in slowly, the basket on her arm.

Master Gavyn was sitting in a chair, with Delwyn in his lap. One of his meaty hands was resting on her son's stomach, the other was caressing his knee. Delwyn's face was covered in tears.

"Leuel, what are you doing here?" Gavyn said, going white as a sheet. He jumped up, throwing her son away like he was a burning iron. "You're supposed to be at the games."

"What are you doing to my son," Leuel whispered. "What are you doing to my son!"

"Now don't do anything rash," he said, scrambling away.

"Rash..." Leuel repeated, dropping her basket to the floor. She rushed up to him and kicked him as hard she could between his legs. Then again, and again. "Don't do anything rash!"

Master Gavyn groaned and dropped to the ground, tears running down his cheeks in a steady stream. "Please, I'm sorry," he said. "I tried to stop, I tried, and I just couldn't. I never meant to…Please have mercy. They'll kill me."

"You deserve to die," Leuel spat, kicking him again. "You deserve it more than Tjabo himself."

"I know," Master Gavyn wept. "I know, I know, I know." He cried and cried, and Leuel found herself disgusted with the sight of him, bile rising in her throat. And he looked up, and his gaze fell on something behind her, and he put his hands up in fear, and Leuel turned to see her son, her precious Delwyn, rushing in with a butcher's knife raised over his head.

And she almost stepped aside. And she almost hesitated. And she almost flinched just long enough for justice to be done. And then Shem felt the cold sucking him away, and he stepped in front of the fat shining blade, and it cut into her shoulder blade with a wet thunk.

And there was pain.

He clung to a mast in the midst of nothing, and Meridia stood at his side. And now there was a figure with her, a figure that Shem could not see so much as feel. For the figure radiated an awful power and spirit, a heat and light that seemed to keep the darkness at bay.

"Quite amazing," Meridia said. "I don't know if anyone else has done that. Now come on Shem, you've got to tell me the truth. Why did you do that?"

Shem wept as the pain of his wounds, the others' wounds, burned within him. He wept and could not answer. He wept and had nothing to say.

"Come now," Meridia said. "What is that thing you people always say? I wrote it myself, for occasions such as this."

Shem could think of only one thing. "Love is one life laid down for another," he said.

"There, that wasn't so hard," Meridia said, smiling. "Is that satisfactory?" she said to the figure Shem could not see.

"Not yet," the figure said, and Shem realized who the presence was, and that, oddly, he had always known, for the figure had always been there. And the heat and light came upon him, and in him, and joined the pain.

"Let us try another."

Shem lost himself.

He lived a thousand lives, he died a thousand deaths. He was a cobbler, a baker, a man of the Tower Guard. He was the High Defender, the Wizard, The Clock, the Stranger. He was a mother, a father, a sister, a son. He was a criminal, a victim. He had everything, he had nothing. He lived in every free city and every chained. He saw the endless grasses of the dark things, the foothills of Pratum, the wide River Osku shining by the light of the moon. He died for brothers and criminals, children and old men, soldiers and captains and traitors and thieves. He stepped in front of blades and clubs, fists and whips, arrows and asps and streaks of fire. Each life ended in death, and the pain of every death stayed on him, and in him, until there was nothing left, nothing left to give, except the light, and the heat.

And then he gave more.

And after every death, he came back to the wooden mast and the darkness and Meridia and the man.

And Meridia said, "Is that enough?"

And Ior said, "Let us try another."

Shem drifted in the endless agony of love.

"Let it be done," Meridia cried, weeping as she looked down on him. "Make him let go, blessed one."

"There is more," Ior said. "If the man so chooses."

The horrors shoved Shem in the back, sending him sprawling to the floor. He was himself. He was Shem.

Another body was thrown to the floor next to him, and Shem turned and saw that it was Jair Thorndike. But not the Jair Thorndike he remembered. This man was a shell of his former self, gaunt and hollow-eyed, looking more than half-starved.

And then it came flooding back to him, the memories. How the High Defender's weapon had opened a gate to the Nightmare instead of killing it, and how they had flooded over the city, killing and burning. How they had taken Jair captive, along with Shem and ninety-eight others of the guard, hauling them to Tjabo's tunnels as a prize of war. And now they were the last two left, and Shem looked up, and there he was.

Tjabo, the one whose true name is forgotten.

He sat on a throne of darkness, his blind eyes glinting in the light of the single blue lantern the horrors carried behind them. Plates of armor covered every inch of him, save for his face, for that was shrouded with a mask of ice. And thick, black chains bound him to his throne, wrapped around his chest and neck like choking snakes. And the chains whispered and moved, and Shem realized with a shock that they were alive, that he was looking at the whispering things of legend, the creatures of the grass.

The last free men, Tjabo mocked, his voice echoing strangely, as if both outside and inside Shem's head, all at once. **Come to kneel before me.**

"Never!" Jair said, defiant and brave to the last. "We will not bow to you. We will die free men."

Freedom is a lie, Tjabo said. **Death is the only truth. I alone have escaped death. I alone am free. Tjabo, king of the earth.**

"Do you not see the chains that bind you?" Shem said, his voice a hoarse mumble. "Do you not see?"

I have no chains, Tjabo said.

"Then rise from your chair," Shem said. "Stand up, and show us."

It looked for a moment as if Tjabo might do it. He shifted and leaned forward, putting his hands on the arms of his throne, bending his knees. But the chains tightened and whispered, and he sat back, clanking in his armor.

I do not wish to, Tjabo said. **I do not take orders from old fools.**

And somehow in that moment, Shem felt pity for this creature, this poor, pathetic man, hiding behind his armor and his mask, bound by his whispering chains, kept from the Heights for a few thousand years. And he knew what he had to do.

He turned to Jair. "Can you fight one last time, General?" he asked.

Jair nodded, and smiled, showing a mouth full of jagged, broken teeth. "Until my last breath," he said.

"Then do it," Shem said.

And then he was running forward, sprinting as fast as his tired, miserable old legs would carry him, and he could hear the sound of Jair throwing himself on the horrors behind him, giving him time to run, and Shem rushed to Tjabo's black throne, and seized a whispering chain in his hand, and pulled and pulled and felt it give way.

Then the chain was unwinding itself from Tjabo and wrapping around Shem instead, and the whispering things slid around his throat and began to choke, and Shem pulled and pulled, trying to free his enemy from the grip of the chain, until…

…until at last the darkness overtook him, and Shem let go of the wooden mast.

But he felt two pairs of strong hands catch him, and then he was being borne up, then he was flying, then he was leaving the pain and death behind, and the darkness broke around him and all the world was shimmering light.

CHAPTER FORTY TWO
And Such Love Will Always

Jair limped to the head of the column, tears standing in his eyes. There were a few hundred soldiers left, drawn up in a triple file behind him, standing shoulder to shoulder. A few hundred men still alive, still holding weapons, still ready to fight. Behind them stood a thousand or so others, old men and teenagers, mothers and maids, grandfathers and house masters, and hundreds upon hundreds of goats, their bells ringing. Some of the people had picked up pikes and crossbows from fallen soldiers, some held kitchen knives or wood axes, Jair had even seen a stout mother of six with a massive two-handed great sword. She claimed it was one of the swords from Tarn Harrick's own ship, a sword that had cut down the grasses for the first city. Jair had sent most of the civilians west, telling to them make for Cairn Doxia as best they could, but these men and women had refused to leave. They would stand with the soldiers, to defend their city to the last.

He felt a hand on his arm, and turned to see Willow, holding a short battle axe. Bryndon was with her, wearing an over sized helm and carrying a sword and shield. And next to him was Robin, with a loaded crossbow, cocked and ready to fire. The girl was braver than any man he had ever met.

Except perhaps one.

For the Low Tower still stood, still shone with silver light. Shem Haeland had given them the time they needed. All night he had stood, and into the morning, for hours and hours, as the Tower Guard had battled in the streets of Meridia, and hunted every creature of the Nightmare to death. Long enough for the last survivors to gather here, where the High Tower once stood, and make their last stand.

Far off in the city, the House of Time rang sext, twelve hollow booms.

And the light of the Low Tower winked out.

Jair drew his sword and held it aloft.

"Shem Haeland!" he shouted. "Honor to the lambs!"

There was a whispering of steel and wood as the people raised their weary arms, not a dry eye among them.

"*Honor to the lambs!*" they replied.

"Love is one life laid down for another!" Jair said.

"*And such love will always prevail!*"

And he turned, and faced the Nightmare as it came roaring through the Low Tower's northern gate, the storm howling at its back. Jair thanked Ior for Shem Haeland, and readied himself to die.

Then there was a sound that Jair had heard once before, like a great scream. The rolling tide of black that was coming toward him collapsed, and the storm broke apart overhead. The creatures of the Nightmare fell to the ground, as if stricken dead. There was a popping sound behind him, and Jair turned in time to see the shame objects disintegrate in his gunners' hands. He looked back to the south, and then he saw him, like a walking stone, a living tower, a sword of light.

Shem lived, his body burning with the white fire of the crucible. And at the sight of him, the Nightmare died.

Shem walked through the fields of the slain, north of where the High Tower used to be. So many dead. So much life destroyed. There were living soldiers all around him, too, but he paid them little attention, for now. He knew he was looking for something, but he didn't know what it was. His eyes were gone, but that didn't seem to matter. He remembered the storm, remembered death waiting for him in the darkness. But Ior had snatched him away from that darkness, had kept him from death, for a little while. So that he could do what he needed to do. He could feel blood dripping from his elbows, but he did not hurt. With every step he took, he thanked Ior that he did not hurt.

He paused by a mound of dead, most of them darkstones, their last snarls frozen on their faces. He could see them, though he had no eyes, for it was like the whole world was made of light. There was something beneath their bodies, the something he was looking for.

He seized one of the darkstones and threw it to the side, handling the massive creatures as easily as he might a child. This didn't seem strange to Shem. Wonderful, but not strange. He had the strength that he needed to have. He tossed more bodies aside, digging into the horrible mound, until at last he came to a stone table. A small woman lay on the table, pierced by a bed of cruel iron spikes. Shem reached down, and lifted the spikes away.

She was a horrid, unrecognizable mess. But Shem knelt beside her, placed his hand over her pierced chest, and began to pray.

CHAPTER FORTY THREE
The Assembly

It was three weeks since the last Nightmare, still many years before the next, and the day dawned bright and clear over the valley of Cairn Meridia. Bryndon was already up, and working, taking the goats out to the pasture land on the western slopes. He had let Robin sleep in. Last night, he had given her the dream bell seed, figuring she could make the choice to use it or not. She had proved herself more than capable of leading, even at her age.

But she was always sleeping in, anyway, since the end of the Nightmare. Her dreams had been bright and happy, and Bryndon thought it only fair to let her enjoy them. Besides, she always slept next to Willow now, and the trader was as grumpy as Lunker when he tried to wake them.

But Bryndon liked walking alone. The smell of smoke and ash had finally faded, and the air was clean and fresh and warm. The new kids were frisking about, scaring up butterflies and taking turns pouncing on their mother. Bumble took all their horseplay with a kind of stoic silence, concentrating on her feeding, occasionally pushing one of them away with her head. Bryndon gave them a tap with the crook every once in a while, reminding them to feed. They were nearly weaned from their mother now, but sometimes they seemed to forget that the morning time was for grazing.

"Bryndon!" said a voice over the field.

Bryndon turned and looked up the slopes, and saw Jair Thorndike sitting on a small outcropping of rock, dressed in plain brown. He waved back and drove the goats up toward him, smiling.

"High Defender," Bryndon said, bowing. "It is good to see you."

"Ah, don't call me that," Jair said. "You know my name." He drew Bryndon into an embrace, patting him on the back. "How is the family getting along?"

"Better than most," Bryndon said. "We all miss Gran, of course, but we're proud of her, too." Somehow, nearly everyone from House Claybrook had survived. Mother and Rhys and Teagan had hid in the basement of Old Bael the blacksmith, who had ushered them in with his father when he had seen the first fires begin to rise, and heard the thunder. Gran had been away from them at the time, looking for needles, and they hadn't known what had happened to her—until a Redcrag man had brought them the story, a week or so after the Nightmare, of how Gran had stood in front of a masked one and whacked her with her basket, giving the other Redcrags enough time to escape their burning house. "It is a miracle from Ior that everyone else is still with us," Bryndon said. "Father especially. There are some families that lost nearly everyone."

"It has been a grievous time for all of us," Jair sighed. "Never before has the city seen such treachery."

"Do you know what Shem is going to say today?" Bryndon asked, not wanting to talk about Praeses. The word had gone around the city all week, that the Living Tower had called for the whole city to gather in the Grove.

"I have an idea," Jair said. "But Shem is much changed from his time in the crucible."

"Changed how?" Bryndon asked. He hadn't spoken to Shem since the battle. For some reason he had felt nervous about it.

"He is more himself," Jair said. "Or maybe his self is somehow more." He shrugged. "I don't know. There is much that I do not know. But I think our time in this valley is coming to an end."

They gathered at the ringing of the noon bell, the survivors of Meridia, funneling into the Grove with baskets and bottles, food and drink, walking and lying among the massive stone trees, rising up around them like living towers. For today was a celebration, a feast, a time to honor the fallen and thank Ior for life.

Saerin sat on the eastern edge of the grass bowl surrounding the

Flower Fountain, munching on honey bread. She reached out her hand, and another hand took it, warm and alive.

"Do you want some more wine?" Zoe asked, offering the bottle. "It's nearly out."

"You can have it," Saerin said. Her house sister was nearly back to her normal self. The weight she had lost while hiding on the mountain paths had been restored by three weeks of hearty meals, and Saerin had finally explained to her what had happened, why she had been in danger of her life, why she had met her outside the House of Summerflower and told her to leave at once for the mountains. Zoe had forgiven her immediately, of course, thanking her for saving her life, not seeming to remember the fact that Saerin had been the one to endanger it. She was a wonder, Zoe, as kind a heart as any Saerin had ever met.

She could almost forget about the High Tower, on a day like today. The sun was shining, and people were abuzz with conversation and good food. She could almost forget the pain of the spikes, the cold of death, the scars that marred her skin in a hundred different places, the odd angle of her ankle. She could almost forget. Almost.

But then she remembered the sight of Wynn, mouthing silently as he fell from the window, and a chill took her. How long had she thought him unworthy of her, how long had she feared and hated him as her enemy? But it was she who was unworthy of him, she who should be dead. Often, she had sat up late into the night, and thought that Shem had brought back the wrong person, that he should have saved Wynn instead of her. Though in truth, she did not know what kind of person she was. That was his real gift—a second chance to choose who she would be. A second chance to find courage.

So she drew her house sister into a hug, and tried to think of Shem.

Oded dozed in the afternoon heat, resting his back against the trunk of a stone tree. He was dreaming of flames and falling stones, flames reaching for him, to burn him apart. But when they reached him, they turned into flying blue moths, and fluttered around Oded like feathers. Something tickled his face, and Oded woke slowly, finding a blue crook on the end of his nose.

"Excuse me," Oded said, gently transferring the little insect onto his finger. "That's not a proper spot for you."

The moth flexed its wings and flew to Oded's shoulder, realizing perhaps, that this was a more acceptable spot.

"Wizard Oded," Halat said, the young man approaching from the other side. "The meeting is about to begin."

"Thank you, Brother Halat," Oded said. "Perhaps you would be kind enough to help me up?"

Halat did so, pulling Oded gently to his feet, and handing him his walking stick. He had been even slower than usual, since the battle at the House of Summerflower. Hours spent lying on the ground in the snow do that to an old man. They made their way slowly to the Flower Fountain, walking through the crowds of people feasting on the grass, under the trees. He had to lean on Halat and the walking stick both, though he didn't mind that so much. The moth rode comfortably on his shoulder, enjoying the view, perhaps, of those creatures unlucky enough to be bound to the earth.

The rest of the remaining Seven were already gathered. The House of Time had not chosen a Keeper to be the new The Clock yet, but High Defender Thorndike was there, smoking a pipe by the Flower Fountain, with Stranger Willow at his side. The new General of the Tower guard, a bearded man from House Greenvallem named Ryna, was speaking with Shepherd Pilio's son, a serious young lad named Cedrik, who had taken over his father's position. And the young Claybrook girl, what was her name again?

"Robin, Wizard Oded," Halat replied. Oded hadn't realized he had spoken aloud. "New Mistress of the House of Moonlight."

"I remember that part," Oded said. Halat often seemed under the impression that Oded was incapable of remembering anything. "She's got a robe to fit her, at last," he added. The girl had been forced to dress in clothes many sizes too big for her at previous council meetings, and had complained non-stop about it. This one looked well suited for her, a rich violet made of linen. Her mother must have set a weaver working on it right after the Nightmare ended.

When Oded had settled into his chair, Jair stood and raised a hand for silence, looking out over the crowd that surrounded them.

"Meridians, we are here at last to declare the Nightmare ended," he said.

The people erupted in cheers, clapping and whistling and whooping with joy. Oded clapped quite a bit himself, though he took care not to do it too vigorously, not wanting to disturb the moth.

"It is a time of great rejoicing," Jair went on, when quiet at last returned. "And a time of great sorrow too, as we remember those that have fallen to defend us. Love is one life laid down for another."

"And such love will always prevail," Oded added.

Jair smiled and nodded at him. "So it was written long ago, by blessed Meridia. Yet for many years now we have not lived out such love. Indeed, our failure was our downfall, for we broke our sisters on a rock of lies, drove them to rebellion through the shame of our own fear. And now change comes to us at last, this place that has known the safety of stability these two thousand years. For seventy years are no longer given to us for our peace. And, more important still, the living tower now walks among us, the one who has spoken to Ior himself. It is he who has called this assembly, Shem Haeland. And so I ask him to speak."

Jair sat, and there was a commotion as Shem stood up from among the crowd and walked to the Flower Fountain. The people gave voice to a great cheer, even louder than before, and the sun shone down on them with golden light.

When Shem at last reached the fountain, he stood on its marble rim, and waved for silence. A white bandage was wrapped around his eyes, and two more were tight around his elbows, stained with blood. Yet he was smiling, and Oded thought he had never seen a stronger or healthier looking man in his life.

"My friends," he began. "I have been blessed by Ior with a great gift. Many of you know, now, what I saw in the crucible, what I felt and did. How I did not die, but suffered with Ior. How, at the end of my strength, he lifted me away from the darkness of death and restored me to you. But before he sent me here, he showed me a hard truth, that our way of life is ended. That the time of the towers is over.

"Too long have we sat in our valley and let the Nightmare of Tjabo oppress the south. Too long have we thought only of protecting ourselves, defending our own power, instead of raiding the house of the enemy. The council has deliberated long and in much prayer about this, and we stand unanimous. We must go, each and every one. The city of Meridia must be abandoned."

Shocked silence greeted this pronouncement, and everywhere Oded looked he saw stunned faces. Except when he looked at the moth on his shoulder, who seemed unconcerned, like it was all part of his mothy plan.

"This will be a hard time," Shem said. "And no one will be forced to leave against their will. Yet to stay here means death, that much I have seen. To go is a risk, but it is a risk we must take."

"But where will we go," a man said from the crowd, a young man in the uniform of the guard, the petal of diligence on his chest.

It was Stranger Willow who replied. "To my home, for a start, Garrett," she said. "There is much we could learn from one another, I know. I have already found that myself."

"And from there, we do not know," Jair added. "We shall let Ior guide us. It may be that he makes a new home for us there, for a time. But make no mistake, the day is coming when we shall have to face Tjabo himself. And challenge the whispering things for rule of this land."

"The people of the south will join us," Willow said. "Not all, and perhaps not most, for many of them live in fear of Tjabo or in thrall to the wealth he gives them. But there will be enough."

"Do not fear," Shem said. "Look to the Heights, and know that Ior looks down upon you with great care. He did not abandon me, and he will not abandon you. Even when I am gone."

There was a sharp outcry at this, but Shem waved it down. "Yes, I must go," he said. "Even now, I feel the Heights calling. The crucible claims the life of the one who chooses it. Ior delayed that for a time, to heal what he could through me, to give you this council. But you can see I bleed still. My life is leaving me, friends. I must go, and I go gladly."

Oded, waiting for this moment, coughed and rose to his feet. "I will go with you as well," he said. "My time is long past, and I have only one journey left in these old bones. I am a poor man, much at fault for what happened here. Yet I would like to make what little climb I could."

Shem nodded, looking like he had expected Oded to say as much. He turned his bandaged eyes to the crowd one last time.

"My friends, you are more precious than rubies," Shem said. "Do not forget what has happened here, that your life is a gift from Ior. Trust in him now. You will find much hardship, no doubt. But you will find much more joy."

And with that Shem stepped down from the fountain, and walked to Oded's side, offering his arm to lean on. Oded took it, not minding the blood. And slowly, slowly, they walked from the Grove together, the two old men, one strong and small, the other bent and wizened, leaving the rest behind. The little blue moth fluttered away, and disappeared into the branches of a tree.

APPENDIX

Time of Day
The Meridians have a standard 24 hour clock, with each day beginning and ending at noon. The hours are marked by the bells of the House of Time and are often referred to by name, rather than number.

The midnight hours of Mare, First Mare, and Second Mare are often thought of as "evil hours" when the power of the Nightmare is strongest. Conversely, the six hours from Terce to Second Sext are considered "grace hours," when the graces of Ior are strongest. Thus the Meridian day begins and ends with "grace time," with the "evil hours" in between. A complete list of time names is below:

Sext - Noon
Second Sext - 1 hour after noon
Third Sext - 2 hours after noon
None (pronounced the same as "known") - 3 hours after noon
Second None
Third None
Vespers - 6 hours after noon
Second Vespers
Third Vespers
Compline ("cahm-plin") - 9 hours after noon
Second Compline
Third Compline
Mare - 12 hours after noon, midnight

Second Mare
Third Mare
Vigil - 15 hours after noon
Second Vigil
Third Vigil
Lauds (rhymes with "odds") - 18 hours after noon
Second Lauds
Third Lauds
Terce (rhymes with "parse") - 21 hours after noon
Second Terce
Third Terce

Meridian Calendar

Dates are marked in terms of the number of Nightmares since the founding of Meridia and their distance from the most recent Nightmare. For example, an event that happened *during* a Nightmare would be written as: *"In the year of the fifteenth Nightmare, such and such came to pass."* In most circumstances, this date would be written in short-hand as "15N." In total, this would be 980 years from the first Nightmare.

An event that happened between Nightmares would be written as: *"In the thirty-third year of the twenty-first peace, such and such came to pass."* Again, this would likely be abbreviated as "33Y-23P." (1577 years after the first Nightmare)

The sequencing of dates is a bit odd. By way of example, the twenty-third peace (23P) *immediately follows* the twenty-second Nightmare (22N) and *immediately precedes* the twenty-third Nightmare (23N). The surrounding sequence is thus 22N - 23P - 23N - 24P - 24N, etc. The very first date on the Meridia calendar is 1N, or the year of the first Nightmare, when Tarn Harrick died as the first lamb. This is immediately followed by 1Y-2P (the first year of the second peace). The first peace (1P) is not a part of recorded time.

Each Nightmare lasts approximately three to five days, and each peace lasts exactly seventy years from the moment the last creature of the previous Nightmare dies. Over the centuries, this has led to some confusion and blurring of dates, though only the Timekeepers really bother themselves about such things.

Jair Thorndike becomes General of the Tower Guard of Cairn Meridia in 30Y-29P (the thirtieth year of the twenty-ninth peace) and fights in 29N (the twenty-ninth Nightmare).

Made in the USA
Monee, IL
22 January 2022

89605869R00213